Through It All

a novel by

Giselle Mills

GOM Press

ISBN: 978-1-7325701-0-8 (Paperback)
978-1-7325701-1-5 (eBook)

To my mother, Patrice

Chapter 1

"Give me back my diary, you little pest!" Andreide shouted at her little brother as he dashed down the stairs, waving his stolen treasure above his head. She ran down the stairs after him, stumbled on the last step then fell flat on her chest.

"Nah nah nah nah nah! I have your stupid diary. I wonder what I'll find inside it … today!" Marques teased his older sister. He turned around and saw her lying on the floor. His teasing demeanour quickly changed to one of concern when he realized that she was not moving.

"Andy? Andy get up! You're supposed to chase me remember? I have your diary!" Marques inched forward towards his motionless sister. When he was directly above her, he leaned down and whispered, "I don't think Mom will like it if I tell her where you and Alisa went yesterday after school!"

Quick as a flash, Andreide rolled unto her back, raised her legs then kicked Marques in his groin. He dropped the book, doubled over and howled.

"Ow Ow Ow OWW! I'm going to tell Mom, you murdered my royal jewels!"

Andreide laughed.

She grabbed her diary then stood up and looked down at her cowering brother. She sighed. "Why are you so annoying? Why can't you just behave and leave me alone? Then, I wouldn't have to hurt you."

"I'm going to tell Mom. I mean it!" Marques shouted at her, his eyes watering with pain and anger.

"Like I care," Andreide retorted.

"I *will* tell!"

"I really don't care, you little brat!" She was now truly angry with him.

"Oh yes, you will care when Mom punishes you. Especially if I tell her about what I read in your diary last week Friday!"

Andreide screamed in frustration. She raised her fist to hit him but Marques anticipated her action. He ducked as her fist connected with the wall behind him.

"Oh shit! Oh shit, that hurts! Shit shit shit!" Andreide hopped and cursed in pain, cradling her right hand.

Marques stared at his aggrieved sister, shocked at her outbursts. He wasn't sure what to do, run for help or run for cover. However, he was relieved of making the decision when his mother came running in the hall from the kitchen doorway.

"What's the matter? Why is there so much noise so early in the morning? You both know that I need silence when I'm in my office. I was on the phone with my publicist for goodness sake! Don't you know that –" Whatever she was going to say was cut off when Andreide shouted.

"Mom! That boy made me hurt my hand. It's paining like hell!"

"Watch your language when you're talking to your mother, child."

"She did it herself," said Marques.

"No, I didn't!"

"Yes, you did!"

"Both of you be quiet."

"But *he* started it. He stole *my diary*! He invaded *my* privacy. He violated *my* human rights!" Andreide cried.

"Privacy is a civil right, not a human right," the eleven-year-old boy responded with a snooty air.

"Oh, hush up, you know-it-all —"

"I said BE QUIET!" the children's mother shouted.

They fell silent immediately. Rose Marie D'Averette was a firm, respected woman who was known to be strict at times, but never had she shouted at her children in such a manner. They stared at her, their mouths slightly agape.

She looked at her children's shocked faces and then realized that she had spoken too harshly. "I'm sorry but I had to get your attention." She sighed. "You know I've been very busy recently with my book. I know it's been difficult for all of you as well, but bear with me please. It will soon be over. By next week, it will be smooth sailing. No more coming home to see the living room, dining room and kitchen packed with editors and littered with manuscripts. That part of production is over. I was just talking to my publicist about all of that and we agreed to move office to downtown."

Andreide and Marques exchanged looks of relief. Rose Marie saw their expressions and smiled. She too was tired of having her entire staff at her home almost everyday. She knew how it inconvenienced her family and was glad that it was over.

"So ... that's it? Your book is finished now?" Andreide asked, her hopes rising.

"Umm ... the editing is finished, yes."

Her children looked at each other again. They knew that their mother was withholding information and were curious to find out what it was.

"But ..." Andreide prodded.

As Rose Marie was about to answer, the telephone rang. She looked relieved. "Oh, that's probably for me ... you know, my publicist. I'll take it in my office," she said, then hastily retreated to her study.

"What was that all about?" said Marques.

"How am I supposed to know?" Andreide snapped. "Do I look like a blasted psychic?" She had had enough of her brother's company. She turned around and returned to her bedroom, stamping up the steps. She was still upset with Marques.

Having a younger brother was very exasperating for Andreide, especially one who constantly interfered and bothered her. However, Marques was not her only sibling. She had another brother to deal with daily – her seventeen-year-old brother, Omarion. He was not as troublesome as Marques but annoyed her in different ways. His recent mood swings were at the moment, the most challenging to deal with. Some days he would be as happy and as bright as sunshine but others, angry and depressed. Her mother told her that it was normal for a boy Omarion's age to behave that way but Andreide was not convinced. He was seventeen years old! Wouldn't he be used to the ups and downs of adolescence yet?

Andreide knew that her older brother's disagreements with their father would have contributed to his worsened mood, for she often heard them arguing. The main reason for the clash was Omarion's career choice and educational decisions. He wanted to become a professional chef but their father thought otherwise. Their father wanted him to become an accountant and be directly involved in business. Andreide believed that their father wanted them to be everything that he never was or could be and have everything that he could not achieve. She understood this but thought it was unfair of her father to be so selfish and not care about the desires of his children. She knew for sure that he would not force her to become anything she didn't want to be.

As a matter of fact, she thought it ironic that her father was so controlling in the matter of his children's career choices, when he himself did not possess a white-collar job or try to improve his career prospects. In fact, Charles David D'Averette was a landscaper in a small-scale landscaping firm. A landscaper – not a doctor, lawyer, professor, engineer or architect. To make matters worse, he was the laziest man on Earth. Andreide was almost ashamed of her father. He never did anything much to contribute meaningfully to the family. All he did was work when he had to, sleep, eat, watch television and occasionally read a newspaper. He hardly ever interacted with his children. This didn't bother Andreide much for she did not enjoy being in her father's company for any period of time, anyway. She normally spent most of her leisure time at home, in her bedroom reading, talking to her friends on the Internet, watching television or with her mother when she wasn't involved with her book.

For the past six months, her mother, Rose Marie, had been occupied with her new book on psychology, 'From a Psychologist's Point of View'. It was soon due to be released to stores and Rose Marie was under pressure to make sure that it was properly publicized so that sales would accelerate quickly. This made her very anxious and tense and she could hardly wait to hear the feedback. Andreide knew that her mother had worked hard on her book and hoped that it would be a success.

When Andreide reached her bedroom, she grabbed a clean bath towel from her closet, and then checked the time on her alarm clock on her desk. She muffled a scream. It was 7:15 a.m. She was going to miss the bus if she was not ready in fifteen minutes.

"That little pest made me late! Why couldn't I have been an only child? Why were little brothers invented? Why God, why?" Andreide looked up towards the ceiling, as if asking for a divine response. However, she heard no reply.

Twenty minutes later, she was dressed and ready for school. She made a general announcement of her departure, made a sandwich to carry then left. Fortunately for her, she did not live too far from her school. Convenient location was one of the advantages of living on a small island.

She had been born in Trinidad but lived in St. Kitts, in St. George's parish her whole life. She usually visited her home country with her family every year so she was familiar with both countries' cultures. In comparison to Trinidad, the pace of life in St. Kitts was very slow but she had gotten used to it.

As she walked along the sidewalk, Andreide breathed in the fresh air which soothed her agitated nerves. She often felt peaceful whenever she walked to school; the scenery was quite beautiful and the air always smelt as fresh and clean as spring.

As Andreide neared Duncan Street, she quickly crossed to the wider side of the pavement and mentally prepared herself for the usual taunting remarks from the rich, obstinate, conceited students of Duncan's Academy. Every morning at 7:45 a.m., the Duncan's Academy school bus for boys, cruised by Duncan Street on the way to the prestigious school; the Duncan's girls' school bus took a different route. Almost every time that Andreide walked to her school, the Duncan's boys' bus passed by; every time they passed, they left a stream of rude, teasing and often derogatory remarks behind for her. Most times, she ignored them and kept her head held high but sometimes their comments really affected her.

This Friday morning, they cruised by as usual, their bus driver deliberately slowing down as they approached Andreide. The boys on the west side of the bus slid open their windows then stuck their arrogant heads out of the air-conditioned silver bus and began their customary greeting.

"Good morning, princess!" one shouted.

"Hey, sweetness! Gimme some sugar, baby!" another teased and puckered his lips at her, making an obscene noise and gesturing with his fingers. Another boy wolf-whistled at her.

"How does a hot thing like you stay cool in this weather?" They laughed, angering Andreide.

"Hop in our bus darling. We'll keep you 'cool'!" taunted a wavy haired boy. Andreide recognized his shiny, golden-blonde hair, thin sharp nose, and piercing blue eyes and knew at once that he was Richard Carlston, the son of the president of Carlston International Development Bank. His father controlled the finances of her father's landscaping firm; she often heard her father complain about Lloyd Carlston's severity and lack of compassion for his boss' financial situation. The dislike between Mr. D'Averette and Mr. Carlston was mutual.

With this thought in mind, Andreide glared at Richard, matching the intensity of his piercing, mocking eyes. Surprised by her challenging stare, he looked away for a split second then chuckled nervously. However, he soon resumed his bravado and returned Andreide's glare.

"Have a nice day at 'Garbage High', *ma cherie!*" he smirked.

All the rich boys laughed then Richard signalled to the bus driver and they sped away, their black exhaust fumes dissipating into the atmosphere like an evil spirit seeking its next victim.

Andreide held back the angry tears which threatened to burst forth. She glowered at the back of the posh bus as it disappeared into the distance. She felt like screaming at the impertinence of those infuriating boys. They made her feel like cursing every rich teenage boy alive and damning them to hell. She wished that there were no wealthy people in the world, so that there would be no class divisions by financial status or skin colour.

Normally, Andreide would not allow those boys to bother her but today was different. Richard Carlston made it different. It wasn't just what he had said that bothered her, but how he had said it too. He almost made her feel like she was less than human, ridiculing her for what she could not control – her family's financial and social status. Not only was he mocking her lowered social and economic standing, but reopening old wounds that had never quite healed in both of them.

Andreide and Richard were good friends until two years ago. In fact, she had begun to like Richard in more ways than one until their relationship went sour. Her father had been employed by Mr. Carlston and worked as his junior assistant at his development bank. They became very good friends as well and began to socialize together, inviting each other for lunch at each other's home and spending days-off at social clubs. Mr. D'Averette's popularity had begun to soar as his new best friend's power almost matched that of the Prime Minister's. Naturally, Richard and Andreide became friends as well and saw a lot of each other, in and out of school. At that time, they were both attending St. George's Public High School.

Disaster struck one day, when an envelope containing ten thousand dollars vanished from Mr. Carlston's locked safe then reappeared on Mr. D'Averette's desk. Without properly investigating the matter, Mr. Carlston accused Mr. D'Averette of theft and immediately dismissed him from his job. It later came to light that one of Mr. Carlston's business partners 'borrowed' the money, using a copy of the safe's original key and 'accidentally misplaced' the envelope on Mr. D'Averette's desk.

However, after this revelation was made, Mr. Carlston never apologized to Andreide's father or tried to make amends. Mr. D'Averette told his family that he suspected his former friend was too embarrassed to admit his mistake. Even though Mr. Carlston had betrayed him, which led to his public humiliation and lowered social status, Mr. D'Averette never sought vengeance. Even when his former friend started spreading lies and rumours about him, he still did not seek retribution. Many of Mr. D'Averette's friends thought that his unfair dismissal was racially motivated as Mr. D'Averette was a black man and his boss was white. Mr. D'Averette did not fully support this theory because he did not believe that his former friend was a racist. Andreide thought otherwise. Nevertheless, her father had not totally forgiven him either and both men shared a common dislike for each other.

A couple months after the incident, Mr. Carlston transferred his son to Duncan's Academy while Andreide remained in St. George's Public High School. From then their enmity blossomed. A few months later, they had met at a party and had exchanged the most abusive words aimed at the other's father. Before their quarrel had ended in violence, the host of the party intervened and sent them home. This unpleasant parting had increased the animosity between the two.

Andreide shook her head and forced herself to clear her mind. She began to think of the day ahead of her and continued on her way to school, thankful that it was the last day of the week.

*

Andreide arrived at school five minutes before the bell rang at 8:30 a.m. She climbed the flight of stairs to the second floor where her home room class was located. She placed her schoolbag on the rack under her desk then slumped in her chair, exhausted and still somewhat angry from her morning ordeal.

"Hey gyul, wha' happen to you this morning?" Keisha Taylor asked in her usual dialect. She was from Conaree, a village south of St. George's parish where the dialect was rather raw.

"Yeah girl, wassup? You look like you vex with the world," Harietta Green commented, entering the classroom after Keisha. She waddled to her usual desk then squeezed into her chair, two seats to the left of Andreide.

Andreide gave a tight smile. "Just the usual – the pest at home and the white supremacist."

Keisha rolled her eyes. "Gyul, why do you let them ole DABs trouble you so? They just making you vex-vex all the time. If I was you, I would ah done buss he face, kick him in he ole bleach ass then spit pon he face! They think they still own us, you know!"

Andreide smiled at her friend's enthusiasm and zeal for vengeance. She believed Keisha would do as she said and 'buss he face …' if she were in Andreide's position. However, Andreide was not a violent person although she could become quite incensed at times.

"I mean it, Andy. Stop letting them white boys rule you so. Slavery done and we free since 1838. It's the twenty-first century now! Gyul, you got to remind them who the boss be now! Is we chile, is we! Is we de boss now!" Keisha pounded her desk for emphasis.

9

"Calm down girl, what's your problem? Andy ain't letting them DABs rule her! It's Richard she meant anyway," said Harietta, turning to Andreide for confirmation.

Andreide looked from one girl to the other, slightly amused. The 'DABs' her friends referred to was an acronym for 'Duncan's Academy Bastards/ Bitches'. Andreide hesitated before she responded, not wanting to set Keisha off on her daily ranting campaign.

"Well yeah, I mainly meant Richard but those other rich idiots are almost as bad as he is."

"Well, what you gonna do 'bout it? I tired ah hearing 'bout them harassing you so. You don't do sumt'ing, I will!" Keisha warned.

"Girl, please! What can you do? You with your lil bony self," said Harietta.

"Gyul, just hush you big mouth! You ain't going to do nothing with you ole fat ass, so who better than me?"

Harietta flicked her hand dismissively at her. "You just jealous that I look better and got a higher grade on the English test than you. And anyway, who died and made you Queen Protector, Miss bony-black-broomstick?"

Andreide laughed to herself as her two friends started their habitual squabbling over whom was the smarter and better looking one. Andreide knew for sure who was the smarter of the two and that was Harietta. However, when it came to looks, she was not too sure.

Harietta was big and meaty but was well proportioned. What she lacked in shape, she made up for in physical beauty. She had a round face dark brown smiling eyes, and skin a chocolaty–brown. Her kinky, dark brown hair was thick and long, which she normally kept plaited and well-oiled.

On the other hand, Keisha was dark in complexion, scrawny and as thin as a stick, which had earned her the nickname, 'Broomstick'. She was shorter than Harietta with dark, slightly bulging eyes and a small, up-turned nose. Her mouth which seemed to never rest, contained two thin lips which habitually pouted. Today, like most days, she had styled her short hair in twigs. Keisha was not ugly; her beauty was just not as apparent as Harietta's.

Their personalities were just as different as their physical appearances. Harietta was bubbly, pleasant and peaceful. She had great self-esteem and was a very mature and wise sixteen-year-old. In contrast, Keisha was cantankerous. Almost everything bothered her and she was hardly ever pleased with anything. She was an outspoken girl and was very quarrelsome, which often led to her disrespecting her elders. However, she did possess positive qualities. She was a firm believer in equality and was conscious of her African heritage.

Andreide thought over her friends' differences and smiled to herself. She knew their argument was futile for they never came to a conclusion.

Five minutes later the bell rang, ending Keisha's and Harietta's quarrel. As the fifth form classroom filled, Andreide noticed that the seat to her right was empty. She leaned backwards in her chair and whispered to Harietta, "Where's Alisa?" Harietta shrugged then motioned to Keisha seated in front of her.

"Hey Keisha, where's Alisa?" Andreide whispered.

"Don't know. I ain't seen she for the morning."

"Yeah, neither me," said Harietta. "I looked out for her when I was leaving home but she didn't meet me as usual by the corner."

Before Andreide could reply, Mrs. Smith, their elderly home room teacher marched in and slammed the blackboard eraser on her desk. "Quiet back there! I don't want to hear any noise coming from you all, this morning. And you Keisha! You better don't start anything today, you hear me?" She shook a withered index finger at Keisha.

Keisha rolled her eyes, turned away and steupsed rudely – making a sucking noise with her tongue against her teeth.

"Child! Don't you suck your teeth at me! What, you didn't brush them this morning?"

"Well, excuse me! Look who talking, Miss rotten mouth wit de stink-stink breath and dutty rotting teeth!" exclaimed Keisha, her eyes widening as they usually did when she was riled.

Everyone tried his and her best to stifle giggles. However, Andreide was not as amused as her fellow classmates. Although their old-aged teacher really had foul breath and revolting-looking teeth, she did not think it was appropriate for Keisha to state this to their teacher, in such a rude and disrespectful manner. It had become the norm now that Keisha and Mrs. Smith sparred verbally almost everyday, and each day it seemed that the former became more proficient at it. Ever since they entered fifth form and received Mrs. Smith as their home room teacher, Keisha and their elderly educator clashed constantly.

Andreide understood why. Mrs. Murielle Smith was a seventy-seven-year-old teacher who was decades passed her retirement age. She was short, wiry, grey-haired and her skin was as shrivelled as an over-dried prune. It was rumoured that if a person touched her skin a trace of dust would remain on his finger, and her putrid odour would seep into his body and slowly poison him – a belief which frightened and repulsed many of her students. Her age deceived her appearance. She looked more like she was ninety-seven than seventy-seven but she had the vitality of a thirty year-old woman. She was very crabby and extremely annoying to students like Keisha who disliked the 'old-time' ways of elderly people and had no patience for it. Mrs. Smith was also very old fashioned so she often conflicted with Keisha's outspokenness and self-governing attitude. As a result, the two were constantly at war.

Mrs. Smith glowered at Keisha through her large, owl-like glasses, her arms akimbo. The wrinkles on her forehead multiplied and rippled as the thin worn out muscles beneath her ancient skin contracted in indignation, making her countenance appear more horrific than was usual.

"You … you … you …!" she sputtered in rage. "How dare you disrespect me so? Child, I am more than fed up with you! No teacher should have to deal with such a devilish child!" Mrs. Smith's eyes bulged beneath her thick bifocals.

Keisha sucked her teeth again. "Then leave nuh ole woman! I certainly ain't stopping you."

All the humour of the situation disappeared from the faces of the onlooking students, as they stared in a mixture of disbelief and awe at their classmate. Andreide tensed, angry at Keisha's audacity and wary of the repercussions that were knocking at the door. She looked over at Harietta and saw that she too was not pleased.

"That's it! I've had it! I will not deal with you anymore. You test me too much. Go to the headmaster's office!"

Keisha returned Mrs. Smith's glower, looking her up and down, her manner very challenging. She folded her arms, leaned back in her chair and pouted, all while glaring at her incensed teacher. Her attitude reeked of defiance and insolence.

"I said go to Mr. Williams' office!" the teacher shouted. Still, Keisha refused to move.

"Go now, you impertinent wretched wench!" she shrieked.

Keisha stood up abruptly. Her cool insolent state quickly changed to one of pure vehement rage.

"*Don't you ever call me that again!*" Her voice was low and trembled with heated fury. She began to shake with anger, her fists balled at her side. Andreide stared at her friend in utmost disbelief and shock. She had never seen her react so irately before, which frightened Andreide significantly; she was afraid for Keisha's sake.

As Mrs. Smith was about to respond, the classroom door flung open. In the doorway was Mr. Williams, the principal. He was very tall and always bore a serious expression on his face. He was known for his severity, especially in issuing punishments to offenders. He stood in the doorway, his presence very intimidating, then spoke in his deep yet quiet voice.

"What seems to be the problem Mrs. Smith? Why is this class creating such a racket, disturbing the whole school?"

"Mr. Williams, it's not the class, it's this *child!*" Mrs. Smith proclaimed, pointing a crooked finger at Keisha as she rounded her desk to approach the principal.

"Well ... what did she do?" Mr. Williams looked down at Mrs. Smith expectantly.

"What did she do? What did she do? WHAT DID SHE DO!" Mrs. Smith bellowed with rage, spittle flying from her frothing mouth. "This child is the devil incarnate! I will not tolerate her rudeness and attitude anymore!"

"Mrs. Smith, please control yourself."

"But sir, you do not understand the gravity of the situation! This child is a fu –"

"MRS. SMITH!"

Everyone stared in shock at the scene before him and her. Keisha's mood lifted slightly as she grinned at her teacher's loss of self-control. She knew that Mrs. Smith had triggered the principal's nerve and would surely face his wrath. Andreide looked on, somewhat fearful.

"Mrs. Smith, follow me to my office, now." Mr. Williams' voice was forcefully controlled.

"But sir ... that ... that ... insolent ... *creature!*" Mrs. Smith sputtered, her gnarled finger pointed at Keisha, shaking with rage.

"That's enough! Come now!" Mr. Williams barked. His patience was at its limit and he could no longer tolerate Mrs. Smith's delirious, unprofessional behaviour.

Mrs. Smith glared at Keisha one last time then grudgingly followed the headmaster out.

Andreide sighed in relief. She leaned back in her seat and massaged her temples.

The tense silence was pierced by Keisha's mirthless laugh. "That ole hag going to get it now!" The class laughed along with her. Keisha strolled up to the teacher's desk, grabbed a stick of chalk and began to draw obscene cartoons of Mrs. Smith, along with profane descriptions of each drawing. The class roared with laughter as Keisha added an audio commentary to her art.

Andreide stood up and approached her friend. "Keisha, this is not funny. You need to stop it and sit down."

Keisha paused from her artwork and turned to Andreide, not surprised by her friend's admonishment. "Aw c'mon gyul, gimme a break. Ah just expressing myself. At least I ain't going on like that ole bitch!" Again the class laughed.

"Listen to Andreide. She's telling you the right thing. You really getting out-a-hand, child!" said Harietta. She too got up and followed Andreide to the front of the classroom.

Keisha raised an eyebrow. "Since when you two become my mother? Y'all sounding like that ole prune now too. *That child is the devil!*" she mocked while making distorted faces. The room rocked with hearty laughter.

After the class settled, Andreide continued. "Keisha, you really need to stop being so rude to Mrs. Smith. Yes, she's a pest and an old bag, everyone knows that. But you don't see us reacting the way you do. You have to control yourself. If you're not going to respect Mrs. Smith, then respect yourself and bite your tongue."

"Yeah girl, you have to watch your temper," said Harietta. "It won't get you anything but trouble."

Keisha turned away from her friends and resumed her drawing. Her face was set like the weather and her mouth was in its usual pout.

"Girl, you hear us?" asked Harietta. When Keisha did not respond, she grabbed her arm and shook it.

"Gyul, lemme go!" Keisha jerked her arm away from Harietta's grasp.

"Keisha, please listen to us! We're only trying to help you," said Andreide.

"Help me? Help me with what? Everybody think they can help me and they know what's best for me. If it ain't you two, is

Granny. Why y'all don't just lemme live me life my way? If y'all want to be smart, stick-by-de-rules people, then go ahead! I know I want to enjoy myself before I die and that is just what I going to do. So leave me 'lone!" She dropped the chalk and turned to return to her seat. However, before she could sit down, Ms. Brown, the English teacher entered the room.

"Keisha Taylor, the principal would like to see you in his office immediately."

Andreide and Harietta exchanged worried glances. Keisha rolled her eyes then left the classroom. Ms. Brown remained in the room.

"Okay children, settle down now. I will be substituting for Mrs. Smith for the rest of the day. You two take your seats," she said indicating to Andreide and Harietta. "The rest of you get out your Geography books and read chapter twenty-three in turns, starting from Clarice and ending with Stephen."

Andreide returned to her seat and prepared herself for the humdrum events of the day. However, her friend's situation dominated her mind.

*

At 3:30 p.m., the bell rang signalling the end of yet another day of school. Andreide and her schoolmates gathered their belongings then exited the building as quickly as possible, excited that it was finally the weekend.

When Andreide reached the front gates, she saw Harietta waiting for her at their usual spot across the street. However, she was not alone. She was accompanied by one of Keisha's cousins, Jamila Hughes. Andreide became wary as she approached them – she did not like or trust Jamila at all. The main reason was Jamila's loose and immoral behaviour, which gained her much popularity on the streets.

"Ey gyul wha' goin on?" Jamila greeted Andreide.

Andreide hesitated. "Nothing. I'm good." She then turned to Harietta and gave her a questioning look.

"Jamila was just telling me about Keisha. She said she saw her going home earlier today and asked her what happened. Keisha said that she was 'taking the afternoon off.'"

"Yeah, my gyul looked vex though. She say something how she ain't finished with that ole witch yet," Jamila added.

"Oh," Andreide replied. She glanced around the street, thinking of a subtle way to disengage herself from Jamila's company. She didn't have to however, for a gang of boys strolled up the road – their arrival immediately caught Jamila's attention.

"Hey tits, come here!" the gang leader hollered.

"Yeah, bring yuh big ass over here wit' them milk pumps too!" The other hoodlums laughed.

Jamila grinned, an excited, desperate look in her eyes. "See y'all later!" She pushed up her triple D cups then quickly wined her way over to the gang. The leader grabbed her then the pack turned down a side street and strolled away, leaving echoes of their boisterousness in their wake.

Andreide and Harietta stared at the retreating figures until they disappeared from sight.

"What is she planning to achieve?"

Harietta sighed. "Girl, I really don't know to tell you the truth. All I know is that she must be real desperate for attention for the way she acting."

They turned in the opposite direction and began the walk home.

"Harietta, I really don't like that girl, you know. Aside from her ways, I just don't trust her and I can't stand her."

"Yeah girl, I know. I feel the same way too. But you still have to deal with people you don't like, no matter what you feel about them."

"But she's such a *slut*."

"True, but she's still a person. Oh and you better make sure you don't call that girl that in front of Keisha." Harietta warned. The girls continued on their journey home in quiet reflectance.

Two streets before Andreide's house, Harietta turned off on Collins Lane. Her house was the fourth one on the right, where she lived with her mother and several younger brothers and sisters. "See you later, girl." Harietta waved goodbye to Andreide. Andreide waved then continued to her house on Blossom Lane, while she thought of the weekend ahead.

Chapter 2

"Hello, good afternoon. May I help you?"

"Oh hi, Mr. Bretford. This is Andreide. Is Alisa there?"

"Um, yes she is. Hold a minute, dear," Mr. Bretford replied.

"Okay, thank you."

It was 4:15 p.m. and Andreide had just arrived home when she remembered that her friend had been absent from school that day. Before she changed her school uniform – a pale brown buttoned shirt, a dark green plaid skirt, green socks and brown shoes – she dumped her school bag in a corner of her room then dialled Alisa's home number on her cell phone.

Alisa was Andreide's best friend and had been since they entered secondary school. Her coyness complemented Andreide's self-assurance quite well. Although Alisa was a loyal friend, she could at times be too naïve and dependent on her friends; Andreide often felt the need to protect her.

After a three-minute wait, Alisa came to the phone. "Hello?" She sounded a bit hoarse.

"Hey girl, how are you? Didn't see you at school today. Are you alright? You sound funny." Andreide flopped unto her desk chair and kicked off her shoes.

"Oh, I wasn't feeling well. But I feel much better now, thanks."

"You sure?"

"Yep."

"So what disease did you have?" Andreide joked. She searched through her desk drawers for a hidden snack.

"Huh?"

"Gosh, dum-dum! You were sick, weren't you?" She found a pack of Lays barbecue chips, her favourite.

Alisa laughed. "Yeah, just a little cough though."

"That's it? A 'little cough'? A 'little cough' kept you from coming to school – the 'most finest institution in the world, in which we love to learn all things righteous'?" At this statement, both girls burst out in laughter. It was a concrete fact that Andreide and her friends disliked their school. What made the joke even more hilarious was that Andreide had quoted Mrs. Smith; it was part of their elderly teacher's routine school-loving speeches.

The girls sobered. "Yeah, Mrs. Smith really is something, eh?" said Alisa.

Andreide laughed. She opened the pack and started to eat some chips.

"Speaking of that old bag, you missed her melt-down this morning."

"Really? What happened?"

"She had a ring-ding-ding with Keisha."

"As usual. Go on."

Andreide then proceeded to inform Alisa about the events of the day, Keisha's behaviour, and the encounter with Jamila and the boys. As usual, Alisa agreed with Andreide's views.

"Yeah that Jamila, we know what she is –"

"A *slut*."

"And as for Keisha," Alisa continued, "well … like you said … she needs guidance."

Both girls grew silent. After a while, Andreide spoke. "I wish she would listen to us. We're trying to help her and she's acting as if we're against her. It's for her own good that we're helping her. I mean, we're telling her the right thing, aren't we?"

"Of course you are!" said Alisa.

"Yeah, I guess." Andreide sighed. There was a pause in the conversation.

"Hang on a sec' Andy, my mother's calling me."

"Ok."

A couple minutes later, Alisa returned on the line. "Hey Andy, I gotta go. My mother is reminding me to take my cough medicine. Yuck!" Alisa shuddered. Andreide laughed.

"Alright, enjoy it. See you Monday, right?"

"Hopefully."

"Ok later."

"Bye."

As Andreide hung up, she heard footsteps approaching her door. Before she saw who it was, she recognized the scent of the perfume. It was her mother. She quickly stuffed the empty chips package in her top desk drawer and dusted the crumbs from her fingers. Mrs. D'Averette knocked on the door before she entered.

"Hey darling, how was school?"

"Hi mom, school was ... well, nothing out of the ordinary happened," she said with a grin, thinking about Keisha's and Mrs. Smith's brawl earlier that morning.

"Ok, that's good." Rose Marie seemed distracted and Andreide noticed it. Her mother gazed out of Andreide's bedroom window with a slight frown on her face.

"Mom, are you alright?"

Mrs. D'Averette refocused on her daughter. She gave a fleeting smile. "Yes dear, just work on my mind. I'm fine." She paused before continuing. "We're going out to dinner tonight for 8:00 p.m. All of us. So be ready by 7:30 p.m., ok?"

Andreide frowned. "Tonight? Why?"

Rose Marie sighed. "Please, not you too. Your brother is in one of his moods and it was difficult enough to get him to come. Please don't give me any trouble as well." She sounded very tired.

Andreide started to reply, but her mother held up her hand and cut her off. "I know you won't give me any trouble. I'm just reminding you that it's an important dinner. My publicist, Jean and one of my editors, Victor Wilson will be there. They said they have something important to tell me and think that the whole family should be there to hear it." Rose Marie appeared both nervous and worried.

"So be ready by 7:30 p.m. You know how long you take to get ready for everything so please, be ready early. For once!"

Andreide began to rebut her mother's accusatory remark but thought better of it. She simply agreed to be ready on time.

After her mother left her bedroom, Andreide changed out of her school clothes then went down the hall to the bathroom, wrapped in a bath towel. When she got there, the door was locked. She knocked on the door but received no answer. She tightened her towel then pressed her right ear to the door. All she heard was the sounds of a low voice talking. She frowned.

"C'mon Marques, get out of there!" she yelled.

"Get out of where? What did I do?" Marques poked his head out of the door of the bedroom that he shared with their older brother, Omarion.

Ignoring him, Andreide rolled her eyes and muttered to herself. "Oh great, then it's the next one. God only knows how long he'll spend in there." She turned around and headed back to her room.

"Hey Andy, I can tell you when he comes out of the bathroom, if you want?" said Marques.

Andreide turned to face him and gave him a quizzical look.

"Why? What do you want?"

Marques seemed confused by her question. He thought that it was obvious – he only wanted to help her. In fact, he felt guilty about his behaviour earlier that morning and wanted to be in his big sister's good books again.

"Nothing, I just want to be kind," he said quietly, his eyes lowered.

Andreide laughed.

"Yeah right. As if you're ever kind to me, you little pest! Up to now my hand still hurts from this morning. I haven't forgotten that. You want to be kind – fine! How about this, why don't you take your kindness and shove it up your –"

"Andreide Melissa D'Averette!"

Andreide spun around as her mother hurried up the stairs. Rose Marie was stricken with disbelief at her daughter's language.

"Andreide, what is going on here? Why are you using such inappropriate figures of speech to your little brother?"

"He's such a nuisance mom! He deliberately tries to annoy me and I'm really fed up of him!"

"I was only trying to help her."

"Well I didn't ask for your *'help'*, now did I?"

"Look, I don't have time for this! It's 5:30 p.m. and I'd like to have some quiet time to think before we go to dinner. You two need to stop the quarrelling and stop being so selfish. And you Andreide, I don't want to hear you speaking to your brother like that again. Understood?"

"But mom that's not fair! You always take his side. You haven't even heard what he's done!" Andreide said indignantly. "He –"

Mrs. D'Averette's cell phone rang, interrupting her daughter's complaint. She glanced at the screen then seemed startled by the caller ID. "I have to take this call," she said quickly. She opened the line then hurried down the stairs to the privacy of her office.

"Argh!" Andreide threw her arms up in the air in frustration. She turned around to face her brother and glared at him, full of resentment. Instead of venting her rage on him, she stormed into her bedroom, slamming the door behind her.

As she released some steam, her mind raced back to Keisha and her hatred of Mrs. Smith and adults in general. Andreide still did not agree with Keisha's methods of handling similar situations but she began to understand Keisha's feelings of disgust and frustration with adults, who were much too busy with their own business to take the time to understand their children.

*

At 7:45 p.m., the D'Averette family left the house and drove to one of the finest restaurants in the town near the coast. 'La Grande Cuisine' was a posh, international five-star restaurant owned and operated by professional French chefs. Only on rare occasions did the D'Averettes dine at the first-class restaurant.

When they arrived, they were greeted by one of the several foreign hostesses who showed them to their table; Jean and Mr. Wilson were already seated. Andreide noted the attire of the other guests and felt self-conscious. She also didn't fail to note the attitude of the hostess who regarded them with a condescending manner.

After they were seated and pleasantries were exchanged, Andreide glanced around the restaurant. It was very large and impressive. The walls were beautifully painted with portraits and murals, and classical music filled the air.

Andreide gazed at the other guests in curiosity. It was obvious from their appearance that they were financially well-off. The majority of the men wore black tailored suits and the women were dressed in gowns of black, white, red or royal blue. The diamonds that adorned their pale skin sparkled like the stars in the sky. Andreide felt uncomfortable.

When they had ordered their meals, the adults began their discussion of Mrs. D'Averette's book. Andreide sat back and tried to appear inconspicuous, without much success. She felt as if everyone was watching them. Her family was an oil spill among the sea of white faces – a stain, ruining and intruding in their perfect world of rich and idle life. Andreide felt disgusted and wanted to leave the enemy-zone as quickly as possible. Her family didn't belong there and she knew it.

"So what's the big news that couldn't be told over the phone or at home?" Mrs. D'Averette asked with a nervous grin. Andreide perked up and listened closely.

Jean Chang, the publicist and Victor Wilson, the executive editor, exchanged excited looks. "Well, Rose Marie, we have very, very good news to share with you all that may change your lives forever!" Jean announced dramatically. Her dark slanted eyes danced with merriment as she kept the D'Averettes in suspense.

Mr. Wilson laughed at their anxious expressions, a happy laugh which caught Andreide's attention. "Jean, would you just tell them already." His grey eyes smiled amiably in his handsome face and Andreide couldn't help but gaze at his appealing features – sharp regal nose, thin smiling lips, smooth, clean-shaven face. He even smelled gorgeous! She noted his dress style and knew at once that he too was among the affluent; he wore a long-sleeved, light blue designer dress-shirt, a silky grey tie, and dark blue dress-pants with polished, black, Italian leather shoes. He spoke with an accent and Andreide was not sure if it was American or British.

Jean grinned. "Alright." She turned to Mrs. D'Averette with a serious expression. "Rose Marie, your book is attracting a lot of attention in the medical field. Everyone's reading it and everyone's loving it! Even before it's released to the public it's getting a lot of attention."

"Yes, it is!" said Mr. Wilson. "We were considering bringing the release date forward to increase the sales that we predicted –"

"*We* predicted?" Jean cut in. "Since when do *we* work together?" she said, turning to face Mr. Wilson with a slightly challenging look.

He laughed then smoothly flicked back a lock of shiny, black hair from his forehead. Andreide followed his every movement.

"I'm the publicist and you're the editor, Victor," Jean continued, pointing at him as she spoke. She could not help but grin as Mr. Wilson focused his laughing eyes on her in an amused expression.

"So what are you saying?" Mr. D'Averette interrupted as if waking up from a stupor. Everyone looked at him blankly. Andreide rolled her eyes, annoyed at his thoughtless questions and embarrassed that she was related to him. She hoped that Mr. Wilson had not noticed.

Jean paused before continuing. "Well, Mr. D'Averette, this means that your wife's book is a guaranteed success. And at the rate it's going, it's bound to be number one in medical literature pretty soon," she stated. "Definitely number one in the Caribbean."

Everyone reacted gleefully to the news.

"Wow, this is so cool, isn't it Mom!" Marques exclaimed as he fidgeted in his chair.

"Well done dear. I knew you would succeed," Mr. D'Averette kissed his wife on the cheek. Rose Marie smiled faintly.

Andreide eyed her hypocritical father before she gave her sentiments. "Yeah Mom, this is really great." She was truly happy for her mother.

Even Omarion, who had remained silent and cross since they arrived, reacted positively to the news. He smiled awkwardly and congratulated his mother, much to her delight. His mood brightened a little throughout the rest of the evening.

Fifteen minutes later their dinner was served and they ate amongst lively chatter. Everyone was happy and excited about the good news. During dessert, while the adults paused from their conversation to sample the delicacies, Marques asked excitedly, "So does this mean that Mom is going to be famous now? Like a celebrity? Is she gonna be on TV? Is she going to Hollywood? Are we all going with her?"

Everyone laughed. "Calm down will you? She hasn't even sold a book yet," Andreide said, annoyed with her little brother, as usual.

"Andreide!" Rose Marie cautioned her daughter. Andreide rolled her eyes and sighed. Unlike the adults, she did not think Marques' behaviour was cute or amusing at all.

Jean set her fork down and brushed the chocolate cake crumbs from her mouth. "Well Marques," she said thoughtfully. "It is a possibility that your mother will become famous, but it's only her first book and it hasn't been released yet, like your sister said. I don't want you to get your hopes up so –"

"Oh, you joy-stealer!" Mr. Wilson cut in with a laugh. "Don't listen to Jean, son. She's always too practical and wicked. Yes, your mother will become famous! She'll be the most famous psychologist-author ever known!" he said with gusto, shooting his right fist in the air in a triumphant gesture.

Everyone at the table laughed at his zealous expression. Andreide's feelings of annoyance with Marques vanished as she gazed upon the joyous face of her mother's executive editor. She sighed contentedly.

An hour later, after the last dishes were removed, their waitress brought the bill. On cue with its arrival, Mr. D'Averette excused himself from the table to visit the Men's room, a move which nobody failed to notice. Mr. Wilson raised his eyebrows and glanced at Rose Marie, who looked away, clearly embarrassed. Andreide glared at her father's retreating figure with strong distaste, until her mother nudged her from under the table.

Mrs. D'Averette took the bill and stared at it in shock. However, she quickly resumed her composure. Before Andreide could peek at the sum, Mr. Wilson gently took the bill from Rose Marie's hands.

"Tonight's on me," he said quietly.

"But Victor –!" Rose Marie began to protest.

He held up his hand and gave a determined smile. "No no no, ma'am, I insist. It's my treat." He looked Rose Marie in the eye for a few seconds.

Jean looked on quietly. As Victor signed a cheque, she tried to change the subject and lighten the mood once more. "So Rose Marie, what do you think about us moving the release date forward by two weeks?"

Rose Marie looked away from Victor as she focussed on Jean. She smiled weakly. "Well, if it will boost sales like you said, then sure. I'm fine with it."

Jean grinned. "Hell yes, it *will* boost sales! And not only that – imagine the media attention we'll get – you'll get!" she added quickly. Mr. Wilson glanced up from reviewing the cheque with a slight frown on his countenance. Jean continued, "But by bringing forward the release date to the last week of this month, January, we'll also have to bring the date of your book tour forward as well, to at least the middle of February."

Rose Marie seemed startled. "What? But that's so soon! You're telling me I'll be going on the book tour a month from now?"

"Oh no no no no! That's just an approximation. But you get what I'm saying anyway," Jean said hastily. She looked at Victor for support but he did not respond. He placed the cheque along with a tip in U.S currency in the bill holder then handed it to the over-eager waitress, who hustled over to their table.

As they were exiting the restaurant on the way to the parking lot, Mr. D'Averette hurried towards them from the opposite end of the building. Andreide and her brothers were not the only ones who showed visible revulsion at the sight of him. Rose Marie stiffened and Andreide saw a vein throb in her temple.

Oblivious to the change in his family's mood, catching up to them, Mr. D'Averette said, "So … what did I miss?" He grinned at them all. Everyone stared at him incredulously and halted their steps. Andreide gritted her teeth, trying to restrain the string of obscenities which were at the tip of her tongue. Omarion clenched and unclenched his fist, looking daggers at his ignorant father.

When no one spoke or moved, feeling awkward, Mr. D'Averette hurried ahead of them to 'warm up' their car. Rose Marie released a tight breath and Jean patted her sympathetically on her back. Andreide ran to catch up with Omarion who had stomped off ahead of them.

"Do you believe that man? He can't be serious!" she said when she was on par with her brother. Omarion glanced back at his mother and her colleagues before he responded.

"He's lucky he left so soon just now, or else I would've knocked the crap outta him! Let him try that again and he'll see." Omarion said vehemently. He cooled down a bit then continued. "That man really makes me angry. Damn! I can't wait to be eighteen in April and see the back of him – the ole bastard!" He swore then stormed off ahead of Andreide. She let him go. She felt the same way.

Meanwhile, Jean occupied Marques in conversation to distract him from the hostile mood of his family members. She walked him ahead of his mother and Mr. Wilson.

Rose Marie felt physically and mentally exhausted. She sighed deeply and gazed into the distance as she walked. Victor slowed his pace and looked over at her, concern in his eyes.

"Are you all right, Mrs. D'Averette?"

She focused on him and forced a smile.

"Yes, I'm fine thanks."

Victor was not convinced.

Before he could ask another question, Rose Marie said while averting her eyes, "I'd like to apologize for my husband's behaviour tonight. And I'm sorry for whatever inconvenience it may have caused you with footing the bill. I'll pay you back first thing Monday morning and –"

"Rose," said Victor quietly.

She looked at him and caught his eyes, surprised that he had called her by her first name, for he was always formal in addressing her. He continued, "You don't need to repay me. I meant it when I said that it was my treat ... Ok?" He waited for her response. She looked away and hesitated. When she did not respond, he added even more quietly, "And you don't have to apologize to me, ever."

After a while, Rose Marie stopped walking and cleared her throat. She looked up at him; their eyes locked. He saw the moonlight glistening in her dark brown eyes, enhancing her beautiful features. They looked at each other for a few seconds, before Rose Marie answered him.

"Thank you," she said softly, in almost a whisper.

Before Victor could respond, she resumed walking and quickened her pace to catch up with the others who were nearly at the car. Victor smiled slightly as he watched her go before following her to rejoin the others.

At the D'Averette's car, Victor and Jean bid the family goodnight then proceeded to their own vehicles. Victor drove away in a black BMW and Jean in a red Mercedes-Benz. The D'Averettes drove home in their old, grey, 1997 Toyota station wagon.

Andreide noticed that her mother seemed distant and distracted on the journey back home and was not sure if that was a good or bad thing. She knew that something other than her book was troubling her, and Andreide had an inkling of what it was. She glared at the back of her father's head the rest of the drive home.

***

Rose Marie splashed some cold water onto her face and gasped at its frigidity. It soothed the agitated muscles in her face, which were a result of the recent weeks of stress over the publishing of her book. She had never known that writing a book could be so stressful until she experienced it for herself. She longed for the day when production would officially be complete. She was glad that Jean was releasing the book two weeks ahead of schedule. But then, there was the book tour so quickly approaching. She really was not keen on travelling to the USA so soon; it meant that she would have to leave her children for weeks with their father, Charles – the second source of her stress.

After removing her make-up, Rose Marie changed into a light blue cotton nightgown. She undid her long, black, straightened hair which was styled in a chignon and plaited it into a long braid. She looked in the bathroom mirror and heaved a sigh. She could see her weariness. Tiny stress lines were beginning to form near her eyes and she noticed her forehead seemed creased in a subconscious frown. The circles under her eyes were also more prominent and darker than before.

Yet beneath these recent signs of over-work, Rose Marie was a very beautiful forty-three year old woman. Her skin was a smooth, firm, cocoa brown which made her appear more youthful than her age revealed. Her face was oval-shaped and her features were neatly proportioned.

Since she had begun to write her book six months ago, Rose Marie had joined a fitness club in an attempt to ease her stress and as a means of distraction and relaxation. Every Saturday morning and Wednesday evening, her club met at the town's Community Centre to jog through the hills at the south-east end of the island. The results of such arduous exercise had begun to show on her body, a fact which Rose Marie was very proud of. She had lost a total of forty pounds so far and felt like a new woman. One morning, while in the shower, she realised that she could see the curve of her waist again – it had disappeared since the birth of her last child – which raised her spirits tremendously. In addition, she had developed more muscle tone which attracted the stares of many men, several of whom were quite young, which both alarmed and pleased her. The admiring comments from her friends and family also encouraged her to continue her hard work. She smiled as she thought of her accomplishments.

After she finished preparing herself for bed, she switched the light off and came out of the adjoining bathroom. She stopped as she saw Charles already lying in bed asleep. She felt resentment and disappointment brew within her as she looked at her lethargic husband and remembered his shameful behaviour that night at dinner.

It was a known fact that Charles D'Averette was a stingy man but Rose Marie did not expect that he would show it so publicly and shamelessly in her presence, especially in front of Victor. She still felt embarrassed and her face flushed as she pictured Victor's look of surprise and disbelief that night at dinner. Even if Charles were awake, she was not inclined to speak to him about his habitual miserly attitude. She sighed and strode across the bedroom.

She slept on the pull-out sofa on the opposite side of the room.

***

The next day, Andreide awoke at 7:30 a.m. and began her usual Saturday morning routine. She made her bed then quickly neatened her room. She rushed to use the bathroom first, before her brothers woke up and locked themselves in there for what seemed like hours.

Half an hour later, Andreide went downstairs to the kitchen to prepare herself some breakfast. As usual, she chose the fastest means of food preparation and made herself a ham and cheese sandwich with wheat bread – she hated to cook. She poured some apple juice in a glass while she microwaved her sandwich.

As she entered the living room with her breakfast tray, she halted in the doorway. Marques was sprawled out on her favourite couch directly in front of the television watching Saturday morning cartoons. A vein twitched in her forehead.

"Boy, what do you think you're doing?" Andreide demanded.

Marques whipped his head around, startled by her sudden entrance. "Watching TV," he said curtly. He grabbed the remote from the coffee table and readied himself for the impending onslaught.

"I can see that, you moron! I mean why are you watching TV here? You know that I watch what I want on Saturday mornings on this TV. Go in Mom and Dad's room!"

"Well, Dad was still sleeping in there, alright?" Marques said in an impatient tone.

Andreide rolled her eyes. "Wow, that's a surprise. So what else is new?"

Marques turned back to his cartoons and ignored her sarcasm. He wished she wasn't so argumentative and fussy, especially with him. However, at the moment, he didn't feel like having her order him around.

"Well?" Andreide demanded, one hand on her hip, the other balancing her food tray.

Marques turned back to face her. "Well what?"

"Go use the TV upstairs!"

"No," he stated, his tone defiant. He turned back around and raised the volume on the television set.

Andreide stared at him in disbelief and confusion. How dare he disrespect and disobey her? She was older than him and had the final say!

"Argh! You pest! I hate you!" she shouted at him. She picked up a cushion from a nearby sofa and threw it at his head. Her aim was accurate. She stormed out of the living room while Marques shouted back at her.

"Ha! Well, I still get to watch TV here," he teased, "And I'm gonna tell Mom you threw that cushion from her new sofa at me!"

Andreide cursed him under her breath as she entered the dining room. She dropped into a chair then moodily ate her breakfast, wishing yet again that she was an only child. When she finished eating, she washed her dishes then went back upstairs to her room. She took out a pink, close-fitting t-shirt with purple stripes and her favourite pair of dark blue jeans.

She checked her desk clock then went to take a shower, still fuming over her annoying brother. It was 8:10 a.m. She was going to visit Alisa and hopefully, she could watch TV there while she vented her emotions out to her best friend.

By half past eight, Andreide was dressed and ready to go. It took her a while to pick out a matching handbag from her *Kipling* collection to go with her pink and purple t-shirt, but she eventually decided on a plum-coloured shoulder bag. She took her cell phone, house keys and a colour coordinating wallet and put them in her bag.

Before she left the house, she peeped in her parents' bedroom to check if her mother had returned from her early morning walk. However, there was no sign of her presence and Andreide's father was fast asleep in their bed. Andreide rolled her eyes then shut the door. How could her intelligent, industrious mother marry such a dull, slothful man? Andreide knew that opposites attracted but her parents were beyond opposite. It was ridiculous! Shaking her head in incredulity, she descended to the ground floor and exited through the front door without further ado.

*

"How does this look?" Alisa twirled around in her wall length mirror. She was wearing a light green, short-sleeved dress with white polka dots. The hem swirled around her knees as she turned in the mirror, examining her new outfit. She had tried on three other new dresses before she chose this one, and she liked it very much. The tapered-waist styling of the dress made her appear slimmer than she actually was, which gave her some hope.

Andreide was lying on her friend's queen-sized bed which was decorated with fluffy pink sheets and multi-coloured heart-shaped pillows, and was flipping through an *Ebony* magazine. They were in Alisa's bedroom on the second floor of her house. The room was quite spacious and artistically designed. The walls were painted in pastel colours with vine-like designs bordering the floor and ceiling. Alisa's room made Andreide's appear rather dull and diminutive.

In one corner of the room, there was a Mac desktop computer and in another corner sat a polished, medium-sized wooden desk, on which many of Alisa's school books lay in neat piles. Towards the southern end of her room, a large built-in cupboard stood from floor to ceiling, almost occupying the whole wall space. Alisa's bed was perched on a separate tier, in the middle of the room.

Andreide was not envious that Alisa's room was bigger and had more luxuries than hers. In fact, Alisa's entire house was larger and better equipped than Andreide's house. It had greater yard space and was located further away from Andreide's home, in the 'Upper Middle Class' residential area.

In St. George's Parish, there were three main social and economic divisions – Low Class, Middle Class and High Class. The 'Middle Class' division was subdivided into the 'Upper Middle Class' and the 'Lower Middle Class'. Andreide's family was part of the 'Lower Middle Class' category and had been ever since her father was fired from Carlston International Development Bank.

Alisa's father was a highly-qualified dentist and her mother was an interior decorator, who worked with an international designing firm. Both her parents had migrated from the USA several years ago, and brought their jobs with them. Alisa was their only child and as a result, the Bretfords lavished all their money and attention on her. Even though there was a difference in the financial and social standings of their families, this did not affect Andreide and Alisa's relationship – they treated each other as equals.

Andreide looked up from an article entitled 'Ten Ways to Tell If Your Man Is Cheating on You' to critique Alisa's outfit. She inspected it for a few seconds before she responded, without much interest.

"It's nice – perfect for a picnic." She returned her attention to the article.

Alisa laughed. "C'mon, Andy! Really, what do you think?" She spun around once, her hands out for show.

Andreide looked up again. "Ok ok, the green looks nice against the brown of your skin but I don't like the white spots. Polka dots aren't my thing." She resumed her reading.

Alisa looked at her friend intently. "What's wrong Andy? Did I do something?"

Andreide looked at her friend and sighed. "No, you didn't do me anything. It's just …" she paused. "I'm tired."

"You're tired?"

"Yes, I'm tired. I'm tired of everything!" She closed the magazine and sat up. "I'm tired of the way things are – my annoying brother always bothering me, moody Omarion and that lazy man who's supposed to be my father!"

Alisa joined Andreide on the bed. "What about your mother? Are you tired of her too?"

Andreide sighed. "No, not really. Just that, you know she's been busy with her book and hasn't really been bothering with me. It's that annoying boy who's been getting all the attention. You know, last week when Mom had to travel to Puerto Rico for a conference, she took *him* and not me." Andreide frowned and slapped at a purple pillow.

"Well, Marques is younger than you and I guess your mom thought he would need her more than you would," Alisa said tentatively.

"I don't care! I'm the one who always supported her since she decided to write the book two years ago. I should be the one getting the benefits, not him!" Andreide pounded the pillow.

Alisa remained quiet while she let her friend cool down. After a while, Andreide continued.

"You know, sometimes I wish I was more like Keisha. I could tell off anyone who bothered me at any time, then they'd know not to mess with me."

Alisa watched Andreide for a while then stood up. "No, you don't want to be like Keisha, not at all."

Before Andreide fully digested what her friend said, Alisa pulled her off the bed and dragged her to the cupboard. "Here, try this on. My aunt sent it for me yesterday but it's too tight. You're thinner, it will fit you." She picked a black and red jersey with three brown buttons at the neckline from her closet and handed it to Andreide. Alisa grinned at the puzzled expression on her friend's face.

"Go on, try it! I know you will like it."

Andreide took the jersey then removed her t-shirt behind the partitioned area near the closet, which served as Alisa's changing room. She pulled on the new top then frowned thoughtfully as she examined it. Somehow, it seemed familiar to her.

"Well ... How does it fit?"

Andreide came around the partition and stood in front of the body-length mirror.

Alisa clapped gleefully. "It looks marvellous! It fits you so perfectly – like a second skin!"

Andreide frowned. "Where have I seen this before?"

Alisa grinned. "Ah, you remember! Last week Saturday, when we were in town, you pointed it out in the display window of 'Lana's Boutique'. You didn't have enough money to buy it at the time and I knew you really liked it so I went back for it, later. But, when I went back they were all sold out."

"But –"

"So," Alisa continued excitedly, "I called my aunt up in the States – who works for a clothing distributor that supplies 'Lana's Boutique' – and described the jersey to her and asked her to send it for me and here it is! It's all yours, girly!" She pointed at Andreide's top with a flourish.

Andreide stared at her friend in wonder. She certainly liked the jersey but she couldn't get over the fact that Alisa had gone through the trouble to have her aunt post it here for her. She smiled at her beaming friend and took the moment to really appreciate their friendship.

"It's great, thanks Alisa. You always did know how to cheer me up." She smiled and spun in the mirror like Alisa had done earlier. Alisa laughed and hugged her best friend.

"Alisa! Alisa, will you come down here for a moment please?" a pleasant female voice called from downstairs.

"That's Mom. I'll go see what she wants," Alisa said. "I'll be right back!" She hurried out of the room.

Andreide turned back to the mirror and inspected her new shirt. She really did like the design. The shirt was long and narrow and was made of a stretchy material. The sleeves were cut in a Capri style, which revealed Andreide's long slender arms. She revolved in front of the long mirror and examined her physical appearance and the effects the shirt had on her body.

The black and red colour combination gave the top a classy look; the contrast of the dark colours fit perfectly with Andreide's light brown complexion. The red horizontal stripes across the shirt made her small breasts appear larger than they actually were. Andreide smiled at the thought and turned sideways to view her profile.

Andreide was thin and she knew it. She had long slender arms and legs, and except for her rounded butt and thighs, she did not have a trace of extra fat on her. What she lacked in general body size, she made up for in facial appearance. With a heart-shaped face and warm brown eyes, she was a very beautiful sixteen-year-old girl. Although she greatly resembled her father in features, she had her mother's feminine beauty.

She soon heard Alisa coming up the stairs. She turned from the mirror then flopped unto the fluffy bed, quickly grabbing the *Ebony* magazine as Alisa entered the room.

"I'm back!" Alisa announced cheerfully. Andreide looked up from the magazine at her friend.

"So, what did your mom want?" she asked.

"Oh, she said that she's going out for a few hours and that we'd be here all alone, 'cause Dad's at the office." Alisa plopped unto the bed near her friend and was silent for a few minutes as Andreide continued through the magazine.

"So, what do you wanna do, Andy?" Alisa asked after a while. Andreide closed the magazine and sat up.

"Well, it's Saturday and usually at this time I'd be watching *Vh1* or *MTV* or something. Thanks to that lil pest at home I probably missed this week's new videos." Andreide frowned.

Sensitive to her best friend's feelings, Alisa tried to distract her from her resentment. "C'mon Andy, let's go out. Take your mind off all this." Alisa stood up and picked up both of their hand bags from her desk. She returned to Andreide who was still sitting on the bed and handed her her bag and patted her encouragingly.

Andreide took her bag and sighed. She supposed she could do with the distraction. Besides, it was time for a new *Kipling* bag anyway. She stood up then followed Alisa out the door.

*

"Ooool Look at that one! Isn't she pretty Andreide?" Alisa pointed excitedly at a porcelain doll perched in the shop window of Royal Toys. "I've never seen her before. I have to buy her! I'll just charge it to Mom's account. Oh my God, she's like so awesome!"

Andreide laughed. "Girl, calm yourself. You sound so blonde!" She followed Alisa who had already dashed into the store.

As she waited near the front of the store by a row of Army action figure dolls, she spied a black Rolls-Royce town car out of the corner of her eye. The sleek car slowed to a stop in front of a four storied office building, opposite the toy store. Her curiosity aroused, Andreide inched towards the glass display to get a better look.

One of the back doors opened and a tall, handsome, curly-haired, well-built teenaged boy stepped out of the vehicle and unto the sidewalk. Andreide's heart skipped a few beats and then hammered madly. She quickly concealed herself from view behind a display of toy trucks near the window. However, her sudden excitement affected her coordination and in her haste to hide, she knocked over a few boxes that were directly in front of the display window.

As she realised that she was in full view of the street, Andreide threw herself across the floor, just as the boy looked in her direction. She scrambled on her hands and knees and sought refuge near a rack of posters. She leaned against the wall, closed her eyes with her hand over her heart and breathed out deeply.

As she regained her composure, she heard the door of the luxury car shut and the car accelerated. She then took the opportunity to peek out the window from behind the rack. She saw the curly-haired boy disappear through the large entrance doors of *Michaels & Michaels'* law offices.

"Andy! What are you doing on the floor?"

Andreide whipped her head around. Alisa was standing at the top of the aisle with a Royal Toys shopping bag in her hand. She almost forgot why she was in the store until she noticed the porcelain doll's box printing through the bag in her friend's hand. She stood up quickly and brushed her clothes.

"I … uh … fell down." She barely made eye contact with her confused friend.

"Oh, well you must've knocked over those boxes too." Alisa pointed at the toy trucks scattered on the floor. "I'll help you."

"No, it's ok. I'll get them." Andreide bent down and picked up the toys then arranged them as best as she could on the pile on which they originally sat. As she replaced the last truck, she took a quick peek out of the glass display and her heart resumed its frantic pounding. The boy had reappeared on the sidewalk in front of the building and was talking on a cellular phone.

Andreide's hand shook and slipped as she stared at the attractive young man; the toy fell with a loud thud.

"Andreide! Be careful!" Alisa squeaked nervously as she saw one of the store's employees approach them from a nearby aisle, a frown on his face.

"Do you ladies need any help?" He glanced from Andreide's guilty/anxious face to Alisa's, then at the toy on the floor.

Andreide bent down and picked up the truck, then hastily positioned it back on its pile. She smiled apologetically at the employee.

"Oh, I'm sorry! I just knocked this toy over as I was passing by. No harm done though. Ok bye!" Andreide grabbed Alisa's arm then steered her to the exit without waiting for the worker's response. The employee's frown was one of bewilderment as he watched the girls flee.

Back on the sidewalk, Andreide exhaled in relief as they continued walking. She glanced back and saw the boy still talking on his cell phone. She turned back around quickly before he noticed her watching him.

"Andy, would you mind telling me what that was all about just now?" Alisa asked as they neared a strip of boutiques. She looked backwards but the boy had already disappeared from view.

"What are you talking about?" Andreide feigned ignorance.

"Back there at the store. You were all flustered and nervous-like. And what were you looking at through the window?"

Andreide replied quickly. "I told you, I fell, alright? I got distracted – I saw something outside and I just wasn't watching where I was going." She shrugged her shoulders dismissively then began to comment on the items of clothing displayed in the boutique windows before Alisa could inquire further.

After admiring several flared skirts and light cotton blouses, the girls ended their window shopping and entered Andreide's favourite store, *L'Ambiance*. Andreide headed straight for the *Kipling* section, passing through the perfume, jewellery, bath soaps and scrubs, designer sun glasses and cosmetics sections. It was one of the few stores on the block which sold designer products and attracted many of the wealthy residents.

After quickly eliminating the styles which she already had in her collection, she spotted a shelf with eight new bags. She rushed over to them and began her usual adoration, declining the help of a sales attendant who was standing nearby.

"Oh, wow! Just look at this one!" she said excitedly, holding a moss green long-strapped bag with lime green stripes in her hand.

"Oooo! And look at that one! It's so different!" She took a dark blue multi-pocketed hand bag with white edgings from the shelf and compared it to the one in her other hand.

She examined each of the other bags in turn with much interest and delight until she came to the last one. She shrieked with surprise and elation as she grabbed the eighth bag, which was by far the most beautiful.

It was a short-handled hand bag with one main zipper and two front pockets with white Velcro straps. The bag was multi-coloured with a mixture of red, white and pink and swirled with designs. Andreide sighed in awe as she gaped at the treasure in her hands.

Alisa looked at her stunned face and saw the depth of Andreide's obsession with the *Kipling* line as her eyes filled with moisture. She stared at the bag clutched in her friend's arms.

"I take it you really like this one, huh?"

Andreide nodded her head slowly.

"How much is it?" Alisa inquired.

Andreide hesitated before she checked the price tag on the bag. Her eyes bulged and almost fell to the floor as she read the alarming figure.

"Two hundred and thirty dollars!"

"No way!" Alisa exclaimed. She too read the price tag and was just as shocked. "That's crazy!"

"Yeah. There's no way I can afford to buy it now. I spent my last savings on some gold earrings about two weeks ago and I haven't gotten any allowance since Mom started her book – you know, with all the production costs and all." She paused. "And there's absolutely no chance of getting *Mr. Krabs* to break his penny-pinching and give me the money." She sighed, defeated.

"Hey, my mom shops here all the time and she has a credit system here. We can charge it to her account like what I did to buy Susie here!" Alisa indicated the doll in her bag and smiled, pleased with herself for thinking of the solution.

Andreide shook her head and frowned. "No, we can't do that. Well, we can but we shouldn't. Even though it's the last of its kind." She sighed. "I won't charge it to your mom's account."

Alisa protested. "But I'm sure she wouldn't mind!"

"It doesn't matter. We don't have her permission and I'm not buying it unless I can pay for it *myself*," she said. When she saw her friend's fallen expression, she added, "Thanks for the offer though."

Alisa nodded disappointedly.

Andreide replaced the bag then led them out of the store. Both girls did not feel like doing any further shopping for the day.

Chapter 3

The next morning, Sunday, Andreide awoke at quarter to eight to loud knocks at her bedroom door. She rolled over and tried to block the sounds out which were becoming more and more frequent and annoying.

"Andreide! It's eight o'clock and church starts in half an hour. Get yourself up now!" her mother demanded from outside the door.

Andreide opened an eye and gazed lazily at her bedside clock. It was 7:47 a.m. She grumbled, annoyed. Her mother always exaggerated when it came to time.

"Andreide, do you hear me? Get up now, it's late!"

"Alright, alright! I'm up, I'm up!" Andreide shouted back. She threw back the covers and dragged herself out of bed, wishing she had at least another hour to sleep. She searched through her closet until she found a yellow dress that did not need ironing then draped it on her bed. She grabbed her towel and toothbrush then proceeded to the bathroom; it was actually unoccupied.

As she was closing the door, she heard her mother's voice travel up from downstairs. "Why can't she ever be ready on time, for once, without me waking her?"

Her father then said something that Andreide could not hear properly. Her mother responded angrily.

"Well, it's not like she has to wake up at all hours of the morning to go over piles of edited scripts with ceaseless thoughts running through her mind!"

Again Mr. D'Averette responded but too softly for Andreide to hear.

"What school work? When was the last time you saw that child up late studying? I'm the tired one, not her!"

Mr. D'Averette reserved his comment.

"And why do I feel like I'm the only one who cares about anything in this house?"

Her husband then spoke up. "Come now, Rosie, you know that's not true. You're just tired now and the stress from your book is making you upset and —"

"Charles, don't you start with that!"

Andreide sighed and closed the bathroom door, shutting out her mother's angry voice.

Twenty-five minutes later, Andreide was clean, dressed and ready to go. She chose a matching sunflower yellow purse then quickly went downstairs to find her parents waiting in the living room. Her father was sitting on a sofa, sipping his morning tea while her mother was pacing the ground behind him, in a navy blue skirt suit, her high-heels striking staccato pitches against the tiled floor. She turned abruptly to face her daughter as Andreide approached them.

"Do you have any concept of time, young lady?" Rose Marie asked in a controlled voice.

Andreide hesitated before she answered. "It took a while to comb out my hair and pull it together — it's just so thick and annoying!"

"Nothing's wrong with your hair!" Rose Marie snapped. "You just take too long to do everything. Now, let's leave and hopefully we'll make it before 'Amen'!" She hurried Andreide outside where her sons were already waiting in the car. Her husband's 'See you later, Rosie', went ignored as she slammed the front door and marched to the car.

*

They arrived ten minutes after the service started. Rose Marie led her children to their usual bench in the north-eastern side of the Cathedral and tried to ignore the disapproving glances of her fellow church-goers. However, she did notice the smug smile on the middle-aged woman sitting behind her amidst her string band of children. Rose Marie paid her no attention until during the second gospel reading when the pretentious woman leaned forward and whispered to her.

"I see we got held back this morning, hmm? I thought maybe something was wrong at home when I didn't see you here on time." The woman spoke with a lilted island accent, which greatly annoyed Rose Marie.

Without turning, Rose Marie said, "Well Eugenia, not everyone can be an early bird like you are." There was a forced note of cheeriness in her voice.

Eugenia Richardson kept her ostentatious smile painted on her dry, leathery face as she brushed over the younger woman's comment. Her face looked even more comical than usual, as her short, frizzy grey hair was yanked backwards in a tiny low bun; it made her broad, shining forehead more prominent than ever.

"How is the husband, dear? I see he's not here today." Her smug smile broadened as she glanced over at her own husband sitting about seven children away from her; he was staring into the distance with a dazed look in his spectacle-framed, protruding eyes, his mouth hanging open. Eugenia Richardson smiled back at Rose Marie as if to say, "Hah, at least my husband is always at church with me and my ten million children."

Rose Marie stilled her tongue from lashing out at the hypocritical woman. She placed her hands in her lap and clasped them together. She prayed for the strength to deal with such a woman and still set a positive example for her children. Even in church, God's own sacred house, the woman persisted in her pretentious ways! Eugenia Richardson could make a nun swear.

Rose Marie turned her head slightly and replied with a guarded tongue, "*Charles* is fine. We can't all be as dedicated in attending daily mass like yourself. However, I do expect that such a spiritually devoted woman like *you* would know that there are other *acceptable* means of receiving religious guidance than by attending weekly or daily mass."

Quick to the punch, Eugenia Richardson hastened to reply. "Yes, yes, of course. I understand...." Her irritating voice faded into the background as she pondered on Rose Marie's implications.

"Good," Rose Marie said with a note of finality in her tone. She re-focused her attention on the service as the priest began the homily. However, she was quite aware of the wretched woman's penetrating stare behind her back.

*

At a quarter past ten, the Mass finally ended. It had seemed longer to Andreide as she inhaled fresh air on the entrance steps outside the church. It was only so much croaking and high pitched old lady voices she could bear on such a hot day; the senior choir was especially bad this Sunday or at least in her opinion.

As she was propelled down the steps by the jostling crowd of overheated bodies, she searched for her mother and brothers, whom she had forgotten about in her haste to escape the heat and stiffness of the church. While picking through the crowd, many of her mother's acquaintances decided to press their large, bosom-heavy bodies against her in an embrace which almost stifled the life out of her slim body.

Finally detaching herself from the meaty arms of a squat woman, who claimed to be one of her fourth cousins on her father's side, Andreide spotted one of her classmates near a mango tree. She hurried over to her, neatly avoiding colliding with three of the Richardson's rat pack; they scuttled by to rejoin the main brood.

Shauna was the only other classmate besides herself who was a Catholic, which limited her after-church companionship.

"Hey Andreide," said Shauna as she neared her. "Church was really some thing, eh?"

"Yeah, really hot, torturous and boring." Andreide rolled her eyes and Shauna laughed.

They talked for a while about recent happenings, until Andreide glimpsed Omarion's head above the crowd moving in her direction. As she was about to end their conversation, Shauna quickly switched subjects.

"Gyul! You hear 'bout that new guy?" Shauna's eyes lit up excitedly as she spoke.

Andreide returned her attention to her friend, her pulse quickening as she immediately thought of the boy in the black Rolls-Royce.

"A new guy? Really?" she asked innocently.

"Yeah! And he's real hott!"

"How do you know that?" Andreide tried to suppress her excitement but her curiosity got the best of her. "Who is he?"

"Well, Tonya tell me that she hear it from Risha who hear it from Shonetta, who neighbour have a cousin who does go that rich people school, that she tell them that when she was at school she saw some white man that she never did see before, talking to the principal 'bout he son. And she say that she hear that —"

"Andreide! Girl, come ahead and stop wasting time with your stupid gossiping." Omarion rudely interrupted. "We've been looking for you for the past twenty minutes and Mom's anxious to leave. Hurry up and let's go!" He stalked off with the expectation that his sister would follow.

Andreide scowled. Who the hell did he think he was to talk to her like that in front of her friend and disrupt their conversation? He had some nerve!

She reluctantly said good-bye to Shauna then followed her brother. She did not even get to learn the boy's name or hear the rest of Shauna's story. She would just have to wait until the next day at school to find out from Shauna or some other reliable source of gossip.

She climbed into the car to meet three disgruntled faces – her mother's the most irritated of the lot. However, Mrs. D'Averette said nothing to her and drove home in silence, much to Andreide's relief. Andreide sat back and stared out of the window, hoping against hope that she might see the handsome, curly haired boy again. She looked out for the shiny black Rolls-Royce.

*

After changing out of her church dress, Andreide went downstairs to have a late breakfast. She found the kitchen deserted. She hummed a hymn and prepared a sandwich of turkey bacon and melted cheese.

As she sat at the dining table to eat, she realised that the house seemed still and the atmosphere so peaceful. She guessed that her father was doing his favourite activity – sleeping, and her brothers were in their room doing whatever it was they did that kept them quiet. As long as they were silent and away from her, Andreide did not care what they did (providing that they were not interfering with her things, of course).

While eating, Andreide heard the familiar shuffling of papers coming from her mother's study. She sighed as she thought of the pressure her mother had been under in the past six months. She wished that she could take it away from her – all the stress, deadlines, headaches, frustration. She longed for the middle of February when her mother would go on the book tour and have less stress and worry to deal with. Then, Rose Marie would be happier and naturally, everyone else would be too.

The telephone rang suddenly, shattering the silence, startling Andreide. She quickly reached for the receiver.

"Hello?"

There was no response.

"Hello? Who is this?"

The caller took a while to reply.

"Ahhh … Thissssss … Rosie?" The person's speech sounded slurred and heavy. The voice sounded somewhat familiar but Andreide was not sure to whom it belonged. She became cautious.

"What's your name please?"

The man paused.

"Ahhh … Peter? … Yeah … Peter," he said slowly.

The name rang a bell in Andreide's head. Surprised by the caller, she put him on hold then hurried to her mother's study.

"Mom!" Andreide burst into the room startling her mother. Rose Marie dropped her pen and looked searchingly at her daughter.

"What is it? What's wrong?"

"Uncle Peter, he's on the phone."

"What? Are you sure?" Rose Marie looked as surprised as her daughter, but was more confused and worried by the call. Her brother lived in St. Vincent and he rarely ever called her. She had not seen him in over five years and his sudden call put her on edge.

"Yes Mom, but he doesn't sound good. You know, like he's drunk or something. His words are all slow and slurred and it took him a while to speak," Andreide said. "Why do you think he called? I mean, we haven't heard from him in a long time. Do you think he's ok?"

Rose Marie exhaled heavily. "I don't know. I'll take the call in here though, so hang up the phone in the dining room." She ushered Andreide out of her study.

As Andreide closed the door behind her, she heard her mother pick up the phone in her office. She was tempted to stay by the door and listen to the conversation but remembered that she could get better results using the other line in the dining room. She hurried back to the other room.

She was about to lift the phone to her ear when she heard footsteps descending the stairs. She quietly replaced the receiver on the cradle, then dashed to her previous seat where her three-quarter eaten sandwich still lay.

"Man, I'm hungry!" said Omarion as he and his younger brother entered the dining room through the kitchen.

"Yeah, me too," said Marques. "I can eat a cow!"

Andreide rolled her eyes. She drained the last of the orange juice in her glass then took her dishes to the kitchen. Marques followed her.

"Mom cooked yet?"

Andreide ignored him as she washed her dishes.

"Huh? Did she?" he asked again. He opened the fridge and looked through it aimlessly.

"Does it *look* like she did? Do you *smell* anything cooked?" said Andreide, who was beginning to feel annoyed as she usually was with her brother. He gave her a surly look then grabbed an apple from the fridge. He bit into it with his rather large front teeth, threw back his head then bellowed, "I'M HUNGRY!"

"Shut up, you idiot!" Andreide shouted back at him.

"What's wrong with you two now?" Omarion appeared in the doorway.

"This retard is shouting down the place and Mom is on the phone in her office!"

"Don't call me a retard!"

"Well you are one, making so much noise in the place."

"I didn't know Mom was on the phone!"

"Well that's not the only thing you don't know, now is it?" She placed her hands on her hips and raised an eyebrow, a smirk twitching at her lips.

Marques started to retort but Omarion cut him off.

"Will you two stop it? You're both making noise so just hush!" He glared at his siblings in turn, his six foot six inches frame towering over them.

Andreide returned his glare, irritated and unaccustomed to his interference; he usually isolated himself from the rest of the family and hardly ever assumed the 'big brother' role.

"What were you saying about Mom on the phone?" he asked her.

She released an exasperated sigh before answering him.

"Uncle Peter called and Mom is talking to him now. She seemed nervous about him calling and I was about to listen in until you two showed up."

Omarion ignored her tone. "Uncle Peter? He called? What does *he* want?"

"How am I supposed to know? I was gonna find out until you two came in exclaiming how hungry you were."

"Who's Uncle Peter?" Marques inquired, his face confused.

"He's Mom's younger brother," said Omarion. "He lives in St. Vincent. You might not remember him – you would have been five or six when we last saw him."

"Oh. So why are you all so surprised that he called?"

"Duh, you dummy! We haven't heard or seen him in years. Of course we'd be surprised that he called. Plus he doesn't exactly have the reputation to –"

"Andreide, be quiet and don't tell him anymore. Let's wait until at least Mom is ready to tell him," Omarion instructed.

"Ah c'mon, tell me! I wanna know!" Marques wailed.

"Shush! I hear Mom's door," said Omarion.

They hurried out the kitchen, through the dining room, down the hall and waited at the corner near their mother's study.

Rose Marie emerged looking drained and upset. She looked at her children with a contemplative frown on her face and sighed. How would they handle the news she had to tell them? Why did her brother have to do this to her right at the moment when she was so stressed already? Why did he put her in such a difficult situation? Why did he always do that to her? And why had she accepted? Was there no reward for her hard work? She faced her children.

"We need to talk. We *all* need to talk." She sighed. "Marques darling, wake your father up for me please. Tell him it's an emergency and maybe he just might stir."

Marques hastened to do his mother's bidding.

"In the meantime, let's sit in the living room. We don't have much time."

Andreide exchanged a quick look with Omarion who was just as confused and as curious as she was, then followed their mother. Andreide and Omarion sat on the sofas but their mother remained standing, one hand leaning against the back of a chair for support.

Marques returned with his father close behind him, looking ruffled. Charles took a look at his wife and children and knew that something was not right.

"Rosie, what is it?"

Rose Marie looked at him then at her children before she spoke.

"My brother called –"

"Peter? Isn't he in St. Vincent?"

"Yes, he is ... or was." She sighed again. "He ... he's having some problems. You know like last time. But this time is worse."

"Is he sick, Mom?" Marques asked.

Rose Marie hesitated.

Charles looked at his wife's expression. "Rosie, maybe we should talk about this together first."

"No." She shook her head then thought for a while. "Well, yes maybe we should," she recanted. She instructed the children to remain in the room while she talked to their father. She led Charles to her study then shut the door.

"Man! This seems serious," said Andreide. She leaned back on the sofa and looked at her brothers.

Marques glanced at Omarion. "Think we should follow them and listen?"

Omarion gave him a disapproving look then turned his head away and remained silent.

Ten minutes passed and their parents had not returned. Another five minutes crept by and Andreide and her brothers' anxiety increased. Just as they were about to burst with frustration, the adults re-entered the room. Charles appeared angry rather than weary like his wife. Rose Marie sat while her husband stood off to the side.

"Ok children. As I was saying, your uncle has been experiencing some problems and they have gotten so bad that he can't handle them by himself," she said. "Over the years, he has had problems with gambling and drinking and they have gotten worse these past few months."

Her children looked at her with concern in their eyes.

"His wife recently divorced him and moved away. She left their daughter with him and it's very difficult for Peter to manage his addiction to gambling and manage a daughter on his own." Rose Marie's voice was heavy with tiredness. "His daughter, Chrystal, is a lot to deal with. She is seventeen now and she gives him a lot of trouble." She paused and glanced at Charles who remained angry and silent, staring at a spot on the wall.

"His main problem is financial. His wife took most of his assets in the divorce settlement, and his gambling drained him of the rest. He is practically living off government assistance as his friends are all gamblers too. And his daughter is not any help – she just adds to his money problems." She sighed.

Andreide noted her father's angry expression and her mother's one of unease and tiredness. She sensed that her mother had more worrying news to tell.

Rose Marie took a deep breath and prepared herself for their reaction to the main cause of her new stress.

"So ... Peter called and explained all this and asked for my help."

Andreide glanced at her brothers.

"He sounded very desperate and I just couldn't say no." She paused and gathered herself. "He asked to move in with us so he could have a chance to recover himself and turn a new leaf."

Just as she expected, her children did not take the news very well.

"What! Are you serious, Mom?"

"You're joking!"

"Move in with *us*? Now? Is he crazy?"

"My sentiments exactly," Charles muttered.

"But Mom, he can't move in with us! Not now at least. You're still dealing with your book. How much stress can you take?" Andreide exclaimed.

"Yeah, and how can *we* help *him*?" Omarion asked incredulously. He stood up and started to pace the room. "We're not some blasted rehab centre!"

"Watch your language!"

"Where would he stay? This house is not even big enough for the five of us!" said Andreide.

"For real!" Marques put in.

"He can't stay in our room that's for sure. It's cramped enough with me and Marques."

Rose Marie sighed and shook her head. "Your father and I agreed that he will use the guestroom –"

"But that's packed with our old stuff!" Marques whined.

" – and Chrystal will stay in Andreide's room."

"WHAT!" Andreide shouted. Everyone looked at her, startled by her outburst. "He's moving in with his daughter too?" She now understood her father's anger. She remembered her cousin to be a nuisance, nosy and annoying, even worse than Marques. There was no way she could share her room with *her*.

"Andreide, there's no need to shout," her mother admonished.

"But where will I sleep?"

"Don't be ridiculous. You will still sleep in your room. It is only for a while – they won't be staying with us for long. Just until Peter can steady himself."

"Yeah and when will that be?" Andreide asked, a little too insolently.

"Don't you question me with that tone, young lady! This is not a debate. Peter is my brother and I love him and I will help him in any way I can. Your father and I have agreed to let him and his daughter stay with us and our decision is final. However long they will stay, you all will *live* with it and *deal* with it. They're our family for goodness sake!" said Rose Marie, glaring at each of her children in turn. She pretended not to hear Charles' sound of disgust.

There was a brief moment of silence. Omarion sat down again and leaned back, stony-faced. Everyone looked at each other, wondering what he or she should say when the obvious occurred to Marques.

"Uhh … When are they coming here?" he said timidly.

Rose Marie glanced at her husband before responding, aware of his negativity. She felt mentally and physically exhausted.

"Around four this afternoon. They are already in the country, but are staying in a motel somewhere or other." She paused. "I'm going to need you guys to help clear the boxes from the guest room and put them at the end of the hall." Omarion and Marques exchanged uneasy looks. She turned to Andreide. "And Andreide, clean out your room. Your father will go to town and buy a new mattress for Chrystal."

If Andreide's face was riled with defiance and displeasure, her father's was none the better.

"What? You didn't say anything about buying a mattress for them!" said Charles, his nerves on edge at the thought of spending unnecessary money.

"And my room *is* clean Mom!" said Andreide.

Rose Marie stared at the both of them in disbelief. "What's the matter with you all? I ask a simple thing as cleaning your room and you can't just be humble and do it. I am your mother and what I say goes. Don't you contradict my instructions, especially when you know I'm so stressed as it is!" Her eyes flared with anger.

Andreide looked down at the floor and kept quiet, silently wishing she had stilled her tongue.

Rose Marie stood up abruptly, her arms stiff at her side. "I've said what I've said now you all get to it. We only have a few hours to clean this place and get everything ready." She looked at her sons who avoided her eye, then shot a fierce look at her husband; he returned her look with cool insolence.

"I need to speak to you, now," she stated. Although her voice was firm, Andreide heard it tremor with a mixture of annoyance and anger.

Rose Marie turned on her heel and left the room, her husband following her shortly. Marques looked at his older siblings and sighed.

"I guess we better get the house ready, huh?"

Omarion scowled and cursed under his breath. "Why the hell did this man have to come here now? He just ruined my plans of going out later. Uncle or not, I don't want him in my house! And he better not plan to be staying here long." He got up and stormed out of the room, pounding up the steps as he headed for the guest bedroom.

Marques glanced at his sister then sighed. He stood up and followed his brother to begin their arduous chore. Andreide was left alone in the living room.

She thought over what her mother had told them and concluded that she too did not want them to come. She absolutely resented being inconvenienced at such short a notice and the thought of sharing her room with her older, nosy cousin brought forth anger from inside her. Like her brother said, they had better not be staying long!

*

While Andreide was sweeping under her bed, she heard the squeak of the old station wagon and knew that her father had returned from town. She looked out of the window and saw him untie a plastic-covered mattress from the roof of the car, then drag it to the back door with much difficulty. He muttered a few obscenities before he managed to yank it through the door.

Andreide shook her head in disbelief and awe of her mother, as she thought of what Rose Marie must have said to Charles to make him buy the mattress. Andreide estimated that it must have cost more than two hundred dollars and knowing her father, he would have purchased the cheapest one he could find.

She returned to her sweeping, glad that she had already tidied her closet and made space in her dresser for her cousin's things. As she was scooping up the dust and crumpled balls of paper, she heard her mother's shriek from downstairs.

"Do you see what time it is? They're going to be here any minute now and you two haven't finished cleaning the guest room. We don't have much time left you know!" She heard two pairs of feet stomp up the stairs.

Andreide looked at her clock and gulped. It was 3:35 p.m. Her mother was right – they did not have much time until Uncle Peter and his daughter arrived.

"Andreide, where are you? Come down here and help me, please!" Rose Marie called her voice full of anxiety.

Andreide emptied the garbage into her dustbin then quickly took it downstairs. She transferred the contents into the bigger garbage bin in the kitchen then dashed upstairs to put it back in her room. When she returned downstairs, she found her mother in the living room, hurriedly mopping the floor.

Rose Marie looked up when her daughter entered the room. "Have you finished cleaning your bedroom?"

"Yes, Mom."

"Good. Grab a broom and sweep out the dining room. I already swept and mopped everywhere else. And hurry up please!"

Andreide took a broom from the storage cupboard under the staircase then did as she was instructed. When she was done, she went back to the living room but her mother was not in there. Rose Marie had apparently finished cleaning the room, as it was spotless and the aroma of the apple-scented disinfectant lingered in the air.

Andreide checked the time on the kitchen clock and became nervous. It was five minutes to four o'clock. She hurried through the house to locate her mother and eventually found her upstairs in the guest bedroom.

"Why is it taking you two so long to fix this room? I had time clean the whole of downstairs and you haven't even finished with the *one* room I told you to clean!" Rose Marie stood inside the doorway with her hands on her hips.

"But Mom, these boxes are heavy and awkward to carry downstairs!" Marques complained. Omarion remained silent and moody standing by the dust-covered closet.

Rose Marie closed her eyes and placed one hand against her forehead and sighed. Her head throbbed and her eyes hurt. "Just push the rest of the boxes into the corner by the dresser and move the bed nearer to the window. We will have to clear the rest of this stuff some other time. Now please hurry! They'll soon be here." She turned from the doorway and headed towards Andreide's room, leaving her grumbling sons to continue their task. Andreide followed her.

"Where's the new mattress? Why isn't it in here?" She glanced around the room, her patience running out.

"I don't know Mom. I just cleaned my room like you said. I haven't seen Dad since he came back with the mattress and shoved it through the backdoor."

Rose Marie groaned, her hand massaging her temple. "Why is this man doing this to me?" she muttered.

"What?"

"Nothing."

Andreide looked at her mother with concern in her eyes. "Mom, are you alright? I mean, besides all the stress with your book and I guess this new stress with Uncle Peter moving in with his daughter now." She paused. "Is there something else?"

Rose Marie gave a weak smile at her daughter's simple but loaded question. She patted Andreide's shoulder then descended the stairs slowly, her movement slightly stiff and weighted with worry. Andreide wondered what was bothering her mother so much that she could not tell her most faithful confidante.

She turned around and headed back to her bedroom. She had already cleared a space for the new mattress and she wanted to have it settled in her room as soon as possible; she hated to see her room rearranged. She kicked at her dustbin by the door then turned back around. She was going to find her father.

As she neared the top of the stairs, she halted in her tracks at the sound of angry voices below her. She climbed down a step then peeped over the banister. Her parents were in the corridor near the back door where the mattress lay propped against the wall.

"Charles, it's after four! Why is this thing still down here?" Rose Marie pointed at the mattress.

"I know what time it is, thank you!" Charles snapped. "This thing is damn heavy you know." He slapped the mattress.

"But you brought it back more than twenty minutes ago. You could have gotten it upstairs by now!"

Charles looked away and muttered under his breath.

"What were you doing all this time, anyway? Sleeping as usual? Buying a mattress tired you out so much?"

Charles glared at his wife. "What, you think you're the only tired one around here?" His voice rose with his anger. "I'm just as stressed as you are!"

"You're as stressed as I am?" Rose Marie repeated incredulously, her voice also rising. "*You're* stressed? *You?* What the hell brought on *your* stress then? Been working hard, have you?"

"Don't mock me, Rose Marie! I don't have to be smart and write a book to be stressed."

"Oh, really! Then tell me, what's the source of your *stress?*"

Charles glared at Rose Marie. He started to respond but decided against it. Rose Marie returned his glare.

Instead of retorting, Charles marched past his wife and headed for the front door. He grabbed the car keys from the rack on the wall then stormed out the door, slamming it behind him.

"What's going on?" Marques appeared next to Andreide's shoulder. He peered over the banister where Andreide's fingers were tightly gripped and saw his mother staring at the front door, her hands clenched at her side.

"Mom, are you alright?" he asked quietly.

Rose Marie glanced up at her children and forced her brow muscles to relax. "Call your brother, Marques. I need you boys to take this mattress upstairs to Andreide's room now, please."

Marques looked around quickly. "Where's Dad?"

Rose Marie sighed and rubbed her forehead. "Just call your brother for me please!"

Marques turned around and hastened to their bedroom. A few seconds later, he returned with his brother. Omarion glanced at his sister perched on the step then at his mother posed rigidly below.

"Something wrong?" he asked with not much concern in his voice.

"I need you and Marques to take this mattress into Andreide's room right now. And please hurry up, it's after four." Rose Marie turned to leave.

"But … what about Dad?" Omarion asked his mood worsening at the prospect of doing more manual labour.

Rose Marie turned her head sharply. "What *about* him? If you want to end up like him – a lazy useless creature, then you can just follow him out that door!"

Rose Marie turned on her heel and left the room. Andreide heard her mother's study door slam shut a few moments later.

Andreide and her brothers stood on the stairs immobile by shock. They were not used to hearing their mother talk about their father in such a derogative manner, especially in front of them. After a while, Marques broke the silence.

"She didn't mean it, did she?" he asked.

Andreide glanced at Omarion's hard expression then looked at Marques with a glimmer of sympathy in her eyes.

"She couldn't have meant it, right?" he asked again.

Omarion grumbled under his breath then went down the stairs. He tried to pull the mattress towards him but without much success. After several more tugs at the plastic covering, he swore vehemently then gave the mattress a mighty kick. He bent down and found the seam of the covering, then ripped the plastic apart with long powerful fingers.

As Andreide looked on, a strange feeling trickled through her. She had the growing suspicion that there was more stress to come.

"Well, don't just stand there! Come and help me!" Omarion growled while yanking the plastic off the mattress.

Marques hurried down the stairs. They pulled the cover off and threw it aside. Omarion stood in front of the mattress while Marques positioned himself behind it.

"Push it from the top. We need to turn it on the other side," Omarion instructed his younger brother.

"What?"

"Push it from up there!" He pointed at the top edge of the mattress.

"But I can't reach that!" Marques complained.

Omarion swore again. All patience was lost as he shoved his brother aside and assumed his position behind the mattress. He pushed it from the top edge until it fell on its horizontal side with a dull thud. He resumed his original place at the front of the mattress and began to drag the heavy object towards the stairs.

"Well, come on and help me!" he ordered Marques who was standing aside looking on, feeling a bit intimidated. Marques hastened forward and lifted the end of the mattress.

It took them ten minutes to get the mattress from the bottom of the stairs to the top. Andreide thought that it would have taken longer but was glad that it had not. The moment that the mattress touched the top stair, a car horn blew outside.

"Oh no. It's them, isn't it?" Marques gasped as he struggled to catch his breath. He clung to the end of the mattress for support, weak from his exertions.

Omarion leaned against the wall and breathed deeply. The underarms and neck of his t-shirt were darkened with sweat and his forehead glistened.

Again the car horn sounded from outside. Andreide looked over the banister and saw her mother hurrying from the corridor below. She adjusted her blouse before she opened the front door. An *Oscar* winning smile appeared on her face as she stepped unto the threshold.

A car door opened and slammed shut. Andreide and her brothers remained fixed at the top of the stairs. They heard voices outside, including their mother's which sounded unusually happy for her previous disposition. As the vehicle's ignition started and the voices drew nearer to the house, Andreide realised that they should move.

"Hey, you guys still have to put the mattress in my room. They're almost at the door, hurry up!"

They managed to push the mattress across the landing and into Andreide's room just as the front door opened.

"Yoo who!" a female voice rang out from downstairs.

The siblings looked at each other anxiously. They were here and they had no choice but to face them.

"Omarion, Andreide, Marques!" Their mother called from the ground floor.

Again they exchanged worried glances.

Andreide prodded her brothers. "C'mon guys, they're here. We have to go and greet them."

"Do we have to?" Marques whined.

"Yes, so come ahead. We're gonna have to see them sooner or later so let's get this over with."

"But they're gonna be here for a while anyway, so why can't we just stay here and wait for them to leave then tell them bye?"

"Boy don't be stupid! We don't even know how long they will be here for. If you want to wait up here for weeks and weeks then you will stay here alone because I'm going down." Andreide stated. She started for the door then stopped and looked back at her grumpy and forlorn brothers.

"Oh yeah and I think you two should change before you come down. You're not exactly appealing to the sense of smell at the moment and you know how Mom's senses are on alert around guests."

Marques pouted sourly. "I smell alright," he grumbled.

Omarion looked at him and frowned. "No, you don't. I don't know about you but I think it's a good idea." He left for his room.

Marques followed him to change, mumbling under his breath.

"Make sure you put on some strong deodorant!" Andreide called after her little brother. He looked back at her and his pout elongated. Andreide laughed.

Before going downstairs, Andreide checked herself in the mirror. She brushed her hair and fixed her bun in place then examined her outfit. Her pink t-shirt and light yellow cotton skirt seemed appropriate enough. However, aware that her uncle was not in a very stable condition, she decided to change her skirt for something longer and less revealing. She chose a pair of blue jeans.

When she reached the bottom of the stairs, she heard a slightly familiar voice coming from the living room. Andreide braced herself before entering the room where her mother sat with her niece and brother on opposite sofas.

"Ah, here's Andreide now." Rose Marie pointed to her daughter.

The girl sitting near to Rose Marie looked over at Andreide in surprise.

"That's her? That's little Andreide?" She laughed. "Yuh kidding me Tantie!"

Andreide restrained herself from retorting thoughtlessly. *Little Andreide?* She was about the same size as her when they last met! Plus, how much older did she think she was from her anyway?

Rose Marie gave a light laugh. "It's the same Andreide."

"Same? No way Tantie!" She stood up and examined her cousin. "She get *big* eh?"

Andreide raised an eyebrow. *Big? Her?* If she was only referring to her butt, Andreide would not let her get away with it.

"Wait till you see the boys! They're the ones who've done the most growing." Rose Marie glanced at Andreide and silently cautioned her to remain civil.

Andreide gritted her teeth and entered the room. She sat on the opposite side of her mother away from her cousin's direct line of vision. On her right, her uncle sat in a single-seat sofa seemingly half awake, his head resting on the back of the sofa. She looked over at her mother questioningly, who shook her head. Apparently, her uncle was not in any state to talk much.

"So where the boys anyway?" Her cousin resumed the conversation.

"They should be down any minute now," said Rose Marie. She glanced at her brother who lay silent and half-conscious and her forehead creased.

"So Andreide, how things? Do you remember me? I'm your cousin Chrystal." She gave Andreide a friendly smile.

Andreide wasn't sure if she was amused or annoyed with her cousin now. How could she not remember the irritating girl who talked incessantly and who was responsible for the decapitation and destruction of several of her most beautiful and treasured Barbie Dolls? She could remember the exact day when it happened about eight years ago.

It was a beautiful Saturday afternoon around three o'clock, for the ice-cream truck was passing by. Uncle Peter and Chrystal were visiting them for the weekend. Andreide's uncle went fishing with her father while Andreide was stuck with her cousin and forced by her mother to play with her in her room. Unfortunately for Andreide, she had forgotten to lock the door of her doll house and seeing this, Chrystal darted to it as soon as she entered the bedroom.

Before Andreide could have stopped her, her cousin had already pulled five of her Barbie dolls out of the doll house and had them strewn across the floor. Like a hurricane, the little girl left no stone uncovered. Her fierce winds and storm waves washed over the little doll village, drowning everything in its path. Baywatch Barbie never saw the wave which hit her, leaving her comatose body contorted and weirdly disfigured. Within five minutes, Nurse Barbie and Surfer Ken were doomed to the infirmary as their amputated legs were crunched according to Chrystal, by 'the big nasty green monster' which was nothing more than Military Ken's lifeless army truck.

The Destroyer did not stop with the disabled nurse and surfer; she continued her campaign of mayhem with Teacher Barbie and Student Stacy. These unlucky dolls were the first victims of decapitation. When questioned as to why she had committed such an act, the Destroyer responded in her most pathetic little girl voice with, "But Tantie Rosie, Teacher Barbie was giving Stacy too much homework so Stacy had to do it! She had to make Teacher stop!"

As to why Student Stacy was beheaded, the accused blamed the doll's owner. "That wasn't my fault! It was Andreide! She grabbed Stacy from me. She made me do it. She made me rip her head off. It wasn't my fault, I swear!" When this was declared so boldly and unremorsefully by her cousin, Andreide threw herself on her mother and cried her little lungs out. She could not believe that her cousin had done that to her dolls, to the precious beings she treated as her sisters, to her friends whom she treasured more than the life of her wretched cousin.

Andreide thought back on this and felt the old hurt resurface after so long. To make it worse, her cousin had not been adequately punished, in Andreide's opinion. She had gotten away with only a stern scolding. Andreide had never forgiven Chrystal, even when she had apologised profusely when she had spied the new Barbie dolls that her mother had bought to replace the destroyed ones. Andreide had never allowed her to touch her toys again and her mother never forced her to again either.

It took great effort on Andreide's part not to curse her cousin at that very moment. In response to her question, she simply stated, "Yes, I remember you." She looked her cousin square in the eye and a nerve ticked in Andreide's head as she saw the incomprehension on Chrystal's face. Of course she would not remember, and why would she? She was always self-centred and insensitive anyway.

Rose Marie watched her daughter carefully.

Before another word could be said, Omarion and Marques trudged down the stairs and stepped into the room.

Chrystal looked up and squealed.

"Oh, my gosh! Look at these big people! Wow." She walked over to the boys with her mouth open in shock.

"Omari boy! Where you going with that height? You play basketball nuh?" she exclaimed standing next to him, her head barely reaching his shoulder.

Omarion mumbled to himself. "It's Omarion." He looked over at his uncle lying unresponsively in the armchair and frowned.

Their cousin then turned to Marques.

"Well, eh eh! Who's this handsome young man?" Chrystal placed her hands on her hips as she looked Marques over.

Marques smiled shyly. "I'm Marques."

Chrystal shook her head and smiled. "Marques, last time I saw you, you was a lil baby!" She turned to her aunt. "Tantie Rosie, what you feeding these chirren eh?"

Rose Marie gave another light laugh. Andreide rolled her eyes. Omarion was expressionless. Marques smiled shyly.

"So where Uncle Charlie?" Chrystal asked her aunt.

Andreide was not the only one to tense at the mention of her father's name. Omarion's face grew hard and stony and the pleasant expression in Rose Marie's eyes turned ice cold. Marques was the only unaffected one; he seemed too enthralled by his cousin to react to her question.

"He went out," said Rose Marie. Without giving her niece a chance to inquire further, she changed the subject abruptly.

"Well, Chrystal, I'm sure you must be tired from travelling. Why don't you go upstairs and get settled in – Andreide will show you up."

Andreide darted a quick scowl at her mother who returned it with a warning glare.

"Oh, I'm not really that tired!" Chrystal smiled jovially at her aunt.

"Oh, but I insist. You need to unpack and settle in and the sooner done the better. Plus, you and Andreide can catch up while you're at it. And don't worry about your bags, I'm sure Omarion and Marques will be happy to take them up to your room for you." Rose Marie glanced at her sons. Marques nodded vigorously while Omarion frowned from his corner. He stuffed his hands deeply in his pockets as his brother ran forward to collect their cousin's belongings.

"Ok Tantie," said Chrystal. She turned to Andreide, who quickly assumed a semi-pleasant expression. "Lead on cuzz!"

As soon as she looked away, Andreide rolled her eyes. Her cousin was still annoying, only this time it seemed that she matured with it. This new annoyance of hers bordered on bossiness, which already pulled at Andreide's nerves. Her cousin had better watch herself. Andreide was not going to let her take over and challenge her authority as the only girl in the house.

Chapter 4

"It's only been a day. She can't be *that* bad, can she?" Harietta asked. It was Monday morning and they had just escaped from their History class as soon as the midmorning bell rang, freeing them for their fifteen minute break. They assumed their usual liming spot under the mango tree on the hill, where they had the best view of the school ground and the road beyond the fence. With a venomous glare from Keisha's bulging globes, she had scared away a couple of second formers who had dared to linger by their tree.

"Yeah gyul, she only with you for a day so far." Keisha yanked up her skirt and gathered the cloth between her legs before she threw herself down on the sparse grass under the mango tree. With more decorum, Harietta carefully placed herself beside Keisha who had already found a juicy, ripe mango to sink her teeth into.

"Andy, maybe you should give her a chance," Alisa said. She remained standing near her best friend who frowned at the thought.

"Y'all don't know this girl. True she's only spent a day so far, but in that day she already thinks she's the Queen! She has Marques doing everything for her – showing her around the house, taking her bags for her, showing her how to do this and that. And that stupid lil boy is only too happy to jump to her call," said Andreide. "He'd never do anything like that for me, even if I pay him. But as soon as she snaps her fingers, he's there at her heels like some retarded dog!"

Keisha laughed and mango pulp flew from her mouth.

"Girl, what you laughing for? And watch where your nasty mango going, nuh!" Harietta flicked a piece of Keisha's mango off her arm and scowled at her in annoyance.

Undaunted by her friend's insensitive outburst, Andreide continued her complaint. "And you know what else? As soon as she reached my room, she dumped all her crap on my bed even though I showed her which bed was hers, then she went to my cupboard and started searching through my clothes!"

"Well, excuse me!"

"No, she didn't!"

"Well, she forward, eh?"

"Yeah and that's not all! I showed her where she could put her things in the drawer that I cleared out for her, and you know she went and shoved my clothes aside and hang up her whole suitcase full of clothes in my cupboard anyway?"

Harietta, Keisha and Alisa stared at her in shock.

"Yeah, then she piled the rest of her suitcases on top of my cupboard and had the nerve to smile at me when she finished unpacking to tell me how glad she is that she'll be sharing a room with me and how she can't wait to meet my friends and hang out with me," Andreide said with her hands on her hips. "Can you believe that girl?"

Keisha steupsed. "She jus' reach and she doing all of that? Me arm! She must think she home." She threw the devoured mango seed aside and snatched another recently fallen one lying near to Harietta, who had been eyeing it hopefully a few seconds before.

Robbed of the fruit she was about to claim, Harietta darted a jealous look at Keisha whose thin lips were smeared with the yellow pulp of the sweet fruit, before turning to her distressed friend.

"Andy girl, don't bother with that child. You know how she is already and you know she'll never change. She'll be gone soon anyway so don't let she get to you."

Andreide rolled her eyes. "That's easy for you to say – you don't have to live with her."

"*Live?* She *living* wit' you now?" Keisha paused from her noisy sucking and raised an eyebrow.

Andreide released an exasperated sigh and threw her arms up in the air. "Well I don't know! She brought like five suitcases and she talking 'bout finding a work. And her dead father just lying 'round the place all moody and depressed. I already asked my mother how long they would be staying with us and she herself doesn't even know. She said something 'bout how until Peter can catch himself or something like that."

Alisa looked at her friend sympathetically. "Don't worry Andy. I'm sure they'll be gone soon."

"They'd better be! Cause I can't deal with this girl again, not after what she did last time. And my mother already has enough stress as it is with her book and all. She doesn't need them to add to it. That girl better watch herself this time 'cause she ain't ruling me again!"

Keisha nodded her head. "Fo' real!" Harietta and Alisa remained silent. A few minutes elapsed in which Andreide thought over what was to come with her cousin and uncle.

A cool breeze blew over the school yard, rustling through the leaves of the mango tree, bringing with it a peaceful sense of calm which washed over Andreide, relaxing her tense body and mind. She inhaled deeply and closed her eyes, feeling the therapeutic currents flow gently along her skin. She felt a strange sense of happiness, a sense of peace that she rarely ever felt so strongly and distinctly. She basked in this new feeling until Alisa broke the silence with a squeal.

"Ooo! Look!" She pointed towards the road where a sleek, black Rolls-Royce town car appeared around the corner. Andreide's eyes flew open and she stared intently at the car, aware of the sudden increase in her heart rate. She knew without a doubt that it was the same luxury car that she had seen the day before in front of the toy store – the same car that the tall gorgeous boy had stepped out of.

"That ain't the new rich people car that Shauna was telling me 'bout earlier this morning?" said Keisha, the mango in her hand forgotten now as she too stared at the approaching vehicle. Harietta and Alisa were too distracted by the grandeur of the car to respond.

The girls were not the only ones captivated by the shiny car. With one shout of, "Check dat trans!" the school ground buzzed with excitement as the students swarmed to the fence to get a better look at the foreign vehicle. Bodies pressed against bodies, arms and legs shoved and kicked at their neighbours' limbs in an eager attempt to be closest to the object of such great interest. As the vehicle drew nearer, all movement ceased as the many pairs of eyes stared at it, transfixed with a mixture of reverence and stupidity.

The sleek vehicle cruised to a stop in front of the wrought iron entrance gates. The driver's door opened and a young Indian man fully clad in a black and grey driver's uniform stepped out of the vehicle. He hurried to the rear passenger door and quickly removing his grey cap, he stretched forward to open the door. He stepped backwards hastily as a man in an expensive suit emerged from the cool comfort of the dark air-conditioned vehicle.

The man winced as his pale face was struck by the intense sunlight. He donned a pair of designer shades and scowled as he took in his surroundings. He turned to his driver and raised an eyebrow. The two spoke briefly. Whatever they said was lost on Andreide and her friends as the wind blew their words in the opposite direction.

The man in the suit soon slid back into the comfort of his luxury vehicle, shutting out the nosy looks of the school children, behind the dark tint of the car's windows. His driver quickly followed suit. Within a few seconds, the engine purred back to life and the black shiny car was a figure in the distance.

A minute later, the bell rang signalling the end of break.

*

"I wonder what they were talking about," Alisa pondered out loud.

"What who were talking about?" said Andreide. She unwrapped the ham sandwich in her lap and reached for her bottle of water by her knees.

"The men from that black car," Alisa replied.

"Oh, you mean that snooty-lookin' white man and he driver?" Keisha asked. She shrugged her shoulders and bit into the hamburger she had just bought for her lunch. "I ain't get to hear what they did say. You know how rich people does talk soft."

Harietta rolled her eyes. "Maybe you should take a lesson from them then and shut yuh mouth when you eating."

Keisha dismissed her comment with a flick of her hand. "Gyul please!"

"Please what? It's true! You always eating and talking at the same time. One of these days here you going to choke you know. And I tired tell you must stop it."

"Lawd gyul! Leave me 'lone nuh! If I want to chat wit me mouth full is me business it be!"

"Well, we don't want to see the contents of your dutty mouth so ah beg you keep it shut!"

Keisha sucked her teeth in annoyance and turned her back away from Harietta who was sitting at the base of their mango tree.

Andreide chuckled to herself. Her friends were so argumentative yet so amusing.

"Right so, Andy gyul, you hear what they did say?" Keisha turned to Andreide.

"I wish I did, but no. I don't think anyone heard. And I don't think that man wanted to be heard anyway."

"Why you say that?" Harietta asked. She brushed bread crumbs from her mouth and looked at Andreide inquisitively.

"Well ... Didn't you see the way he looked at us? Well, not exactly at *us* but at the other children then. As if we're not worthy to hear what he has to say. Like he's too good for us, sort of way."

Alisa frowned. "Are you sure? I didn't notice that."

"Well I can't be sure of anything but that's what I saw. I hope I'm wrong though."

"Why? Ah sure you right! That's how them people does go on when they by us people. Acting as if they so important and precious and we're not. That man there in he big ole rich-man fancy suit an' he big flashy rich car an' he driver. He must think he something see!"

Harietta laughed. "Girl, you don't even know the man. What you going on so for?"

Keisha dropped her burger and turned her large eyes on Harietta.

"He's white. And that's all I need to know!"

Harietta's amused expression disappeared from her face now. She took a moment before she responded. "Girl, not all of them are like that. My great-great granddaddy was a white man and he was real rich but he was a good man. My mama told me that."

Keisha placed her hands on her hips and stared Harietta in the eye. "Well your mama's wrong," she said harshly. "Ain't none of them good!"

Harietta glared back at Keisha and Andreide realised that that was the first time she had seen Harietta look so angry. Before Andreide could interject to prevent the situation from getting any worse, they were disturbed by a group of girls from their class.

"Hey, you see that rich people car? It look good, ent?" Shauna came towards them from behind the tree. She had two other girls with her.

"Yeah, and that man look sweet too eh?" one of the girls said. She giggled with her friend next to her.

Keisha rolled her eyes. "Oh please! What wrong with your eyes?"

"Talking 'bout gorgeous! Have y'all seen his son? He's daaaaaamn fine!" said Shauna excitedly. Her two companions giggled and agreed profusely.

At the mention of his son, Andreide's heart rate quickened once more as she flashed back to the attractive young man with the curly hair, whom she'd seen from the toy store window. She felt a ball of excitement grow within her chest, right next to her heart and lungs, creating a pressure, making it difficult for her to breathe normally.

"He's unbelievably handsome!" one of Shauna's friends said.

"Lawdamercy! He drop-dead gorgeous! I could jus' lick 'im so!" said the other.

Andreide, Alisa and Harietta laughed along with Shauna and her friends at this exclamation. Even Keisha seemed to crack a smile.

"Yeah man, he's like sugar and I got a sweet tooth! Ya know what I'm saying ladies?"

They laughed again.

"But serious now," Shauna said, "He really is sumt'ing special. He has a nice kinda mixed look, you know? Real nice looking, man. If that white man is he father then he mother got to be mixed, 'cause he ain't look pure white to me or to anybody who say they see him."

"Yeah fo' real," one of her friends concurred. The other girl nodded in agreement with a far-out look in her eyes.

A few seconds of silence took over the conversation until Shauna chuckled.

"What happen girl?" Harietta asked.

Shauna grinned at them with a conniving gleam in her eye. "Imagine if one of us could have him."

Andreide shot a quick glance at Alisa and Harietta before hastily asking, "What do you mean?"

Shauna rolled her eyes but kept grinning. "I mean as a boyfriend, duh! Wouldn't that be sweet?" Her two excited friends squealed in agreement.

Alisa smiled. "Yeah, that would be so great. What if he was my boyfriend by Valentine's Day? Such perfect timing!"

Shauna placed her hands on her hips and arched an eyebrow. "Gyul please! You? Who talking 'bout you? I mean him for me. He would never want *you*."

Harietta laughed but Andreide's lips barely twitched. She did not like the way this conversation was going and her feelings of excitement were slowly turning into something else – unease and a growing sensation of something she was not sure of. Whatever the new feeling was, it was not pleasant and at the moment it was directed at Shauna.

"Now, if he was my man! Mmmm!" Shauna continued, her grin spreading from ear to ear.

Keisha finally broke her silence and turned to face Shauna with her nails razor sharp, on the brink of bursting the conceited girl's bubble.

"Gyul! What make you think he gonna want you? You wit' you ole big black ass self. You ain't know white man like they flat ass white chic? Eh? He ain't gonna want you!"

A deafening silence rang out.

After Andreide's initial shock at her friend's outburst wore off, she smirked to herself, appreciative of Keisha's bold and frank nature. Shauna deserved it. How dare she think that gorgeous boy would choose her of all people! And how dare she think he would choose her over Alisa, who had a much better character than she. Plus, Shauna was hardly attractive in Andreide's opinion, anyway.

In less than a second, the grin vanished from Shauna's face and was replaced by a mean, ugly scowl. She stuck her hands on her hips and looked Keisha up and down with a venomous glare.

"Wha'? And you think he gonna want you! You with you scrawny bony self. At least I got shape and he could tap my ass. What you got? You ole dry bones gonna make man think you got AIDS! You done so ugly and bun-up black an' all. White boy ain't want shit in he milk!"

If looks could have killed, Shauna would have been a grossly dismembered, disembowelled corpse on the ground, having surely suffered a long, excruciatingly painful death. In rage, Keisha's eyes bulged past her eye sockets and her wispy eyebrows contorted in synchronisation with her forehead's agitated muscles. She flew to her feet and took a few steps towards Shauna, who just as quickly shifted backwards, having seen the murderous intent in Keisha's dark, bulging eyes.

Andreide and Harietta jumped to their feet in an attempt to restrain their angered friend. Alisa looked on nervously. Harietta grabbed Keisha's taut right arm, which was posed just about to pummel the other girl, and yanked her arm backwards.

"Gyul! Lemme go!" Keisha shouted, trying to wrench her arm free of her friend's unyielding grip, while still looking daggers at the alarmed girl in front of her.

"Keisha calm yourself! It doesn't need to go this far," Andreide warned her. She turned to Shauna who was slowly but steadily retreating along with her two cronies.

"And you, Shauna! You didn't have to say that! That was uncalled for. Y'all friends long time and you can't be dissing each other like that because of some boy nobody even know or talk to yet! And anyway, how do you know if he doesn't already have a girlfriend?"

Shauna and her sidekicks just stared at Andreide with an 'I never thought about that' expression on their faces. However, Shauna quickly resumed her look of confidence and her smirk grew back on her face.

"Well Andreide, I'll jus' have to see 'bout that. No man can resist my goods!" She laughed along with her followers as she turned to leave. After a few steps she turned back around and added as an after note, "And for the record, that boy is mine. I saw him first an' y'all lucky I told y'all anything 'bout him so y'all better don't get no ideas yuh hear! Right Keisha?" She arched an eyebrow and smirked at Keisha who bared her teeth at her as she shook with fury. It took all of Harietta's strength and willpower to keep a steady hold on her rage-blinded friend. Keisha was using all the pent up energy in her bony frame to try to break her binds and tear at Shauna's taunting face.

"See y'all later!" Shauna laughed as she walked off with her two disciples.

As they disappeared from view, Harietta released Keisha who snatched her arm away at the same time. She gave Harietta the evil eye before marching away from her. She stormed down the slope by the mango tree until she reached the boundary fence of the school compound. She clung to the wire and looked out into the distance, her face set like a stormy sea. Any additional provocation was sure to cause a tsunami disaster.

Andreide prepared herself for the imminent onslaught. She took a deep breath and released it slowly before following Keisha a few moments later. Harietta and Alisa did the same.

"Keisha?" Andreide approached her cautiously from the side. She gently placed her hand on her left shoulder but was hastily shrugged off. Andreide exchanged a slightly worried look with Harietta who pulled Alisa from Keisha's potential line of fire.

A few seconds later, as Andreide expected, Keisha exploded.

"Who de *hell* does she t'ink she is!" she shouted. A few first formers who were chatting nearby looked over at Keisha in alarm then hurried off to a safer spot. She banged at the wire fence before turning to face her worried friends.

"Who de hell does she t'ink she is?" she repeated but lower and more forcefully this time, glowering at each of her startled friends in turn. "What make she t'ink she so special and all that?

What de hell wrong wit' she, eh? All yuh done know how I be with white people so you done know I would neva want no white boy. And she there throwing him in me face like I want him! Shit man! That bitch get me vex see!"

Andreide started to say something but Keisha continued.

"And who tell she she look good eh? 'Bout how I ugly an' how I look like I got AIDS. She too damn outta place! Ah mean, I know I skinny an' blacker than auntie Mary backside, but she ain't got no cause to be telling me that! I only diss she cause she was t'inking she all that an' dissing off Alisa. And I ain't even diss she good enough for she to go on so! 'Bout I is shit in he milk! Naw, she gone too far wit' that!"

"But Keisha," Harietta managed to cut in. "Why you letting her get to you so? You don't normally bother with what people say about you."

"Yeah, for real," said Alisa quietly.

Andreide withheld her comment as she carefully studied her friend. She knew what Harietta said was true as Keisha hardly ever took personal insults seriously to heart. She normally laughed them off or fired back a more hurtful response which would wound her adversary deeply and deter him/her from continuing to attack her. It was strange that Keisha would take this incident personally. She normally got along well with Shauna and Andreide could not identify what exactly upset her so badly. She knew that Keisha was always sensitive when it came to the topic of white people and after all these years of asking her and getting no concrete answer, she still did not know why this was so. Could that be it? Was it because Shauna had brought up the gorgeous white-looking boy that Keisha had become extra sensitive? If that was it, it still did not make sense to Andreide.

"Keisha, what is it? What's really wrong?" Harietta asked, trying to make eye contact with her friend who continued to stare into the distance. Keisha turned away from their searching eyes and her scowl deepened. She refused to look at her worried friends.

"C'mon Keisha, tell us what's really bothering you. Please?" Andreide said.

Keisha swung back to face them suddenly and Andreide saw a mixture of pain and anger in her eyes which were now alarmingly, filling with moisture.

"I DON'T HAVE AIDS!" she shouted at them. "I DON'T!"

The girls jumped in fright. Quickly recovering, Andreide hurried to soothe their friend.

"We know you don't have AIDS, Keisha. We know that. Is that what bothered you? You think we believe that you have AIDS?"

"No," said Keisha quickly.

"Then what is it?" Harietta asked.

Keisha's face seemed to relax somewhat as she gazed out in thought at the school grounds where the majority of the students were gathered.

"Keisha?"

The troubled girl sighed heavily and remained silent.

"C'mon Keisha, talk to us. Tell us what's wrong!" Harietta pleaded.

"Yeah girl, talk. Whatever it is you know we'd help you," said Alisa.

Whatever peace that was calming Keisha, only lasted momentarily. The old anger and hurt raced back through Keisha's veins. "I don't want yuh blasted help!" she shouted at Alisa before turning away from her friends and dashing across the grounds to the school gate.

"Keisha!" Andreide made to follow her distraught friend but Harietta stopped her.

"Don't," Harietta said as she caught her arm. "Let her go. Whatever it is that's troubling her, she needs to deal with it herself for now."

"But Harietta! You know how she gets when she's angry. Who knows what she's gonna do if we don't stop her!" Andreide said. She frowned anxiously as she saw Keisha squeeze through the gate and run off. She was now out of sight.

Harietta sighed. "Keisha needs to learn how to control her anger and we can't always be there to control it for her. This is just one of those times when we have to let her handle things herself."

"But Harietta, didn't you see how angry she was? You gotta be crazy to let her go like that!"

"Andy girl, if you want to go and chase after her then go ahead, but you'd only be making things worse. Keisha needs to cool down by herself. And while she's cooling down she also need to try and adjust that attitude of hers 'cause it ain't getting her anywhere."

"How can you just stand there and say that without trying to help her? She needs help! She needs *our* help. We're her friends!" Andreide exclaimed. She looked over at Alisa who was sitting on a rock biting her nails, her eyes swimming with tears.

"Yes, Keisha does need help," said Harietta. "But sometimes we have to ask for that help."

Andreide rolled her eyes and released an exasperated sigh.

"But Keisha isn't the type of person to ask for help. You know that."

"Yes, I know."

"Then do something!"

"Well, what do you want me to do?"

"I don't know! Just do something to stop her. She might go and do something stupid. Doesn't the Bible say that we are our brothers and sisters' keepers?" said Andreide, attempting to appeal to her friend's religious side.

Harietta sighed. She looked up in the sky and weighed her words before saying them.

"Yes, the Bible says that we are our brothers and sisters' keepers. And that's true to a certain extent. It doesn't mean that we're Keisha's shadow and conscience. We've done what we can for her and now she has to do for herself. But I'll keep praying for her. She's in God's hands and that's the safest place she can be."

With that said, the bell rang ending their lunch break and the usual noise and commotion ensued. The ground vibrated and shook as multitudes of children stampeded toward the building, leaving a cloud of dust in their wake. Andreide walked back under the mango tree where she had left her lunch and picked it up. She looked down at her half eaten sandwich and instead of finishing it, she threw it in the garbage on the way to her classroom. She had lost her appetite.

Chapter 5

Rose Marie was sitting in a field of buttercups, wearing a sunflower-yellow, sleeveless dress. Everywhere she looked, she was surrounded by endless hilly fields of buttercups and butterflies. Suddenly, the wind blew strongly. Rose Marie closed her eyes; she revelled in the cool sensation of the wind along her skin. The gust only lasted a minute and slowly died down to a light breeze.

Something brushed her palm; she opened her eyes. She looked down and saw a Monarch butterfly – the only Monarch in the field – on her hand. As she stared at it, she felt a growing sense of peace and tranquillity. A feeling of warmth flowed throughout her body till she glowed with happiness.

It was as if the butterfly was bestowing upon her this wonderful sensation that she had almost forgotten existed. This heart-lifting feeling brought joy to her stressed soul and gave her the peace she so often prayed for. It was amazing how a creature so simple and small could make her feel so blissful. She almost felt like a child again, surrounded by such beauty and merriment. She smiled as she watched the other multi-coloured butterflies dance before her eyes.

Something in the distance distracted her. She glanced at her palm but the Monarch butterfly had already taken flight. Slightly perplexed, she searched the clusters of butterflies above and around her but without success. Her friend was not there. Just as she felt her hope fading, a brilliant light appeared ahead. Rose Marie shielded her eyes from the glare. She blinked several times to make sure that her eyes were not deceiving her. But there was no mistake. Out of the glowing light, emerged a man.

Rose Marie was entranced as she stared at his approaching figure. A series of mixed emotions blossomed within her as the man drew closer. The nearer he came, her excitement and curiosity grew. The glow of the light around his body gave him a heavenly appearance and it almost seemed to Rose Marie that he himself was the energy source. Only until he was a few feet from her, did she realise that the Monarch lay serenely on his shoulder.

The butterfly took flight and glided down to rest on Rose Marie's lap. She looked at it in wonder, before returning her attention to the man who stood in front of her. As she gazed up at the tall, masculine figure before her, she felt her heart flutter and a new feeling of happiness bloomed within her core. She could feel the joy, hope and goodness emanating from him and she had a strange feeling that she knew the man.

He slowly bent before her, lowering himself onto his hunches until they were at eye level. A gentle breeze blew from behind him and Rose Marie closed her eyes as she took in his wonderful scent. He smelled fresh, pure and untainted, mixed with the sweet, succulent aromas of the blossoming flowers. No other scent could compare to this one. Rose Marie was lost within it.

As the wind died down again, she opened her eyes and gasped at the man before her. He was unnaturally beautiful. His beauty was too divine to be human ... or could it be? Rose Marie was speechless. Never had she seen such a handsome man in all her life. His face was radiant. As much as she squinted to make out his facial features, in the glow of the light she could not be sure of who he was.

Rose Marie was so enraptured by his aura that she did not notice that he was holding something. She looked down as he brought his arm forward and held a single red rose in his hand. It was the most perfect rose she had ever seen. He held it so tenderly between his thumb and middle finger, as if it were the most fragile and most precious gift in the Universe. Rose Marie stared at it in awe before realising that he was offering it to her. For the first time, he spoke.

"A rose for *my* Rose," he said softly. His sweet breath brushed against her cheek.

Rose Marie's eyes glistened and filled with emotion. She took the rose from his hand just as he leaned forward and kissed her gently on her cheek. She felt his lips linger near her cheek after their bitter-sweet departure from her skin. She sighed and closed her eyes once more, savouring the sweet sensation of his lips upon her skin.

Then ... she woke up.

She knew it was only a dream but it seemed too real to have been only a figment of her imagination. But then obvious facts like the endless fields of buttercups and butterflies made her realise that it really was only a dream. There were no places like that in the country. And how could she not be able to see the man's face clearly and he was so close? And yet he was still so handsome! Of course it was a dream.

Rose Marie sat up and tried to organise her thoughts. She could not let this fantasy distract her from the work she needed to get done. She had not meant to fall asleep but she had been up late the night before familiarising herself with the information she needed to know for her interview. Jean had insisted that Rose Marie accept whatever interviews she was offered to increase publicity for her upcoming book. Her interview with a local radio broadcasting corporation was scheduled for the following week Tuesday and she was quite nervous – it was her first public interview. She was also feeling mentally exhausted but the marketing aspect of her book was not the only contributor to her fatigue.

Only the weekend had passed and she was already beginning to doubt her decision to allow her brother and his daughter to stay with them. Since the moment he had arrived the day before, all Peter did was sleep. That was not so much of a problem she supposed, but seeing the effects of his past life on him troubled her. He had barely said a word to her after arriving. She knew his hardships even before she saw them etched so clearly and deeply on his prematurely hardened face. She hoped he recovered soon or at least that his mood would lighten by the end of the week; his dismal appearance did nothing to help raise her spirits. She also did not want her children to have to see their uncle in such a state and gather a bad impression of him.

Chrystal was another story. Quite the opposite of her morose father, she just would not shut up. Everything seemed new to her and there was always a question after every sentence. It was only by the grace of God that Rose Marie managed to restrain herself from shouting at her niece to quiet her. That night, she prayed long and hard for the patience she would need for the next couple of weeks.

Rose Marie sat back in her desk chair and closed her eyes. She listened to the stillness of the atmosphere. She felt that same sense of peace she had felt in her dream flow through her again, calming her mind. The house was very quiet at the moment as she was the only one home. The children were at school, Chrystal went out to look for a job and took her father with her, and Charles was at work, thank goodness! Only God knew how much Rose Marie enjoyed the calming silence of the air when everyone was gone. She was a very peaceful and independent person who could not operate in noise or crowded surroundings. She needed her own space and time to accomplish what she had to do without the constant interruptions from her husband and children. As much as she loved her family, sometimes she really wished that they would just disappear so that she could hear her own thoughts for a while.

Rose Marie knew that she herself was to blame for some of the distractions as she gave in too easily to her children's interruptions. She was a very patient and understanding woman and she cared for her children too much to ignore their problems.

Sometimes she just had to stop her work to listen to Andreide's wining about her brothers or her father's annoying behaviour or her belief that she had no real friends; it might be Marques crying outside her door, complaining about the shove his brother gave him or the abuse he received from his sister when she found him listening in to one of her phone calls. The sounds of his sniffles tore at Rose Marie's maternal instincts to run and comfort her little lamb. But then it might be Omarion fuming and steaming about his 'ignorant ass' father and how he was trying to crush his son's dreams of becoming a professional chef.

All these complaints and more disturbed Rose Marie's peace of mind and more than added to her stress. Her husband who should be sensitive to her situation gave her no relief. In fact, he was just as bad as or worse than their children with his selfish questions and demands. It was only so much she could do not to retaliate blindly and do something she might regret later on.

She needed to de-stress. What she needed was a vacation and she knew it. She needed to get away from it all, leave her children, husband, paperwork and all her other responsibilities behind. She needed to go far away from them so that she could think clearly and breathe for her and her alone. She would give anything right now to find a place that would serve as her sanctuary, where she would be undisturbed by everyone's self-centred, inconsiderate demands on her body, mind and soul. But of course, the likelihood of that happening was as great as her dream becoming a reality.

Rose Marie jumped, startled as the phone rang suddenly, splintering the silence of the afternoon air. Annoyed by the disturbance of what seemed to be an interruption-free afternoon, she picked up the receiver.

"Hello?" Her tone was less than friendly.

"Rosie?"

Rose Marie rolled her eyes. It was her husband. Leave it to Charles to ruin what was probably the only afternoon she would have to herself for the rest of the month. She should have known that the initial peace and contentment she experienced from her dream was too good to be true.

"Yes, Charles, what is it?" she snapped.

"Is everything alright? You seem a bit edgy."

"Yes, everything's just *perfect*."

"Uh, ok."

Rose Marie struggled to keep her mounting rage in.

"Well, what do you think Charles? I have my first interview to prepare for next week Tuesday and I'm hardly ready for it. I was trying to prepare for it then I fell asleep."

"Weren't you working on that last night? I thought you'd be finished with that already." He gave a light chuckle. "I mean, even if you aren't finished with it yet, you still have a whole week again to be ready for it, right?"

Rose Marie bit back the oath she was about to release and closed her eyes. She needed to centre herself. She was used to his insensitive behaviour and careless remarks and she could not let it bother her now. Not when she still had so much work to do and deadlines to meet.

"Rosie?"

"What?" she nearly spat out.

"Why aren't you answering me? You'll be ready for it next week, right? I know you will anyway. You always get things done."

Rose Marie could hear him grinning stupidly through the phone. If he thought his attempt at a compliment would please her and lighten her mood, he thought wrong. In fact, it did quite the opposite. She felt a sudden urge to reach through the phone and slap him continuously; her annoyance with him was so great. His compliment only reminded her of how dependent he and everyone else were on her and how they viewed her as 'She who can do all things'. And how did they think she did all that with their constant hindrances? It was a miracle she got anything done at all!

"Well, you know I probably won't get more work done if I'm always interrupted whenever I try to start anything."

"Really? Well I did say having your brother and niece staying with us was a bad idea in the first place and –"

"I wasn't referring to *them*, Charles!"

"The children –"

"Nor them!"

"Well, what are you saying Rosie?"

Rose Marie gritted her teeth in anger and disbelief. How could one man be so incredibly dim-witted and possess little if no powers of deduction? And why in God's name, did she end up married to him?

She released an exasperated sigh.

"I'm sure you had a good reason for calling me after one in the afternoon when you know I'm usually busy at this time with my publishing team."

"Oh, I'm sorry. I didn't realise they were there. This doesn't mean you're busy does it?"

Rose Marie stifled a growl of frustration.

"Rosie? Is there something wrong with the phone line?"

"No, there isn't! And no my publishing team is not here and yes, I *am* busy! I'm always busy in case you haven't noticed lately, Charles. And whether my staff is here or not doesn't indicate whether or not I'm occupied with my work. And that's not even my point!"

"Your point?" Charles asked, confusion in his voice.

"Just forget it." She sighed. "Why did you call me again?"

"Oh right." Charles cleared his throat and assumed what Rose Marie presumed was his business voice.

"Rosie, I left an envelope on the dining room table containing some very important business documents for my boss, Mr. Rapier. I didn't realise I forgot them home this morning until a few minutes ago when Mr. Rapier asked me for them." He chuckled nervously. "He said he needed them on his desk by two o'clock this afternoon."

"Uh huh. And?"

"Well, uh, I told him he'd have it by two o'clock."

"Okay… so why are you telling me this?" She feigned ignorance.

"Rosie, could you bring the envelope for me, please?" Charles asked.

Silence was his answer.

"Rosie, please?"

Another dose of silence.

"Rosie, this is very important to me. My job may depend on these documents getting here on time!"

Rose Marie could not sustain her silent strike any further. She had to get some of her pent up feelings off her chest.

"And don't you think *my* job is very important to me too? Huh? Don't you? You think because I don't formally go to work in an office like you do and push papers all day and work for some old, fat man who's got a stick shoved up his ass that I don't have a real job? That's what you think, don't you?"

"No, Rosie wait, I –"

"Don't you 'Rosie wait' me! What part of I-AM-BUSY don't you understand?" She was a few decibels lower than screaming.

This time, Charles allowed the silence.

"Rosie," he said quietly after a few seconds had elapsed. "It would mean so much to me if you could bring the envelope for me."

Rose Marie had cooled down somewhat during the seconds of silence. She allowed a few more seconds to pass before she responded. "You took the car to work, Charles." She sighed tiredly.

"Yes, I know. And that's another thing I'm going to buy when I get my raise. Remember I told you about that?" His voice was eager and anxious, as if desperate for his wife's concurrence.

Rose Marie vaguely remembered him mentioning something to her about a raise sometime last week. As usual, he had not gone into much detail with her about it so it barely registered in her mind.

"Things are going to change once I get that increase and I need those documents to secure it for us."

Rose Marie tried not to sneer but she could not help but laugh dryly to herself at his words. He spoke as if he were planning on saving the world with his raise. Charles the humanitarian!

"I don't think it would be wise for me to leave the office at the moment since Mr. Rapier isn't in the best mood with me right now. So I was going to ask Freddy here to take the car and pass by the house to collect the envelope from you … Because it would be absolutely ridiculous for you to take a taxi to drop it off here for me," he added quickly.

Rose Marie laughed out loud. If only he knew what she was thinking at the moment.

He continued on, encouraged that her mood seemed to have improved. "So I'll give Freddy directions to our house and you'll look out for him in a few minutes, okay?"

Rose Marie shook her head in disbelief.

"Charles."

"Yes?"

"Are you for real?"

"What do you mean, Rosie?"

"Are you listening to what you're saying?"

"Well, of course I am!"

"Well you don't seem to be!"

"What's that supposed to mean?" he snapped.

Rose Marie replied in an even more annoyed tone. "How could you just tell me that you're sending some guy over here to collect your envelope for you?"

"But all you have to do is hand him the envelope!"

"Charles, that's not the point!"

"Well, what *is* the point this time?" he nearly shouted.

Rose Marie could not believe it. How could he be so unaware?

"Charles, you're telling me that you're sending some Freddy guy over here to our house and I'm the only one home at the moment and you know that. You feel comfortable with that? You feel comfortable sending a strange man to your home where your wife is the only one present? And for what? Some envelope for your boss? You would risk your wife's life to ensure your pay raise?"

"Oh c'mon! Don't be so dramatic. And you wonder where Andreide gets it from."

"Charles, I don't know this man! What if he attacks me, shoves me into the house and rapes me?"

"Rosie, you're overdoing it."

"No, I'm not Charles! These things happen. This is the real world. It is what it is and not what you want it to be!"

Charles did not respond after these words and in the silence that permeated the distance between them, Rose Marie could tell that he was angry. She did not care. She wanted him to be angry; he was too foolhardy.

After what seemed like ages, Charles finally responded.

"Does the fact that I trust him mean nothing to you?" he asked.

"Can your trust save me when he has me in a choke-hold?"

Another bout of silence then Charles made a noise of aggravation.

"Let's not fight over this."

"Fine."

"I'll just instruct Freddy to stay in the car since I have such a fussy wife who does not trust her husband's judgment. That way he won't even have to make it to our front door. Happy? It's almost 1:30 p.m. He should be there shortly – he left a few minutes ago.

Thank you in advance for all the *danger* I'm putting you in." He ended the conversation.

Rose Marie stared at the receiver in her hand as the dial tone buzzed in the background. How dare he be so bold? He had some nerve calling her fussy. She had made her view quite clear and yet he had still ignored her wishes. And then mocked her on top of that. If that was not disrespect, she did not know what was!

Infuriated with her husband, she slammed the phone into its cradle then stormed out of her study. She did not know what she was going to do, but she was going to do something and it surely was not delivering that envelope!

As Rose Marie entered the dining room, her eyes searched the table for the envelope. Surely, lying smack in the centre of the dining table was a long brown packet. She marched over to it and stared at it with distaste, her hands at her side, not touching it. As she stared at it, surprisingly, her anger seemed to melt away. She could not explain it but the more and more she stared at the envelope, the more she felt calm.

As she reached out to examine the object, she heard a car pull up outside the house. Her hand froze in mid-air directly above the envelope just as her heart commenced a frenzied beating. He could not be here already, could he? Panic shot through her veins faster than venom from a snake bite as she heard the car door open.

If she had not been so alarmed, she would have noticed that the sound of the car's engine was nothing like the family's car. This car was brand new and well cared for while their car was too old, squeaky and dilapidated to enter a museum.

Rose Marie grabbed the envelope off the table and clutched it to her chest as she heard footsteps on the concrete path. It was only a matter of seconds before –

Ding Dong. The door bell rang.

Rose Marie started.

Freddy was here to kill her!

Again, the door bell rang.

She could not answer it. She was not ready to die. And her children! What about her children? Who would look after them when she was dead? All of this just for some blasted envelope for her selfish, irresponsible husband!

A dart of anger shot through her as she thought of this. She was being ridiculous. No Freddy man was going to take her away from her children! And she bloody well was not going to let him if he tried!

She marched towards the front door, the envelope clamped in her hand at her side. Her anger fuelled her determination to live which strengthened her bravery. As she reached the door, she took a deep breath then yanked it open, her face fierce and ready for the battle.

But her face froze with shock as she stared at the man in front of her; it seemed like that was the second time for the day that she stared in shock at this man. But then, it could not be. And then she realised.

It was Victor.

"Good afternoon, Mrs. D'Averette."

The breath she held seemed to stick in her throat. The envelope slipped to the tips of her fingers.

"Are you alright?" He looked at her curiously.

It was then she realised how absurd she must have appeared and she quickly disposed of her battle composure, relaxing her facial muscles. Her cheeks flushed with embarrassment. She could not believe she had let Victor see her looking so silly! She had to brush this off at once.

"Oh, hello Victor!" She flashed on a smile. "You startled me."

He returned her smile. "Who were you expecting?"

She forced a laugh. "Not you."

She certainly had not been expecting him, no doubt about that. And as he stood before her, she felt all her negative emotions flow out from her body, just as smoothly and freely as the wind was blowing around them. She had to force herself not to close her eyes and bask in the sensational, aromatic scents emanating from him.

Slightly weak at the knees, Rose Marie leaned against the door frame. As she did so, she could not help but take in Victor's appearance.

He was dressed in his usual office style except something looked different to her. His long navy blue trousers and shiny black shoes were as pristine as usual, as well as his immaculately white, long-sleeved shirt. Then she realised that he was not wearing a tie and his top collar buttons were undone, revealing a few of his black chest hairs. She pulled her eyes away from them as her heart pounded faster again, but to a whole different rhythm. Then she noticed that his sleeves were rolled up just below his elbows, exposing his tanned, muscular forearms which were evenly layered with dark hair.

Her face flushed even more as she glanced up at his handsome, clean-shaven face and saw his sparkling grey eyes stare as intently into hers. He had seen her looking at him, she was sure and she could not remember the last time she felt this embarrassed. She wished she could run inside and hide from the man in front of her but that was childish. Plus, she could not move her legs even if she wanted to – they were glued to the spot. If only she could quickly say something to break the awkward silence between them. However, Victor did it for her ... to some extent.

"Hot ... isn't it?"

Rose Marie's eyes widened in surprise.

A slow smile spread across Victor's lips and his gaze darkened suddenly and flickered downwards; but just as quickly, as if nothing happened, his eyes lifted and resumed their smiling, boyish charm.

"The weather – it's a bit hot, wouldn't you say? At least it's hot down at the office in town. See?" He raised his arms at the elbows to show her the skin the heat had caused him to reveal. He laughed cheerfully. "Sooner or later I'll be reduced to going to work in a vest, slacks and sandals!"

Rose Marie joined in his laughter but not before noticing with slight apprehension, that serious look behind his amused eyes – a look that told her he was aware of what just took place between them and he was not about to forget it.

However, his laughter was deliberately aimed at relieving her anxiety and it did just that. She smiled, feeling more at ease.

"If that happens, imagine the number of single women Jean would have to beat off to get to you." She grinned at him then immediately regretted her words. She was practically his boss and here she was on the verge of flirting with him. And what was she implying about her publicist and friend to her editor? She could just slap herself!

Before she could say anything more to correct her statement, Victor took the opportunity to continue her unintentional flirtation.

"Well, Jean would have to take a number and wait in line like all the others. But beautiful VIPs like you, madam, get the red carpet and first touch." He opened his arms out wide before placing his hands slowly into his pockets, all while smiling at her with that heart-fluttering boyish grin.

Victor laughed.

Rose Marie could only stare at his gorgeous face. Her eyes wandered from his captivating eyes, his smiling lips and then to his sleek, black wavy hair which rested on his head, not a hair out of place.

He had called her beautiful. Beautiful! Well, she knew that she was beautiful already but hearing it from Victor made her feel like the Queen. And those arms! Wow, those arms! If he had held them open a bit longer she would have thrown herself into them. But why was she taking it all so seriously? He had not meant it anyway – he was only teasing her. She needed to get a grip on herself – she was a married woman!

"Oh yes." He cleared his throat and resumed his business-like persona. "Jean sent me by to drop off these papers. She said she had them for you for some time now." He had a clear plastic folder in his right hand that she had not noticed before.

He paused. "Well actually, I volunteered to come and give them to you. Anything to get out of that heat!" He laughed then tugged at his open collar.

She smiled then realised they were still standing at the door. She slapped her palm against the side of her face and gave him an apologetic smile.

"Oh gosh. I'm so sorry Victor. Where are my manners? Please, come inside. I have you baking out here in the sun!" She stepped aside to let him pass.

"Oh, it's no problem. I like a good tan." He gave her a sly smile and a wink, then stepped into the hallway.

Rose Marie smiled at him and shook her head as he stepped pass her. She never realised just how charming he was and even more so with his accent. She also realised that she did not really know him personally either. She did not know much more about him than his credentials. She did not even know if he was married! In the three months since Victor had joined them as her main editor, all they ever talked about at their meetings was her book and matters related to it. Everything was professional and now that she thought about it, this was the first time she had ever been alone with him.

"So ... Where's Jean? She normally comes here with you." They were standing in the hall near the front door.

As she glanced at Victor for his response, she was not sure if she had imagined a fleeting look of irritation in his eyes. But whatever it was was gone when he turned to face her.

"She said she couldn't deal with the heat. She left around lunch time and went home. All the better anyway. With the air-condition unit broken and hot air coming in, stress levels were rising and creating problems. The more people leave, the better it is for everybody," he stated. He looked over at Rose Marie before continuing.

"I don't mind the heat that much since I'm accustomed to the cold. Hell, I welcome it!" He smiled. "So she left this folder on her desk for you." He indicated the plastic folder in his hand. "And then she went home. I stayed behind to finish up some work I was doing then took the folder, hopped in my car and here I am." He spread his arms slightly before letting them drop to his side again. He smiled faintly at her.

Rose Marie returned his smile.

"So!" Victor clapped his hands together. "Here is your folder, ma'am." He extended it to her and Rose Marie took it.

"Thank you for your delivery service, kind Sir."

"Always at thy service, muh Lady." He tried his best medieval accent and sounded quite authentic. Adding to the theatrical charm, he bent low in a bow while twirling his right hand in front of his chest and his left arm stuck out majestically at his side.

Rose Marie laughed. This man surely had a great sense of humour! From his bowed position, he raised his head slightly and peeped at her from under his eyelashes. He wiggled his eyebrows and flashed on a comical smile. Rose Marie laughed even harder. He straightened up and joined in her laughter.

After they had sobered a few moments later, a comfortable silence filled the gap between them. Then Victor noticed the brown envelope.

"I think you had that in your hand since I came." He pointed at it.

Rose Marie looked down at the envelope in her hand. She had almost forgotten that she was holding it the whole time. Victor's arrival had distracted her from it and lightened her mood. Now that she had been reminded of its existence and subsequently, her previous argument with her husband, she felt her old anger stir.

Victor sensed the change in her disposition.

"Mrs. D'Averette, are you alright?" He looked at her carefully, his eyes full of interest.

"Yes, yes. I'm fine," she said. She tried to cover it up with a reassuring smile but it was weak.

"It's just some papers my husband wants me to give to some friend of his – who I never met and know nothing about – who's supposed to be passing by here to collect them." She released a tight breath. "He called a while ago, beating around the bush until he finally got to the point. I knew he wanted something of me, he always does. He wouldn't call me just for the sake of it." She looked away, her face filled with disgust and her voice full of resentment. Victor's caring look encouraged her to continue.

"He knew what he wanted the whole time and he just pretended to care enough to ask me my opinion. And thinking that he would persuade me with the prospect of his getting a raise! Did he think I was that low? That money would make me jump? Victor, I don't care about money the way a lot of people like my husband do. And after twenty long years of marriage you would think he would know that by now. There's so much he doesn't seem to know or he just doesn't care about. Like me!" She paused. She was breathing heavily now.

"I'm sure he loves you, Rose," Victor said softly.

Rose Marie looked at him quickly, aware that that was the second time he had ever addressed her by her first name. She did not mind, she just had not been expecting him to at that moment. It made her heart feel lighter. But she was still upset.

"Love? *Love?* He doesn't know what love is! If he did, he wouldn't be treating me like this. He would be sensitive to my emotions and care for my feelings if he loved me. He would know when and when not to bother me with his self-centred and infantile dilemmas." Before she could stop herself, she found herself telling Victor about the telephone call she had had with her husband. When she was finished, she turned away from Victor, hating for him to see the angry tears that were welling up in her eyes.

After a while, she continued.

"Victor, I'm just so tired." She sighed heavily. "This book ... Jean said that things were going to get better and I believed her. But it's not getting better."

"It *will* get better."

"But when, Victor? When?" Rose Marie looked searchingly into his eyes. Her own eyes were on the brink of overflowing.

"I thought by now I would be enjoying the fruits of my labour. I have my first public interview to finish preparing for and after that it would be more interviews. And then before I catch myself, it's time for my book tour. I need a break somewhere. This is driving me crazy! And to add to it all, my brother and his daughter just moved in with us for I don't know how long. It's only been about two days and my niece is already harassing me and Peter just lies around the house all day. As if I needed two more people to add to my list of dependents. And that *husband* of mine isn't giving me any help at all. I'm so frustrated, Victor!" Her voice trembled then she broke down in tears.

She cried like she had not cried in a long time. She covered her face with her hands as her tears flowed abundantly down her cheeks, mortified that Victor was seeing her in such a state. She could not believe that she was crying in front of him. She had not meant for their conversation to end up like this. What must he think of her? How vulnerable she must appear!

Victor's arms were soon around her. Rose Marie clutched to his chest as she cried out her frustration.

Several minutes later, her tears finally abated. As her breathing returned to normal, she started to become aware of their close proximity. He had not released her, and his arms felt so strong and comforting. With her head against his chest, she could feel his warmth and the firmness of the muscles beneath his shirt. She shifted her head a bit and his arms tightened around her. He felt and smelled good ... too good.

Rose Marie pulled back suddenly.

"Oh, Victor, I'm so sorry. You must think I'm an emotional wreck, don't you?"

Victor frowned slightly as he tried to reassure her. "No, not at all. You're just going through a rough spot. You needed to let it out. And it's good that you did. It's not healthy to keep all that frustration bottled up in you."

"But you didn't ask for this. You just came to deliver these papers and here I am crying all over you like some weak, helpless woman!"

Victor's expression suddenly became serious.

"You're not weak!" he said, firmly looking her in the eyes. "Or helpless. So don't think that – not for one minute." He stepped nearer to her, closing the gap she had created when she had broken their embrace. His eyes flickered down to her trembling lip and lingered there, indecisively.

Rose Marie could only stare at him; her senses were numb and she felt weak from crying. She had not even noticed when the envelope had slipped from her fingers. He was staring at her, but he was not looking directly into her eyes. His gaze was focussed intently on her lips. She saw something flash through his eyes which made her heart beat even faster. She shuddered.

It was this movement that brought Victor back to his senses. He caught himself just as he was about to raise his hand to her cheek to caress it. He smoothly lowered his hand and stuffed into his pants pocket. He looked away from her for a moment, his brow creased.

Rose Marie saw the darkness in his eyes dissolve as he looked at her again. "Why don't I take you for a drink? My treat." He smiled at her. "Take your mind off your book and interviews and everything else for a while. We'll just talk and forget about it all, just for this afternoon. I know a great place where we can go – completely stress free, I promise. Perfect for relaxing. Hmm?"

Rose Marie hesitated. She had not planned to go out that afternoon. In fact, she had intended to spend the rest of the day preparing for her interview, locked in her study, undisturbed for at least another hour until the children came home. But Victor's soft smile and that look in his eye made it really hard to decline his offer. She needed the break. And she could surely do with a drink about now.

"Yes, thanks. That sounds like a great idea."

"Great then! Shall we leave?"

"Just a minute. Let me get my handbag."

"Sure."

Victor watched her turn and head towards the stairs. His eyes followed her up each stair until she disappeared from view. He smiled to himself. Rose Marie was smiling too.

Chapter 6

A week had elapsed since the incident with Keisha and Shauna. During that week, Keisha had absented herself from school for four days straight. She had also refused to answer all of her friends' phone calls and appeared to be 'out' every time one of them went to visit her. Andreide became so worried that she resorted to asking Jamila, Keisha's wayward cousin, to check on her friend for them. Jamila told her not to worry and assured her that Keisha would be back out to school soon. And sure enough, she was back that Tuesday morning.

Keisha looked the same to Andreide. She had not lost or gained any weight nor did she appear to be depressed. Andreide was relieved. In fact, Keisha had resumed her usual disposition and carried on as if nothing had transpired that previous Monday morning. They were cautious about asking her about Shauna, but when they did, she agreed that she had overreacted but blamed it on hormones. She told her friends that she had had PMS. Andreide and Harietta were doubtful but they did not want to upset her again so they had dropped the subject.

Since Keisha's episode with Shauna and her alarming reaction to it, Andreide had been preoccupied with worry for her friend for the whole week. She was so worried and afraid for her friend's safety that she hardly had time to think about anything else. In fact, she had been so distracted that she had not thought about the new boy since that incident with Shauna. As a matter of fact, neither Harietta nor Alisa had mentioned him in the wake of Keisha's absence; now that she was present, it seemed wiser to continue to keep him out of the subject of discussion. It was not until that afternoon when his existence came crashing back into Andreide's memory.

The bell rang as usual at 3:30 p.m. ending that Tuesday's classes. The four girls strolled out of the school building, arm in arm, each with a happy smile on her face. Andreide was especially relieved that Keisha had not done anything to incriminate or endanger herself during their week-long separation. She was also quite proud of her friend for the way she had behaved that day in class. For once, Keisha had not had a brawl with Mrs. Smith.

Mrs. Smith seemed to have been deliberately on Keisha's case that day, or so Andreide believed. That morning, when Keisha had given their home room teacher her excuse note for her absence that week, Mrs. Smith had taken the liberty to read the note to the class, much to Andreide's embarrassment. When she had looked over at Keisha for her reaction, what she saw surprised her. Keisha was looking out of one of the windows with a cool calmness about her. It did not even appear that she was listening or affected by her teacher violating her privacy. When Mrs. Smith had reached the end of the note, she crumpled it into a ball then threw it in the bin beside her desk. Andreide had braced herself for the explosion. But it never came. Keisha had merely glanced at the taunting expression on their teacher's old, disintegrating face then looked back out the window.

After being blatantly ignored and obviously feeling rather foolish, Mrs. Smith had continued to teach the class with a huff, her back turned to Keisha and her temperament worse than ever. Keisha had kept her face blank after that, which only increased the old woman's rage. By the end of the school day, Mrs. Smith left the classroom with her teeth chattering with fury.

The girls exited the school gates and crossed the street, chatting happily with one another.

*

Twenty minutes later, the four girls were seated at a table in Jenny's Ice-Cream Parlour. Andreide had been in the mood for a soft-serve chocolate and vanilla swirl but since there was not any, she had settled for a regular scoop of chocolate ice-cream. Harietta was crunching the last pieces of a coconut cone, Alisa was slowly licking her strawberry ice-cream and Keisha was scooping chunks of peanuts and almonds along with pecan flavoured ice-cream into her mouth. Alisa had volunteered to pay for their dessert.

"Mmmm. This is sooooo good!" Alisa licked a dollop of pink ice-cream from her cone and closed her eyes as she savoured the taste.

Andreide chuckled. "You're acting as if you never had ice-cream before."

"Andy, my dad's a dentist. That should tell you enough."

"Please! My God-cousin is a doctor and he does smoke so … yuh point is?"

"My point, Keisha, is that my dad is a really dedicated dentist and he monitors what I eat most of the time."

"That must be a pain." Harietta shoved the end of her cone between her lips.

"Yeah, it is. He watches my sugar intake as if I'm diabetic or something. And of course, I can't eat any sweets in his presence. When I was younger, my mom used to take pity on me and hide some candy to give me as a treat whenever he got me upset over not being able to have sweets like a normal child."

"So he doesn't even let you eat ice-cream?" Andreide asked in disbelief. She could not picture having a childhood robbed of such sweet pleasures. And even worse, not having chocolate! Life without chocolate was like life without oxygen.

"Hardly ever," said Alisa. She swivelled her tongue through her ice-cream, enjoying the sweet-cold sensation of it.

"Gyul! Why you never did tell us how serious this was? We coulda give you all the candy from Christmas and Valentine's that we had left over. You coulda hide them in yuh room and eat them whenever you want. Ah can't believe you let youself suffer like that!"

Alisa laughed.

As she finished her ice cream, Andreide looked aimlessly around the shop. Her eyes settled on a woman and her young daughter, who were sitting nearer to the door. Andreide smiled as she watched the little girl lick her multi-coloured ice-cream cone. The child reminded her of herself when she was that age – about five – sitting in that same parlour eating ice-cream with her mother.

Before she could wander further down memory lane, a dark object outside the shop caught her attention. She spied it out of the corner of her eye. She felt her heart stop as she turned her head and saw what it was.

The black Rolls-Royce cruised by and as if by magic, or so it seemed to Andreide, its aura placed a damper on all the activity occurring in the streets. It barely hummed as it passed by.

"What you looking at so intently, Andy?" Alisa asked. Both she and Keisha turned to look out the window, following Andreide's gaze. However, the sleek car had already vanished out of sight, much to Andreide's relief. She had not even realised when they had stopped talking.

"Nothing," she said quickly. She was glad they could not see how fast her heart was beating.

Alisa gave her friend a curious look.

At that moment, Andreide's cell phone rang, saving her from further inquiry. She took it out from her bag just as it began its third ring. She got up from the table and moved away from her friends.

"Hello?"

"Hi, Andy. It's me." It was her mother.

"Oh, hi Mom."

"Hi honey. How was school? Is everything okay?"

"Yes, everything is fine. School was alright, I suppose. The best part was that Keisha came back. In fact, we're all here at Jenny's having ice-cream in celebration."

"Ok that's nice, love." Her mother sounded distracted.

"Are you still at that interview, Mom?" Andreide remembered that her mother had to attend her first public interview that day and she had been gone since morning.

Mrs. D'Averette sighed.

"Yes, I'm still here. It's actually halfway through, can you believe it? We're on a break now."

Andreide glanced at her watch. "But Mom, it's almost four! And you're now halfway through?"

Mrs. D'Averette sighed again.

"Yes, unfortunately. It started on time but we had several breaks in between. One delay after another."

"Oh, I see. Well, I hope you finish soon. You sound really tired, Mom."

"Well, I am, darling. I am. I'm exhausted."

Andreide sympathised with her mother.

"Well, anyway. I just called to see how things are going. Marques is supposed to be at football practice until around 5:30 p.m. and Omarion has class until 6 p.m. Chrystal and Peter are out visiting one of his old friends so they shouldn't be back till late. And you know your father is at work or wherever it is he goes."

Andreide picked up the slight bitterness in her voice at the mention of her father. Her parents were not in the best of moods with each other ever since they had argued last week Monday. Andreide had only heard pieces of the argument and would have heard more if Chrystal had not been snoring so damn loudly. From what she had heard, it was about some envelope that her mother had not delivered to him or something like that.

"What time do you think you'll be coming home, Mom. Marques will be bugging me to know."

Mrs. D'Averette did not respond right away. "I don't know, Andreide. I really don't know. But I'll come home, when I come home. Alright?" She sounded more tired than Andreide had heard her in a while.

"Ok."

"Well, I have to go back on in five minutes. Jean's calling me. See you when I get home, whenever that will be. Oh and don't go home late. You have to be there before Marques comes home. He shouldn't be coming home to meet an empty house."

"I know, Mom, I know." Andreide restrained herself from rolling her eyes. He could not come home to an 'empty house' but no one cared if she did. And why was that? Because he's a baby, of course! Mama's little baby. And who was Andreide? The middle child. It was always the first and the last children who got the most attention.

Andreide fumed after she hung up. All thoughts of the black car and the cute guy were evaporated from her mind as pictures of her little annoying brother burned holes in her thoughts.

"Andy. You look upset. Is something wrong?" Alisa asked as she approached their table.

The answer quickest at her tongue was "No shit!" but she shook her head instead.

"Nothings wrong?" Alisa asked.

Keisha grinned at her. "You need a next ice-cream, that's all. Let's split a rum an' raison, eh?"

Andreide gave a tight smile.

"No. I have to go home." She was not in the mood for any more ice-cream nor did she feel up to Keisha's humour. She just wanted to be alone.

She sighed. If only she could find a place to be alone. If she thought sharing a small house with five people was bad, with the additional two, it was torture. And even worse, she had to share her bedroom. There was hardly one moment of privacy for her to enjoy before someone barged in to disturb her. And Chrystal was pretty good at that.

Andreide turned towards her friends. She gave them an apologetic smile.

"That was my mother. Since she's out all day with her interview business, she called to remind me of my substitute duties." Andreide rolled her eyes.

A look of recognition dawned in Alisa's eyes. "Oh! It's him isn't it? Marques."

"Yeah ... *him*," Andreide sneered.

Keisha made a noise in disgust. "Gyul. I tell you. Lemme come over and deal with de lil brat for you, nuh! One good taste of auntie Keisha knuckles and you will see how fast he could behave heself!"

Andreide and Alisa laughed while Harietta rolled her eyes. Maybe she could deal with Keisha's sense of humour for a few more minutes. But then the thought of Chrystal arriving home early and occupying her room before her with more time to search through Andreide's things, propelled her towards the door.

She said her final goodbyes, grabbed her schoolbag off the back of her chair then headed out the door.

*

Shortly after leaving her friends, Andreide realised that she had forgotten her keys at home that morning. Something which she never did. All because of her nosy cousin Chrystal, who had distracted her. As her father's workplace was along her route, she decided to pass by his office to borrow his set.

When she arrived at the two-storey, cream-coloured building, she greeted the secretary then headed upstairs.

"Dad." Andreide swung open her father's office door. Charles D'Averette sat at his desk, bent over some papers in front of him. He looked up in surprise at his daughter standing in the doorway.

"Andreide! What are you doing here? Are you alright?" He pushed his chair back as his daughter walked in.

"I'm fine. I'm fine. Just came to borrow your keys." She dropped her bag on the floor near his desk and flopped down into the chair next to it.

"My keys?" Charles looked perplexed.

Andreide struggled not to roll her eyes.

"Your house keys. I left mine home this morning. What's her name – Chrystal – kept me back this morning with some nonsense about helping her find her MP3 player and I ended up leaving my keys in my room."

"Oh. Ok, sure. I have mine in my briefcase, here." He leaned to his right and pulled the bottom drawer of his desk open then lifted out his black briefcase. Just as he was about to unlock it, a large man barged into the office.

"D'Averette!" the man boomed.

Andreide and her father quickly looked up, startled. It was Mr. Rapier, her father's boss. She recognised him instantly. He was quite a fat man, so large in fact that he gave obese a whole new meaning. His triple chins, along with his bad brown toupee jiggled with each step he took as his massive frame approached. His small, puffy dark eyes focussed on the skinny man in front of him. At that moment, his snout-like nose appeared even larger than ever to Andreide. He was a pig in a wig in a suit.

"D'Averette!" he boomed again. "I need you to come out here and meet somebody. Same man I was telling you about earlier. He just moved here and I can smell his money!" The fat man laughed, his tiny eyes consumed by the overhanging blubber of his eyelids. His chins wobbled. His great belly shook. Andreide looked away from the sight in front of her, her stomach beginning to feel slightly queasy.

"Now, come on D'Averette! Can't keep potential investors waiting!" His great frame turned and marched back towards the door. Andreide swore she could have felt each vibration his beefy feet made against the concrete floor.

"Yes, sir."

Charles turned towards his daughter and gave her a weary smile. He took his briefcase off the desk and replaced it in the bottom drawer. "I'll have to give you the keys, when I come back. I'll only be a while so wait here, ok?" He stood up and headed for the door, closing it behind him. Andreide rolled her eyes. As if she had anywhere else to wait.

A few seconds later, the sound of voices not too far away lured her to her feet. She was somewhat curious to know who her father was meeting and the voices emanating from so nearby were a temptation that she could not resist. She inched quietly towards the door. She grasped the doorknob and turned it, pulling it slowly towards her. She placed an eye to the opening and searched the hallway for the source of the voices.

Near the end of the corridor, close to the stairs stood four men. She recognised her father and Mr. Rapier at once. As she looked closely, she was a bit alarmed as she also recognised the third man. It was her father's former friend, Mr. Carlston. What was *he* doing here? He stood alongside another man whom Andreide could not identify. However, his pale face, dark eyes and even darker hair seemed familiar to her, as if from a vague memory. He had an aristocratic look that she had seen only on one man before – a man wearing designer shades, looking snobbishly around at his surroundings. And then she remembered.

"Ah, Alfred! Pleased to see you again." Mr. Carlston held his hand out to Mr. Rapier who shook it with little pleasure. Andreide knew from her father that Mr. Rapier disliked the president of Carlston International Development Bank almost as much as he did.

Mr. Carlston barely glanced at Mr. D'Averette before acknowledging his presence with a stiff nod. Andreide saw her father return it with as much aloofness. If the stranger had detected the hostility between the two men, he either pretended not to have noticed or really did not care. His face showed no interest. Mr. Carlston turned back to Mr. Rapier.

"May I introduce you to my friend, Mr. Michaels?"

The man beside him moved slightly forward as he reached for Mr. Rapier's short outstretched arm. He hesitated for a split second before grasping the fat fingers before him.

"John Michaels. Pleased to meet you." His voice was cool, calm and crisp. He spoke with a distinctly English accent.

"Alfred Rapier. The pleasure's all mine." Mr. Rapier smiled eagerly, his porky eyes disappearing beneath crinkled fat. Andreide was sure that by what little light entering his hidden pig-like eyes, he was seeing dollar signs.

"I was just telling John here about your establishment. Told him you're one of the best landscapers in this country. Isn't that right, Alfred?"

"Yes yes, of course!" Mr. Rapier's chins seemed to bounce with excitement and pride on receiving such a compliment from Mr. Carlston of all persons, the man who was so difficult to please.

"Well, then maybe one day I'll have the opportunity to view your fine work. Perhaps even have you do something with my courtyard and that awful bit of earth that my wife insists on having as her garden. Women and their gardens," he scoffed, "Lord, help us."

He shook his head and chuckled. Mr. Carlston laughed and also shook his head as if he knew exactly what his new comrade was talking about. Mr. Rapier quickly followed suit, his booming laughter the loudest of them all. Mr. Michaels glanced at Mr. Carlston before sweeping his eyes from the bouncing man in front of him to the only man who had remained silent.

"I'm sorry, I didn't get your name." Mr. Michaels caught Mr. D'Averette's eye.

Before he could introduce himself, Mr. Rapier grabbed the microphone.

"Ah! How could I forget!" He dramatically raised his arms and shook them for emphasis. "Mr. Michaels, this is my right hand man, Charles D'Averette. Almost forgot you were here – staying so quiet-like eh, Charles?" He laughed, his loose chins wobbling.

"Pleased to meet you, Charles." Mr. Michaels said as he shook Mr. D'Averette's hand.

"Well, now that we're *all* acquainted," said Mr. Carlston, "why don't we get down to business? Alfred, I trust that you have flyers or some kind of brochure to show our guest? If Mr. Michaels would like to have his yard done by your company, he would need to see what you have to offer, I'm sure." He spoke like a man schooled to power and domination. He raised a well-trimmed eyebrow at Mr. D'Averette's boss.

"Why, yes yes, of course! I have plenty. We recently did a lawn for one of the government ministers and it turned out marvellous, if I do say so myself. The minister was quite pleased himself! Gave us a lot of publicity. We have many pictures – I can show them to you right now if we step into my office around the corner –"

Mr. Michaels held up his palm, cutting off the eager man. "Yes, that's fine, thank you, Mr. Rapier. But we'll do business shortly. I left my boys in the car and they must be bored stiff by now. I think they would enjoy the fresh air."

"Yes, yes! But of course! Let them out. By all means, it would be my pleasure to have your sons here. They can explore the compound and view my tropical specimens which I'm sure you will find to your liking. In fact, I can recommend a new rare flower, home to the South American jungles of Peru that they examine. I imported a few and have them under my shade cloth to the south of the compound along with several anthuriums, ranging from deep red to –"

This time, it was Mr. Carlston who interrupted his speech.

"That's all fine, Alfred. But Mr. Michaels isn't interested in your *flowers* at the moment." He glanced apologetically at Mr. Michaels who returned a polite smile.

Andreide's neck was beginning to ache. Her head was twisted at an angle such as to maximise the scope of her one-eyed vision. She pulled her head backward and began to massage her knotted neck muscles as best as she could. However, as she heard footsteps hurrying up the stairs, she jerked her head forward and rammed her eye to the crack at the sound of young male voices.

"Dad!"

"Nick, wait! Stop!"

The men turned in the direction of the voices as a young boy came hurling up the stairs. He was closely followed by an older boy. Andreide twisted and turned as much as possible to see their faces but she could not. The stairs were out of her line of vision. She felt her heart beat faster as her interest grew into more than curiosity.

"Boys! What are you doing?" Mr. Michaels looked sternly at his sons.

"I tried to stop him, Dad. But he just would not listen," said the older of the boys. Just like his father, he spoke with an English accent, but his was not as strong.

Mr. Michaels turned to his younger son and frowned, his dark eyes focussed on him. "Well?"

The younger boy looked up at the men around him then up at his father. He was obviously uncomfortable. He mumbled something that Andreide could not discern.

"Speak up! I can't hear you," his father commanded.

"I ... I ... I have to go," he said quietly but more audibly. His face reddened and he looked down at the floor as his legs squirmed. His father looked as if he were struggling between being annoyed and amused. He gave Mr. Carlston a rueful smile before addressing Mr. Rapier.

"Excuse my son, but his bladder seems to have the best of him at the moment." Mr. Carlston laughed at this and the boy turned an even darker shade of red. "May he use your bathroom?"

Mr. Rapier grinned widely and his jowls stretched. "Of course, of course! He can use my bathroom in my office. Good thing we're on our way there eh, young fellow?" His booming laughter ricocheted off the walls. The small boy jumped and barely contained his fluids. "Right this way, follow me." His large body monopolised the hallway as he led them down the corridor.

As they neared her father's office door, Andreide could now see the boys, who were trailing after their father. The smaller of the two looked to be around Marques' age. He was cute with a dark olive complexion and big, black curly hair. Unlike him, his older brother was quite tall. He was the last one in the group and as he came into Andreide's line of vision, she gasped. Her heart did a double back flip. It was *the* boy! The new, rich, gorgeous boy whom all the girls were talking about. Andreide could not believe it. Her heart began to pound faster than an African war drum. What was she going to do?

Without conscious thought, she quickly stepped backwards. Her right foot collided with the waste paper bin near the door, knocking it over with a loud thud; its contents spilled unto the floor, just as the boy passed by the door. She stumbled in a hurried attempt to hide and fell clumsily on the floor. She heard his footsteps pause as she lay stock-still on the ground. She closed her eyes and prayed fervently that he would continue walking and follow the other men. As she laid there, her breath stuck in the alveoli of her lungs, all she could hear was the ticking of the clock on the wall and the pulsing of the blood in her veins.

But luck was on her side. She heard him move and his footsteps continued down the corridor. She did not budge until the last echo of his movements dissipated.

Andreide exhaled slowly, releasing the pressure in her lungs. She had come so close to being discovered in such an embarrassing position and she could not afford to take that risk again. She felt like such a fool. What if the boy *did* see her? What if he had found her lying on the floor surrounded by crumpled and ruined paper, old pens and an overturned bin? What kind of a first impression he would have had of her? She did not want to think about it; she already felt quite foolish.

She stood up and rubbed her back. She had to get out of there. She could not stay there in case they came back and saw her – in case *he* came back. She needed to breathe. She needed to think. Without taking her schoolbag, Andreide left the office. She raced as quietly as she could towards the stairs and descended them in quick succession. She darted pass the secretary without a word and out into the surrounding grassy compound.

*

Andreide sighed. She felt calm. The breeze was cool and refreshing as she sat in the shade of a large tree. Her legs were crossed at the ankles and her back rested against the trunk of the tree as she gazed out at the attractive landscape. She had full view of the quiet street below and its neighbouring buildings. Everything was peaceful. She closed her eyes and leaned her head against the tree as she tried to empty her mind. She was not thinking about her father and the men inside Mr. Rapier's office nor was she thinking about the two boys. She especially was not thinking about the older, tall, handsome one. She let her mind wander. She pictured birds flying in the sky and a little boy playing with a puppy. She smiled. The birds began to change colours and multiplied just as the little boy began to grow. He suddenly became tall and as he turned, she saw his face, closer than she had ever seen it. He smiled at her and she began to feel warm. Just as suddenly, her eyes flew open as she heard the sounds of approaching footsteps coming from behind.

She sprang to her feet and dusted her school skirt, just as the person rounded the tree. She felt like screaming but her voice stuck in her throat. It was the boy.

"Oh, hello! Didn't see you, there. I'm so sorry. I hope I didn't give you a fright!" He smiled at her with the most perfect set of teeth she had ever seen.

Andreide could only stare at him. She never imagined she would meet a boy who was so good-looking but yet here he was standing in front of her, wearing a turquoise blue polo shirt, khakis and white *Nike*'s. If she thought he was handsome from afar, he was even more so up close. He was gorgeous. No other way to put it but gorgeous. He personified male beauty.

He had short, curly brown hair that shined golden in the sunlight. His light brown eyes complemented his soft curls and as they focussed on Andreide, they seemed to sparkle with warmth. His nose was straight and centred, his lips perfectly shaped and sized. His skin was not as pale as his father's – it had more of a creamy hue to it. And if his gorgeous facial features were not enough to make her melt into a puddle, he dared to have a dimple to go with that smile.

He extended his hand to her, looking her in the eyes.

"I'm Dominick Michaels."

He introduced himself with a confidence that she had never heard or seen from teenaged boys his age. His voice was strong, even and masculine, underscored by a slight English accent. He had hardly said much but she had already fallen in love with his voice. Enraptured, she slowly raised her hand and shook his. She was tongue-tied.

She breathed in sharply as their palms met. It felt like a warm surge of energy had flowed between them, entering her body from his. It instantly revitalised her and she regained control of her body. However, her senses seemed even more aware of the striking young man before her. She swallowed quickly.

"I'm Andreide D'Averette." She hoped her voice did not sound as breathless and shaky as she thought it did.

He smiled at her and inclined his head slightly.

"*Andreide*. What a beautiful name. Pleased to meet you, Andreide."

She smiled and lowered her eyes. She could feel a blush creeping up her face. He thought her name was beautiful! Again she felt like screaming.

"Have I seen you before?" He gave her a curious look, his lips still smiling. "Somehow you seem familiar to me."

Andreide felt her pulse race. "Umm, I don't know. Have you?"

"I'm not sure." He gave her a thoughtful look. "Maybe it was the day I registered at Duncan's Academy – Friday. You were there, weren't you?" His eyes were so bright and alive.

"No. Actually, I go to St. George's Public High School."

Andreide felt quite disappointed as she realised what he had said. He was registered at Duncan's Academy – the rich people school. The school of snobs. She did not know why she felt so disappointed. She should have known that he would have attended that school. After all, he was rich. Rich and white. Or almost white.

"Oh. I see." He almost sounded as disappointed as she felt. "Well, then it must have been somewhere else." He said this more to himself than to her.

A few seconds passed in which they both looked out at the landscape and the road below. With each passing second, Andreide felt more and more self-conscious. So much so, she could hear her blood pounding in her ears. She itched to move. But she felt so ensnared by the gorgeous boy standing in her presence. She wondered what he was thinking. She took a quick glance at him just as he also glanced at her. He grinned nervously. She smiled shyly.

"So ..." he said while looking at her.

Andreide tried hard to think of something smart and impressive to say but her mind kept drawing blanks. She had to say something soon. She could not remain there all quiet and have him think of her as some overly shy, stupid little local girl. But still nothing came to mind. She had finally met him but now she seemed incapable of saying a few sentences to introduce herself. She felt like kicking her own behind.

"Did you say your surname was D'Averette?"

She nodded. Speak Andreide, speak!

"There was a man with Mr. Rapier in his office. Charles D'Averette. Are you related to him by any chance?"

"Yes, I am," she spoke up quickly. "He's my father."

"Oh, really?" He looked interested. "Well, he seems like a nice man. Knows a lot about landscaping. He was happy to tell me the difference between the varieties of ferns on Mr. Rapier's desk when I pointed them out to my Dad. In fact, he told me where to find more out here. I've been looking for a couple of minutes but I haven't found any yet. But I found you though!" He smiled at her, exposing those dazzling pearly whites. His brown eyes sparkled.

Andreide felt her heart flutter; if it could have talked it would have been screaming. This boy – Dominick Michaels – was unbelievably stunning. And he was charming too! She could not believe that he was standing there talking to her, smiling at her with those warm friendly eyes. Andreide felt her cheeks grow warm.

"So Andreide. What brings you here?"

"Umm, I'm waiting for my father. I have to get something from him before I leave. I was in his office earlier.... Was that little boy your brother?"

"Nick? Yep, he's my brother. Almost wet himself just now trying to get to the bathroom." He chuckled. "I warned him to go before we left home, but he said he was fine. He thinks he's a man, that's what, but he's surely not." Dominick laughed. Andreide watched him – his eyes, his nose, his mouth.

"I have a little brother who sounds just like that. His name is Marques and he thinks he's as old as everyone else and can do whatever we can do. That's what annoys me the most about him." Andreide paused. She did not want to say more about Marques because once she started, she would keep going on about him and that was the last thing she wanted to do. He could not be the subject of her first ever conversation with Dominick. The most important thing was letting him learn about her attributes more than anything else.

"Oh. Well, Nick annoys me loads, too. But he's generally a good brother. So is Marques your only sibling?"

"No. I have an older brother too – Omarion. He's seventeen."

"Seventeen? Cool. It must be nice to have a brother around your age. Especially an older one."

Andreide grimaced. "No, not really."

Dominick grinned. "So, how old are you if you don't mind me asking?"

Andreide smiled. So polite. What a guy!

"Sixteen. I'll be seventeen in October. You?"

"I'm sixteen too. Seventeen in August."

"Oh, that's nice." Andreide was secretly glad that they were the same age. "So I know you're new here. Where are you from?" She was dying to know everything about him. Ever since she first saw him from the toy store window, her curiosity had been aroused. Now she was hooked more than ever.

"Oh, I'm from the UK. England actually. I was born there and lived there up until Nick was born. Then my Dad became a senior partner in his father's law firm and that's when we started to move. We moved all over actually." Dominick looked over Andreide's shoulder and gazed into the distance. "We first moved to Scotland and spent about three years there. Then my Dad was transferred to Austria to manage the firm's branch there. When we moved there, we had to start all over again. New house, new school, new friends, more adjustments. It was hard but it's been like that for a while. But it's different now. After staying two years in Austria, we moved back to England, back to our old neighbourhood in Cambridge. We were happy, especially my Mum who had friends and family there. And me, I got to reconnect with my old friends. We didn't think we'd be moving again until my grandfather got sick and my Dad had to take over for him. My Mum begged him not to move us again but he said he had to. It was his job, his duty – running the family firm. So we moved again. And we went all over. Hong Kong, South Africa, France, Germany, Italy. We probably hold the record for the most relocated family in the world." Dominick chuckled.

Andreide looked at him in awe.

"Now, how did we end up here?" he said with a slight smile. "Well, we were in Australia for six months when I first found out. Dad said we were moving again but this time it was going to be for a longer time. We asked him how long and he said perhaps permanently. You can't imagine how happy we were then to hear that!" He caught Andreide's eye and smiled. "Then when Dad told us we were going to the Caribbean that was about the best news we'd had in a long time. We didn't know anything about St. Kitts though, but we were glad all the same. Everywhere else we went was bloody cold most of the time. We were really looking forward to living in a tropical climate."

"My Mum insisted though that we go back to England to visit before coming here and my Dad agreed. We packed what we needed from our old home in Cambridge, said our goodbyes to friends and family and flew down here. We came here on the second of this month, January. So we've been here about three weeks." He looked at her and smiled. His eyes looked like golden honey in the sunshine. Andreide smiled.

"Wow," she said. "You've really been around! It must have been tough moving all the time, leaving all your friends and loved ones behind."

"Yes, but I can always make new friends. I'm pretty good at that actually. When you move as much as I do, you either make loads of friends or have none at all." He grinned at Andreide. "And I've got plenty of love to go around."

Andreide felt herself blush. She did not know why she was feeling so coy all of a sudden and Dominick's handsome face and subtle charm was only making her feel weaker by the second. No boy had ever had such an effect on her. There was something different about him. Something that made him unique, special from everyone else. And she was going to find out what it was that attracted her so much, even if it was the last thing she did.

A voice called out in the distance and both Andreide and Dominick turned in its direction. A boy was hurrying towards them from the building's exit. It was Dominick's brother. He stopped halfway across the lawn and called out.

"Dominick! We're leaving now. Dad's on his way down. Come on!"

He turned around and ran back down to the building where his father, Mr. Rapier, Mr. Carlston and Andreide's father were now exiting.

Dominick turned back to Andreide. He smiled. "Well, it was great meeting you, Andreide." He held his hand out to her. She shook it. "I really enjoyed talking to you."

"I liked talking to you too," she said with a girly grin.

"Well, perhaps we can talk again soon."

"Definitely."

"It's a pity we won't be attending the same school. It would have been nice though. I'd already have a friend then."

He gave her a boyish grin then started walking backwards. Andreide could not take her eyes off him.

"Alright then, Andreide. I'll see you around then, won't I?"

"For sure." She was going to make certain of that.

"Swell then. See you, Andreide."

"See you later, Dominick."

He turned then and walked across the grass to meet the others who were now walking down the path to the parking lot. Before he rounded the last corner and disappeared from her view, he turned and waved. She waved back, then watched him turn the corner. A few minutes later, the black Rolls Royce pulled out of the driveway and cruised off into the distance. Andreide could not stop smiling.

*

"Did I tell you how cute he was?" Andreide was ecstatic with glee.

Harietta and Alisa watched each other and rolled their eyes. It was Friday at lunchtime and the girls had chosen to eat in their homeroom class. Since that morning they could not get a break from their friend's excited chatter.

"Yes, Andy you told us. You've been telling us all week since Wednesday. Surprised you didn't tell us Tuesday after you got home or the moment he left." Harietta sighed. She drank the last dregs of her orange juice then threw the bottle into the nearby garbage bin.

"Oh, she told me though. Called me Tuesday night and had me listening forever." Alisa shook her head and grinned.

"Poor you," said Harietta. Andreide slapped her shoulder and Harietta laughed.

"Oh, c'mon! You girls supposed to be my friends." Andreide looked from one to the other.

"Yeah, we are. But does that mean we gotta listen to you talk 'bout that boy non-stop all the time?" asked Harietta.

"Yes! Like duh!"

They all laughed.

"Well all yuh happy eh! Wha' goin' on?" Zenicia, one of their classmates walked over to them and sat on top of an unoccupied desk. She threw a stick of gum in her mouth and started chewing it.

"So where me gyul, Keisha? She normally with y'all." She blew a bubble and popped it with a loud smack.

"She went home for lunch," Harietta said.

"Oh. So what y'all talkin' 'bout?"

Before Andreide could stop her, Alisa broke her news.

"Andreide met that rich, gorgeous boy who everyone's been talking about!" she announced proudly.

"Wha'! Fo' real, gyul?" Zenicia stared at Andreide in shock.

"Yeah, she did! And they talked and he told her about himself and they're friends now – he said so! And he smiled at her like she was the only girl in the world –"

"Alisa!" Andreide hissed.

"– and he said he wants to see her again!"

"Wha'. All ah that? Me arm. He say that fo' real?" Zenicia stared at Alisa.

"No, he didn't!" Andreide said hastily.

"Yes, he did," Alisa insisted. "You told us Andy!"

"Alisa, girl why don't you just hush?" Harietta glared at her.

"But ... Andy ..."

Zenicia slid off the desk and called out to a group of girls, who were giggling and peeping out of one of the open windows.

"Ey! Trisha, Meeky, Tonya! Guess what? This gyul here, Andreide, she talk to the rich boy!"

All three girls whipped their heads around. They stared at Andreide in disbelief.

"You lie!" Trisha exclaimed.

"She jokin' man!" said Tonya.

Meeky just stared.

"Is true. Alisa here jus' tell me. Come lemme tell you outside. Bell goin' go ring jus' now!" Zenicia beckoned the girls and they hurried over to her excitedly, eager to hear the new gossip.

"Eh heh! Wait till Shauna find out!" said Trisha as they hastened towards the door.

"Wait till Shauna find out wha'?"

They all stopped moving momentarily and looked towards the door. Keisha had appeared in the doorway, looking at them with an expectant, almost challenging glare. Andreide held her head in her hands.

Without answering her, the three girls and Zenicia hustled past her and out the door. Keisha walked in.

"Well?" She stared at Andreide, Harietta and Alisa in turn. "Y'all ain't gonna tell me good afternoon or wha'?"

They stared at each other then burst out laughing.

"What? Y'all think I was gonna get upset 'cause she mention Shauna, nuh?" Keisha asked amidst the laughter. They quieted down and looked at her.

"Well, I ain't upset. In fact, I got something to tell you, Andreide."

"Keisha –" Harietta interjected.

"No, wait. Lemme talk."

Andreide braced herself.

"Andreide, all ah got to say is Shauna ain't own nobody so whateva crap she saying 'bout that boy is hers is plain ole crap! She jus' want notice see. She neva even talk to the boy and she acting like she with him. And don't let she frighten you wit' any of she shit, 'cause I ain' 'fraid nobody! She want to trouble you or any of y'all, you jus' lemme know, you hear?"

Andreide tried to keep a straight face. She had not expected this from Keisha and right now she was finding it hard to breathe from suppressing laughter. Keisha watched her fiercely and she nodded her response.

"Lemme hear it from yuh mouth!" Keisha commanded.

"Yes, Mommy, yes!" Andreide burst out.

Harietta and Alisa erupted in laughter. Andreide joined in. Keisha watched them and her mouth formed its habitual pout.

"Ah serious you know! You jus' tell me if she starting any crap with you. 'Cause ain't nothing wrong with you being friends with the boy. Jus' don't let she trouble you."

"Ok. Thanks Keisha," Andreide replied after they'd settled down a bit. She exchanged a look with Harietta before turning back to their defender. "So, Keisha. Did you have a change of heart or something? You're fine with me being friends with Dominick?

Have you seen him? He looks white you know." She struggled to stifle a giggle. Harietta and Alisa were both fighting the same battle.

"Gyul, don't trouble me soul, nuh! I know he white or look white, whateva! Ah jus' saying I ain' got no problem with him. Is true he look alright an' all –"

"Aha! So that's why you don't have a problem with him! You think he's cute too?" Harietta grinned. "You got a soft spot for the boy now, eh!"

Keisha steupsed but could not hide the smile forming on her lips. "Gyul, run 'way!"

They laughed.

The bell rang a minute later, ending their lunch hour. As the classroom began to fill with students, Andreide thought about Dominick. She still could not believe she had met him and actually talked to him. And before all the other girls too! She felt so lucky and happy at that moment that she felt giddy. She knew that because of Alisa's over-eagerness in spreading her news, Shauna was bound to find out soon that she had met him. But Andreide did not care. She was not afraid of Shauna or anybody else. Keisha was right – Shauna did not own him. And as long as Andreide had breath in her body, she was going to make sure that Shauna never would.

Chapter 7

January ended on a harmonious note. February began just as peacefully. It was Saturday 3rd February, and Andreide and her friends had decided to spend the day hanging out together. Like most of their peers, their minds were occupied with the significance of the 14th of February.

"Can you believe January's over already?" said Andreide.

"Yeah, it went by quick see!" Keisha agreed.

The four girls were walking through the local Square on their way to town. It was mid-morning and they had just left Andreide's house after eating breakfast together. They were spared from Chrystal's presence that morning as she had not yet woken up. Andreide was immensely grateful as she had not felt like dealing with her cousin's bossy and selfish behaviour, especially in front of her friends.

"You girls know what this means, don't you?" Alisa said with a big grin.

"What?" Harietta glanced at her.

"Valentine's Day!" Alisa shrieked with excitement.

Keisha rolled her eyes. Andreide and Harietta laughed.

"I just don't know why y'all does go on so much 'bout that as if it's something. Some dum American thing and all yuh Caribbean people so quick to eat it up."

"Keisha! How can you say that? Valentine's Day is celebrated all over the world. Plus, it wasn't created by Americans.

It just became a big thing over there. It's a Roman tradition, started by St. Valentine who was a priest in the third century. He was imprisoned by the emperor for going against his wishes and marrying soldiers, or so they say. When he was in jail, before he died he wrote a letter to his love and signed it 'from your Valentine'. And people have used that expression ever since. So that's how Valentine's Day came about."

Keisha stared at Alisa blankly. "But ah didn't ask you."

Andreide bit her lip and chuckled.

"Well the girl was just telling you so you could stop sounding so ignorant," said Harietta.

Keisha steupsed.

"Keisha, Valentine's Day is all about giving love and showing each other how much you care for them," Alisa continued. "It's the one day in the year that's dedicated to love. Why can't you just enjoy it like everybody else?"

"'Cause it's a waste of time, thats what. Is just a dum trick by all them business people to try and take everybody money. And every year y'all people does get trapped by them and go and waste yuh money on all kinda crap that people neva gonna even use! If you count up de amount of money y'all people does spend every year on that one day buying gifts, you will see how much money y'all waste. That money coulda been used to help the poor black people in Africa or poor people in Asia. Just imagine that and now tell me ah wrong!"

"You're not wrong. You have a point. But you taking the thing way too seriously, chile," Harietta replied.

"Yeah, Keisha, she's right," Andreide agreed. "Giving gifts is just symbolic of the love you have for that person. It's true that people waste a lot of money on gifts but the point of gift-giving is to make others happy and feel loved. Once you accomplish that it doesn't really matter how much money you spent 'cause the aim was to make your loved ones happy. And there's no price on happiness."

Keisha was silent.

"So, what do you say Keesh?" Alisa watched her intently. "How about giving Valentine's Day this year a try, huh? You just might like it. And who knows, maybe you'll get a Valentine!" She grinned.

Andreide and Harietta laughed. Keisha pouted her lips, but nevertheless, smiled at the same time. She playfully shoved Alisa to the side.

"Gyul, please."

Alisa laughed. "I'm serious! What if you get a Valentine. What if we all get a Valentine! That would be soooo sweet!" She squealed excitedly.

"Gyul, you're just a big chile, you know that?"

"She's right though. It *would* be nice to have a Valentine. At least for once." Harietta sighed.

"Oh c'mon, Harietta! You're sounding as if you never had a Valentine before." Alisa watched her incredulously.

Harietta steupsed. "Girl, how long you know me? You well know I ain't had a Valentine since primary school, so what you saying? If it's anything, it's you who does have all the Valentines. You and Andreide. Always had boys running down y'all."

"But Harietta, I haven't had Valentines for the past couple of years. You're confusing me with Alisa."

"Gyul, boys always used to give you things on Valentine's Day! What you talking 'bout?" Keisha butted in.

"But that's different. They weren't really my Valentines. Your Valentine should be someone you love, someone –" Andreide broke off and sighed exasperatedly. She was not sure how to explain it.

Alisa watched her carefully. "You mean like a boyfriend then?"

"Well ... sorta ... yeah! A boyfriend."

"I kinda see what you mean, Andy," said Harietta. "Your Valentine should be more of a permanent figure than a one day thing, right?"

"Yeah. That's what I meant."

"But we don't have boyfriends. None of us do," Alisa said.

"I know. But it would've been nice if we did. Not just for Valentine's Day. Don't you think it's time we actually had ourselves a boyfriend? I mean, look how old we are. We're sixteen going on seventeen and we're single like old maids!"

"Andy, girl. What's with this all of a sudden? It never used to bother you before." Harietta watched Andreide curiously.

"Well, we're not getting any younger you know. I just feel ... I feel ... like – Well, haven't you girls ever felt the need for companionship? Male companionship?"

Alisa looked at Andreide with her eyes wide. She whispered, "You mean, you mean like, like ... *it*?"

Andreide rolled her eyes. "No, Alisa! I don't mean sex."

Keisha burst out laughing. Alisa chuckled nervously and looked away.

Harietta looked at them and rolled her eyes.

"I know what you mean, girl," Harietta said. "It's a kind of a lonely, empty feeling. Yeah, I know the feeling." She reflected for a while. "But let's not make it upset us. Even if we don't have a man, Valentine's Day is for friends and family too. And girls, let's promise we'll make this Valentine's a special one, alright? Together. You included Keisha."

Keisha grunted while Alisa and Andreide agreed.

"Good. Now let's hurry up and check out the new Valentine's stuff. Clothes first!" Alisa exclaimed.

The three girls laughed before hurrying after Alisa who was already across the street.

*

"Gosh, this pink dress is too much! Just look at those lacy frills – they're gorgeous!" Alisa's face was filled with the excitement of window shopping. She had dragged her friends into the store with her after the dress caught her eye from the display window. She took the dress of its rack and draped it against the front of her body.

"How does it look?" She twirled around so her friends could see.

Andreide looked over at her and smiled.

"It's really pretty. You'll look good in it."

Alisa grinned. "You think so?"

"Would I lie to you?"

Alisa smiled. She turned to face Harietta who was busy searching through a rack of red, white and pink halter tops.

"What do you think, Harietta?"

She paused from her searching and glanced up. She frowned a little and tilted her head to the side. "Well, I guess it's alright. For you that is. You wouldn't catch me dead in that though."

Andreide laughed but regretted it when she saw the disappointed look on her best friend's face.

"Why not?" Alisa asked her in a slightly hurt voice.

"Girl! You know I hate pink. That colour is too girly-girl for me. It's fine for you if you wanna look like some baby doll but I wouldn't wear it. Not with my size anyway. Those frills would make me look ridiculous! Think about it. A big girl like me wearing a pink frilly dress. I don't think so, girl!" Harietta shook her head and turned back to her rack. She grabbed the last top in line and checked the size. She steupsed, slammed the top and its hanger back on the rack then marched off to a different area of the store.

Alisa gave Andreide a look then turned to Keisha who was leaning up against an unpacked pile of boxes.

"What do you think Keisha? I know you don't hate pink that much too right? So what do you say? Doesn't it look good?" she asked eagerly.

Keisha did not even look up at the dress. "Yeah, whatever." She flicked at a spot of dirt under her finger nail.

Alisa huffed.

Andreide laughed at her friend's expression. "Why did you even ask? Girl, just go and try it on. I'm sure it'll look good. Go on."

Alisa smiled and hurried to the back of the store to the dressing rooms with the dress clutched to her chest.

"Keisha, it wouldn't hurt you to try and be nice you know. You know how Alisa values our opinions. Yours too. So could you try and compliment her when she comes out?" Andreide said as patiently as she could.

Keisha glanced at her then returned her attention to her nails. She grunted her response.

Andreide sighed and moved away from her. Keisha's lack of consideration and insensitive ways were serious character flaws for her. Andreide wished she could get her to realise that and try to change it but so far she had not been successful. She just hoped Alisa did not take her response or lack of it seriously.

Andreide walked towards the front of the store and gazed out of the glass display windows. Except for the increase in the number of teenagers in town and the arrival of new Valentine's Day merchandise, it was a regular Saturday. She looked out at the pedestrians passing by and recognised a few of her classmates. She also saw a couple of her Church members and much to her surprise, her parish priest as well. What made it even more surprising was the unmistakeable red and white paper shopping bag in his hand, bearing the logo 'LLL' in soft pink designs. Andreide grinned deviously but tried not to assume the worst. 'LLL' stood for Luscious Ladies' Lingerie.

A couple of minutes passed by and Alisa still had not returned from the dressing room. Andreide did not mind – she was enjoying her view of the street's activities. After watching more people pass by, she was about to turn away from the window when she saw a fair-skinned boy walk by with curly hair. She immediately thought of Dominick. She knew it was not him for this boy was too short and his expression was hard. But still, her mind raced to thoughts of him and an image of his handsome smiling face hovered before her eyes. She sighed and flashed back to the last time she had seen him.

Since she had met him that Tuesday afternoon at her father's workplace, she had seen him twice after that blessed occasion. Once, while she was in town with her mother last week Saturday – they were driving by looking for a parking space on Bladen Street when Andreide saw Dominick and his father coming out of *Michaels & Michaels'* law offices. She had waved timidly at him and he had smiled and returned her gesture, almost as awkwardly but not quite.

The second time was the following Monday when Andreide was walking to school along her usual route. The Duncan's school bus had already passed by a few minutes earlier and as usual, the uncouth Academy boys had left a trail of teasing remarks for her to digest. Distracted by thoughts of them, she had hardly heard a vehicle drive up alongside her. She only noticed it when the window rolled down and a recently familiar voice called out, "Good morning, Andreide". She had been completely startled and all thoughts of her previous encounter with the Duncan boys had been swiped from her mind. Dominick had smiled at her from the backseat of the town car and asked her how her day was going and how she was feeling that day. After replying quite shyly with a "I'm fine, thank you," and then with a 'I can't believe this gorgeous boy just pulled up and asked me how my morning was and he's smiling at me with such a dazzling, sexy smile and those honey coloured eyes are looking at me,' kind of smile, she noticed that there seemed to have been something he wanted to say. But he withheld it.

After this, someone had spoken but Andreide could not see who it was. Dominick had glanced to the front of the car then back at Andreide. He had given her a small regretful smile and shrugged his shoulder as if to say, "I wish we could talk more but ..." then he waved at her and said good-bye. She had waved back and as the car drove away and turned in the direction of Duncan's Academy, she felt like nothing could take away her happiness. The image of Dominick's face looking up at her with such a lovely smile had remained with her for the rest of the day.

Andreide sighed. If only she did attend Duncan's Academy. They would probably be in the same class and then they would definitely be able to interact with each other more. But then, that was only wishful thinking. Her parents could not afford to send her to that school and she would rather be uneducated than attend it anyway. Duncan's Academy was a school filled with snobs and racists. She did not belong there. If that was not enough of a turn-off, the ratio of black to white students definitely was. She could count the number of black students there on one hand. She would never want to be a pupil of such an institution – to have to be subjected to all the pressures and pain of being a member of the minority.

"Hey, Andy."

Andreide turned from the window. Alisa had returned from the dressing room but she was not wearing the dress. Andreide frowned.

"What happened to the dress?"

"Nothing. It was too big and the zipper couldn't zip up properly in the back. Kinda disappointed but, oh well." She shrugged. "It doesn't matter, anyway. Guess it wasn't meant for me."

"Oh. Well, it did look good on you. Maybe you'll find it in a smaller size in a next store."

"Yeah, hopefully. I really liked that dress."

"Oh great! Lemme guess. We're going to search through every shop until we find the damn dress then, eh?" Harietta shoved a rack of purple pants aside and walked towards them, her hands on her hips. She looked truly annoyed. Andreide found this both strange and amusing but something told her not to laugh.

"What's wrong with you?" Andreide asked.

"Yuh mean besides what was wrong with she before?" Keisha looked up from her nails and grinned at them. Harietta did not look pleased.

"Girl, just hush yuh mouth! Nobody asked you anything."

"Whoa! Gyul, mind you bite off me head see! Lawd gyul, what wrong with you? I ain't do you nuttin'."

Harietta sighed and seemed to calm down a bit.

"I know. It's not you. It's this stupid store. In fact, it's this whole world!"

Andreide and Alisa exchanged a quick look.

"No one seems to care 'bout people my size these days. Everywhere you turn is some small short-up piece of clothes for all yuh skinny ass, no figure, no shape people. But what about me? What about women like me? What do we wear then? Why can't they make clothes to fit us plus size women? Something to fit our meat and curves. Clothes to make us feel comfortable in. Everybody's not the same! They can't be making the same size clothes for people. This is ridiculous! And then when we buy the small clothes and squeeze into them and walk down the road in them, they gonna want to say how nasty and vulgar we are. Well, it's them who made us look that way. It's them who won't cater to us big women. And you know what? I'm sick and tired of it. I'm tired of it all. I don't want to go into a store and have to choose from a bunch of small clothes. I got shape and size! I wanna be able to go into a store and find a top and bottom that are stylish and in a size big enough to fit me. I wanna be able to go into a store and not have to look for the biggest size to try on. I want to choose a size knowing that there are even bigger sizes. Do you girls get what I'm saying?" Harietta looked at them, as if pleading with them to understand.

"It's alright, girl." Andreide patted her shoulder. "Don't mind. I hear you. I know what you're going through."

"No, you don't." Harietta pulled away from her friend. "You don't know what it's like to be fat. And you probably never will with the way how you look. You got skinny genes. You'll never know what it's like to have to struggle with society, being big like me."

The girls were quiet for a moment as they thought over this. Andreide knew Harietta was right but she did not know what to say to her. She did not know personally what it was like to be overweight but she could only imagine.

"I know this though," Harietta continued. "I love myself and I love my body. And nobody's gonna make me feel bad about the way I look! I've always been fat and maybe I always will be. But to tell you the truth, I don't care! Shit, I'm quite comfortable with the way I am and if anybody think different, well to hell with them! I'm not gonna adjust my body to suit anybody. Or to suit these clothes. If they wanna keep making clothes to fit the *ideal* size and shape woman then fine, they can continue. But somebody gotta tell them that big women got curves! And this woman here ain't buying into their nonsense. No no no. If they won't make my size then I'll have to do it myself!"

Harietta's heavy chest heaved as she looked at her friends as if challenging them to oppose her. They could only stare at her, shocked. A few other customers who had been listening in to the conversation also stared at her; two of them who were rather large themselves seemed to smile with pride at their spokeswoman. Harietta glanced at them before returning her attention to her friends.

"Well, then. If you don't mind, I won't be joining you on your search to find your small size dress. I feel too annoyed as it is and I don't mind if I never set foot in another clothes store again." Harietta turned and started towards the door.

"Harietta wait!" Alisa called out as she hurried behind her friend. "Please don't go! I'm sorry. It's all my fault. I didn't realise you weren't having fun. You normally seem okay with shopping."

Harietta sighed and turned around.

"It's not your fault, Alisa, so don't go blaming yourself. I just don't feel up to anymore clothes shopping, that's all."

"But we don't have to go clothes shopping again! I can get that dress another time. Or if I don't get it before Valentine's Day I can have my auntie send it down for me. So come on, let's do something fun. Something that you want to do." She smiled at her frowning friend.

"Alright, fine," Harietta agreed. "Let's just get out of here and then maybe I can think straight."

They left the store.

*

Andreide felt a sense of déjà vu as she looked out through the glass window at the Michaels & Michaels building on the opposite side of the street. She remembered the last time she was standing in front of the same display window and saw Dominick emerge from the sleek black Rolls Royce and unto the front steps of his father's workplace. She smiled and imagined him standing on the steps there looking at her with those beautiful honeyed eyes. She felt the familiar flutter in her stomach at the thought of seeing him again so near. She grinned then turned around, narrowly avoiding two little boys who raced pass her with ninja dolls in their hands.

They had ended up in Royal Toys toy store. Surprisingly, it was Harietta who opted to go there; she wanted to see what new toys the store had that she could buy her younger siblings for Valentine's Day. Andreide admired her thoughtfulness and kindness towards her brothers and sisters. In fact, her friend's selflessness almost inspired her to do the same for her younger brother, Marques. Almost.

"Hey, Andy, you just have to come and see these cute new Valentine teddies. They're so sweet!" Alisa squealed as she hurried towards Andreide. Before she could reply, Alisa grabbed her wrist and pulled her in the direction from which she came. Andreide almost tripped in her friend's haste.

"Gosh! Will you slow down? What's the big rush? You're acting like you never saw red and white teddy bears before," Andreide said while trying to keep up with her friend as they hurried past two aisles of board games. Alisa ignored her until she turned down the fourth aisle and halted at the entrance to the passage.

"See? Aren't they all so beautiful?" she whispered in an awestruck voice. Her head revolved slowly as she took in the shelves of colourful stuffed animals on her left and right. She looked over at Andreide for her response who looked back at her with an amused expression.

"You know you need help, right?" she teased her.

"Oh, c'mon Andy! Tell the truth. Don't you find them pretty too? I don't think I've ever seen any prettier Valentine's toys!"

Andreide looked at the toys on the shelves to her right and then her left. The first thing that struck her was the intensity of the Valentine colour scheme of red, white and pink. She approached the shelves for a closer examination and on inspection, she had to agree with Alisa. These toys really were pretty. Extraordinarily so compared to the usual toys the store brought in for the occasion. Andreide now understood her friend's over eagerness and great interest in them. Even though she wasn't much of a 'stuffed toy' person, she did see the appeal it had to people like Alisa, whose childhood pleasures seemed to overextend its limit.

Alisa gently took a fluffy pink teddy bear with red hearts stitched into its fur from the shelf and hugged it against her chest. She closed her eyes as she embraced it and rubbed her cheek against its fluffy coat.

"It's so soft and cuddly," she sighed out loud. "I wish I could get this one for Valentine's Day."

Andreide watched her and smiled. "You're right," she said. "They are something special."

Alisa opened her eyes and grinned at Andreide with her head still pressed against the stuffed toy in her arms.

"So you agree then? You like 'em too?"

"Yeah, they're cute –" She paused as her eye caught a stuffed dog on a shelf opposite Alisa. "– especially this one." She walked over and took the toy off the shelf. It was a white fluffy dog with big brown dreamy eyes, pink ears, paws, tail, tongue and nose – to her surprise. Its paws were beanbag-like, its ears droopy. But the rest of its body was posed in an upright sitting position. She smiled at its innocent expression and felt too like hugging it. It looked so peaceful and comforting. It reminded her of her childhood – her room filled with cute soft toys.

"Adorable, don't you think?" A male, slightly British-tinged voice spoke behind her.

As if responding to the firing of a pistol, Andreide's heart shot in the direction of her throat. She knew who it was before turning sharply to face him.

Dominick grinned at her, his eyes sparkling amiably. Andreide stared up at him, temporarily at a loss for words. Although she had been thinking about him all afternoon, she had not been prepared for such a sudden meeting. She especially was not prepared for the effects his gorgeous smiling face, sexy accent and alluring cologne had on her. She tried her best to dislodge her heart from her breathing passage.

"Oh, and that toy dog's pretty cute too." He gave her a mischievous grin.

Andreide felt her heart do a light flutter.

"Dominick! Wh-What are you doing here?"

"Oh, I'm here with Nick. The little chap wanted to see what toys there were in here that he doesn't have already. Honestly, I don't see the point of him buying more toys. With the amount he has he could start his own toy store! Both his bedroom and his playroom are packed with all sorts of things. But he asked my Mum and well ..." Dominick sighed and shrugged his shoulders. "She gave in as usual."

Andreide shook her head in understanding. "I know what you mean. Same with my brother. He gets what he wants, especially from my mother."

Dominick grinned. "Maybe we should start our own anti-little brothers association. We could recruit members from all over the world as long as they have an annoying little brother who pesters them all the time."

Andreide laughed.

"No, c'mon, I'm serious!" Dominick laughed along with her. "We'd have so many group members. We could do things like petitioning our countries' governments to legalise sibling trading or the auctioning of little brothers. Hmmm, I wonder how much Nick's worth." Dominick rubbed his chin and looked up at the ceiling, pretending to calculate figures in his mind.

Andreide laughed even more. Dominick grinned.

"Naw, I wouldn't sell Nick. No matter how much he gets in my hair. He's a good little brother," he recanted.

Andreide looked at him and smiled slightly, wishing she could say the same for hers.

"So Andreide," Dominick refocused on her. "Who's that cute thing for – if you don't mind me asking?" He pointed to the pink and white dog which she still held in her hands.

Andreide felt her cheeks grow warm and her heart resumed its racing. She didn't even realise she still had the childish stuffed toy in her hands and she felt the beginnings of embarrassment creep up along her skin. What made it more embarrassing was the fact that it was a Valentine's Day toy. She could imagine how childish she must appear to him standing there holding it like it was the most precious creature in the world. She was sixteen years old. She was not interested in toys!

But what was she to say? She could not tell him it was for her boyfriend because she did not have one. And even if she did tell him that, he might lose interest in her because of that fact. But then again, he might not. But if she told him it was not for anyone, he might think she did not have someone to give it to and think that she was pathetic *and* lose interest in her. These thoughts swirled through her mind as she fidgeted with the toy in her hands.

"It's um ... um ... nothing. I was just admiring it – it's so pretty and cute." She glanced at it once more before quickly replacing it on its shelf.

Dominick smiled. "Yes, it is."

There was something in his eyes that Andreide could not quite put her finger on. Before she could think of what it was, he spoke again.

"Well, Andreide. It was great meeting up with you again, but I should go and check on Nick. Don't know what he's up to and he likes wandering off, you see. I hope we could do this again soon." He grinned sheepishly. "Well, I don't mean exactly *this* but to talk again, you know."

Andreide smiled. "Yes, I know."

"Hopefully, next time we'll have more time. It would be nice if we could talk more."

"Yeah ..." Andreide then felt stupid for her loss of sensible words.

"Well then, I'll see you 'round Andreide." Dominick smiled at her. He took a last glance at the shelf of toys next to her then back at Andreide before waving slightly and heading down the aisle. Andreide watched him walk his tall confident walk, until he turned the corner and disappeared from view. She had barely exhaled before her friends – who had been listening in and watching the two of them from the top of the aisle – came rushing towards her. All three of them were bursting with excitement.

"Girl! Wooo! He's hot!"

"He's on fiya!"

"Wow, Andy! I see why you go on so much about him now!"

"Gyul! Ah sorry if I did go on bad 'bout the boy, see! Gyul, you right. He really sumt'ing sweet, eh?"

"Well, eh eh! Look at that. Even Keisha could see the boy look nice. What is this!"

"I can't believe I never saw him so close up before. He's so sweet! Oh my, God!"

"Lawd gyul, Andreide! You struck gold chile!"

"What are you talking about?" Andreide managed to cut in.

"Gyul! What yuh mean what ah talking 'bout? You got a rich white boy into you! How much luckier you could get?"

"How 'bout a rich black boy?" said Harietta.

"Gyul please! Nobody ask you anything. Getting a rich black boy is like getting a piece of fry chicken from you – as in neva!"

Harietta steupsed. "Chile! Don't let me have to break yuh dry bones for you right here and now!"

Andreide laughed.

"Hey girls! Could we get back to Andreide and Dominick?"

They all looked at Alisa then started laughing.

"You right."

"But Andy, you're really lucky you know! You could always attract the best boys. You done have this one already."

"What are you talking about? I don't *have* him. I barely even *know* him. He barely even knows me. I'm sure he doesn't even like me like that anyway."

"Andy, girl! Are you nuts? Of course he likes you!" Alisa exclaimed.

"Chile, didn't you see the way he looked at you and how he kept smiling at you? You already got him hooked, girl!" Harietta clapped her hands together and grinned.

"No. You girls just exaggerating. That's how he is. He smiles at everyone."

"*That's how he is?*" Harietta quoted her. She placed her hands on her hips. "I thought you didn't know him?"

"And how do you know if he smiles at everyone? He didn't smile at me. And I was the second closest one to him just now," said Alisa.

Andreide rolled her eyes but could not stop the grin from spreading across her face. Her friends' excitement and enthusiasm with Dominick and herself was only adding fuel to her already excited fire.

"Wow. I just can't believe this!" Alisa looked at her best friend with amazement in her eyes. "This is it, Andy. It's him! He's the guy you've been waiting for – the boyfriend you always wanted, remember. Wow, and we talked about this just this morning."

"Alisa, you really need help. You're crazy."

"You know, Crazy Girl might be on to something," Harietta mused.

Keisha cackled.

"No, really! Just this morning for real you were talking 'bout wanting a boyfriend and not just a Valentine. And look at that! The cute boy shows up. It's a sign, girl, it's a sign. What if he becomes your boyfriend, Andreide? And he's interested in you too and I know you like him."

"Who says I like him? And you still don't know if he really likes me."

This time it was Harietta who rolled her eyes.

"Oh c'mon, chile! Stop being stupid! You interested in him and he interested in you. You're blessed, chile!"

"Fo' real."

"Yeah, Andy."

Andreide tried not to let her excitement show but she could hardly cover it up. She really wanted what her friends were saying to be true; at least on her part she knew that it was. She liked

Dominick. He was cute and from what she knew about him and what she had perceived, she liked that too. If only she could spend time together with him so they could get to know each other more.

As if she could read her thoughts, Harietta said, "We just need to get you two together sometime so you guys could talk and so, you know. But we gotta get it done fast before some hoochie try to snatch him. And it's worse 'cause you'll have competition from both our school and his rich people private school."

Andreide nodded but she wasn't really listening to her friend.

"This is so cool!" Alisa squeaked. "Imagine if you two could be an item by Valentine's Day. That'd be romantic and *so* sweet!"

Andreide gave her a look. "Again, I say you need help. Valentine's Day is only eleven days away. Unless you're some kind of magic woman, I can't see that happening."

Alisa started to reply but Harietta cut her off.

"Girl, don't you worry yourself 'bout it. A lot can happen in eleven days. That's almost two weeks. Who knows what could happen between now and then?"

"True," said Keisha.

Andreide looked at her and shook her head in amusement and disbelief.

"Keisha, since when is it alright with you for any of us to associate with people like Dominick? And not just you but all of you! Why y'all so interested in my relationship with him, anyway? What do y'all have to gain from it?"

Her three friends stared at her incredulously.

"What do we have to gain? Are you nuts, chile?" Harietta arched an eyebrow at her, her arms akimbo. "We're your girls! We don't help each other out to gain from it. You know that, Andreide."

"Yeah, Andy, c'mon. We just wanna help you be happy, you know. All for one and one for all, right?"

Keisha gave a dry laugh.

"I don't know 'bout y'all but I know I got something to gain from it all. And I'll tell you what it is." She paused dramatically and Harietta shot her a warning look. "Peace and silence! Won't have to hear you bitchin' 'bout not having a man and all ah that, that's what."

The girls looked at each other before bursting out in laughter.

"Keisha, you're too much, you know that?" Andreide chuckled.

"Well, am right, ent it?"

They continued laughing.

"Well, anyway," Keisha said. "It's lunchtime people and am hungry. Leh we go from here and find sumt'ing to eat."

"You always hungry. And yet you does talk 'bout me eating so much!" said Harietta.

Keisha rolled her eyes.

"Gyul, please. You too greedy that's what. I does burn food faster than you. All you does do is store yours like some hibernating pig."

"Pigs don't hibernate, brainless!"

"Whatever, fat ass."

"Girl! I'll –"

"Will you two shut up?" Andreide cut in. Alisa giggled at her side. Harietta eyed Keisha menacingly before turning away from her.

"Fine," she said. "Let's go."

Keisha smirked as they headed towards the exit. "You well know you want food too, ent it? Admit it. You think I can't hear them big growls yuh stomach was making, or wha'?"

Harietta almost knocked Alisa and Andreide aside as she charged past them to get at Keisha, who darted ahead of them.

Andreide shook her head as she watched them fly out the store, chasing each other like two little children. Alisa watched her and grinned before she too followed them out the door, but in a more dignified manner. Andreide glanced around the store one last time before turning for the exit as well.

*

"Where's Mom?"

"Out."

"Out where?"

"I dunno."

"What you mean you don't know? You were here when she left weren't you?"

"Yeah, so?"

"Boy! Don't you use that tone with me! Now, did she tell you where she was going or what?"

"No."

"No, what?!"

"No, she didn't tell me where she was going! I was still asleep when she left, alright? Now, I'm trying to watch this show so if you please –"

"But it's Sunday! Where could she have gone? She didn't say we weren't going to church this weekend so how could she just go without saying anything? We always go to church. Well, we usually do anyway. Why didn't she wake me and tell me where she was going?"

"I don't know. I'm not her! Maybe she didn't want to see your ugly face so early in the morning. Did you think about that?"

"Boy! I will come over there and slap you if you don't shut up!"

"Well, you asked."

Andreide growled in frustration, turned on her heel and stormed out of the living room. At that moment, she wished she could throttle her little brother. He was so annoying! At times like these, she really wished he had never been born.

She marched up the stairs, walked along the landing then turned into her bedroom. Chrystal was awake, sitting up in her bed, propped against her pillows. She was reading a plain brown covered

147

book. Andreide was shocked when she realised it was a Bible. On seeing Andreide, Chrystal placed the string bookmark between the pages, closed the holy book and looked up at her roommate.

"Morning, cuzz!" she sang out and smiled at her cousin.

Andreide tried not to roll her eyes as she crossed to her side of her room. She flopped unto her bed and stared up at the ceiling. She wondered where her mother was.

"So, did you have a good night's sleep?"

Andreide ignored her question. She could not get over her mother's leaving and not telling her where she was going. Was it supposed to be a secret? But her mother did not have any secrets. Well, as far as she knew, anyway.

"I see you're not as happy as you was yesterday," Chrystal commented. "Wassup?" There was a sort of glee to her voice.

This time, Andreide rolled her eyes and sighed. She turned unto her side with her back to her nosy cousin.

"Oooo! I know what it is. I know what it is!" she sang out.

"Good. Now keep it to yourself. Some things aren't worth sharing," Andreide replied dryly.

"It's a boy, isn't it?" she said nevertheless. "It's that new rich boy, isn't it?"

Andreide momentarily forgot about her mother's whereabouts and whipped her body around to face her cousin. How could she know?

"No, of course not! What are you talking about?"

Chrystal squealed in delight. "Oh, I knew it! It *is* him. He's why you were so happy yesterday! What happened? Did you girls see him in town or something? Did you talk to him?"

"Yes. No! Mind your own business."

Chrystal grinned. "So, what did he say? Did he ask you to be his Valentine? You know Valentine's Day is only like a week-plus away. Is he really as cute as you and them other girls say he is?"

"Look. How do you even know about him? I never told you about him and you don't go to our school or his school to know anything about him."

Chrystal did not answer.

"Well?" Andreide prodded.

"I heard you talking 'bout him."

"You what? You mean you listened to my phone calls?" Andreide stared incredulously at her.

"Well, is not like you were trying to keep it secret. You were talking loud enough for me to hear."

"I was in my room! I expect to have some kind of privacy in my own room, don't you think? I shouldn't have to be cautious of eavesdroppers listening in to my conversations when I'm talking in my own personal space. But now I guess I should be. Seeing as I have a fast-ass big ears girl living in my room now!"

Chrystal looked a bit shocked at her cousin's outburst. She lowered her eyes and stared at the floor for a while before meeting Andreide's eyes again.

"Is that how you feel?" she asked timidly.

Andreide bit down on her bottom lip to keep from cursing. "No, I usually just express my opinions and feelings for no reason – what do you think!"

"I think you're angry at me," said Chrystal.

"Well, of course I'm angry at you! I'm more annoyed than anything. First of all, I didn't even want you to move in here with us and even worse, not with me. But I got stuck with you anyway. And if that isn't bad enough, you're a terrible roommate! Why can't you respect my privacy and stay out of my things and my business? Yes, we're cousins but that doesn't mean we got to share everything. You're not my sister. And I don't want you as my sister either. We're cousins by blood and that's it! I don't want you in my space. So as long as you're here and staying in my room, keep to your side and I'll keep to mine. Just mind your own damn business!"

Andreide did not wait for Chrystal's response. She got up from her bed, grabbed her cell phone from her desk and marched out of the room. Marques was bad enough – at least he did not share her room. But Chrystal, now? She felt like screaming or hurting something. She stamped down the stairs, marched to the front door, flung it open then proceeded outside.

*

It was early afternoon when her mother came back home. Andreide heard the sound of their old car pulling up in front the house and jumped off the couch to peer through the window. It was her mother alright. She hurried to the door, opened it then ran down the path to meet her.

"Mom! Where've you been?" she said as her mother stepped out the car.

Rose Marie took her handbag and a blue folder from the passenger seat then shut and locked the car door. She turned to face her daughter.

"Excuse me?"

"I mean, you weren't here when I got up and you were gone for so long. I didn't know where you were and I was worried, Mom! I thought maybe something happened to you. You don't normally miss church. When I tried your cell phone it just kept ringing and you didn't answer."

"Well, I'm alright, Andreide. I left my cell in the car. There was nothing to worry about. I had a meeting to attend at the main office in town – about my book and the book tour. So that's where I was."

"A meeting? On a Sunday?"

"Yes." Rose Marie frowned at her daughter. "Why are you so concerned? You know I work all hours with my book so there's nothing unusual about me working on a Sunday."

"Oh. Well, it's just that you never had meetings on a Sunday before, that's all," Andreide said.

150

Rose Marie smiled. "I'm sorry if you were worried about me. I should've told you I was going but you looked so peaceful sleeping. I didn't want to disturb you. It was so early too."

Andreide nodded. "It's ok, I understand. Anyway, if you'd woken me that nosy Chrystal probably would've woken up too and start asking all kinds of questions. She's so annoying, Mom! She got me so mad this morning."

Rose Marie sighed. "Andreide, don't you think you should give her a chance? All you've been doing is complaining about her. Can't you just get along with her? It's true she talks a lot and interferes where she shouldn't but can't you find anything good about her? She's not all that bad, you know."

"But Mom, she's always in my things. She listens to my phone calls!"

"How do you know that?"

"She admitted it when I asked her this morning. And I know it's true 'cause she knows things that I didn't tell her about."

Rose Marie exhaled slowly.

"Look. Just try to be patient, ok? Try putting yourself in her position and see how she feels."

Andreide gave her an irritated look.

"She may be lonely now that she's not in her home country with the people she knows. What she needs is a friend and not someone to be at war with her because of her little annoying ways. We all have annoying things about us, Andreide and you do too. Don't you think she might find some of the things you do to be annoying as well? So she's occupying half of your room now and it's a bit discomforting for you but it is only temporary. The thing is you've had your own room for so long that you don't know what it's like to share with someone else. Dealing with these small inconveniences helps to build character, Andreide. And if you can't handle it and keep focussing on her faults you're just going to make yourself unhappy, harming yourself and eventually affecting everyone else with your foul mood. So be reasonable and try to remember that she's your family. Start treating her like she's your cousin and not like some intruding outsider. Do I make myself clear?"

Andreide looked her mother in the eye and recognised the seriousness in her expression. She nodded.

"Yes, Mom."

"Good. Now, if you'll excuse me I'm very tired, hungry and this sun is giving me a headache." Rose Marie adjusted the folder in her hand and started towards the house.

"But Mom," said Andreide. "What about what *I* feel?"

Rose Marie turned and looked her daughter in the eye.

"The world doesn't revolve around *you*, Andreide."

She turned and continued walking towards the house. She opened and closed the door, leaving her daughter outside. Andreide stood there looking at the house, feeling rather foolish. Her cheeks felt hot.

Chapter 8

It was 11:42 a.m. the last time she checked. Andreide looked up at the circular clock mounted on the wall above the blackboard and sighed. Only three minutes had passed. She still had fifteen more to go till she was free from Mr. Black's boring Biology class. It was Monday and they were reviewing the digestive system which Andreide could hardly pay attention to. It required all of her concentration to distinguish between the different digestive juices and at the moment, she felt like she could not even tell a stomach from a heart. She tapped her pen against her notebook where she had drawn a nearly perfect replica of the large and small intestines and counted the minutes down till her freedom.

Suddenly, a wad of paper flew through the air and landed on her desk, distracting her from her countdown. She looked around for the sender and saw Zenicia wave at her, pointing to the paper. Andreide looked down at it curiously and unfolded the scrunched up paper ball. There was a short note scribbled between the lines which read:

'Hey gyul, guess wa? There's a football match on Frydee 'tween we school dem an dat rich people school, Duncans Akadamee. Ah no you gon want go cause you know who playing!'

Andreide read the note twice before realising what it said. She frowned slightly. *You know who?* She could not be referring to –

Bbbbring Bbbbring!

The bell rang.

Before the last note faded into the distance, all books and papers were packed away, the seats vacated and the room empty of every student, regardless of the teacher still writing notes on the board.

Andreide followed the crowd to their homeroom where the majority of students deposited their belongings and prepared for lunch. Some left for the canteen while the others stayed to eat at their desks. Andreide wanted to be clear on this note Zenicia gave her before thinking about eating or anything else. She placed her bag on the rack beneath her chair then headed over to Zenicia where she was seated with several other classmates around her.

"Hey, Zenicia," Andreide greeted her.

"'Ey gyul. You read the note?"

"Yeah. That's what I want to know about."

"Wha' you mean? You want to know 'bout the football game?"

"Yeah, and also –"

"You gyuls hear 'bout we match too, eh?" Jason, a fellow classmate of Andreide's, strolled over and placed himself in their conversation. He was the captain of their school's football team and Andreide was not fond of him. She found him to be too conceited and arrogant for her taste. However, he was always polite with her and she tolerated him mainly for that reason.

"Yeah boy. I was just telling Andreide here 'bout it," Zenicia responded with a grin on her face.

"Good, good," he said while looking at Andreide. "Tell everybody too, eh. We gotta spread de word 'cause it was a short notice thing. Coach only tell us 'bout it last Friday."

"Yeah, fo' true." Another boy walked over and joined their conversation. He was also one of the members of their football team. Two of his friends accompanied him.

"Yeah boy, Harris. I still can't believe who we playing 'gainst."

Harris nodded. "Yeah, Duncan's Academy. How Coach could do us so bad, eh?"

"Yeah, man. What we do to deserve playing 'gainst them lil wusses. Ain't gonna be a fair game, at all. We gonna have the lil gay boys crying!" Jason laughed and slapped hands with one of his team mates, who chuckled along with him.

"No, boy." Harris shook his head. "It ain't gonna be like that. I hear they get better, man. I hear they play 'gainst Canyon and beat them!"

Jason laughed. "Oh please! That ain't nothin'. Anybody could beat Canyon. They worse than them white boys."

Harris still shook his head.

"No, man. I'm serious. They playing good now."

"Who tell you that?" Jason asked with irritation in his voice.

"Somebody."

"You see them play?"

"Not recently."

"Then is what you goin' on 'bout? People like to talk! They only playing with yuh head, man. Them white boys can't play we football. They can't even use they two foot to kick a ball but they say they have team."

"Well, that ain't all I hear," Harris said.

Jason laughed.

"You like to hear things, eh?" He looked at the girls and grinned. Andreide ignored him. Zenicia smiled back at him.

Harris continued nevertheless. "I hear that the reason they playing better is 'cause they have a new coach."

"So? They coach can't give them skills what they don't have."

"And that's not all."

Jason gave him an irritated look.

"I hear that they also have a new player. He trained with one of them English football clubs and he real good too."

"Yeah, I hear that too. I hear he's they secret weapon," one of the boys put in.

"Yeah, man. He deadly!" the other boy added.

Jason looked both annoyed and frustrated.

"Who is this boy?"

Harris shrugged.

"Don't know his name. But I hear he's new at the school – started a few weeks ago."

On hearing this, Andreide's heart began to beat faster.

"I hear he's the best player them boys got now, though. And he real popular up there," said a boy sitting near to Jason.

"Man, he so good, I ain't too sure 'bout this game on Friday see," another boy commented. The other students listening in began to nod and mumble their agreements. As the buzz became louder with pessimistic opinions, Jason stood up abruptly and shouted out, silencing the audience.

"Hey! What's wrong with y'all?" he said in disbelief. "Y'all acting like some scared lil sissies 'bout this game. Them lil rich boys can't beat us! Not even if they have a new player. He only one person. You think if they couldn't beat us before with all of them, they could beat us now with only one good player on they team?" He looked at all of them. "We the best and the best there ever will be. We the best football team in this country and ain't no rich lil white boys gonna take that away from us! Now y'all wit' me or what?" Jason looked at his team mates in turn.

They all nodded vigorously.

"Of course we with you, man!" Harris grinned.

Jason slapped Harris on his shoulder and nodded towards the other boys.

"C'mon boys, let's roll. Leh we get some practise in before the bell ring."

"But, Jason. I thought you ain't worried 'bout this game? So what we practising for?" one of the boys asked.

Jason turned to him and gave him a look.

"Boy, you sound so dum. Practising ain't got anything to do wit' them. It's for us. Now haul all yuh asses out on the field. Let's go, let's go!"

A mixture of groans and laughter filled the air and Andreide smiled at their reactions. Probably assuming that her smile was directed at him, Jason turned and caught her eye as his team mates brushed past him to the door.

"So … Andreide." He smiled at her. "I looking out for you on Friday in the front row, right?"

Andreide forced a smile. "Yeah, maybe. We'll see."

"Naw, girl. You gotta be sure. It's our team! C'mon. You got to be there. Everybody got to come. We ain't a team without our supporters." He looked across at Zenicia and turned his charm over on her. "How 'bout you, babe? You comin'?"

Zenicia grinned stupidly. "Yeah! Of course, Jason."

Jason beamed at her then winked. "That's my girl. See y'all later. Make sure y'all gonna be wearing our colours, eh." He turned and left the room.

Zenicia and the others then launched into an animated chatter.

As her friends were not in the classroom, Andreide took her lunch and headed outside. Just as she expected, she found them sitting under their usual mango tree. She filled them in on the football match. Andreide tried to hide her growing excitement at the prospect of seeing Dominick at the match. She was almost certain that he was the new player the guys had been talking about.

"This going to be an interesting game. Finally, something to look forward to. I can't wait till Friday, man!" Harietta groaned anxiously.

Andreide laughed. "Me too. Haven't been to anything in a while."

"Yeah, all you been doing is studying whenever we ask you to go somewhere. Thank God for Valentine's Day an' this new boy 'cause if it wasn't for them, you would still be stuck up in yuh room say you studying. Imagine that. And is now only February."

"Keisha, you're making me sound like some kinda nerd. Yeah, I've been studying and we all have to, you know. CXC exams are just around the corner in May, girl," Andreide warned.

"Yeah, that's true," said Harietta. "We have to buckle down."

"Yeah, ah will. But not now. After the match." Keisha grinned.

Andreide rolled her eyes and Harietta and Alisa shook their heads.

"Girl, you have to get serious. We're in fifth form. This is our last year in school."

"Ah know, ah know! Gosh! It's not like I ain't start studying. I start some and ah gonna continue later. It's only February, gyul. Take a chill pill. I jus' want to enjoy meself a lil bit before ah have to start the real studying. Now let's drop this studying talk for a while nuh? We gonna have all the time to talk 'bout studying later, but how many times do you get to talk 'bout or actually go to a football match between our school and Duncan's?"

Andreide thought for a while then sighed. "Alright, Keisha. You're right. You win."

Keisha grinned. "Good. Now, Harietta, you going to finish that patty or wha'?"

All three girls burst out laughing. Andreide watched with amusement as Keisha stealthily snatched the half-eaten patty from Harietta's lap before she could even blink twice. With a sly grin, she shoved the patty in her mouth before Harietta could react. A few seconds later, she gulped it down; not a trace of a crumb could be found. Harietta gazed at her in disbelief, her mouth hanging open in shock. The girls continued laughing until their cheeks hurt.

*

The week could not crawl by any slower. With each passing day, Andreide felt more and more excited. She had never felt this way about a football game before. In fact, she did not even really like the sport. But what really had her so interested in this particular match was the uncertainty of the identity of the new player on the rivalling school's team. She could not be completely sure, but who else could it be? She really hoped it was Dominick. It had to be. The thought made her giddy with excitement.

Finally, Friday arrived. Much to everyone's delight, classes were ended early at midday to allow the students and staff to attend the match. Andreide even believed she saw crabby old Mrs. Smith crack a smile.

As soon as the bell rang, the school emptied in an instant. Andreide and her peers raced home to get ready. They had all agreed to wear their school's colours of green and brown but Andreide opted not to wear the brown. She had chosen a navy green blouse and a matching navy green, three-quarter length cargo pants with army green sneakers. Her handbag was also a matching shade of green and her silver hoops and necklace complimented her outfit quite nicely. She lightly sprayed on her *Tommy Girl* perfume before leaving her room.

"Where are you going?"

Andreide paused abruptly at the front door and turned to see her cousin walking towards her from the kitchen. What was she doing here at this time?

"Didn't you hear? There's a big football match on this afternoon. My school against Duncan's Academy," Andreide replied.

"Oh ... football. Well, I wouldn't know if you didn't tell me. After all, I don't go to your school and you don't let me hang with you and your friends so ..." Chrystal sounded so mellow and meek as she said this and it somehow moved Andreide. She flashed back on what her mother had told her.

"Well, you know. You can come if you want," Andreide said. "I don't mind, really."

Chrystal watched her for a while then smiled slightly.

"Thanks for offering but I can't. I've got stuff to do."

"Oh, ok. Well, maybe another time."

"Yeah, maybe. Enjoy your football game." Chrystal turned and headed for the stairs.

"Yeah, ok." Andreide watched her climb the steps until she was out of sight then sighed. She was relieved that she did not take up her offer but somehow, at the same time she felt disappointed. With a last glance at the stairs, she opened the front door then proceeded outside.

*

The noise in the stadium greeted the girls with almost the same intensity that its appearance did. Andreide stared in shock at the size of the stadium and could not believe what she was seeing. Never before had she been in such a large arena and in especially one so majestically and stunningly built. It was open roofed and as far as she could tell, the field looked like the same size as football fields she had seen on television in real professional matches. There was a refreshments bar at the entrance along with other canteens and bathrooms. As they walked in stunned silence through the entrance and into the stands, they stared in amazement at the vastness surrounding them. The stands were filled with blue and white seats which shined in the afternoon sun.

"Wow," Alisa said. "This is crazy."

"You took the words out of my mouth," said Andreide.

"Same here," Harietta murmured.

"Yeah ... Wow!" Keisha's eyes bulged as they struggled to take in all aspects of their surroundings.

"This place is soooo big! It's amazing. Imagine what their school building must look like if their play area looks like this."

"Yeah, I bet their school is all gold and the floors are marble," Andreide scoffed.

"True. I hear de prefects have gold toilets," Keisha said raising her voice above the noise.

Andreide, Alisa and Harietta laughed.

"I wouldn't doubt it, though," Andreide said. "I bet they're spoilt rotten up there."

"They must be. Just look at this stadium. They could hold the FIFA World Cup in here!"

Again they laughed.

"C'mon, girls. Let's go find us some seats," Harietta suggested as she led the way towards the stands.

"Hey, Harietta, wait," Andreide called out to her. "Let's sit close to the field so we could see the players, ok?"

Harietta watched her and smiled knowingly.

"Uh huh … I bet I know who you want to see in particular."

Andreide tried not to blush. She rolled her eyes.

"C'mon. Let's go down to the field before everybody else takes those seats."

"Yeah, let's go," Keisha agreed and took over the lead from Harietta.

After ten minutes, and after several shoves and glares administered by Keisha, they managed to settle in four seats three rows up from the field. Andreide beamed happily at their luck and mainly Keisha's determination and aggression in securing them ideal seats. From their position, they had a great view of the field and could see action going on in both ends of the grounds. The closest player on the field to their section would only be a few metres away from them. Andreide grinned, nervous and excited to be there. The match was scheduled to commence at three o'clock and she could hardly wait for the time to arrive.

"Lawd! I feel like I gon pee meself. What time it is?"

Andreide checked her watch. "Nine minutes to go."

"Lawd! Ah wish they would hurry up."

"Keisha, chile. Hush up and wait like everybody else, nuh!"

"Gyul, Harietta. I gon –"

The crowd suddenly released a great roar, cutting off Keisha's next words. Andreide whipped her head around to the field and looked down at what had excited the spectators. She felt her heart beat faster as her own excitement pounded within her chest as she watched the football players jog out unto the field, each team entering from a different entrance. Her eyes followed the eleven players clad in dark green – with the exception of the goal keeper who wore all brown – unto the grounds. She spotted Jason waving to the crowd with his red captain band on his arm, waving and grinning like the football star he wished and could only dream of being. Andreide grinned.

"Wow! Andy, check out the Duncan's' uniforms!" Alisa poked her in the arm. Andreide switched her attention to the opposite team and felt her eyes widen in a combination of awe and disbelief.

The Duncan's Academy players were dressed in white and gold, a dazzling combination under the bright rays of the sun. Andreide stared at them in shock. Their shirts were white with a gold stripe along the shoulders, sleeves, necklines and the sides of their shirts. The pants like the shirts were white with two matching gold stripes on the sides, one on each pant leg. Their goal keeper wore royal blue with the same pattern of gold stripes on his shirt and shorts, with the addition of gold gloves. Andreide watched them as they strutted along the field and proceeded to warm up. She could feel their conceit even from where she sat, without watching it on their smirking faces.

She felt her pulse quicken even more as she recognised the player wearing the captain's armband. His golden blonde hair stood out like a beacon in a sea of dark-haired comrades, shining brightly in the sunlight. He was not far away from where she was seated and as he turned in her direction, Andreide felt bitter resentment stir within her. As if sensing her stare, his focus shifted and his piercing blue eyes met her smouldering dark ones and seemed to linger on her far longer than was appropriate. She saw his mouth curl in his usual sneering greeting to her before he turned back to face the opposite set of stands where most of the Duncan's Academy fans and supporters were congregated; they were colour co-ordinated in their blue, white and gold. Andreide released a tight breath.

"Andy, what's wrong? You look so tense." Alisa watched her closely.

"Nothing." She shook her head. "I'm fine."

Andreide averted her eyes from the golden spectacle now flexing and pruning himself for his supporters and the cheerleaders whom Andreide had not noticed before. They too wore all white and were striped with gold but had blue pompoms. Andreide watched them begin their routine then looked in the other direction at her own school's cheerleaders who were dressed in dark green and carried brown and green pompoms. They were looking over at the opposing cheerleaders with distinct expressions of disgust and annoyance. Andreide grinned. This was going to be one special game!

"Andy, Andy, Andy!" Alisa exclaimed, pulling on Andreide's arm excitedly.

"What, what, what?" Andreide tried to shake her off.

"Look! Look, it's him. It's *him!*" On the edge of her seat, Alisa seemed to bounce up and down elatedly as she pointed at the field. Andreide knew at once whom she was referring to and felt her heart leap with excitement as she hurriedly scanned the field.

"I don't see him. Where is he?" She could hear her nervousness in her voice.

"He's right there! Look … right *there*." She pointed towards the south-east end of the field.

"There where?" Andreide felt even more anxious as she searched the grounds with no success.

"Hey, Andy, I see him. Wow, does he look great in that uniform!" Harietta smiled broadly.

"Oh yeah, ah see him too. Look yuh rich boy over there, Andreide. He doing some stretching by the red head boy in the corner. Wait, look a man coming over to him. Who he be, eh?"

"He looks Italian."

"He must be their new coach."

"You know, I still can't find him!" Andreide was beginning to feel frustrated now. All three of them had already found him but she could not, yet she was the one with the greatest interest in him. She frowned as she followed Keisha's outstretched arm.

Suddenly a deep voice boomed out over the loudspeakers announcing the beginning of the match. At the same time, the players on the field began moving towards the centre of the grounds. Andreide sighed disappointedly. She could not find him now.

Alisa turned to her and gave her an encouraging look.

"Don't worry, Andy. You'll see him just now. They're scoring on this side of the field so he's bound to come down here soon." Alisa gave her a reassuring smile. Andreide just nodded.

A few minutes later, the ball was brought on the field, the first kick awarded and play began. For the first ten minutes, St. George's mainly had possession of the ball and Andreide watched the game with semi-interest. She could feel Alisa watching her every now and then but did not feel like talking to her or anyone else at the moment. In fact, even if she desired to, she would only strain her voice to make herself heard over the increased volume of noise generated by the excited and cheering crowd. Keisha shouting at the players as they ran by and taunting the opposing team only made Andreide's head throb as a headache threatened to take over. Harietta crunching on peanuts and chips did not help either.

Then a commentator made a remark over the sound system which caught Andreide's attention. She perked up and listened closely. And then she heard it, she heard what had caught her interest.

"*... and there goes Dominick Michaels, the newly added British player to the Duncan's team. Some say he's the fresh new talent they've been needing for years and some say he's their secret weapon ... But time will surely tell.*"

Andreide's heart did a somersault in her chest. It was true – Dominick *was* the new player for Duncan's Academy. She looked over at Alisa and catching her eye, she grinned excitedly then turned her attention once more to the field, her interest tweaked.

"*And now Davidson has the ball ... he passes to Burk who passes to Estridge – Ow! He didn't see that coming. And now Estridge is down ladies and gentlemen but will the referee call this one? No, he doesn't and Carlston of Duncan's Academy has taken possession ...*"

Andreide watched as Richard Carlston manoeuvred the ball past his opponents and was surprised at his skill. He had certainly improved tremendously from the last time she had seen him play over three years ago. However, he still had that arrogant, self assured way about him and underestimating the skill of the opponent in front of him, he lost the ball. Keisha laughed and threw insults in his direction. Andreide shook her head and snickered.

"*... Once again, Duncan's has lost possession and control is back in the hands of – or should I say, the feet of – St. George's. Pemberton has the ball now, he passes to the captain, Warner, who sends it a long way to Samuels ... Samuels is at the goal with only one opponent in his way. He aims for the goal, he shoots ... and scores!*"

The entire stands behind Andreide erupted in jubilation. Every person wearing green or brown in the stadium was on his or her feet, yelling and cheering, slapping fellow supporters on their backs. Surprisingly, Andreide too was one of them. She did not even realise that she was on her feet, let alone shouting elatedly and being squeezed by Harietta's large bosom and punched by Keisha's bony knuckles. Alisa was jumping up and down, performing her own cheerleading dance.

"And there it is ladies and gentlemen! The first goal of the match, scored by Samuels of St. George's High. I'm sure his team mates are very happy – wow, would you listen to the crowd! St. George's supporters are ecstatic!"

Andreide watched her school's team rejoice their first goal and she could not help but grin. As she watched Jason hug and pat his fellow footballers and saw the joy in their faces, she forgot about her past disappointment in not finding Dominick and took the moment to revel in their happiness.

Play resumed a few minutes later and with the success of their first goal under their belts, the St. George's players were more confident and controlled the ball even more. However, their monopoly was soon broken by the rivalling team.

Andreide watched as the Duncan's players kicked the ball back and forth to each other and as she did so, she noticed how organised they were. Her eyes trailed the movements of the white and gold players until she felt she was temporarily blinded from the glare. She was relieved when St. George's took possession once more – glad for the change. There was a limit to the amount of dazzlingly bright colours she could take in all at once.

She suddenly bolted to her feet. She was almost certain that she had just seen him at the end of the field near the goal closer to her. She scanned the players hurriedly, anxious to locate him. What she had not realised before was that the majority of the Duncan's Academy football players were of similar appearance – light or white skinned with dark hair. There were only the odd few like Richard with his shiny blonde hair and a red haired boy who stood out amongst the others. Otherwise, the other players were not easily recognisable. Andreide almost felt like giving up hope.

"... Ferdinand passes to Burk. Cornered, Burk passes back to Ferdinand ..."

Andreide sighed.

"... It's Davidson ... Burk ... Estridge ... Closely tailing Estridge, captain Richard Carlston, who swerves to steal the ball. But Estridge is saved by team mate and fellow mid-fielder Pemberton ... St. George's in possession – but what's this? Pemberton fumbles! Quincy slides in to take the ball –"

Why couldn't she find him? Why could Harietta, Alisa *and* Keisha find him but not her?

"Duncan's in possession ... Quincy passes to Mitcham ... Mitcham to Paul ... Clark ... Clark side kicks to Rodgers –"

Alisa was telling Andreide something but she could not hear her. She slumped in her chair and tried to block out all the noise. If only she could block out Alisa's annoying poking of her arm too.

"– Rodgers has the ball, ladies and gentlemen and it looks like he's not letting go of it either! He side-steps Brown ... swerves past James ... he looks for a team mate to pass the ball to but is surrounded by opponents ..."

Andreide now felt like slapping and cuffing Alisa – she was really getting on her nerves. Why couldn't she express her excitement over a lame ole football match some other way than by repeatedly shaking Andreide's arm?

"... and here comes Michaels to the rescue ... he darts in, ruffling St. George's defenders, relieving fellow striker, Rodgers of the ball. And look at him go! This young man certainly has talent indeed! He dodges past Brown, feints a move to the left then abruptly turns and whizzes past another opponent –"

One more time, if she shook her arm one more time, Andreide was not going to hold back her frustration. She would –

Michaels? Did the commentator just say Michaels?

Andreide was suddenly aware of what Alisa was trying to tell her. She did not have to look at her to hear her words or feel the eager desperation in her voice.

"It's Dominick, Andreide! Look! You can see him now. It's Dominick!" Alisa shouted.

Andreide suddenly lost all feeling in her body as she looked down at the players headed her way and immediately spotted him. Alisa was right. The commentator was right. It *was* Dominick! It was Dominick wearing white and gold, his brown curls glowing golden in the sunlight as he raced with the ball and opponents surrounding him. Andreide had finally found him and as she stared at him feeling senseless, she realised why she could not have found him earlier. She was looking for a dark haired boy not realising that under the bright sunlight his hair appeared lighter.

Her senses came crashing back to her like a tidal wave upon the shore. She could hear every sound around her with the highest detail; she could smell every distinct scent permeating the air; she could feel the vibrations of the emotional spectators; she could taste anticipation in the atmosphere; and she saw everything with utmost clarity. Her senses were reborn.

"Michaels dashes to the goal with incredible speed – just look at him go! James comes at him from the side but he anticipates the attack and abruptly changes course. He passes to Rodgers –"

Andreide felt her heart hammer madly against her ribcage. She could not believe what she was seeing. Apart from the fact that she was still shocked from the discovery that he was Duncan's new player, she was completely enthralled by his skill in the game. He moved with such grace and agility, with such familiarity and confidence which she would not expect from such a young sportsman. His movements were smooth and supple and he flowed with such elegance it appeared that he was dancing a quick-step. Andreide watched him move, awestruck.

She could see him clearly now that he was closer to her side of the field. Harietta was right – he looked great in his uniform. As he ran, the wind whipped at his clothing and his shirt clung to his chest, outlining his athletic build. Andreide could not take her eyes off him.

"Rodgers passes back to Michaels. Michaels moves in quickly, darts past Rawlins –"

Andreide's pulse raced faster as she watched Dominick head closer to the goal. He was so close! If he was not intercepted soon, with one well-aimed kick he could score one for Duncan's.

But why did she feel so excited and hopeful that he *did* score? He was on the opposing team. She did not support Duncan's Academy in the least. She was there to cheer for her school, St. George's and not Duncan's, no matter who was playing on their team.

"*– Michaels is inline with the goal now with no opponents in his way, Rawlins having fallen back. He faces the keeper ... with James closing in, Michaels makes a quick-second decision, aims at the goal and – Oh! He feigns it! Both the keeper and James take the bait ... keeper Adams lunges to the right and Michaels shoots to the left ... he scores!*"

If Andreide thought her stand was the noisiest when her school had scored, she was definitely wrong. The stands seating Duncan's supporters dressed in their blue, white and gold exploded in roars at their school's first goal. The St. George's fans seemed more stunned than upset at their rival's goal and were shocked into silence. This stunned silence was a deviation from the norm of booing and rude gesturing usually warranted at other matches. Andreide could see the faces of many of her fellow supporters looking unbelievably at the scoreboard and the field where the Duncan's players were delighting in their accomplishment. She watched as his fellow white and gold clad team mates slapped Dominick on the back, some tussling his hair. She grinned as she watched the joy on his face and had the sudden urge to be one of the players on the field, hugging and grasping him. With slight apprehension, she watched as Richard jogged over to him; he placed his hand on Dominick's shoulder and spoke into his ear. Dominick grinned on hearing whatever it was Richard told him.

Richard then pointed to the bottom of their supporters' stands where their cheerleaders had just begun cheering. Dominick looked in the direction and smiled. The other players also looked over at the Duncan's cheerleaders. It was a minute later when Andreide realised what was happening. The cheerleaders were chanting but not their usual cheers. It was only until the stands of Duncan's supporters behind them picked up the chant did Andreide hear what they were saying.

"Dominick! Dominick! We love Dominick!"

Andreide was at a lost for words or thought.

"Dominick! Dominick! We love Dominick!"

They continued the chant until it increased in volume and tempo, spreading to the other Duncan's Academy stands.

Keisha stared at Harietta who looked at Alisa who passed the look to Andreide. She knew how they felt, for she felt the same way. It was mostly disbelief mixed with amusement and wonder. She felt like laughing but was unable to emit the necessary sounds.

Play resumed amidst the chanting. From the looks of the St. George's players, they were quite annoyed with the opposition's cheer tactics. However, this did not interfere with their playing as they soon reclaimed their control over the game. Andreide followed the match with renewed interest. Every few seconds she scanned the field for Dominick and every time she located him, she felt her heart do a light flutter. At one moment she had a terrible urge to call out to him but she resisted, not wanting to distract him from the game. She wished he would look up in her direction. She had her attention focussed so much on him that she was startled when the stadium rang out with cheers and drumming, mostly coming from her stand and the surrounding ones. She saw her school's team jumping up forming one big group hug, saw the slaps of appreciation and realised that they had just scored their second goal. And she had missed it. She felt silly for having missed witnessing their second goal – it could have been a memorable shot. She then promised herself that she would focus more on her team and less on Dominick. But that proved to be easier said than done.

Ten minutes later, the whistle was blown signalling half-time. The players exited the field to their respective quarters.

"It's half-time now, ladies and gentlemen with the score at 2 to 1. St. George's leads by one having scored their second goal by the captain, Jason Warner –"

Andreide rolled her eyes and sighed. Leave it to Jason to score the goal that she missed. Hopefully, it had not been spectacular so she would not have to lie too much when he asked her about it.

"— *the first goal having been scored by Dijon Samuels. The host, Duncan's Academy trails only by one, having scored quite memorably by the new recruit, Dominick Michaels …*"

During the break, both team's cheerleaders performed their dance routines for the entertainment of their supporters. Andreide watched them having nothing else to distract her thoughts from Dominick. She paid more attention to the Duncan's Academy cheer routines as she was already familiar with her own school's. They amused her.

The first thing that struck her was the fact that it was an all white squad and at least half of them were blondes. Andreide noticed one of the blondes in particular who was apparently the leader of the squad, doing the most elaborate dance moves. She obviously wanted to be seen and she was doing a good job of making herself look like a fool, or at least in Andreide's opinion.

About half an hour later, the players returned to the field and the match resumed. Within the first fifteen minutes of the second half, St. George's scored their third goal much to the delight of their supporters who pounded their joy on makeshift musical instruments, some creating their own chants. Andreide laughed at a group of bare backed boys who had painted themselves green and were trying to spell St. George's with their bodies.

Unbelievably, less than five minutes later, Andreide and her schoolmates were going wild once more, as their team scored yet another goal. Andreide's cheeks hurt from laughing and she tried not to spill the drink she had just bought as Keisha did her own little victory dance in the aisle.

However, the Duncan's fans were given a turn at celebrating when the St. George's keeper, Adams, dived and missed the ball shot by Rodgers of Duncan's Academy. Boos and hisses rained down from the opposing supporters. Duncan's Academy was now two goals behind. Andreide found it much easier to focus solely on the game as the excitement it created was mounting ever so quickly. She followed the match with hawk-like vigilance, completely engrossed in it.

As time was coming to an end with only twenty minutes left in the game, emotions were building high and aggression became a problem on both sides. The referee called several fouls some of which included minor offside fouls while the major fouls were for tackling and the sort. A yellow card was issued to a player of St. George's which incited quite an uproar in the crowd – Keisha being a major contributor to the protest. As a result of the foul, a penalty shot was awarded to Duncan's and they scored their third goal. Keisha was beside herself with expletives. Two minutes later, the score was tied. The St. George's supporters were enraged.

The whistle blew as the Duncan's Academy football coach signalled for a time-out. He apparently called Dominick and Richard as they both jogged over to him at the boundary. Andreide took this time to note her team's expressions and saw the worry, nervousness and agitation that they all felt, mirrored on their faces. Jason in particular looked the worst and as captain, Andreide thought that he should have had more control over the display of his emotions, especially in front of his team mates. They could not afford to have low morale at this crucial time.

A few moments later, the match continued with St. George's in possession. Andreide could see the strain on the players as they were constantly denied an opportunity to advance towards the goal. The Duncan's players were ruthless and unwavering in their defence – they blocked their adversaries at every chance, angering them.

They were now into overtime. Neither side was relenting in their possessive defence of the ball.

Three minutes were left.

Andreide felt her heart pounding louder than the clamour created by the anxious crowd. Still no one had scored.

Two minutes left.

Andreide shot a nervous glance at her friends, not wanting to establish eye contact for fear of seeing the truth beneath their worried thoughts.

One minute left.

Gasps were heard in every direction. With stealth unknown to the most cunning fox, the Duncan's pilfered the ball from their rivals. In the blink of an eye, they dashed through the field.

"Quincy ... Mitcham ... Paul ... Rodgers ... Clark ...!"

Andreide could barely hear the commentator as she waited with baited breath, on the edge of her seat, her eyes wide and unblinking.

Twenty seconds left.

Andreide watched as the ball zoomed to Richard Carlston and as he approached the goal, time seemed to suddenly play in slow motion.

Ten seconds.

Richard was accosted from the rear. His opponent lashed out at the ball a second too late – Richard had already sent it on its forward journey.

Five seconds.

Andreide suddenly realised she had no emotional energy left. She watched with a blank mind, her body a hollow shell as Dominick received the ball. With speed and accuracy beyond her comprehension, he slammed the ball past the immobile keeper and into the palms of the awaiting net, just as the clock hit zero.

Everyone froze.

Silence reigned.

The shrill whistle of the referee signalling the conclusion of the match was the spell breaker, shattering the reverie. The titanic explosion which ensued was deafening.

There were screams. There were shouts – all mixtures of immense relief, joy, disappointment and anger. Andreide did not know which one she felt but she knew she felt something. Keisha spluttered at a lost for words; Harietta just sat there blinking; Alisa was looking around, her face full of disbelief and bewilderment. No one knew what to say.

"And there you have it, ladies and gentlemen – in a stunning and emotionally charged game, Duncan's Academy has won the match! Who would have thought? Just listen to their supporters. This is one game that will definitely be recorded in the books!"

Andreide looked down at the field. The boys in white and gold were ecstatic. They looked so innocent and youthful as she watched them jump for joy, hugging and thumping each other elatedly. Their coach had joined them along with several other adults whom Andreide supposed were teachers, parents and family. She watched as more of the proud supporters descended unto the grounds. Andreide spotted Dominick chatting animatedly with his fellow team mates and felt her heart start beating again, not having realised that it had almost completely stopped. It was then she felt a strong pang to be down there, a need more than anything else.

She stood up, picked up her handbag then exited the row, leaving her three friends still seated in a stupor of disbelief. She looked for the nearest entrance to the field and hurried towards it.

The closer she got to the field, the faster and harder her heart beat against her chest. She was nervous and she knew it, but she was also even more excited. Excited to see Dominick. As she thought this, she felt her face flush and she inwardly chastised herself for being so affected. In fact, she should not be feeling this way at all – she should not be feeling a glowing warmth of happiness swelling from within her at the prospect of meeting the player who had caused the demise of her own school's team! She was supposed to be in mourning like the rest of her school, hating the winning team and everybody on it while feeling disappointed and more than embarrassed at her school's out of the ordinary defeat – defeat to a team they were guaranteed to conquer. But she did not feel that way at all. Not in the least.

There were more persons on the field than she had expected and she had to squeeze past several overly-happy supporters to gain access to the grounds. As she walked further unto the field, her attention switched back to Dominick. He was doing a little jig with two of his schoolmates who had descended unto the field to share in the joy. Andreide smiled as she watched them, her eyes focussed on a laughing Dominick. She sighed. He looked so handsome in his happiness.

"Dominick!" someone shrieked excitedly.

Andreide paused abruptly, causing a couple of passers-by to stumble behind her, almost knocking into her. She completely ignored them as she stared at the group a few feet in front of her.

"Dominick! Dominick!" A girl in the Duncan's Academy colours ran over to the group where Dominick stood with his comrades and flung her arms around him. Andreide recognised her as the same cheerleader who was doing the flashy dancing and also as the one who had started the chanting. Andreide was vaguely aware that her breathing had become ragged and her heart suddenly started pounding to a different kind of beat.

"Dominick, you were like *so* totally awesome out there!" she exclaimed loud enough for everyone within several feet to hear.

She clung on to him, grinning.

Andreide did not hear his response but whatever he said kept the girl grinning while locked on to him all the while. Andreide felt a sharp burst of anger shoot through her veins as she watched the girl fawning in Dominick's arms. Her stomach churned with acidity as she turned away from the scene before her. She turned to leave, before they saw her or before she did something she might regret later on – like lunging at the harlot and ripping her bleached hair out.

She could not believe she had been so stupid. Why did she think Dominick was going to be as happy to see her as she was to see him? Why did she think he would have been thinking about her as intensely as she was of him? Why had she fallen for his incredibly good looks and charm which allured her and enticed her into falsely thinking that he was interested in her? Obviously, she was the last thing on his mind as he stood there in his euphoria with that pretty little blonde in his arms. Andreide felt like kicking herself. How could she be so gullible? For all she knew, that *girl* could be his girlfriend.

She fumed as she started back towards the stands. No one paid her anger much attention as they assumed she was one of the irate St. George's fans. She saw one of the white and gold dressed fans give her a sympathetic look and she immediately felt like strangling him. She was so wrapped up in her steaming thoughts that she did not hear someone calling out to her until the person raised his voice.

"Andreide!" he shouted.

She whipped around, nearly breaking her neck in the process as she saw Dominick hurrying towards her. Her system seemed to shut down and restart at the same time. She exhaled and with that breath, released all her pent up anger. How could she be angry as she watched this gorgeous, smiling boy come running up to her, his face alive with joy? Her limbs felt weak as she stared at him, not believing that he was approaching her after she had just seen him in the arms of that blonde, smiling at Andreide as if he found pleasure in her presence.

"Andreide." He slowed to a stop and breathed out deeply, placing a hand on his heaving chest. From the looks of him, he had apparently done some serious running to be so out of breath, Andreide thought. She gazed at him, overcome by his close proximity. She could see the beads of sweat trickling down the sides of his face and his golden brown curls were damp on his head. She sighed as she took in the manly scent of his sweat mixed with grass and the underlying aroma of his cologne.

He stood in front of her and smiled, taking several deep breaths before he spoke.

"Hey!" He gasped. "You're here. You don't know how glad I am to see you!"

Andreide tried to steady her twitching cheek muscles.

"I had a feeling you'd be here. I was looking for you in the stands whenever I got the chance but you know ..." He grinned. "... this stadium is pretty huge! I'd have better chance finding a needle in a haystack than picking anyone out in this crowd."

Andreide felt her tongue go numb. Her heart was like a feather floating in the wind. He had been looking for her! And he was glad to see her? Was this some sort of a dream?

He smiled at her and she saw the sun illuminating his honey coloured eyes. She could melt under their gaze, right about now.

"So Andreide. How are you?"

She struggled to coherently articulate her response. "I'm ... I'm fine. You?" She tried to calm her breathing.

Dominick grinned broadly, his teeth dazzling. His eyes seemed to dance their joy as they sparkled. "I'm great!" he said. "We WON!"

Andreide managed a weak smile. "Congratulations."

Just realising, Dominick lowered his tone and looked meek. "I mean ... we won." He hung his head as he said this and gave her an apologetic look, almost wincing.

Andreide laughed. "Well, of course you won! You don't have to do that – stop." She laughed as he gave her a whimpering, puppy dog look. "I'm happy that you won, anyway."

Dominick's eyebrows shot up. "You are?" His voice was full of surprise.

"Um, yes." Andreide tried not to blush. "You guys played really well and it's only fitting that you won. I mean, wow. I've seen your school play before and honestly, you guys stunk. But now ... wow! You guys really have improved a real lot. Especially to have beaten us!" Andreide gave him a devious grin. "And you –

amazing!" she continued. "I didn't believe it when I heard that you were the new player on Duncan's team and I still didn't believe it until I actually saw you score those goals. Dominick, that was amazing! I've never seen a guy play so well. Compared to these guys here you're like David Beckham!" He chuckled as she said this. "No, really!" She continued. "You really *are* talented. And that's why I'm glad that you won. You deserve it."

Dominick studied her for a while then gave her a soft smile. "Why, thank you, Andreide."

Now, she felt her face redden. Why the *hell* had she said so much? She probably sounded like some worshipping and adoring fan. She wished he would stop looking at her with that heart-melting look in his eyes and that muscle-weakening smile.

"I don't think I've been complimented on my playing as highly as you just did."

His look was killing her. She did not think her face could turn any redder. Why wouldn't he look away?

"Oh, I'm sure you have. You must have a lot of fans now that you've given Duncan's Academy a new name in football. Fans perhaps like that girl who was all over you. She certainly knows how to cheer and chant your name."

She saw something flit through Dominick's eyes and she immediately regretted her words. How could she be so infantile in saying that? Now, he knew that she had seen him with her. Oh God! What if he thought she was jealous?

But Dominick laughed. "You mean Anna?" He chuckled. "Yes, she complimented me but that was more for her than for me."

Andreide gave him a questioning look.

"That was more of a publicity stunt for her than anything. She's head cheerleader you know, so she flaunts herself a lot."

Again, Andreide could not believe what he was saying. He was denying his interest in her and here she was thinking the opposite! It was this disbelief that led her to her next question.

"So … um … she isn't your girlfriend, then?"

Dominick gave a laugh full of humour and youth. "No, no. What made you think that?"

"Oh, I was just wondering."

"Well, no, she's not my girlfriend." He paused as he looked at her. "I don't have a girlfriend – not yet anyway."

Andreide's breath caught in her throat and her heart skipped a beat. He was looking into her eyes as he said this, with an intense, almost piercing look. The seriousness in his eyes and voice scared her but excited her all the same.

"Andreide –" he began but stopped abruptly, distracted by a commotion not too far away. He frowned and Andreide turned to see what he was looking at.

A few metres away, two players were arguing. Andreide recognised both of them instantly – one was Jason and the other was Richard. She could not hear what they were saying but she could sense the impending violence. And she was right. Richard placed his hand on top of Jason's head and laughed. Then Jason shoved him backwards. A second later, they launched into a full-on brawl.

Screams were heard and shouts were bellowed. Jason's three remaining team mates lunged forward, ready to jump in the fight. Two of Richard's friends lurched forward with their fists raised, while the remaining onlookers fled the scene. Alerted by the commotion, the two team's coaches ran to the group with several other persons tailing behind.

"Hey, hey! What's going on here?" one of the coaches demanded.

As they approached, Richard threw himself on the grass and covered his face. He moaned. "Oh, my God, my face! I think my nose is broken." He touched his nose and winced. "It is! Oh, God! I'm dying!"

"Carlston! What happened?" The Duncan's Academy coach hurried over to his injured player and knelt on the grass beside him.

He removed Richard's hand from his face and grimaced. Blood was smeared all over his mouth and a trail trickled from his nose.

"Warner! Boy, are you crazy? What you did to this boy?" Jason's coach rounded on him. He stared at him, his face livid.

Jason did not answer.

"Warner, answer me!" he demanded.

Still, Jason remained dumb.

On the verge of beating the stubborn player himself, the other coach spoke up, stopping him.

"It's alright, Merfe. It was probably just some left over stress from the game, right boys?" He looked at each of the combatants in turn – Jason towering over them with his fists still balled, Richard lying at his knees glaring up at Jason, apparently forgetting the pain of his injuries.

When both boys nodded, the coach continued. "Good. Now let's get on. I'll take you to get cleaned up, Carlston." He bent to help his player to his feet.

"No, wait," Merfe the coach interrupted. "Warner should at least apologize." They all looked over at the coach as if he were insane. However, he persisted. "Warner, apologize," he ordered.

Jason arched an eyebrow.

"Say you're sorry, now."

Jason glanced around at his team mates as if to ask, "Is he serious?" then looked back at the coach.

"Warner, apologize to Carlston right now, or else you're off the team!" the coach bellowed. He had lost his cool.

Jason glowered down at a smirking Richard, bleeding on the ground. Jason grunted an apology but the look he gave him while delivering it, was far from remorseful.

Apparently accepting it, Merfe nodded at Duncan's coach, then instructed Jason and the remaining members of his team to follow him. They turned and left the field, in the direction of their changing room. Richard and his coach did the same.

Andreide released a tight breath and looked up at Dominick. He was staring at the players as they exited the field. He appeared just as shaken by the fight as she was. He turned to face her and gave her a worried look.

"Wow. A lot of hate there, huh?" he said.

Andreide didn't know what the appropriate response was. She merely nodded.

"It's too bad our schools are such rivals. But why is that?" He frowned slightly.

Andreide shrugged. "Too much bad history, I guess. This match will probably be one they'll never forget."

"Why do you say that?"

"St. George's just lost. Dominick, we never lose. And especially not to your school. Like I told you before, your school used to play really bad and it was a joke to have a match with you guys. But now … no one expected this outcome. Never in a thousand years did anybody think that we would lose to you guys. But now we have. And it hurts … it hurts the players, it hurts our school, it hurts our community. Do you get it, Dominick? It's embarrassing for them! No one's going to forget this anytime soon." Andreide sighed.

"Oh. I understand now. You guys were the best then, yeah?"

"Yes, you can say that."

They were quiet after this. Andreide stood there and thought about what school would be like on Monday. She dreaded the aftermath.

The stadium seemed unusually quiet and she looked around curiously. The stands were almost completely empty. Only a few supporters of Duncan's Academy were left behind, still cheering victoriously.

"You looked so peaceful just now." His smile was so soft she could almost feel it.

She looked down shyly, unsure of a fitting response. Then she remembered that he had started to tell her something before they had been interrupted by the ruction.

"Um, Dominick ... you were going to say something earlier?"

"Oh ... that." Dominick's face flushed. "Well, I was ... er ... well you know ... er ... I ..."

"Yes?" Andreide smiled encouragingly.

She had never seen him like this, so unsure and lacking his usual confidence which she found so attractive. But this new vulnerable side of him was also appealing and he looked so very cute as he stumbled.

"Well, I was going to ask you ... if you wanted to –" He paused. He looked down at the ground and kicked at a loose patch of grass.

Andreide looked at him expectantly. Her heart had resumed its mad beating and excitement flowed through her veins. What was he trying to say?

Dominick sighed and looked up at her. He smiled weakly as he caught her eyes and Andreide felt like flinging herself in his arms. She now envied the fact that that girl had beaten her to it. But then she smiled smugly inside at the thought that Dominick had preferred her company.

"Andreide," he said. "I would really like to get to know you better. We hardly see each other and when we do, we don't get much of an opportunity to talk. But I *want* to see you. To talk to you. Just you and I. So, what I want to ask you is ... do you want to see me too? Or am I being too bold?"

Andreide stared at him, not believing the words that had just come out of his mouth. He *wanted* to see her. He *wanted* to talk to her. She could not believe it. This day was just unbelievable.

How could she answer his question? Hell yes, she wanted to see him! She had been yearning for so long. But how could she tell him without sounding desperate?

Andreide looked into his cute, honey-coloured eyes and found it difficult to resist the urge to hug and kiss him. If only *she* was bold enough!

"Andreide?"

"Dominick, I would love that. And no, you're not being bold. Not in the least."

Dominick seemed to release a breath of relief. He smiled at her and she smiled at him. They just stood there smiling.

Chapter 9

Just as Andreide had predicted, on Monday morning, the entire school buzzed with the events of Friday's match. Everywhere she went she heard students expressing their disappointment and the disbelief they still felt over the outcome of the game. To Andreide's surprise, even the teachers congregated in corners to discuss the match amongst their fellow colleagues. Ever since their defeat, the players had been extremely disgruntled; as expected, Jason's mood was the foulest of them all.

However, on Tuesday, the subject of popular discussion was abruptly switched to one of a completely contrasting nature. The school – mainly the female population – was alive with excitement as they eagerly anticipated the arrival of the following significant day – Valentine's Day.

"Can you believe tomorrow is Valentine's Day?" Alisa squealed excitedly as the girls ate lunch in their classroom.

Keisha rolled her eyes. "Gyul, how many times you gonna ask that question?"

"Chile!" Harietta gave Keisha an annoyed look. "Alisa is just happy 'bout it that's all. Now would you stop acting like the Grinch of Valentine's and try to enjoy the season? You've been sour all day."

"What season? You making it sound like it's Christmas. And I could be as sour as I want so jus' leave me 'lone!"

"Grump," Harietta muttered.

Andreide chuckled.

When the bell rang at 3:30, they were all – with the exception of Keisha and most of the boys – anxious for the next day to arrive.

As she was walking home with Alisa chatting spiritedly at her side, Andreide imagined what tomorrow was going to be like. She was not expecting much if anything at all. She had already bought her mother a card and one of those scented candles which she loved so much – a red, cinnamon scented one. Buying anything for her father never crossed her mind. He had no appreciation for gift giving or receiving so she saw no point in wasting her time and money on him.

Andreide sighed as she thought of the romantic aspect of Valentine's Day. She wished so much that she had gotten a Valentine. But more than that, she wanted someone to love – someone who would love her just as much and even more. She was tired of the childish crushes and the shyness of it all. She wanted a real guy, a guy who would make her feel special no matter what. As she thought this, her thoughts turned to Dominick. She saw his handsome face, his cute adorable smile, and those clear, sweet, honey-coloured eyes. She suddenly felt her heart palpitate against her chest and as she placed her hand on the throbbing spot, she saw Alisa give her a worried look.

"Are you ok, Andy?" she asked.

"Yes, I'm fine," Andreide hastily responded and quickened her pace. She did not feel like being under anyone's scrutiny at the moment. She longed to get home to the privacy of her room.

*

"Wake up, sleepy-head!"

Andreide groaned and turned away from her disturber. She hated to be woken up before she was ready and the only person who usually woke her was her mother. Now she had to deal with another alarm clock in human form which unfortunately, was not as easy to break as the inanimate ones.

"Guess what day it is?" Chrystal sang out. "It's Valentine's Day! Happy Valentine's Day, Cuzz!"

Andreide's eyes were still shut. "What time is it?"

"Time to get up."

"What *time* is it?"

"Eight o'clock."

"What!" Andreide shouted.

She threw back the covers and scrambled out of bed. She could not believe it. How could it be so late? She could not be late to school on Valentine's Day!

"Why didn't you wake me up before? You knew what time it is and you let me sleep so late? It's Valentine's Day! No one goes to school late on Valentine's —" She stopped in mid-sentence as she caught a glimpse of the clock on her desk. She stared at it to make sure she was seeing correctly then glared at her cousin sitting on the bed in front of her.

"Chrystal!"

"Yes?" she asked innocently.

"It's *not* eight o'clock! It's seven twenty."

Chrystal looked across at the clock then raised her eyebrows and opened her mouth, apparently in shock. "Oh! Well, I thought it said eight. My mistake. No biggee!" She grinned.

Andreide felt like slapping the grin off her face. "You're lying. You knew what time it was. Why'd you do that?"

"Well, I got you up, didn't I?" She grinned. "I just wanted to see your face when you realised you were late on Valentine's Day. And I got what I was looking for."

"Yeah? What's that?"

"You've got a Valentine, don't ya?" Chrystal's eyes sparkled with excitement. "So, who are you crushing on? Who is he? Is it that same cute, rich guy?"

"*What* are you talking about?"

"Aha! I knew it. It *is* him. Lil Andreide's got a crush!"

"Oh, shut up! I don't have a crush on anybody and stop calling me little! You're just a year older than me so stop acting like you're so much older and wiser than me."

Chrystal laughed.

"Alright, alright! Peace! You're right. But Andy, I'm still older than you and more experienced when it comes to these things."

"What things? And who says you're more experienced than me?" Andreide gave her a challenging look.

"Believe me, I am." There was no humour in her voice as she said this and Andreide realised that she was not joking. She could only imagine what she meant by that and as she looked at her cousin, she began to see the gap between them. She realised she did not know her at all.

"Andreide, all joke aside. What I'm saying is this – I know what it's like to have a crush on a guy and I've had plenty. As your big cousin, I just want to make sure you're alright and safe and I wanna help you if I can."

Andreide suddenly felt annoyed.

"Look. First of all, I don't know where you're getting at thinking I have a crush on anybody. Even if I did, I'm not stupid. I know how to take care of myself and I don't need your help." She stood up from the bed, grabbed her towel and toothbrush and headed to the door.

*

Before she could enter the classroom, something pink and furry appeared out of nowhere and attacked her. She stumbled as the weight of her assailant nearly knocked her off her feet. It was Alisa, squeezing the life out of her body.

"Happy Valentine's Day, Andy!" she cried happily as she released her friend from her tight bonds. She then grabbed Andreide's arm and led her into the classroom.

Andreide was struck by the bright pinks, reds and whites decorating each student. For Valentine's Day, they were allowed to wear whatever they wanted as long as it was appropriate and in the colour scheme. The pretty colours the students wore were such a refreshing change from the usual drab green and brown of their school uniform. Andreide smiled.

"Hey, Andy. You look nice, girl."

"Thanks Harietta. You look nice too. That white top looks good on you. I like the red hearts on it. Where'd you get it?"

"Oh, this ole thing? I made it myself, girl."

"Wha'?" Keisha stared at Harietta's blouse in shock. "You made that?"

"Yes, I did. You got a problem?"

"No, gyul. It's just that it look real nice, that's all."

Harietta raised her eyebrows. "Wow. I gotta remember this moment. Keisha is actually complimenting me!"

Andreide and Alisa laughed. Keisha grinned and rolled her eyes.

"Gyul. Just take it and hush, see."

They all laughed.

As the morning progressed, Andreide and her friends received several compliments on their outfits and all the girls beamed with excitement. It was pointless for the teachers to have classes as no one could concentrate on what was being taught; all that occupied their minds were the gifts they were to receive and the activities they would partake in after they were freed from school. Before the first period ended, Andreide had already heard the news of at least five parties being held directly after school.

By lunchtime, no one could hide their enthusiasm and happy feelings. Even the teachers were overly joyful and were less restrictive with the students. There was a special lunch being served in the cafeteria and those who stayed to eat it received quite a shock – it actually tasted good, to Andreide's surprise.

When she returned to her classroom a few minutes before the bell rang ending the lunch break, Andreide found a package on her desk. She smiled excitedly – she had received her first

Valentine's gift. She approached it curiously and when she got closer, she realised what it was. It was a red, heart-shaped container, wrapped in red tissue paper and without opening it, she knew it contained chocolates. On the cover was a short handwritten note and as she read it, she felt her excitement quickly fade away.

"What's that you got there, Andy?"

Alisa walked in closely followed by Harietta. Keisha strolled in after them.

"Nothing," Andreide sighed.

"It's got to be something. You've gotten a gift already? Can I see?" Harietta asked eagerly.

Andreide shrugged. "Whatever."

"Uh oh. With that expression, I bet I know who it's from," Alisa said. She exchanged a look with Harietta and tried to hide her grin.

"It's from lover boy, isn't it?"

Andreide frowned and did not answer. Harietta read the note and nodded.

"Yup, you're right, girl. It's from Hal alright."

Keisha laughed and threw back her head. "That fat boy don't know how to give up, see. He after you since preschool!"

Andreide's frown deepened. Keisha exaggerated but she was right nevertheless. Hal Chandani was an overweight, extremely irritating boy who had been infatuated with Andreide for as long as she could remember, dating back to at least grade one. Over the years, his infatuation had grown into almost an adoration which frightened and unnerved Andreide to the bone, for he was not afraid to show it. He had tried on several occasions to proclaim his undying love for her and at every attempt, she had turned him down. It was at moments like these that she felt her dislike for him grow stronger and stronger. Hal Chandani did not know when or how to give up which annoyed and frustrated her even more than the fact that she found him repulsive. In addition, his devotion was more than embarrassing.

Andreide dropped the box of chocolates on her desk and was about to pick it back up to throw it in the trash when Keisha stopped her.

"Gyul! What yuh doing?"

"What's it look like I'm doing?" Andreide retorted. "I don't want this crap so why should I keep it?"

"You ain't gonna even open it and eat one?"

"No," Andreide stated. "I don't want *any* of it."

"Well, then damn, gyul, gimme it! Waste not, want not."

Keisha grabbed the box, discarded the flamboyant wrapping paper then ripped the plastic covering off the container. They watched as she shoved five of the nougat filled sweets into her mouth.

Harietta shook her head. "Girl, I thought you didn't like Valentine's Day and stuff, so what you doin' with the chocolate?"

"Ah don't." Keisha chewed on a cream filled one. "But ain't nuttin wrong with the candy."

Harietta laughed and the girls watched Keisha in amusement before returning to their respective seats as the bell rang.

It was midway through English when a knock was heard at the door. Ms. Brown, their teacher paused from marking her students' papers to greet the caller. As she talked to the person, Andreide could tell by the reflection through the glass pane in the door that it was a man. However, his reflection was slightly distorted by an object obscuring his shape. She watched curiously as her teacher allowed the man in. However, as Ms. Brown pointed to Andreide and the man started towards her, she felt her heart leap up in her chest and beat faster. All eyes turned on her.

"Ms. D'Averette," the man addressed her.

Andreide looked up at him and nodded meekly, at a lost for words. She could not believe he had come to her.

"I have a delivery for you and the gentleman who sends it wishes you a very happy Valentine's Day."

Andreide stared at him with her mouth slightly opened as he smiled at her and placed a large basket wrapped in colourful pink plastic wrap on her desk. He smiled once more then turned and left the room. The silence ensuing from his arrival was abruptly replaced by excited and curious chatter as everyone focussed his and her attention on Andreide and her gift.

"Oooo! Andy, what is it?" Alisa leaned over and asked her.

"Who's it from?" somebody asked from across the room.

"I bet it's her boyfriend!" someone else answered.

"Who?"

"Andreide has a boyfriend? Andreide, you have a boyfriend?"

"Ok, class settle down!" Ms. Brown spoke up. However, no one paid her any attention and continued their talking, questioning each other and Andreide about the gift. However, Andreide was as clueless as them about it or its sender ... until she opened it.

She had to stand up to unwrap the plastic comfortably but not wanting to be more of a distraction than she already was, she took the basket off her desk and placed it on the floor in the aisle next to her chair. Alisa watched her keenly as she undid the pink ribbon holding the plastic together at the top.

Andreide gasped as the pink plastic wrap fell away. In the basket, surrounded by dozens of heart-shaped and lip-shaped red and pink wrapped chocolates was a pink and white stuffed dog. As she stared at it in wonder, she felt her heart beat even faster as she recognised the toy's cute face. It was the same white and pink toy dog she had seen in the toy store. The same toy that had caught her attention. The same toy that she had been holding when ...

Andreide gasped again. Her heart pounded wildly as she thought of the possibility that she was correct. There were only two people who knew that she liked that toy. The first was Alisa but it could not be her for she was sitting right next to Andreide, appearing as surprised as she was. And the second was Dominick. Dominick! It had to be him. There was no one else.

191

She looked at the toy dog in complete amazement before realising that there was a small card attached to the basket. She pulled it off and read it, her face beaming. The card read:

Happy Valentine's Day, Andreide!
From: Your Secret Valentine
P.S.
Isn't he adorable? ;)

There was without a doubt that the gift was from Dominick. The post script comment confirmed her belief. But Andreide could not believe it. Dominick had sent *her* a Valentine's gift? She, Andreide? He thought of her *that* much? She felt her cheeks glow and her face beamed with happiness at the thought.

"Hey, Andy! That toy. It's from –"

"I know, Alisa," Andreide cut her off with a grin. "I know."

*

Andreide tried to concentrate on the remainder of her English class but she just could not. No matter how hard she tried, Dominick and the idea of him sending her a Valentine's gift kept popping up in her mind – so much in fact, she could hardly think of anything else. The whispers of her classmates only added to her excitement and every time she looked up, many of the girls were staring at her curiously. It was only when homework assignments were given and Math class began did the class seem to refocus on schoolwork. However, until yet another knock was heard at the door …

Ms. Brown looked up startled at the sudden sound. She turned from writing a simultaneous equation on the blackboard and went to answer the knock. Immediately, the class erupted in sounds of shock and disbelief as a man wearing a Beau Flowers delivery uniform walked in the room. In his arms was a bouquet of red and white roses tied together in fine, pink paper and a pink bow.

Andreide was speechless as the man walked over to her after being pointed out by her teacher, yet again.

"Ms. D'Averette, these are for you. Happy Valentine's Day!"

Andreide stared at the man as he handed her the roses and all she could manage was a stammered 'thanks'. He nodded at her then left the classroom, leaving her feeling completely stunned.

"Well, someone certainly has an admirer," Ms. Brown commented. She looked at Andreide as if expecting an answer but Andreide did not know what to say.

There was also a card on the bouquet and as she read it, her heart did back flips. The handwriting matched that of the writing on the previous card. It was from Dominick. Again. Andreide felt her insides scream with joy. What was going on here? Dominick had sent her a Valentine's toy with chocolates *and* a bouquet of red and white roses. She must be dreaming. This was not real, it couldn't be! Maybe it was a mistake. Maybe he meant it for someone else. But no, it was addressed to her, Andreide – it was written clearly on the card.

"Andy, girl, what's going on?" Harietta inquired.

Keisha and Alisa looked at her with the same questions on their faces. The girls sitting close to them strained their necks to see in the basket and they whispered excitedly to their neighbours.

"Is it from You-Know-Who?" Alisa asked.

Andreide's blush was more than enough confirmation.

*

"Wow, girl, you're so lucky! I wish I'd gotten something like this for Valentine's Day."

"I wish I even *had* a Valentine!"

"Andreide, who is he?"

"Whoever he is must really like you! Look at those roses. Them look real expensive, see!"

"And he give you a cute dog! And me arm! That's chocolate too?"

"Gyul, you too lucky, see!"

"Wish I had yuh boyfriend."

"She ain't got no boyfriend!"

"I bet I know who all this from."

"Who?"

"Is that rich boy, ent? That Duncan boy who score them goals and beat we team on Friday gone."

"That white boy? You crazy? He and Andreide? What you sayin' girl?"

"Fo' chu! I bet he done have he white gyul up in them rich people school."

"Fo' real. White man ain't want black gyul unless is she ass he after."

"Gyul! Ah beg you hush!"

"Well, is true!"

"Then who you think these t'ings here from?"

"Ah don't know. Ask de gyul, nuh."

Andreide sat back and watched her fellow female classmates in amusement as they discussed her and her gifts. She was so elated and felt so light-hearted as if she were floating in the clouds. She could not believe how great her afternoon had turned out to be. The curiosity filled questions and comments only added to her happiness and she felt so very special. Special to be the one attracting so much attention and special to be the one to have received gifts from Dominick. Dominick! She felt like screaming.

It was after school and Andreide sat on a bench outside with Alisa waiting for Harietta and Keisha to join them – they were talking to Jamila, Keisha's cousin and some of her friends.

"Hey, Andy."

"Ya?"

"Isn't that Shauna standing over there with her two cronies by the wall?" Alisa asked.

Andreide looked where her friend was pointing. "Yeah. So?"

"Nothing. It's just that since you got these Valentine's gifts this afternoon, she's been staring at you with that foul look."

"Yeah, I know. I've seen her."

"Well, I just wanted to tell you not to bother with her or let her upset you in any way. She's just jealous of you and jealous that she's too butt-ugly to even have a Valentine. So don't let her get to you, Andy."

Andreide smiled. It was rare that Alisa spoke up like that but when she did, she was most often right. Andreide turned to her.

"Don't worry, Lissy. The way I'm feeling right now, nothing can take away my happiness!

*

Euphoric was insufficient a word to describe Andreide's feelings at the moment. As she walked through her front door, she felt like her whole day had been a dream. She still could not believe that Dominick had sent her those gifts. It had to be him, she was sure of it. But she still wanted to be completely certain – she wished she could see him now. She wanted to see that gorgeous face and throw her arms around him, showering him with kisses. If only she could …

Andreide stood in the hallway and sighed dreamily, looking at the two gifts in her arms – the roses in her right, the basket in the left. She sighed. Dominick had really made her day.

"Wow. I can tell someone had a great day. And you said you didn't have a Valentine?" Chrystal commented as Andreide walked in their room. She grinned. "Now, imagine if you *did* have a Valentine!"

Andreide's look of complete bliss was stuck on her face as she drifted over to her dresser. She placed the two treasured items on the dresser top and looked at them once more before turning and flopping unto her mattress. She inhaled deeply and sighed peacefully.

"Andy, these roses are so beautiful. And this toy doggy is so cute!" Chrystal exclaimed from the dresser where she had just hurried to. "Lawd, this boy must really like you! Who is he?"

Andreide turned over and looked at her nosy cousin who was staring in awe at her presents. But she did not feel her usual annoyance with her. In fact, she felt quite pleased.

"C'mon, Andreide! Spill! Who is he?"

Andreide grinned then rolled back over.

Chrystal gasped. "It's him, isn't it? It's that cute boy – the rich one. Wow. So he likes you too, then!"

Andreide turned back around. "Why'd you say that?"

"What?"

"That he likes me."

"Well, duh Andy! Just take a look at these flowers. They're red and white roses! Like a dozen or so. What guy sends a girl a dozen red and white roses *and* a basket filled with chocolates and a cute stuffed Valentine dog in it, if he didn't like her? None! Andy, this guy is into you."

Andreide laughed but felt her cheeks beginning to blush anyway. "Oh, please Chrystal. He doesn't like me like that. We're just friends."

Now it was her cousin's turn to laugh.

"Just friends? You mad or something? Guys don't send this kind of stuff to girls and are just friends wit' them. Believe me, this guy has more than friendly thoughts on his mind."

"Now why do you say that?" Andreide contended. "You don't know what he's thinking. You're acting as if you know what every guy thinks."

"I don't. But I know how guys roll and this guy ain't only want to be your friend."

"Whatever, Chrystal."

"Andy, I'm serious!"

"Ok! Thank you for the advice, now would you drop it so I can enjoy my gifts in peace?"

Chrystal laughed.

"Alright, fine." She headed towards the cupboard and took out a dark red bejewelled top, a dark pair of jeans and red high heels. Andreide watched with curiosity as she changed into the outfit. Chrystal dumped her used clothes on her bed and as she grabbed her purse and was about to leave the room, Andreide stopped her.

"Hey, where're you going?"

"Out," Chrystal replied as she adjusted her bra strap then heavily sprayed on some perfume.

"Out where?" Andreide twitched her nose at the scent of the strong aroma.

"Well, it *is* Valentine's Day. I'm not gonna be stuck inside all day. I've got a date." Chrystal grinned.

Andreide raised an eyebrow. "A date? With who? You don't know anybody here."

"Well, I do now."

"Who is he?"

Chrystal watched her sceptically. "Why?"

"Well, you've been all up in my business so what if I ask about yours?"

Chrystal rolled her eyes and grinned. "Fine. He's a guy I met when I went to apply for my job."

"So you got the job?"

"Uh, yeah. I start next week."

"Oh, ok. Congrats."

"Thanks. So, I gone. Later."

"Alright. Have fun."

"Thanks." Chrystal turned then left the room.

Andreide laid back and smiled, amused with her cousin and engrossed by thoughts of Dominick.

*

The doorbell rang five times before Andreide woke from her daze and hurried down the stairs to answer it. She forgot that

Chrystal was not there but thought that at least someone was downstairs to answer it.

She raced to the door and quickly opened it before the person could leave. For one crazy, excited moment, she hoped that it was Dominick but on seeing who it was her excitement evaporated.

"Good afternoon. I'm here with a delivery for a Mrs. Rose Marie D'Averette. Does she live here?"

"Yes, she does." Andreide replied, looking at what the man was holding with interest.

"Ok. Sign this please." He held out a clipboard to her and waited as she signed the delivery note. He then handed her a bouquet of a dozen long-stemmed red roses.

Andreide watched him leave before shutting the door then quickly searched the bouquet for a card. When she found it, read it then read it again, she felt very confused and amused at the same time. The roses were indeed for her mother. But what confused her was the sender. It was signed from Victor Wilson, her mother's editor.

Mr. Wilson? What was he doing sending her mother flowers – red roses to be exact? She pondered on this and admired the roses as she headed to her mother's study. They were of the same quality as the ones Dominick had given her. Dominick. She felt her heart flutter in delight.

"Mom?" Andreide knocked at the door.

"Yes?"

"I have something here for you."

"Andy, you're too sweet. You already gave me my gift this morning. You have another one for me?"

"No, Mom. It's something else. This one just came for you."

Andreide heard her mother pushing back her chair then heard her walking towards the door. Andreide stepped back a bit as she opened the door.

"Andy, I ..." Rose Marie trailed off as she caught sight of the roses in her daughter's hand.

"These are for you, Mom. They were just delivered." She handed the roses to her mother. "Guess who they're from."

Rose Marie did not look up. She stared at the flowers in her hands with a look of surprise and awe.

"Mr. Wilson," Andreide replied. She looked at her mother for a response but she kept staring at the roses.

"They're beautiful," Rose Marie whispered.

"Yes, they are. But why would he send them to you?" Andreide asked.

Her mother laughed then. "Oh, Victor! He's too nice. He must know I like roses. I told Jean that once. Such a nice man. You don't come across them so easily these days."

"Oh. Yeah, true. Mr. Wilson *is* very nice and quite funny."

"Yes ... he is. Well, thank you for bringing me the roses, Andreide and thanks again for my gift. I love that candle, it smells great! You always know what gifts to get me."

"You do too. Like mother, like daughter."

Rose Marie smiled then gave Andreide a peck on the check.

"Thanks darling. I have to get back to work now, though. I'm finalising some last minute details with Jean about my tour. You know, we're leaving on Saturday so we're finishing up preparations." She gave Andreide a smile. "You know, I don't think I've thanked you enough for being such a good sport ever since I started my book. You've been so cooperative and helpful through it all – it doesn't seem fair for me to leave you guys now. I hate to leave you and your brothers behind."

Andreide smiled. "I know, Mom. But I understand. Your work is important."

"But it's not nearly as important as you guys are to me. I want you to understand that. Don't ever think that I don't care about you guys or that I care more about my work because I don't. It's just that I'm really busy at the moment. But you know what?

It's going to change when I come back. I won't have to be doing all this paperwork and arrangements and things will be more normal again." Rose Marie paused and looked into her daughter's eyes. "When I come back, we have to spend some time together. When last have we done that, huh?" She smiled. "Just me and you."

Andreide smiled. "I'd like that."

"Me too."

The phone rang behind Rose Marie. She sighed.

"Duty calls." Andreide grinned at her own pun. Her mother smiled weakly then turned and re-entered her office. Andreide closed the door then headed back up to her room.

*

The week could not end on a better note. Since Wednesday, the only gossip topic that the girls in Andreide's class could discuss was her Valentine's Day gifts and the identity of her secret Valentine. This discussion kept up through the rest of the week, heightening Andreide's feelings of contentment. She felt like a queen among them all, being idolised by eager minions. She loved the feeling.

It was Friday afternoon and Andreide was waiting for her father to finish work at his office at Rapier Landscaping Co. She was sitting outside on a white bench near the front of the compound, shaded by several trees nearby. She had been reading a new novel until thoughts of Dominick and the idea of him being her secret Valentine swam through her mind. She felt the usual flutter of her heart as she thought of him and allowed that blushing smile to blossom on her face.

It was then she felt her neck tingle. As she turned around to confirm her suspicions, she gasped out loud. She almost screamed.

"Dominick!"

He was standing a few feet behind her with his hands tucked neatly inside his pants pockets. He stood there, smiling at her.

"Hey." His voice sounded so gorgeous to her, so masculine.

She gulped. "How long have you been standing there?"

Dominick smiled. "Not very long."

"What are you doing here?"

"With my Dad. He's talking to Mr. Rapier about our lawn – he wants him to do the landscaping now."

"Oh."

"Yep."

Andreide looked up at Dominick, not believing that he was right there after she had been longing to see him since Valentine's Day. Now that he was there, she suddenly felt extremely shy and tongue-tied. He looked at her and she looked at him. Then they both blushed and looked away. After a few nervous seconds, they blurted out at the same time.

"How was your Valentine's Day, Andreide?"

"You're my secret Valentine, aren't you, Dominick?"

They laughed awkwardly. Andreide felt her face flush and if she weren't mistaken, Dominick's face was reddening too.

"What makes you think I'm your Valentine, Andreide?" He gave her an amused look.

Andreide laughed lightly.

"Well, by deduction really. Only you and Alisa knew that I liked that toy and it wasn't her who bought it because she looked as surprised as me. Plus, she would've told me if it were her – she can't keep secrets for long. Oh and your card gave it away." Andreide grinned.

Dominick blushed and nodded as he looked down at the grass. He kicked at an odd pebble before responding.

"Well, it seems like my secret isn't a secret anymore." He looked up at her with those honey-coloured eyes and his lips curved to the side in a dashing smile. Andreide was extremely grateful that she was sitting down or else she would have oozed to the ground if she were upright – her legs had been liquefied.

"Those roses were really beautiful too. Thank you."

Dominick smiled and nodded. "My pleasure."

Andreide smiled coyly. They were both silent for a few moments then Dominick spoke.

"Andreide ..." He shifted his hands in his pockets. "There's this party one of my friends is holding next weekend and we're allowed to bring dates or um ... I mean friends ... well um ... as dates, you know. So I was wondering ... if you would like to go to the party with me."

Andreide stared at Dominick feeling utterly senseless. Did he just ask her out? To a party, yes, but he asked her out all the same, didn't he? Maybe her ears had been deceiving her. But he was looking at her with that pleading puppy dog expression that was simply weakening her by every second, waiting for a reply. She swallowed and tried to control her now thumping heart.

"Are you ... Are you asking me out? Like on a date? A party date?" Her heart beat pounded in her ears.

Dominick smiled shyly and Andreide noticed his ears were becoming cherry red.

"Yes, pretty much so."

Andreide ogled at him in disbelief.

"That is if you want to, of course. You don't have to. If you're busy, I understand completely. And if you just don't want to, it's ok. I was just wondering if you –"

"Dominick," Andreide cut him off and smiled. He looked up at her quickly. "I'd love to go with you."

His eyes smiled sweetly as he looked at her. "Great! Perfect. Andreide, I –" He stopped as someone called out in the distance. They both looked towards the front of the building and saw Mr. Michaels at the door beckoning to his son.

Dominick turned back to Andreide and gave her an apologetic smile.

"I'm sorry, I have to go. Dad's got a meeting with one of his clients and he has to drop me off at home first." He sighed. "This happens a lot doesn't it? We get interrupted whenever we get to talk to each other."

Andreide nodded. "I was thinking the same thing."

Dominick gave her a rueful smile then glanced back at his father.

"Hey, you know what? I don't know when again I'll be seeing you but I need to talk to you before next weekend – mainly about the party and where it is and so on. Do you have a number that I can reach you at?"

"Oh, right. Yes, I do."

"I forgot my phone in the car. Do you have a bit of paper?"

"I um …" Andreide looked about feeling a bit flustered – she could not find any. "I don't have any paper on me but skin is a pretty good substitute. Do you mind if I …?"

"Use my hand?" Dominick grinned. "Not at all. Be my guest."

He walked over to Andreide at the same time that she got up from the bench and approached him. They came so close together, that they both felt the effects of their proximity. Their eyes connected and they blushed, each smiling demurely. Andreide fumbled with her pen while Dominick awkwardly extracted his left arm from his pocket. He held it out to her and as she stepped nearer to write on his forearm, she smelled his sensational cologne. She tried her best not to swoon from the effects he was having on her as she quickly wrote her cell phone number on his arm. Just touching his skin alone was doing odd things inside her body.

"So um, that's my cell number," Andreide said quietly. "You can get me for sure on that."

"Great. I'd love to get you."

Andreide stifled a gasp.

Dominick blushed. "I mean, contact you," he said quickly.

Andreide smiled coyly.

Dominick's father called out to him again.

"Well, Andreide. I'll see you later. I'll call you."

"Bye, Dominick."

"G' bye Andreide."

Andreide waved as he followed his father to their car. She watched as they leaved and marvelled at how wonderful her week had turned out to be. It was the best Valentine's Day she had ever had. Dominick's invitation to accompany him to the party made her feel even more ecstatic. This week had definitely been the greatest one she had had in a very very long time.

Chapter 10

Rose Marie leaned back and sighed as the American Airlines jet climbed into the air. They had just taken off and were on their way to Miami, Florida, where she was scheduled to begin her book tour. She felt a sudden pang of a mixture of guilt and sorrow at the thought of leaving her children behind for two whole weeks. She knew that they could take care of themselves but was concerned all the same. What she was most worried about was Charles. He had never been much of a caretaker and whenever she was gone for more than twenty-four hours, she feared the worst for her children. But she had to be realistic. What was the worst that could happen? She cringed at the thought.

She turned and glanced around. Jean had insisted they flew business class although Rose Marie had tried to persuade her otherwise. According to her publicist, it was not about cost; it was about image and comfort.

Rose Marie looked behind her as she heard a raucous laugh. Jean was seated directly behind her, cackling and chatting animatedly with the passenger beside her.

Victor was seated in the row in front of her, near the aisle. Rose Marie's eyes settled on him as she watched him turn several pages of the newspaper he was reading. Although it was not necessary for him to have accompanied them on the tour, Jean had insisted that he did. She had claimed that she needed an assistant and that he would be a good tour guide for them when they travelled to Atlanta, since he knew the city well. Victor had attempted to decline but Jean would not take 'no' for an answer. Rose Marie hoped that the trip had not displaced him too much.

She leaned back in the comfort of her padded leather seat and exhaled. She wondered how her children were faring. She longed for all of this to be over so that she could spend more time with them again. But this was just the beginning of several of her tours.

*

Several hours later, they arrived at their hotel at Miami Beach. Rose Marie sighed tiredly as she dropped her shoulder bag on a table in her room. They had each booked single rooms with adjoining bathrooms on the same floor. As Rose Marie entered hers, the first thing she noticed was the silence. She looked at the double bed in the centre of the room and smiled – no deadbeat lazy husband sprawled out there.

She walked around the room, admiring the designs on the walls before she peered into the bathroom. It was beautiful. The room was painted peach and white and everything shined pristinely. With one glance at the large bathtub, she felt like stripping herself and jumping in it immediately. She stared at it with longing before realising that she had full use of it and could go in it right away if she wanted to. And as she was about to do just that, Jean traipsed into her room.

"Is your room as great as mine? Hey, you got a bigger TV! And look at that cupboard space!"

Rose Marie stepped back into the bedroom and watched as Jean stared in awe at her wardrobe closet.

"Is this oak?" she asked in disbelief.

Rose Marie laughed. "I don't know, Jean. I'm not much of a wood person."

"Well, it sure looks nice – good quality. This would look really nice in my new guest room. I do love the Marriott. I wonder who furnishes their rooms. Anyway ..." Jean turned to face Rose

Marie. "Feel free to use room service, it's all covered. And we're having lunch in about half an hour so you can meet us there when you're ready. There's a restaurant on the second floor that I heard is just fabulous! We have to eat there. So –" She clapped her hands together. "Go and have a nice relaxing bath. I know you must be pooped from that trip. I know I am. But nothing like a little drink can't cure!" She laughed riotously then turned to the door.

"I'll go and tell Victor. Now, you relax and don't hurry yourself down. Just meet us when you're ready!" Jean sing-songed before shutting the door.

Rose Marie shook her head and smiled. Jean was one character – lively, loud, annoying and amusing all at the same time. But Rose Marie liked her for it; it was her personality that made her such a good publicist. She was keen and strong-willed with her work and she was quite proficient at handling all aspects of what her job as publicist detailed, especially at the most harrowing times.

As she walked over to her suitcases near the door, Rose Marie realised that she had not yet turned on her cell phone. After retrieving her cell phone from her handbag, she discovered that she had no missed calls. She arched an eyebrow as she stared at the screen. They had not called her at all? Was something wrong? She quickly dialled her home number and was relieved when Andreide assured her that all was well.

After she hung up, she checked the time. She realised that she should start getting ready to join Jean and Victor for lunch. Although Jean had told her not to hurry, Rose Marie was not one to keep people waiting. She worked to time and hated being late for anything.

Rose Marie sighed. She longed to just flop on the big bed and drift off into a peaceful sleep. But she had to postpone her nap. She had to meet the others for lunch and turning Jean down was not an option. She had last eaten hours ago on the plane and she was quite hungry.

*

When Rose Marie arrived at the restaurant, she found Jean waiting at a table looking at a menu. She was alone. Jean looked up as she approached and smiled broadly.

"Ah, you made it! Good. Did you get to relax a bit?"

Rose Marie sat opposite her publicist. "Hardly. I didn't know which was worse – hunger or fatigue. So, I decided to relieve the hunger first then work on the tiredness later."

Jean laughed.

"By the way, where's Victor? I thought he was joining us for lunch," said Rose Marie.

"Oh, he's not." Jean sobered. "He had an appointment or something like that he said. Frankly, I don't see how that is and we just arrived but anyway, that's what he said. He also said he would probably be out for the rest of the day so not to include him in our plans." Jean shook her head and raised her eyes to the ceiling. "Men!"

Rose Marie thought on this and also found it odd. They had just landed a couple hours ago and Victor already had an appointment? He must have arranged it before they had left. But why? And who was he meeting?

Rose Marie shook her head. But why did she care so much? Victor was her business associate. He was a grown man. He could make other arrangements and do as he pleased, even if they were travelling together. What he did and who he did it with was none of their business – none of *her* business. But why couldn't she stop thinking about it still?

Jean was babbling on about some other topic but Rose Marie was not listening. As the waiter placed their drinks in front of them and flipped his notepad to take their lunch orders, it was then a thought occurred to her. What if Victor was avoiding her? Maybe that was it. But why? As she thought about it, she realised that they had not had a real conversation since that afternoon in January when he had taken her for drinks. True, they had talked after that but their subsequent meetings had been business related and as usual, Jean or other crew had been around. Then maybe he was avoiding her because of Valentine's Day. Perhaps he was embarrassed about sending her the roses.

Rose Marie sighed. The idea was ridiculous. He could not be avoiding her. If he were, he would not have agreed to come on the tour with them. But then he had not seemed thrilled to accompany them and he had hardly said a word to her since they had arrived in Miami. But maybe he was just tired like she was, she thought. But if he were tired, what was he doing going out before they even had time to settle in?

She sighed, exasperated with herself. Why the *hell* did this bother her so much?

*

"Don't you just love it here? It's so sunny and bright and feel the breeze! Oooo I just love Florida!" Jean sighed. She took a sip of her lemonade and looked over at Rose Marie. "What do you think, Mrs. D?"

Rose Marie smiled as she swirled the straw around in her glass of fruit punch. It was mid-morning, Sunday and having spent most of the morning relaxing in the large bathtub, soaking in bubbles and reading a novel she had brought with her, she felt quite refreshed. She had also had the best sleep she'd had in quite some time that night and woke up that morning feeling well-rested. Consequently, her mood had never been better.

They were sitting in an outdoor café which was just around the corner from their hotel. From where she sat, Rose Marie could see most of the street and the surrounding buildings and marvelled at the activity for a Sunday morning.

"Yes, it really is nice. I can see why people like to retire here. It's beautiful."

"Yes, it is! Hmm, maybe I should look into getting a condo up here. One on the beach would be good." Jean grinned.

Rose Marie watched her warily.

"I know what you're going to say next and before you suggest it, the answer is no. No, I'm not going to the beach with you to check out condos ... or to check out anything or anybody else."

Jean laughed. "You know me well, Rose Marie! How do you know I was going to say that?"

"You had that excited gleam in your eyes. You know – that look you get when you're thinking about shopping."

Jean laughed again. "Ok, ok. No condo shopping. But that doesn't mean we can't shop at all."

"It's Sunday, Jean."

"So? This isn't St. Kitts. There are actually places to shop here that are *always* open. Always! This is the real world, Rose Marie. There are malls!" Jean exclaimed excitedly.

Rose Marie laughed. "You sound worse than my daughter. I'd hate to lose you two up here in a mall with my credit card or even worse – my cheque book!"

The two women laughed.

"Now, let's not forget our main purpose," Rose Marie said, calming down. "We're here for my book tour, so let's stay focussed. And you, Jean." Rose Marie slapped at her good-naturedly. "You're the one who's supposed to keep me in check, not leading me astray with thoughts of shopping."

Jean grinned.

"True, true. But it's not everyday we'll be on call. We at least have weekends like today to relax and pretend we're on holiday. And speaking of relaxing, hitting the beach right now sounds like a damn good idea to me. We might even pick up a few hot Cuban guys!"

Rose Marie laughed till her stomach hurt. Her eyes began to water with pure happiness.

"Oh come now, Rose Marie! You can't tell me you haven't thought about meeting up with some cute Cuban guys up here."

"Jean, of course not! I'm a married woman."

"The hell with marriage!" Jean scoffed. "That never stopped me before."

"Well, you're divorced now aren't you?"

Jean held up her left hand, showing her bare fourth finger and grinned. "Oh, yes I am. And loving every minute of it!"

They cackled like evil twin witches. Luckily, there were only a few other people sitting outside the café who seemed more amused than appalled at their lewd laughter.

After they sobered somewhat, Rose Marie drank the last of her fruit punch and Jean finished her lemonade. From their high emotional state, it was hard for an onlooker to believe that their beverages were non-alcoholic.

"Jean, I never knew you were this much of a bad influence. It's a good thing I found out sooner rather than later," Rose Marie said wickedly.

Jean grinned. "Yeah, so you can try to keep me in check, right?"

"Sure, I can try. But I don't see myself succeeding. The damage has already been done."

Jean laughed. "Well then, that's why I brought along Victor!"

"Victor?" Rose Marie said. Her recovering heart rate suddenly began to accelerate.

"Yes, Victor. You know ... your editor? He's – well, well! Speak of the devil!" Jean looked to Rose Marie's left and grinned. Rose Marie quickly turned her head. Victor was strolling towards them from the direction of their hotel.

"Well, what kind of a coincidence is this?" Jean said delightedly. She raised her arm and waved at him as he approached their table. He smiled at them, tall and handsome.

"Good morning, ladies."

"Well, hello stranger!" Jean grinned.

Victor smiled ruefully. "Firstly, let me apologize for leaving you ladies alone here yesterday, although I'm sure you had a wonderful time without me. I had an important engagement I had to keep –"

"Yeah yeah, we know. And of course we had a wonderful time without you! We went out and had us some fun, didn't we Mrs. D? We went club-hopping and rented out some Latino strippers and wow, weren't they hot! In fact, we're rendezvousing with them for a recap in half hours time so if you don't have anything important to say, you know, we're on the move."

They laughed.

"Well, I see you two had a great time. Now, I don't want to keep you busy ladies back so go on ahead with your Latino guys. I'll just wait in my hotel room. I know when I'm not wanted." Victor turned to leave but not before shooting them a mischievous, roguish grin. Jean reached out a hand and pulled him back, forcing him to sit down.

"Aww! Did we hurt Victor's feelings?" she crooned. "Maybe Victor should've thought about our feelings … before he abandoned us yesterday!" Jean threw her scrunched-up straw wrapper at him.

Victor laughed. "I take it you ladies missed me then?" His eyes, which looked brighter than usual, glanced at Jean before lightly resting on Rose Marie. It was then she felt extra warm – a warmth that had nothing to do with the temperature. She struggled to maintain his eye contact wanting nothing more than to hide from his gaze. She suddenly felt like a teenager again – a blushing teenager in the presence of a secret crush.

"Hell yes, we missed you, damn it! How could you just take off on us like that? And on the first day we arrived too," Jean said in mock indignation.

"Ladies, I'm truly sorry about that. It's just that –"

"Yeah yeah … 'important engagement' … blah blah."

Victor smiled. "How can I make it up to you?"

Jean looked at Rose Marie as if she'd just struck gold.

"Well, you can start by removing your –" Jean abruptly stopped as she felt a sharp pain in her ankle. She quickly masked her wince with a tight smile as Rose Marie shot her a 'will you please control yourself' look. Jean cleared her throat.

"I mean, just give us proper warning in advance next time. I'll have to think of some punishment for you so in the meantime, I'll just hold it against you."

"Oh no," Victor moaned in trepidation.

They laughed.

Jean's handbag began to vibrate in her lap. She quickly opened the zipper and dug frantically, upsetting the contents within. She resurfaced clutching her now ringing cell phone. She flipped it open and launched into conversation with the caller.

"Nora, darling! Haven't heard from you in a while. How've you been, dear? Me? Oh, I'm good – swell actually. No. No. Yes, uh huh. That's right. Well, actually I'm in Miami right now. Hold one second, dear."

Jean lowered her cell phone and whispered to her companions. "I'm gonna take this call privately. An old friend of the family!" She chuckled and got up from the table. She headed towards the street.

Rose Marie sighed softly. It was then she realised that she was now alone with Victor. The thought made her nervous. She glanced at him and he smiled at her. She was grateful for the shade of the table's umbrella.

"You know, I really am sorry about yesterday," Victor began. "It was only when we arrived here that I realised one of my old college friends lived in this area of Miami. He's into computers and I saw an ad of his in the paper and it surprised me. I just had to find out if it were him. He was one of my best pals."

Rose Marie nodded. "You don't have to explain. It's alright. I understand. I probably would've done the same, especially if it were a close friend of mine."

Victor smiled at her, making her heart tremor. Why was he having such an effect on her? Just by looking at her!

"I knew you'd understand. I –" He paused as if deciding how to choose his next words. "You know, tomorrow is your first international interview at the Convention Center. There'll be media crews from all over the US there and it will be a lot more intense than you're used to."

"Yes. Jean explained it to me. I also have to do some book signing too, right?"

"Yes, you do. Autographs really." He grinned. Rose Marie smiled feeling a giddy sense of happiness and excitement at the thought of signing copies of her own book.

"Anyway," Victor continued, glancing in Jean's direction. "I could give you a few pointers that may help you with tomorrow's interview ... if you'd like, of course."

"You would? Sure. Thank you! I'd love to get as much advice as possible. Thanks so much, Victor." Rose Marie beamed.

"No problem. Glad to help." His eyes flickered over her face before settling on her eyes. "Shall we discuss it over dinner, perhaps?" His tone was light and friendly. He smiled at Rose Marie with such geniality, there was no way she could resist his offer.

"Um, sure. Yes. Dinner is fine."

"Great then. I would've suggested we discuss it over lunch but ..." He winced regretfully. "I have to go out. Jean will just kill me if she found out but I promised my friend I'd meet him for lunch."

"Oh, that's ok. Jean will just have to bear it." Rose Marie grinned. "I'm sure she'll find something for us to do while you're gone."

"Oh yeah, I forgot about those Latino men." Victor teased. "Aren't you ladies late already? Do they charge by the minute or hour?"

Rose Marie laughed lightly.

Victor's cell phone beeped then and he reached into his pants pocket to check it. After a few seconds, he slipped it back into his pocket and looked up at Rose Marie with an apologetic smile.

"I'm sorry, Mrs. D'Averette, but I have to leave. My friend, Eddy wants me to meet a couple of his business partners before lunch. I should definitely be back by seven so how does dinner at eight sound?"

"Oh, that's fine."

"Ok good. I'll meet you later, then."

"Ok."

Rose Marie watched as he got up from the table. He gave her one last rueful smile before turning and leaving the café. He left in the opposite direction, away from the hotel and away from Jean who was now returning to the café. She looked in his direction with a perplexed expression.

"Where's he going? The hotel's the other way."

"He knows. He said he had to go out – meet a friend for lunch."

Jean shook her head and frowned. "Just wait till he comes back …"

Rose Marie chuckled to herself as she watched her friend's expression. Jean sat for a while and replaced her cell phone in her purse before getting to her feet again.

"I'm hitting a mall – only way to keep me occupied and happy. Are you coming?"

Rose Marie hesitated. She was not really in the mood for much shopping. What she really wanted to do was relax in her hotel room and enjoy her moments of solitude – free from her children, free from her husband, free from everything else. But then her thoughts flashed unto dinner later that night with Victor and it was then she realised that she did not have anything suitable to wear for it. She had brought mainly business attire. The thought forced her in the direction of the pavement where Jean had already hailed a taxi.

*

"So what do you think of this 'spicy lamb with cream sauce'?" said Rose Marie later that evening. They had chosen to dine in one of the hotel's restaurants.

Victor looked down at his own menu. "Sounds interesting. But I'm more of a red meat kinda guy. Ah, like this prime rib steak. Now, that's my beef."

Rose Marie laughed.

After their waiter arrived and they ordered their meal, they began discussing the following day's work. Victor reminded her of the week's schedule before advising her on certain aspects of the interview for the next day, Monday. Rose Marie listened to him in awe of his vast knowledge of the media world. By the time they had finished eating, she felt more confident about the interview. Not even Jean could have equipped her this well.

As Victor was signing the cheque, Rose Marie looked at the couples who were assembling on the dance floor and smiled. A jazz song had begun to play and as the couples moved to the beat, she thought back to the first few years after she and Charles had married and how blissful those years seemed. They used to go dancing and she smiled as she remembered how amusing Charles looked when he attempted a step that was in fashion then. Those were the days when they could afford fun. Now, it would never cross his mind to ask her to go dancing. In fact, they never went anywhere together anymore – just the two of them. Her smile faded as she thought on this and deep within her, she felt an old sorrow stir.

Victor placed the cheque in the bill holder then looked at Rose Marie. He glanced at the dancers before returning his gaze to her. "Mrs. D'Averette …" he began slowly. "Would you like to dance?"

Rose Marie looked at him then, and her smile was one filled with surprise and delight at the invitation. "Victor! I … I um." She chuckled, embarrassed. "I can't dance."

He laughed. "Of course you can. Everyone can dance!"

"Oh, but I haven't danced in years! I don't know if I still can."

Victor smiled. "Yes, you can. And there's only one way to prove it."

He placed his napkin on his plate, stood up then rounded the table to Rose Marie. She looked at him with a mixture of disbelief and amusement. He extended his hand to her and gave her a pleading smile.

"Please?"

Without a word, she slowly raised her hand to his. As their palms connected, their eyes locked. She hesitated a moment before letting him lead her unto the dance floor.

*

Rose Marie beamed at Victor as the music ended and they stood before each other, smiling. She had almost forgotten how wonderful dancing made her feel. But she certainly had not forgotten her moves. The music, the atmosphere, Victor. She felt alive. More alive than she had felt in a long time. Dancing was the medicine she had needed and now she felt cured.

She led the way back to their table. As they sat down, Victor exhaled deeply.

"Wow. That was fun! You're quite the dancer, Mrs. D'Averette. I thought you said you couldn't dance?"

Rose Marie smiled. "Well, I forgot I could dance like that. I suppose you never really forget how to dance once you know how. But you, Victor, you were amazing! I'm impressed, truly."

Victor grinned. "Why thank you, madam. It's a natural gift."

Rose Marie laughed along with him.

"I must tell you though," said Victor. "It's nice to hear you laugh like this. You've been so tense lately and I'm just happy I can give you some relief."

Rose Marie looked down at the tablecloth. Why was he making her feel so coy all of a sudden?

Victor motioned to the dance floor. "This song has a nice beat. How about one last dance?"

Rose Marie tried to hide her delight but her smile gave her away. She nodded. Victor grinned and led them back to the floor.

They danced for a few minutes before the lively music changed to a slow-beat love song. Rose Marie glanced at the couples who were now moving to the slow rhythm, their bodies closer together, their arms and hips amorously conjoined and she felt uncomfortable. This was a dance for lovers, not for an author and her editor who shared merely ties of friendship. There was a certain level of intimacy required for this kind of dance – an intimacy that she and Victor did not possess.

As the seconds passed, Rose Marie felt more and more discomfited as the romantic lyrics played and the couples swayed blissfully to the tantalizing beat. She chanced a glance at Victor and catching his eye, gave him a weak smile watered with embarrassment. She then decided to make the situation easier for both of them and leave the floor.

However, as she was about to turn away, Victor caught her hand and gently pulled her towards him. Rose Marie gasped softly as she felt his palm rest on the small of her back; his other hand smoothly swooped up hers. She had no choice but to place her free hand on his chest. Rose Marie looked up at the man holding her in such a close embrace and felt mildly overwhelmed.

"Victor … I …"

She trailed off as his soft grey eyes penetrated hers with a look so tender, intimate and desirous that she felt alarmed. But before she knew it, his eyes returned to their normal amicable shine. She could sense he was going to speak but her nerves beat him to it.

"Victor, this isn't ... I don't think this is ..."

"Yes?" He arched an eyebrow inquisitively.

Appropriate was the word she was going to use but somehow, she had difficulty articulating it. As she looked into his eyes, she wondered if she had been mistaken by the look of desire he had given her. All she saw right now was the warm, good-natured look he often wore. Was she mistaken by thinking it was something else?

But why was she worried? He had not indicated any other motive than a desire to dance and that was all they were doing. They were *only* dancing. She had to get a grip. She was going to become neurotic if she did not relax.

Victor looked at her expectantly. She sighed and gave him a small smile.

"Victor," she began. "I want to thank you ... for everything you've done for me since you started working on my book. You've been a great editor and not only that but a friend when I needed one. You didn't have to come with us but you came anyway. I don't think I could have managed if you weren't here with me – with us." She looked away as she felt the heat rising in her cheeks.

Victor smiled. His eyes slowly skimmed her face.

"All I want is for you to succeed, Mrs. D'Averette. Giving you advice is the least I can do to help. And I'm glad to help you at any time. It's an honour really. Imagine a couple years from now when you're the most celebrated author in the medical field. I could then die a happy man knowing I had helped such a lovely, talented woman rise to fame."

Rose Marie felt like her cheeks were on fire. She could not dare meet his gaze.

"Thank you, Victor." Her voice was soft, almost a whisper. He smiled and squeezed her hand gently in his. It was then she realised just how close they were to each other and her senses perked up.

There was now, only a sliver of space between their bodies. She could feel his hand on her back as they swayed to the music as if there was nothing separating his skin from hers. The heat radiating from his palm sent tremors up her spine and her heart began to beat faster. As he steered their bodies to the slow rhythm, she felt her pulse race even faster as the scent of his cologne wafted into her nose. It did not help that her palm lay innocently against his chest which felt enticingly firm and muscular beneath her fingertips.

She tried her hardest not to let the effect he was having on her show. But this proved more difficult than she had imagined.

Oh, God! What was she doing? She was a married woman and here she was dancing in the arms of another man, almost swooning over him. This was exactly why they should not have been dancing to this song.

But no – she was being ridiculous. Victor was not affected by their dancing. She was the one overreacting. They were simply dancing to a slow song. There was nothing wrong with that – they were only friends.

It was then Victor's cell phone beeped, startling her from her thoughts. He gave her an apologetic smile and gently released her as he checked his phone. She saw his brow furrow as he read the message. He sighed.

"It's Jean. She wants to know where I am and what I'm doing. Can you believe it?" He chuckled in disbelief.

Rose Marie smiled although she too felt a bit annoyed at Jean's intruding nature. However, the interruption could not have come at a better time.

"You know, I think Jean believes she owns me," Victor mused.

Rose Marie laughed. He grinned.

"But you know what –" He glanced at his Rolex. "Knowing Jean, she'll probably call around to see where I am if I don't answer within the next few seconds. She might even turn up here." He glanced at the door. Rose Marie chuckled. He smiled at her.

"How about we play it safe and leave before she arrives? That is if you're ready to go, though."

Rose Marie nodded. "Sure. I'm ready."

"Ok, let's go."

*

As the elevator arrived at the fourth floor, and Victor led the way to their rooms, a thought suddenly occurred to Rose Marie. She had not thanked him for her Valentine's Day flowers. How could she forget that?

They paused outside her doorway. Victor smiled at her.

"It was a pleasure having you for dinner, Mrs. D'Averette. I can't remember the last time I had such fun on a business date before."

Rose Marie almost blushed.

"Yes, it *was* fun. I haven't danced like that in ages. You've made an old lady feel quite young tonight."

Victor laughed, his eyes lighting up.

"Oh and Victor, thank you for those roses. They added a special touch to my day. They really were beautiful."

"They reminded me of you." Victor's eyes ensnared Rose Marie's. His expression was unforgettable. He stepped closer to her, leaned forward then lightly kissed her cheek. He gazed into her eyes and in a soft voice he murmured, "Good night, Rose."

And with one last look, he turned and left, leaving a dumbfounded Rose Marie in his wake.

Chapter 11

Andreide felt like screaming. She was deliriously happy. She had just finished talking to Dominick and now she was giddier than a three-year-old suffering from ADD who was hyped up on sugar. She was ecstatic! All week she had been waiting anxiously for him to call and now he finally did.

It was Friday afternoon and Andreide had barely gotten out of the shower when her cell phone rang. When she saw the caller ID, she had felt her heart pummel against her ribs and she immediately became nervous. They had first exchanged shy pleasantries then he had asked her if she was able to go to the party. She had eagerly confirmed and his voice glowed with happiness as he then told her the details of the party.

A blissful sigh escaped her lips as she lay on her bed, staring at the ceiling. She was imagining what going to a party with Dominick would be like. But it was not just any party. It was one of Dominick's team mates who was hosting the party and from what Andreide deduced from her conversation with Dominick, the boy was among the richest students in his class. She could tell from the description he gave of the boy's house – a very large, grey and white coloured building in the north section of Lindale, which was an area solely inhabited by the very wealthy. She had seen the house before and she used to imagine what the inside looked like. Now, she would not have to imagine any further.

She sighed. She could not believe her good fortune. She was going to a rich person's party! She had not told the girls in school yet and she could hardly wait to see their faces – especially Shauna's – when they found out about it. This was so great! She pulled her knees to her chest and hugged them in delight. She squealed.

"Well, well, well. Look who's all happy again. What's fanning your flame? Or should I say – who?" Chrystal walked in their room.

Andreide looked at her and grinned. She could not contain it. "I'm going to a party tomorrow!" she exclaimed.

Chrystal raised an eyebrow and grinned. "Oh, really?"

"Yep!"

"Says who?"

"What do you mean, *says who*?"

"I mean, do you have permission to go? Does Tantie know you going to any party?"

Andreide sat up and looked at her cousin in disbelief. "Yes, she knows. When she called the last time, I told her about it."

"Does she know who you going with?"

"Well, she doesn't *know* him but I told her I was going with a friend."

"Aha! So you going with a boy! That's why you told her is a 'friend' you going with. Tsk tsk, Andy!"

Andreide frowned. "Girl! What's wrong with you? Why you acting like my mother for? Who are you and what you done to the crazy, wild cousin I had?"

Chrystal laughed. "I was just playin' with you, girl. It's still me. I was jus' trying to act responsible since Tantie ain't here. Gotta keep a check on everything."

"Chrystal, my mother left *me* in charge and not *you* so drop the act will you? You don't even know what responsible means."

Chrystal laughed again. "True, but going to parties don't make *you* responsible."

"Girl, it's only one party. Plus, it's the weekend. It's not like I'm going out late and partying all the time! I can't afford to do that – I have exams coming up. That's why I'm not even going to stay till this party finishes. I already told Dominick that and he agrees. He wasn't planning on staying for the whole thing either."

Chrystal gave her a long, serious look before bursting out in laughter. Andreide watched her as if she were crazy.

"Andy, girl! You're such a nerd! You're going to a rich people party with that cute boy and you're not planning on staying for the whole thing? Girl, you got it so good you don't even know how good you got it."

"*What?*"

"Andy, I was only joking when I was acting all parental on you. You said it yourself – I'm wild and crazy. I don't care about getting permission to do anything, once it's fun and safe and I know I can handle myself. But you, you're a baby. You have a lot to know about social stuff."

Andreide placed her hands on her hips.

"Excuse me? I am *not* a baby. I know a thing or two. Just 'cause I'm not as worldly and street-wise as you are doesn't mean I'm ignorant. And I really wish you'd stop treating me like I'm so much younger than you 'cause I'm not."

Crystal held up her hands and grinned.

"Ok, ok! I'm sorry, alright? You're right. You're not that much younger than me, I know that. But the thing is, I forget that most times. I treat you like you're younger 'cause I never had a sibling to be a big sister to. And now that I'm here with you all, I treat you like the sister I never had but always wanted." She looked down at her hands and sighed. Andreide suddenly felt a bout of sympathy for her.

"I guess I *have* been a bit too eager and up in your business too much, for real," she continued. "I now see why you don't like me that much and you're right."

"But Chrystal, I *do* like you … not all that much but you're growing on me and I'm getting used to you. It's just the privacy issue and treating me like a lil child that's the main problem between us."

Chrystal was silent as she played with a spot on her bed sheet.

"You know, all you gotta do is respect my space a bit, stay out of my diary, treat me more like I'm sixteen than twelve … and we'll be fine."

Chrystal looked up at Andreide and smiled. "I can do that."

Andreide smiled. "Good." She looked down at her feet and sighed before looking at her cousin again. "Oh, and uh, Chrystal?" Andreide began hesitantly. "I may have been a bit too harsh with you and I'm sorry. Remember when I told you I didn't want your help?"

Chrystal nodded and a smile began to spread across her lips.

"Well … I take it back. I *do* want your help. But only with certain things."

Chrystal laughed. "Andy, girl, I knew you'd come crawling to me some time! It was only a matter of when and why."

Andreide smiled weakly.

"But don't think my advice is free. Nothing's free in life, honey."

Andreide's face fell. Chrystal laughed.

"Don't worry. I won't charge you money. The only condition is – you have to tell me why you want advice on whatever it is you're asking. And you tell me every little detail about the effects of my advice. Every sordid little detail."

Andreide laughed. "You sicko!"

Chrystal grinned. "And since I already know about this party since you couldn't keep your trap shut all week about it, all you have to tell me is the results of this party. You get what I'm saying?"

"Yep."

"So do you agree to the terms of our arrangement?"

"Wait wait. Those were your terms. What about mine?"

"Well, what terms do you want?"

"Whatever I tell you is confidential. You can't tell anybody about it."

"Ok. Agreed?"

"Agreed."

They looked at each other and grinned.

"Well?" Chrystal asked. "What do you want to ask me?"

"Oh, right! What am I gonna wear tomorrow?" Andreide shrieked.

They both laughed and Chrystal grabbed her cousin's arm and pulled her to their shared closet.

"We're gonna mix and match. Girl, when I'm done with you, you're gonna have that boy drooling!"

They giggled as Chrystal flung clothes unto their beds.

*

It was 5:30 p.m. Andreide glanced at her watch and moaned. Dominick was due to pick her up in half an hour and her stomach was dancing with nerves. She had been too nervous to leave the house all day while she counted down the hours and minutes till the time arrived. It was only when Marques wailed that he was hungry and Chrystal dragged Andreide with her to the supermarket did she get any fresh air, which eased her nerves. But now with only minutes to go, her anxiety had returned with full force. She paced her bedroom floor.

"Andy, will you calm down. It's only a party." Chrystal watched her walk back and forth.

Was she crazy? It wasn't just any party! It was a Duncan's party and she was going with Dominick. Dominick! Her heart screamed in anticipation.

Chrystal chuckled. "Girl, you look like you're going to burst. Take a deep breath before you drop dead for me, please."

Andreide faced her mirror and exhaled. Her cousin was right. She was overreacting. It was *only* a party. She looked at herself and smirked. She looked downright chic and stylish. She wore a black pleated jean skirt, a white, V-necked top with black swirly designs, black sneakers and a silver necklace and big silver hoops. Chrystal had insisted on doing her hair and much to Andreide's surprise and pleasure, she braided it impressively well. She gave herself a long admiring look and grinned. She could not remember the last time she had looked this good.

"I told you I'd make you look hot. Now am I good or what? Lemme here it." Chrystal cocked her ears and waited for her praise.

Andreide laughed. "You're the best, Chrystal. You should consider a career in fashion designing or something."

Chrystal grinned. "Maybe I will. Now come here lemme fix your eyes. They could use a lil more highlighting."

Andreide did not even realise where the time went as Chrystal fixed and re-fixed her make-up. It was only when the doorbell rang did she realise how much time had passed.

"Chrystal! He's here! He's here!" she screeched. She waited a second longer for her cousin to finish her eyelashes then jumped up and dashed for her matching handbag. She threw her cell phone in it along with some money, lip gloss, some tissues and whatever else she thought she needed. Chrystal watched her in amusement.

"You're not going to live there you know. Most people go with their hands swinging."

"Well, I'm not most people. I always take a handbag with me. It's a woman's most vital accessory." She grabbed one of her favourite perfumes and generously sprayed herself like Chrystal had shown her to. She checked herself one last time in the mirror then hurried to the door.

"Thanks for everything, girl. See you later!"

"Have fun!" Chrystal called after her.

Andreide raced down the stairs then slowed abruptly in front of the door. She took a deep breath then turned the doorknob. She could have fainted.

Dominick turned as the door opened and on seeing her, he smiled. Andreide stared at him. He was wearing a blue and white chequered shirt with dark blue jeans. On his feet were the newest line of *Nike* sneakers and he sported a matching blue and white cap on his golden curls. His silver watch and chain shined in the late afternoon sunlight, almost as much as his smile dazzled her. He smelled as gorgeous as he looked.

"Hey." He smiled.

"Hi." She managed weakly.

"Wow, you look ... really nice."

Andreide blushed and looked down at the path. "Thank you. You look nice too."

Dominick smiled shyly then nodded towards their transportation. "Are you ready to go?"

"Um, yes." She stepped outside and locked the door behind her. She gave him a nervous smile as he caught her eye. They both grinned as he led the way to the awaiting Rolls Royce that purred in front of her house.

*

Andreide had never ridden in such luxury before. The black Rolls Royce was everything and more than what she had ever imagined. It was nothing but comfort and smoothness. During the trip, they had exchanged light conversation until Andreide had asked Dominick about the car. Then, he immediately launched into a detailed description of the vehicle and as he described, Andreide grinned at his enthusiasm. She looked around as he pointed out certain features.

But the car really was something special. The inside was as dark as the outside with black leather upholstery and gold linings. The backseat was so spacious and comfortable that she felt like she was riding in a limo. She could not get enough of it and was hooked by the time they arrived at their destination. She felt a pang of regret as she stepped out of the luxurious vehicle and watched it drive away. She wished she could ride in it forever.

"Well, we're here," Dominick announced.

Andreide turned and her mouth literally dropped open as she stared at the huge structure before her. Completely surrounded by a white wall that stretched as far back as she could see, the three-storied Rodger's manor stood majestically in the centre of the compound. The well-landscaped lawn was just as eye-catching as the house itself. A gravel driveway led from the main gates to the front of the building then continued to the east where a large garage stood. A smaller path led around the house in the opposite direction. At the foot of that path was a sign which read, 'This way to party' which Dominick and Andreide followed.

As they rounded the side of the house, the first sounds of music could be heard. It became steadily louder the closer they got to the source and was accompanied by boisterous laughter and shouts. Suddenly, someone jumped out from around a corner. Andreide started.

"Dominick! Hey, dude! Wassup?" a red haired boy exclaimed. He had a can of soda in his hand and he nearly spilled it as he slapped Dominick on the back.

"Hey, Tommy. Nice place you have here." He nodded towards the house.

"Oh, yeah, man. Thanks." The boy switched his attention to Andreide. He smiled. "And who's this?"

"Oh, this is my friend, Andreide D'Averette." Dominick smiled at her. "Andreide, meet my pal, Thomas Rodgers."

Dominick's friend gave her a jovial smile as he extended his hand to her. As she shook it, he shot Dominick a quick glance and a grin.

"Pleased to meet you, Andreide. But please, call me Tommy. This British boy and his formal introductions! Pah!" He grinned then beckoned them to follow him as he turned the corner.

As they rounded the corner, the first thing that struck her was the decorations. There were gold, white and blue streamers dangling from every window, doorway and chair with confetti sprinkled on every surface. And as if to ensure that the guests were not confused as to the reason for the celebration, there was a large blue and white banner dangling from the main doorway of the building with 'We are the football champions!' painted in gold lettering. Andreide shook her head and chuckled.

"Cool, huh? Our school's art club did that for us," Tommy commented. He looked at the banner proudly.

"Hey, Tommy, I thought you were going to have the party *in* your house?" Dominick asked his friend.

Andreide glanced around, confused. But this was his house, wasn't it? They were standing just outside the doorway of an annex which seemed to belong to the house as it was painted the same colour and had the same design. However, as she looked at it more, she realised that it was indeed separate from the main building.

Tommy shrugged. "Well, Dad had a fit when I showed him the guest list and he refused to let me have all of us inside. So the only other option was the pool house since Gordon is visiting with his girlfriend and they're staying in the guest house."

"Oh. Well, it's pretty cool for a pool house." Dominick nodded towards it.

"Yeah, it is. And it's private too. We can make as much noise as we want and they won't hear us in the house. That is, unless a bomb goes off!" Tommy grinned. "Come on, let me show you inside. Everybody's in there already."

Tommy turned and headed for the doorway. Andreide and Dominick followed.

As soon as they entered the pool house, Andreide felt like she had just stepped through a portal and into a different dimension. The main room was huge with an arched roof and had several adjoining doorways leading in all directions – through the largest one, leading to the outside, the large blue pool shimmered.

The sea of pale faces highlighted by their colourful clothing and sparkling jewellery, left Andreide feeling somewhat disoriented. The faded effect of the lights in the room added to her discomfort. The music was getting louder in the background.

"Hey, guys! Dominick's here!" someone shouted.

Andreide turned to see a group of boys slouched in a corner, relaxing on beanbag chairs. One of them got up and sauntered over to them.

"Hey, dude! Glad you're here. We've been waiting on the whole team to show up so we can play some ball, man! You ready to get whipped, D? 'Cause you know me and my boys are going to whip your asses out there! Did ya know Tommy has a field that's almost regular size? Wicked, huh!"

Dominick grinned. "Will, all you can think about is playing football, huh?"

"Yeah, Will. Relax, dude. This is a party. We're not here to play football," said one of the boys in the corner. "We're here for the fun – for the chicks, dude!"

The boys laughed.

"Well, if Will is hooked on playing football, we can play my FIFA Championship in the games room," said Tommy.

"Tommy, dude, you got your PS4 hooked up in your pool house?" one of the boys asked in disbelief.

Tommy laughed. "Yeah, of course. I've got PS4s hooked up in all my rooms."

They chuckled.

A loud crash suddenly came from a room nearby. Everybody quickly looked in the direction. Tommy rolled his eyes.

"I'll be back, guys. Gonna see what's destroyed already." He started for the door. "Oh, and Dominick," he turned. "Make yourself at home, bro'. You too, Andreide." He smiled at Andreide then at Dominick before leaving the room.

Will glanced at them both before heading back to his friends; the boys in the corner began to talk among themselves. Dominick turned to Andreide.

"Andreide, are you ok? You haven't said much."

"Oh, I'm fine," she said. "Just taking it all in. Never been to a party in a pool house before." Her eyes swept the room. In fact, she had never even *been* in a pool house before.

Dominick smiled at her. "Yeah, it's cool. And this is only one room. There's a games room down the hall, a kitchen over there, a few washrooms, some rooms I don't know what they're for, and five bedrooms upstairs." He shook his head and chuckled. "This place really goes beyond the average pool house."

Andreide nodded.

"Would you like me to get you a drink? There's a bar outside by the pool. I can get you fruit punch or soda or something."

Andreide smiled. "Thanks. Fruit punch sounds nice."

Dominick grinned. "Well, fruit punch it is. Coming right up!"

Andreide watched as he eased through the throng of bodies towards the opened double doorway to the left. She sighed.

"So, Andreide …" She turned. "It's Andreide, right?" Will looked at her questioningly. He had returned to his seat among the boys who were all looking at her now.

She nodded.

"Well, does Andreide have a last name?" he asked. The boys grinned.

"It's *D'Averette*," a low voice sneered.

They all looked in the direction of the newcomer. Andreide's heart began to pound harder on seeing who it was. A vein twitched in her head.

Richard Carlston stood in the nearest doorway, looking like a model in a fashion magazine. He stood there in a green polo shirt, grey cargo shorts and green-camouflaged sneakers; a diamond stud sparkled in his ear, a gold chain hung loosely at his neck and an expensive gold watch dangled at his wrist. His wavy blonde hair shined almost angelically as his blue eyes bore into hers. She gave him a disdainful look to match his sneering one. Richard stared at her for a few seconds before glancing at his friends. He grinned then strolled over to them, placing himself comfortably in the middle of the largest bean chair. His eyes refocused on Andreide.

Will glanced from Richard to Andreide then grinned at her.

"So, Andreide D'Averette," he began. "I haven't seen you around. You don't go to our school, do you?"

"Of course she doesn't," Richard smirked. "She goes to that public school. You know – the one we beat."

Andreide's insides began to simmer as she stared at Richard's leering face. She should have known he was going to be at the party. Maybe then she would have thought twice about coming. She wished Dominick would come back.

"Oh, St. George's," one of the boys said. "But then what's she doing here?"

"Same thing I was wondering, Hans." Richard's eyes locked on to Andreide's. She tried to swallow her annoyance.

"She's Dominick's date, guys," said Will.

Richard raised an eyebrow. "Oh, really?" His eyes flickered up and down her body. "Well, she surely adds *colour* to the party."

Andreide's eyes darkened as she shot him a cold glance.

"Hey, Andreide," Hans called to her. "Why don't you come on over here and sit with us. Keep us company." He grinned along with the other boys.

Andreide gave a polite smile. "No, thanks. I'm fine where I am."

"Are you sure?" Hans grinned.

"Yes."

"But you look so lonely all by yourself. You sure you don't want to come and sit with us?"

They chuckled. Andreide tried not to show her discomfort. Where was Dominick?

"C'mon guys, leave her alone," Will said. "She's waiting on Dominick."

"Yeah, Hans, lay off," Richard said. Andreide shot him a quick look. He smirked. "She obviously doesn't want *our* company."

They laughed.

"So whose company *do* you want, Andreide?" Hans asked. They looked at her keenly.

Not yours was the first thought that popped into her mind. However, she was saved from answering by Dominick's return.

"Here you are." He handed her a cup of fruit punch. "Sorry I took so long. There's a line out there."

"Thanks. It's ok." She took a sip of the juice.

Dominick glanced from her to his friends who quickly looked away with the exception of Richard whose gaze lingered on them.

"What were you guys talking about?" Dominick asked.

"Hey! What's with the music?" someone shouted from across the room. "Pump up the volume, man!" the person yelled. Everyone laughed.

Immediately, the DJ in the north corner of the room turned a dial and the latest hip-hop songs began to blare from the loudspeakers. Someone hooted and on cue, the crowd began to dance wildly. As the music got even louder and faster-paced, the sounds seemed to reverberate against the walls.

Andreide covered her ears and looked at Dominick. He grinned at her and pointed to the dance floor. He raised an eyebrow. She smiled and nodded, feeling the music vibrate through her bones. Dominick led her to the dancers where they found an unoccupied space near to a thin boy who was being sandwiched by a couple of plump brunettes.

Andreide laughed as Dominick pointed them out. He grinned at her then took her hand, pulling her body closer to his.

She smiled as his eyes met hers and she gave him a sultry look before she started to sway her hips to the music. Dominick smiled slowly as he watched her before he too joined her in dance.

Andreide felt her heart beat in time with the music and never thought she could feel this ecstatic – so carefree and happy. What she could not believe even more was the fact that she was dancing with Dominick, whose eyes never left hers.

Her pulse raced and her heart skipped as his hands circled her waist, luring her even closer to him. They were so close that she could feel his breath and smell his sensational cologne which added to her ecstasy – ecstasy, which overpowered her timidity.

His chest brushed against hers as she turned her back towards him then shimmied down his body. With feline agility, she twirled and pulled herself up, brushing her hips against Dominick's lower abdomen, catching his eyes. His lips curved to the side as his eyes roamed hers, trailing along her body. Andreide watched their progress and felt a tingling sensation spread from her heart and throughout her limbs. It was then, as his arms reeled her in, she had an overwhelming desire to kiss him – a desire which was gaining strength by the second. His eyes lowered then and focussed intently on her mouth and she knew he had similar thoughts. She did not realise how fast she was breathing until the music stopped and all she could hear was her alarming heart rate pulsing in her ears and the rapid, alternating breaths of her lungs. Her face felt hot.

Someone shouted out nearby and applause broke out across the floor, startling Andreide. She quickly looked away from Dominick's gaze and stepped backwards as he released her. However, he did not look away from her now reddening face.

"I ... I um ... I'm going to get some water." She breathed shakily and looked towards the opened doorway.

Dominick smiled lightly. "I can get it for you if you'd like?"

"Oh, no, it's ok, thanks. I can get it." Andreide gave him a shy glance before hastening for the double doorway.

The cool evening atmosphere welcomed her like a refreshing breath of air; a light wind blew along her heated skin. Although the sky was steadily darkening, the surrounding grounds were brightly lit by surveillance beams and porch lights. The bar itself had its own source of neon light which glowed luminously, making it the centre of attraction. Its colourful lights reflecting against the pool's surface looked even more beautiful as the wind blew ripples on the water.

There were only a few people at the bar as the majority of the partygoers were inside dancing. As she sat on a barstool and sipped her water, she looked at a couple sitting a few stools away from her and smiled. She watched the boy whisper in the girl's ear and she giggled before giving him a playful nudge. He then leaned in towards her and quickly kissed her on the cheek. The girl squealed happily.

Andreide gave a wishful sigh. She longed so much to kiss Dominick and wished that she was bold enough to do it. But their dancing just now had revealed a desire greater than wanting to kiss him – a desire which slightly scared her but intrigued her, nevertheless. She was both excited and afraid to act on this longing as she was torn by her natural curiosity and good judgement. Both minds left her indecisive.

A movement nearby disrupted her thoughts and caught her attention. Someone had just vacated his seat but not before clinking his glass on the bar counter. Andreide was almost certain that she saw a blur of golden blonde hair disappear around the corner of the bar. She shrugged it off and returned her glass to the barman before heading back inside.

She found Dominick standing with Tommy near a previously empty table which was now piled with snacks and an impressive range of junk food. Dominick smiled at her as she approached them and she felt the familiar flutter of her heart, just from seeing him.

"Hey." His eyes glowed warmly.

"Hi." Her heart flickered coyly.

"Are you ok?"

She nodded.

He studied her carefully.

"So uh, Dominick. You coming?" Tommy interrupted.

"Oh, right. Yeah, I am." Dominick looked at Tommy and nodded before glancing back at Andreide. "Andreide, Tommy and the guys are going to play some video games and they want me to play with them too. It's a team kind of game and they need me to play. You don't mind if I go with them, do you?" He gave her an apologetic smile.

Andreide smiled. "No, it's ok. You go and play. I'll be fine."

"Hey, you can come too, Andreide. But you'll have to watch though, 'cause it's an all-guy game, you know." Tommy grinned at her.

Andreide rolled her eyes at them and laughed. She agreed and they led the way through the main room and down a corridor. It opened out into an air-conditioned room which was smaller than the previous room but big all the same.

Andreide glanced at the boys already slouched in front of the television and rolled her eyes. She could not understand how boys found such enjoyment out of playing mindless video games all day-long. She thought it a complete waste of time – time which could be gainfully spent on something else, something that actually contributed positively to the world. She could never subject herself for more than a few minutes playing those games, not even when she had an attack of boredom. She looked at the boys and sighed.

Just as she found an empty chair to sit on and resign herself to watching the boys play, a girl sitting near the front of the room called out to her. Andreide recognised her as a cousin of one of her classmates' who attended Duncan's Academy. Andreide smiled at her, grateful for someone she knew who she could talk to. She got up and hurried over to her.

*

Andreide stretched her back as Jocelyn chattered on about her neighbour's new boyfriend's annoying ways. She glanced surreptitiously at her wrist watch and blinked in surprise. She had been sitting there for over an hour and a half! Wow, time surely did fly. And to imagine, Jocelyn had only finished ten topics so far; Andreide was sure she had at least fifty more to go. She looked back at her and gave the required nods and sounds of disbelief before taking a quick peek at the boys, most of whom were still glued to the television screen. The guys who were not playing were stretched out on sofas behind the others, commenting on the game being played, crunching on chips.

Andreide spotted Dominick and smiled. He was in between looking at the television screen and gazing in her direction. He looked so cute. She caught his eye and he smiled back at her, his look soft and warm.

Jocelyn coughed and Andreide regretfully returned her attention to her. If only she could escape from her for a while so she could hear herself think. Plus, she had been sitting in the same position for so long, she needed some exercise.

"Um, Jocelyn," she interrupted her prattling. "I have to go to the bathroom. Excuse me a minute, ok?"

Jocelyn seemed a bit taken aback. Her brow creased. "Oh, ok. Well, I can come with you too, then."

"No, no, no. It's ok," Andreide hastily replied. "I'll be back shortly." She got up quickly and hastened through the doorway and down the corridor.

When she exited the corridor, she sighed. It was such a relief to be away from that room, Jocelyn's chatter and the game-freak boys. She looked out at the crowd where some people were still dancing and others were liming and relaxing on beanbag chairs. She heard laughter coming from outside followed by a loud splash. All eyes turned in the direction and Andreide rolled her eyes. She could only imagine who or what had been thrown into the pool.

It was then she glanced around and decided that she had might as well look for the bathroom. Even though she did not need to use it, she could check her make-up anyway.

After trying several different doors without success, she stepped towards the sixth door then turned the doorknob. It was a storage room but what she saw convinced her that this also was not the room she was looking for. She was completely caught off guard and stared in shock at the scene in front of her.

The sight before her startled her as much as it amused, disgusted and paralysed her. She looked in disbelief at Richard leaning with his bare hips against a table, one hand gripping the table's edge for support; his other hand was resting on the head of a blonde girl, controlling her bobbing movements as she knelt between his legs. Richard's moan of pleasure was not loud enough to mask Andreide's utter of surprise.

Andreide quickly covered her mouth with her hand as Richard's head flew up and his eyes discovered the source of their disturbance. His look of surprise mixed with obvious embarrassment quickly turned to anger as his electrifying blue eyes locked on to Andreide. With one fluid movement, he shoved the girl aside and yanked up his pants.

"Ow! Richard! What's wrong with you? You were like so close to –"

"Shut up!" he roared.

Confused, the girl followed his incensed gaze to Andreide standing transfixed at the door. She cried out in shock and scrambled to her feet.

"I-I-I'm sorry," Andreide stammered. "Wrong room." She hastily turned and exited the room, shutting the door behind her. She ran to the last door, flung it open, hurried inside then quickly shut and locked it. She leaned against the door, closed her eyes and exhaled. What the hell had she just seen?

*

Water sprayed unto the counter as the basin filled from the facet's powerful torrent. Andreide splashed her face with the cool liquid a few times before turning off the stream. She looked up into the mirror and sighed. For the past ten minutes she had been in the bathroom, trying to get over her shock at what she had witnessed. No matter how hard she had tried, images of the girl between Richard's legs and the look of contentment on his face swarmed her mind.

A second bout of nausea overtook her and she dunked her face in the sink, twisted the tap and willed herself to keep from throwing up. She did not know why she felt this sickened. This was the first time she had actually seen something like that with her own two eyes, but she still could not figure out why she felt so dirty, as if she herself had been a participant in the act.

She stood up, turned the tap back off and looked herself firmly in the mirror. She had to get a grip on herself. She did not do anything wrong. She was merely an innocent witness to an act which she had had no intention of viewing nor did she ever wish to see again in the future.

As her thoughts flew to Richard and his reaction on seeing her, she just as quickly dismissed them. So what if he was now even angrier at her and hated her more than he ever did before? She did not care. She hated him too. She hated him even more for allowing her to see that and causing her so much disgust. He could have at least locked the damn door!

She sighed as she stared at herself in the mirror. She took a paper towel from the roll nearby and dried her face with it, thankful that her make-up was water resistant. She only had to lightly reapply her eye shadow before deciding to leave the bathroom. She straightened her outfit before unlocking the door and pulling it open.

Before she could step clear of the doorway, someone appeared from the right, intercepting her movements. He planted himself between her and the entrance, blocking her from leaving the doorway. Startled, Andreide looked up into the livid face of Richard.

"What the hell do you think you're doing?" He glowered at her.

The anger in his voice and the boldness of his action stripped away any fear or intimidation she felt on seeing him. She coldly met his glare.

"I was about to ask *you* the same thing."

"Don't gimme that! What are you doing here?"

"You know exactly what I'm doing here! I'm here with Dominick to enjoy his friend's party."

"Oh hoho! So you're enjoying it, are you?" he sneered. "I bet you are though – lapping up all the free drinks and food you can get."

Andreide tried to edge past him but he prevented her from escaping.

"Your school lost to us and you're here at our victory party. What kind of a patriot are you?"

"The best there is."

"You've got a funny way of showing it."

"That's none of your concern."

"It is when you don't belong here! This is Duncan's territory. Go back to your loser trash school. *That's* where you belong."

Andreide gritted her teeth. She stared Richard in the eye.

"Get out of my way."

"I'm not done with you yet."

"Well, I'm done with you! Get out of my way!"

"No." Richard placed his arms on the wall on either side of her, ensuring that she could not get past him without opposition.

Andreide felt her frustration and anger begin to rise steadily. She could not believe he could be so bold! She glared at him, wishing that she could burn a hole through his brains. He returned her stare with cool insolence.

"So tell me, what's the deal with you and Dominick? How'd he become your meal-ticket to this party?"

"What do *you* care?" she snarled.

"I don't. I'm just looking out for my own kind."

Andreide glanced at the dancers near the front of the room, the couples who were standing close together and the other guests who reclined in chairs. She heard laughter coming from outside near the pool then her thoughts flashed on Dominick and the boys playing video games down the hall. How she wished she was back with them now. She returned her gaze to Richard whose eyes clamped unto hers.

"Get away from me!" she hissed.

"Tell me about Dominick first. I saw you two dancing up a storm over there, giving each other those dirty, hungry looks you probably think nobody saw."

"So, what? You're spying on us now?"

"I wouldn't waste my time." He steadied his arms as she tried to move away from him. "So enlighten me. How'd you get your claws unto him? I bet through your *father*, huh? Oh yeah, my dad told me how D'Averette met Dominick and his father at that landscaping place. Told me how eager your father was to please them too. Subserviently eager ... nothing new there, huh?" He smirked at her.

It was only by the grace of God that Andreide stilled her fists. She clenched them at her side and eyed him with as much hatred as she could muster. "Don't you bring my father into this! This has nothing to do with him!"

"Oh? Well, I think it does. He's how you met Dominick, anyway. So tell me," he continued. "Is this the plan? You were looking for a way outta the dump and jumped at the chance of moving up to high society when Dominick took pity on you by talking to you? Well, let me tell you this." He leaned closer to her. "No matter how hard you try, you're never gonna become one of us 'cause you'll always be one of *them*. Always. That's who you are. So why don't you forget it and leave right about now."

Andreide supposed that it was due to her incensed state of mind, now mixed with the disbelief at what he had just said that kept her from taking his words to heart. Under normal circumstances, she would have broken down crying, completely hurt and embarrassed. But it was the boiling hatred flowing through her veins, accompanied by determination which fuelled her resolve to overcome her tormenter.

A thought then occurred to her and she flashed him a devious smile which she was certain, caught him by surprise.

"You know what, Richard? You're just jealous of me and Dominick. You're jealous that I have somebody and you don't!" It was her turn to sneer.

Richard's smirk quickly faded from his face as he thought over her words.

"Jealous? *Me*? What are you, crazy?" he hastily replied. "Why the hell would I be *jealous* of you when I got all the girls I could ever want falling at my knees!"

Andreide grinned at the ammunition he had given her.

"Oh, yeah, they're at your knees alright. Like that lil blonde 'ho you had dipping there." She gave a spiteful laugh. "I'm sure she didn't even like what you were shoving down her throat – not that it could go far or anything, seeing as it's so damn small!"

She had retorted without thinking and instead of feeling a bit ashamed at what she had said, she felt quite satisfied as she saw Richard's surprised and angry face glow bright red before her. Whatever remorse she was conditioned to feel on insulting someone so personally, vanished as he looked daggers at her. Her uncharacteristic gloat intensified his fury.

He suddenly and roughly grabbed her arm, pinning her against the wall. She could not help but wince at his vice-like grip.

"Don't you *ever* say that again!" he growled, a vein throbbing at his temple. His face was only a few inches from hers, his breath bearable but hot against her cheeks. "Maybe I'll let *you* be the taster next time," he whispered menacingly. "How'd you like that?"

Andreide looked long into his heated eyes before responding with utmost control.

"Do you actually think I'm afraid of you, Richard? You're nothing but a lowlife coward pampered by money. You can threaten me as much as you like but you can't do me anything. And the funny thing is, you *are* envious of the fact that I'm here with Dominick and you're angry because I'm enjoying myself and you're not, when actually you should be angry at yourself. Angry at yourself for your own discontentment and angry at yourself even more for letting me catch you with your pants down."

Andreide breathed quietly as Richard stared at her. Any minute now she expected him to lose it; she waited for the slap. However, no explosion came. He did not even look any angrier. In fact, his rage seemed to simmer down and evaporate as his grip slackened on her arm. For the first time since he had accosted her, he looked away from her and down at the ground. Andreide stared at him, surprised by his docile reaction.

He looked back up at her with a hard expression before completely releasing her arm and stepping backwards. His expression was now so muddled that she could not fully interpret his emotions. He frowned slightly as he looked over Andreide's shoulder and she turned around to see Dominick walking towards them. He smiled as he approached.

"Andreide, I was looking for you." His smile quickly dissolved as he caught sight of their expressions. "Wh-What's going on?" he asked cautiously. He glanced from Andreide to Richard.

Richard shoved his hands into his pockets. He looked from Andreide to Dominick then back to Andreide again before he responded with a cool air.

"Nothing. See you around." His gaze lingered on Andreide before he turned and left them standing at the bathroom doorway.

He headed in the direction of the pool, where he disappeared among the crowd.

Dominick turned to Andreide. "Is everything alright? What was that all about?"

Andreide sighed and forced herself to regain her previously cheery mood. After all, she had gotten the best of Richard, right? Plus, he had deserved what she had told him – he had looked for that himself. How he decided to react to it was his own problem.

"It's fine. Just had a little chat with your friend, Richard, that's all."

"You know him?"

"Oh, he's an old acquaintance of mine. This was just a little 'catch up' talk."

Dominick watched her for a while. "Are you sure you're alright?"

Andreide grinned and tried not to roll her eyes. "Yes, Dominick. I'm fine, I swear."

"Ok, good." His smile was so soft and sweet, she almost completely forgot about her argument with Richard only a few seconds ago. His honey coloured eyes gazed upon her face, and she felt a familiar tingle in her limbs. Her cheeks flushed as his eyes stuck on hers, and his lips curved in a heart-melting smile.

"Andreide, may I talk to you in private?" His voice was low.

She nodded shyly. Her breath caught as he took her hand, leading her to a staircase in the far corner of the room. They squeezed past several couples on the way up the stairs, many of whom were lip-locked in fierce embraces. On passing each one, Andreide's heartbeat increased in tempo. She felt even more nervous as they breached the top of the staircase and headed down a corridor. Oh, God! What was he going to ask her?

Her pulse raced as he placed his palm on a doorknob and turned it, leading them into a prettily furnished, unoccupied bedroom. He shut the door as she tentatively walked in then turned to face her. He exhaled slowly and gave her a coy smile, bordering on nervousness.

"Andreide," he began. Her eyes stuck to him as she waited with bated breath. "I want to thank you for coming to this party with me. Just being here with me made it so much more enjoyable than if it were just me. I don't think I would've come if you hadn't."

Andreide looked down at the carpeting and smiled. She glanced back up as he continued.

"I liked dancing with you, Andreide – very much so. You're a great dancer." He smiled at her. "You're also a really patient person. No other girl would have waited for so long while I played those games with the guys and I appreciate that."

Andreide smiled shyly as his eyes met hers.

"Andreide, I've never met a girl like you. All the girls at my school are so caught up in themselves and mimic each other so much, they're like robots." She chuckled at this and he grinned. "But you, Andreide," he continued. "You're so different. And I like that. In fact, I like everything about you...."

She looked up at him, not quite believing he was saying this. Her heart pummelled against her ribcage as he stepped closer to her.

"Andreide, what I'm saying is I like you. But I don't want us to be friends."

Her heart suddenly stopped. She stared at him. *What?* He brought her up here to break off their friendship? After they had just begun to get to know each other more? How could he do this to her? What about the things he was saying just now, how he liked everything about her? What happened to that? How could he now take it all back and say they could not be friends anymore after he had complimented her like that? How could he –

"I want us to be *more* than friends."

Andreide felt her entire system shut down. She stared at him, unblinkingly. Then, as if being hit by a wave of emotions, her senses and feelings came crashing back to her, swamping every part of her body. Her heart beat faster than ever, pumping her blood to the surface of her skin, as her lungs heaved quickly within her chest. She opened her mouth but nothing came out.

"I like you, Andreide. I like you a lot. I know we don't know each other so well but I can't help but feel I've known you for a long time. I know that's odd but it's just that I feel so comfortable with you. I love being around you. You make me want to smile every time I see you. You just make me so happy, Andreide."

She felt weak with longing on hearing his words and her heart fluttered like a butterfly in her chest. Could this be true? Was her dream becoming a reality?

"So, what I'd like to ask you, Andreide, is … will you be my girlfriend?"

Andreide gasped. Dominick looked at her expectantly, eagerly, anxiously, pleadingly. Her heart stopped again. She must have died and gone to heaven. Was this actually happening?

"I'm sorry, I don't know what's gotten into me," he said with a nervous laugh. "I'm moving too fast, I'm sorry. I should give you time to think. I shouldn't have –"

"Dominick, I'd love to," Andreide breathed. He quickly looked at her. She smiled shakily. "I really like you too and I'd love to be your girlfriend … you don't know how long I've been dreaming of this moment…."

Dominick looked at her as if his most desired wish had been fulfilled. His slow-spreading smile sent shock waves through her body, stunning her mind, trapping her heart and paralysing her thoughts. She gazed at him with an intense longing she saw reflected in his eyes.

"You don't know how happy you've made me."

And with that said, he closed the space between them, stepping forward to bridge the gap. He placed an arm around her waist then gently pulled her to him until her hips met his and her chest brushed his. She gasped softly and his eyes focussed on her face once more before he raised his other hand to her chin, gently tipping it upwards. It was then she became aware of her now pounding heart and could feel his beat just as rapidly beneath his chest. She inhaled sharply before he lowered his lips to hers.

Her heart pounded, her pulse raced. Dominick pulled her even closer, his arm tightening around her waist. His hand at her chin caressed her cheek before tracing a line along her jaw. A faint sound escaped her lips as his fingers traced the length of her throat. She lifted her arms and wrapped them around his neck, his mouth pressing harder against hers. She tilted her head and arched her spine as his hand moved up her back, supporting her, pressing her closer.

Andreide felt like she was in heaven. Never had she been kissed in such a way by a boy that made her heart hammer against her chest, and her limbs languid and weak. It was then as she stood in his arms, kissing him, that she knew that Dominick was the one she had been longing for – he was the boy she had been hoping to meet. And now, she had met him and he had asked her to be his girlfriend. *His* girlfriend. Her dream had actually come true. What more could she wish for?

After what seemed like seconds, though it had been several minutes, Dominick slowly ended the kiss, pulling back gently. Andreide moaned in regret, wishing they could prolong the moment as long as possible; she would give anything to be in his arms for a while longer. He smiled and looked into her glazed eyes.

"You're so beautiful. I've been meaning to tell you that since the first time we met." His voice was low, soft yet completely masculine. Andreide felt her heart glow.

"Thank you," she whispered. "You're quite handsome yourself." Her eyes met his and she blushed. God, he was so gorgeous!

Dominick's eyes shined enchantingly. He gazed upon her with a look that made her heart ache. "Andreide, I'm really happy you said yes."

"And I'm really happy you asked me."

With both arms around her waist, he leaned down and kissed her again – a short, sweet kiss. She sighed contentedly as he rose up. His cologne lingered in her nose.

"How about our first dance – officially as a couple?" His suggestion hinted some sentimentality which Andreide was pleased, almost moved to hear. She nodded her agreement.

He took her hand then led them out the room and towards the staircase. He smiled at her and her heart beat excitedly. Andreide felt like the happiest girl in the world.

*

It was early Sunday morning and Andreide lay on her bed, glowing with delight. For the past half an hour, she had been regaling her cousin on the events of the night before, even though she had been drilled for information the moment she had gotten home. Despite the fact that she had returned after midnight, Chrystal had been up, alert and excited, waiting to greet her at the door. She had bombarded her the moment she stepped through the front door and still her questions and cries of excitement were as abundant as if she had just received the news.

"I can't believe this, Andy! He asked you to be his girlfriend? I told you he was into you. I told you so!" Chrystal squealed.

Andreide grinned as the memories flooded her mind.

"Girl, that outfit musta killed him. You owe me big time!"

Andreide laughed. "Girl, I don't owe you nothing more than I'm telling you right now."

"But he called you beautiful, didn't he?"

"Yeah, so? He meant me more than my clothes, dum-dum."

Chrystal rolled her eyes. "Fine, be that way. But tell me about the kiss, girl! How was it?"

Andreide beamed. "Oh, it was great! Better than great – wonderful. It was just perfect. I've been kissed before but nothing like that."

Chrystal's eyes widened. "You mean he frenched you?"

"No." Andreide shook her head. "It was a normal kiss. But it was so special. I felt like I was soaring in the clouds and my heart beat like crazy! It was just so perfect."

Chrystal laughed. "Girl! You were so worked up over a plain kiss? You're so simple. Imagine if he'd given you a *real* kiss, now!"

"But it *was* a real kiss!"

"Girl, when I say 'real' kiss I mean one with tongue and everything. It's those kisses that are the most meaningful and expressive. You can tell what each other is feeling."

"Well, my *plain* kiss was just fine. The way Dominick held me almost made me faint. His arms are so strong and his hands are big and –"

Chrystal giggled.

"What?"

Her cousin grinned. "You know what they say 'bout guys with big hands, don't you?"

Andreide rolled her eyes and grinned. She threw her pillow at her and laughed. "Chrystal, you're a pervert, you know that?"

"But it's the truth! Does he have big feet and hairy legs too?"

Andreide shook her head and grinned. "You're disgusting."

"What? It's just a question. Don't you wanna know if he's a real man or what?"

"He *is* a real man."

"How do *you* know? Did you see it?" Chrystal gasped. "Oh, God! You *did* see it. When? Where?"

Andreide laughed and flopped unto her second pillow. "Girl, stop. Your mind is too sick. We just became an item. He wouldn't have shown me his … you-know-what, the same day he asked me. What's wrong with you, child?"

"Well, he didn't have to show you for you to know. Did you feel it?"

"Ugh! Chrystal, stop it! You're so nasty! What's wrong with you?"

Chrystal laughed. "Alright, alright. I'm sorry if I upset your precious little ears."

Andreide rolled her eyes. "Whatever. Plus, even if I did know –" She rolled unto her side to face her. "– I wouldn't tell you."

"Aw! Cuzz, you're mean, eh!"

"Whatever. Let's drop the subject now, ok?" Andreide sat up just as her cell phone beeped twice. She bolted to her desk and grabbed it, grinning as she read the text message. She felt like screaming in glee.

"What is it? You win a prize or something?" Chrystal watched her curiously.

"No. Better. Dominick just asked me if I'd like to meet him for ice-cream at nine." She grinned.

"Wha'? You mean this morning?"

"Yeah."

"But that's church time. You can't, girl."

Andreide rolled her eyes. "What happened to the wild, perverse part of you? You get soft 'cause it's church?"

"Andreide, it's different when it comes to church. You can't skip mass to have ice-cream with your boyfriend."

"But it's only this once. C'mon, Chrystal. Where's your adventurous spirit? You're sounding like Mom, now. Missing one sermon won't hurt. Plus, I want to spend as much time with Dominick as I can. I already can't see him during the week so I might as well use whatever opportunity I get. And this is one."

Chrystal sighed. "Fine. I'm glad that the two of you are together now. But don't make this a habit, check?"

Andreide laughed. "How can I? I can only go now 'cause Mom isn't here otherwise I'd be stuck in church anyway. But it's not like I'm going against Mom's wishes – it's just this one time."

Chrystal looked over at Andreide, arched an eyebrow and grinned. "I remember when I used to say that."

"Oh, c'mon! We're always going to church. It wouldn't hurt to miss one mass! Plus, I'm sure it's going to be boring as usual. If Mom were here, she might even have decided to stay home this morning so …"

Chrystal laughed.

Andreide watched her then frowned. "Don't tell me you were setting me up again, Chrystal!"

"No, no," her cousin chuckled. "It's just amusing. I never thought I'd witness you rebelling."

"I'm *not* rebelling. I'm just not going to church this weekend. It's no big deal so drop it will you. I thought you were the one all interested in me and Dominick? How do you expect us to be together if we can't see each other?"

Chrystal held up her hands. "Alright, alright. You're right." She grinned. "Girl, I got you again. I just wanted to see what defence you'd give. But it was pretty good 'though I woulda done it differently."

"Girl, what's wrong with you? You like to annoy me, don't you?"

"Sorry, couldn't help it." Chrystal grinned.

"Yeah? Well, help this!" Andreide threw her second pillow at her cousin, right before leaping unto her bed and playfully punching her. Chrystal grabbed a pillow to block the attacks then swung it at her cousin. Their youthful laughter filled the room.

Chapter 12

"This is unbelievable!"

"Girl, didn't we tell you you had him from day one?"

"Fo' real. Me arm here with this gyul. You even got me happy for you, see."

Andreide grinned. All morning, all she could do was smile as she thought over her wonderful weekend. Her friends' reactions to her news made her even happier. The three girls were basically overjoyed; their delight ranged from Alisa's extreme excitement to Keisha's stunned disbelief. Harietta beamed almost as much as Andreide did. They were all thrilled, ecstatically so.

Andreide leaned against the trunk of their usual mango tree as they sat under its shade. The wind blew gently and cool against their skin, refreshing Andreide's mood. As she listened to her friends marvel at the turn of events, she remembered how her classmates had reacted when they too learned of the party and the fact that Andreide had attended it. She smirked as she thought back on Shauna's expression and the other girls' faces when Alisa accidentally let slip the fact that she had been invited by Dominick. What they were yet to learn was the fact that Dominick had asked Andreide to be his girlfriend. Andreide grinned. She could not wait for them to find out!

"Oooo! I still can't believe it, Andy! Did he really ask you to be his gf? Did he really kiss you?" Alisa squealed.

"Of course he did. What's not to believe? We already knew this was coming, didn't we Keesh?"

"Yeh. Seen it a mile away."

"And he took you for ice-cream. Oooo, that's so sweet! This is soooo awesome!" Alisa shrieked.

Harietta and Keisha laughed. Andreide grinned. She sighed contentedly as her friends continued on for several minutes discussing her new relationship. She too was still a bit overwhelmed, but gloriously so.

"Y'all see the gyul face when she hear 'bout the party?"

"You mean, Shauna?"

"Yeah, that one."

"Yeah, she looked like she was ready to explode."

"True."

"It good for she tho'." Keisha sneered. "She think she own people. Hehe! Wait till she hear that Andreide with him!"

"Yeah, she'll —" Harietta broke off and quickly turned her head at the sound of intruders.

"Well … speak of the devil," Keisha muttered, loud enough for the girls to hear. Her face hardened and her eyes darkened. Andreide glanced at her before turning her attention to their guests.

"So it's true then? You went them Duncan people party?" Shauna walked over to them. Her two cronies flanked her on either side. She stood a few feet from the girls who were sitting under the tree and stared at Andreide. Andreide braced herself.

"Well?" She placed her hands on her hips.

"Well what? Of course she went. You done hear so already so what you acting like yuh deaf or sumt'ing for?" Keisha stared at her, her look challenging and contemptuous. Shauna merely glanced at her before continuing.

"I hear you went out with him yesterday too. Somebody tell me how they see you an' him by the ice-cream shop and then walking through the square. Is true?"

"Well you hearing a lot ah things, eh?" Keisha commented before Andreide could respond. "Before you go mind yuh business!"

Shauna's mouth tightened. She kept her eyes on Andreide.

"I know it's true. And I done know I warn all of y'all to keep yuh hands and eyes off him. 'Cause he's mine!"

"Well, you see, Shauna," Harietta spoke up. "That's where we have a problem." She grinned at her friends. "'Cause you see, he's *not* yours."

"Yeah, thats right! He never was yours and never will be yours."

"Just shut up, Keisha, you skinny, black, broomstick self. I didn't ask you nuttin."

"Well, am telling you anyway so yuh could get yuh facts straight, you skank-ass ho'! That boy is Andreide's now. He asked her to be his girlfriend and she say yes. They done went out and everyt'ing! So what you got to say 'bout that?"

"What!" Shauna stared at each girl in disbelief. "Yuh lie!"

"Oh, no we aren't! Dominick is Andreide's boyfriend now." Alisa beamed proudly.

"Yeah, that's right." Harietta smiled smugly at their nemesis.

Andreide sat back and grinned as she watched the girl sputter before her. Shauna exchanged confused looks with her two companions before returning her gaze to a smiling Andreide. She frowned and her jaw stiffened.

"I ... I don't believe it."

"Well, you better believe it 'cause it's true!" Harietta smirked.

"Yeah. So you better watch yuhself and keep *your* hands and eyes away from him. He's Andreide's now and you better believe it, bitch. Now run 'way and stop bothering us."

Shauna glared at Keisha then at Andreide. She glowered one more time at Keisha before turning on her heel and marching off across the grounds, her followers hurrying behind her.

Keisha laughed, throwing back her head. "Gyul, I so glad you with him now see or else I wouldn't ah get to do that to she! Dum bitch." She laughed. Harietta shook her head and grinned as she watched Keisha cackle. Alisa exchanged a look with Andreide before she too started to chuckle.

Andreide watched them all before turning to look in the direction in which Shauna had stormed off. As she expected, Shauna and her comrades had rejoined their fellow schoolmates near the dusty football field and all of their eyes were now focussed in her direction. There was no need to wonder about the subject of their conversation. But she did not care. Whatever jealous gossip they were surely brewing, could not ruffle her feathers. All that mattered to her was the fact that Dominick had chosen her out of all the other girls in both his school and hers. Nothing could take away her joy now. As she thought this, Andreide closed her eyes and smiled, leaning against the tree. The wind blew lightly across her face lulling her into a daydream saturated with thoughts of her new boyfriend.

*

"Why are you so beautiful?"

"Why are you so handsome?"

"I guess I got lucky." Dominick grinned.

Andreide smiled. "More than lucky. You're blessed."

"You're doubly blessed."

They smiled at each other.

The week had just ended with the beginning of March and Andreide could not be happier. She had been waiting anxiously for Friday to arrive ever since she had received Dominick's text message during the week suggesting that they meet at her father's workplace that afternoon. She never thought she would be so happy to visit her father at his job than she was now.

They were now both sitting on the grass beneath the tree where they had first met. They had been discussing their past week and had been doing so for a while until a lapse occurred in their conversation.

Andreide looked at Dominick as the sunlight filtering through the leaves of the tree cast shifting shadows on their bodies. She gazed at him, basically in awe. She still could not believe they were now together, that their relationship had progressed like this. At the moment, she felt a mixture of shyness and joy which made her heart glow. Her face felt warm despite the cool temperature.

"Andreide, your beauty leaves me speechless. How do you do that?"

She looked at her hand propping her body up on the grass and smiled. "You're going to make me blush, Dominick."

"Go ahead. I like it when your face gets that rosy look." His voice was full of mischief.

Andreide looked up at him, catching him smiling. "Dominick ..." She trailed off with a light laugh.

"Andreide," He looked her in her eyes. "I'm not sure if I told you this before but I'm really glad I met you. You've been such a great friend – actually, you were my first friend here. But now ... you're even more than that."

The smile on his lips made her heart quiver and her pulse quicken as his honey-coloured eyes gazed into her dark brown ones. She swallowed.

"Dominick, I ..." She trailed off as he leaned towards her, kissing her lightly on her lips. Her heart thumped. He withdrew slowly, looking her in the eyes.

"Andreide, you're amazing. I wish I could spend every minute of the day with you, especially now that we're together. I want to know everything about you."

"I feel the same way, Dominick. But we can't." She sighed. "We don't even go to the same school or live near to each other. How can we ever get enough time together?"

"I know. It's a bit of a problem, isn't it?"

She nodded slowly.

"Well, hey, I can always transfer to your school. And maybe we can move in next door."

Andreide laughed. "That's a nice thought but let's be real. That's not going to happen."

"Yeah, you're right. But at least we'll have weekends to be together."

Andreide smiled.

Dominick looked at her and his eyes seemed to sparkle in the afternoon sunlight. "If you're not busy tomorrow, maybe we can hang out if you'd like. My parents are going to a function in the morning and I have to watch Nick. They said they'd be back by noon so the afternoon should be free for me. Is that alright with you?"

Any time with him was fine with her. She nodded. "Sure. What time?"

"Um, how about around three? I might have to do some things with my dad first but I'll definitely be free by then."

"Ok, sure. Three's fine."

"Great." He smiled at her. "I think you're going to like where I'm taking you. It's pretty quiet over there and relatively new so not many people go there yet."

"Where is it?"

He smiled. "You'll see tomorrow. All I'm saying is it's close to where I live and has great scenery."

Andreide laughed. "I don't even know where you live!"

Dominick grinned. "I'll show you tomorrow."

"You're a guy who likes suspense, huh?"

"Among other things."

"Like what?"

"Do you really want to know?" he asked mischievously.

"I want to know *everything* about you, Dominick," she said in a soft voice. "*Every* little thing." Her lips twitched and her eyes glinted just as teasingly.

He grinned. "And I want to know *every* little thing about you too." He leaned forward until their faces were almost touching. Andreide's heart pounded in anticipation. But instead of kissing her, he took her palm and raised it to his mouth, looking her in the eyes. "Every –" He kissed her thumb. "Little –" He kissed her middle finger. "Thing." He kissed her pinkie finger. He held on to her palm and grinned roguishly. "Agreed?"

Andreide stared into his gorgeous face, slightly shocked by his gesture. However, she could not stop the smile spreading across her lips. She giggled as he tugged her towards him, meeting his soft smiling lips with her own.

***

Marques placed the cordless phone back into its holder as Andreide came down the stairs.

"Who was that?" she asked.

"Mom," he replied.

"What? And you hung up? I wanted to talk to her!"

"I didn't know that."

"Yes, you did! I said so last time she called and you heard me."

"Oh. Well, I forgot then." Marques shrugged. "Sorry."

Andreide rolled her eyes. "Yeah, right. Whatever. What did she say?"

"Nothing really. She just called to remind us that she's coming back on Monday and to make sure the house is in order before she comes. And oh yeah, she said make sure we go to church tomorrow and not just me and Chrystal like last weekend."

Andreide was about to respond but paused as she looked at her brother. She placed her hands on her hips and frowned. "And how did she know I didn't go to church last Sunday?"

Marques looked away and fidgeted with his fingers.

"You told her, didn't you?"

"Well, uh ... it slipped out," he said meekly.

"Slipped out? Yeah right. You told her that to get me in trouble, you little pest. What's the matter with you?"

"I-I didn't mean to! Mommy asked if we went to church last week and I told her I did with Chrystal and she asked me about you and I told her you didn't. Why should I lie and tell her you did?"

"Ugh!" Andreide exclaimed. "You're so pathetic! Just buzz off." She turned from him and walked angrily into the kitchen where her cousin was propped on the edge of the counter, scanning through a cook book. Andreide stood at the doorway and watched her, then the stove which held bubbling pots before walking into the aroma-filled room. Chrystal looked up and grinned as she entered.

"Hey, cuzz. You're just in time. Do you know where any basil is?"

"No. What are you cooking? It smells good."

"Thanks." She beamed. "Just trying a little sum'ting for lunch."

"Yeah, but what is it?"

"Uh, vegetable rice, sweet potato pie and stew chicken." Chrystal closed the book and hopped down off the counter. She looked into a pot then glanced at her cousin. "But I really need that basil though. It adds a little flavour to the rice. You sure you don't know where it is?"

Andreide scowled. "Why should I? I don't use basil. Hell, I don't even cook. I hate cooking. I only make basic things when I have to."

Chrystal shook her head. "Tsk tsk. Lazy."

Andreide rolled her eyes. "I'm not lazy. I just don't like cooking – it's time-consuming and annoying. Plus, I'm not exactly skilled in that area."

"You mean whatever you cook burns?" Chrystal grinned.

"Ah, shut up, girl." Andreide smiled as she reached up into the cupboard. She searched a shelf then another before pushing a bottle of pepper aside. She tip-toed, moved a bottle of seasoning then reached for a packet behind it.

"Is this it?" She held the packet out to Chrystal.

"Yeah. Hey, thanks, cuzz. I wouldn't have seen it back there."

"No prob."

Chrystal picked up a pot spoon and stirred the now soft rice before turning off the fire. She opened the packet of herbs then sprinkled some of its contents into the pot. She stirred it again until the rice was completely mixed.

Andreide watched her in amazement. "But since when do you cook?"

Chrystal laughed as she added soy sauce to the white rice. "Since forever. I always liked cooking and got my chance to experiment when Pops started drinking more and Mom started stepping out. I was basically minding myself then. I had to eat so I had to cook."

Andreide shook her head sympathetically. "I'm so sorry, Chrystal."

Her cousin turned to look at her then laughed. "What for? Girl, I've been on my own for so long, it's nothing to me. I like having my freedom to do what I want. I like things how they are."

"You really do?" Andreide asked quietly. "You don't miss your mother or wish that your parents were living together again?"

"No. Why would I want that?" Chrystal scoffed. "They were always fighting when my mother still lived with us. Divorce was the best thing for both of them." She turned back to the stove and lowered the fire beneath the stewed chicken. "Anyway, my life's fine as it is now. But enough 'bout mine, what about yours? How's lover-boy?"

Andreide smiled as her thoughts redirected to Dominick. She was glad Chrystal's back was to her as her face was beginning to flush. She twiddled her fingers. "Oh, he's fine. Actually, we're going out later this afternoon 'round three."

"Oooo! Really? That's nice. Where're you going?"

"Don't know yet. He wants it to be a surprise. If he doesn't call me in the next hour, I'll call him." She paused and grinned. "Chrystal, I really like him. I really do."

Her cousin turned from the stove and faced her. She grinned. "Well, of course you do. You have the most gorgeous boyfriend there is, not to mention rich!"

"It's not only that. He's so ... so ..." She sighed dreamily. "He's so nice. And sweet. And charming. And funny."

Chrystal raised her eyebrows and grinned. "Does he have a great bod?"

"Chrystal!"

"What?" She laughed. "I just wanna know if he's the perfect package. Don't you?"

Andreide grinned, blushing. "I guess. But I haven't seen his body yet to know."

"Yet?" Chrystal teased.

"Oh, c'mon. You know. We haven't been out much and it's not like I've seen him at the beach with his shirt off to know what he looks like."

"But don't you want to?"

Andreide frowned but smiled all the same. "Look. I have a pretty good idea how he looks, alright. His chest was printing through his shirt at the football match, plus he was wearing shorts. When and *if* I do find out, don't worry, you'll be the first one to know."

Chrystal grinned.

"But," Andreide continued. "I'm not setting out today to find out. We're just going to talk about ourselves and so on."

"Yeah, right! If I had a hot boyfriend like yours I wouldn't waste time *talking*. We'd be getting down to business, girl! You know what I mean, ent?" She winked.

Andreide rolled her eyes and grinned. "Well, I'm not *you*, Chrystal. I want to get to know Dominick as a person and not just in a physical sense. Alright?"

"Fine," she sighed. "I guess I'm the only adventurous one here."

"Is that what you call it?"

They looked at each other for a few seconds then burst out laughing.

"What's the joke, ladies? Mmmm, what smells so good? Is that my favourite – sweet potato pie?"

They simmered down and looked up as Charles walked in. Chrystal smiled pleasantly and greeted him as Andreide rolled her eyes. Trust her father to appear when food was cooking.

"What are you two up to today?" He opened the oven door and peered at the golden pie. "The temperature's too high. Lower it."

Andreide exchanged a look with Chrystal then rolled her eyes exasperatedly. He examined the vegetable rice then removed the lid from the pot with the chicken and sniffed. "Hmph! That's salty, eh. I can't eat so much salt. Trying to kill me, Chrystal?" He laughed. Chrystal grinned awkwardly.

Andreide then decided to leave before she lost her cool. As she was about to go, he looked over at her. "Any plans for later, Andy?"

She released a controlled breath. "Yes."

"Where're you going?"

"Out."

"Where?"

"Somewhere."

"With who?"

"A friend."

"When?"

"Later."

"Wait a minute! That's not telling me anything. Where are you going and with who?"

Andreide sighed. "I'm kinda busy, alright. I have homework to do." She turned to Chrystal. "I'll be upstairs." She exited the room before her father could annoy her with any more questions. As if he cared with his false interest. She looked back and saw him rummaging in the fridge with that lazy, irritating look he had when hunger bit him. Thoughts of her had immediately vanished from his mind. She shook her head in disgust as she climbed the stairs.

Once in her room, she decided to choose an outfit for later to pass the time. Still unsure of where they were going but guessing that it was not somewhere fancy, she picked out a pink and white top and jeans. She sat on her bed and thought of the afternoon ahead of her. As she imagined being in a cosy, secluded place with Dominick, her stomach squirmed with anxiety and her heart beat faster. She looked at her cell phone eagerly, willing it to ring. Unable to wait any longer, she snatched up her phone and dialled his number. But he did not answer.

Distractedly, Andreide got up and headed over to her desk where she booted up her old laptop. She swore at it as it took a while for the home screen to appear, making a mental note to beg her mother for her a new one when she came back from her book tour. A few minutes later, the screen was up and Andreide logged into Skype. She bit her lip excitedly as she scanned her list of contacts. Her eyes lit up happily as she saw that Dominick was online. However, her webcam was not working so she could not video-call.

"Hey." She typed. "What's up?" She leaned forward, waiting for his reply. It only took a few seconds.

"Hey. Sorry I missed your call but my little brother has some friends over and they're a bunch of devils. One just took my phone as it started ringing and ran off with it. I just had to chase the little bugger around to get it back before barricading myself in my room."

Andreide grinned then typed, "Lol. Poor you."

"Indeed." Dominick replied. "I've been stuck with the little 'angels' since morning. How about you? How's your morning been?"

Andreide sent a sighing smiley. "Boring. Just passing time until later. I can't wait to see you."

Dominick typed a happy smiley. "I can't wait to see you either. In fact, I wish you were here with me now."

"To help you out with the lil devils?"

"Uh … yeah. That too."

Andreide smiled and blushed. "Lol," she typed. Then she remembered her reason for contacting him. "Oh yeah. About this afternoon. Where are we meeting?"

"I'll come by your house. Do you have a bike?"

"A bike? Um, I used to. But it's Marques' own now. Why?"

"Oh, I just thought it would be nice if we rode there."

"Oh, well I can borrow my brother's. He doesn't use it."

"Really? Great then! So I'll meet you for three?"

"Yes, sure. Definitely." She typed a happy smiley.

"Ok, great." He paused then resumed typing. "I'm sorry, Andreide but I have to go. I just heard a crash downstairs and our housekeeper is about to have a fit. I hope it isn't Mum's new Ming vase."

"Sure. No problem. Good luck with the devils!"

"Thanks. I'll see you later, Andreide."

"See you later."

He logged off. She smiled then did the same.

*

When it was finally heading for three o'clock, Andreide walked towards the back of the house where a little shed stood against the wall. She unbolted the latch and opened the door. She had not asked Omarion to borrow his bike and felt slightly guilty. Nevertheless, she took hold of the blue bicycle's handle bars and led it out of the shed. She locked it back then wheeled the bike across the yard to the front gate.

She waited only five minutes before a figure on a bicycle appeared down the street. Her heart beating steadily, she smiled as she watched her handsome boyfriend ride gracefully towards her. He slowed as he approached.

"Hey, lovely lady. Waiting for someone?"

"Yes. I'm actually waiting for my boyfriend. He's rather handsome. Have you seen him?"

"Handsome you say? Wouldn't happen to be me, would it?"

Andreide gave him a girly smile then nodded. He grinned, climbed off his bike then walked towards her. He kissed her on the cheek. "You look very pretty."

She blushed slightly. "Thanks."

"Ready to go?" His smile was making her heart weak. She gazed at him in his white polo shirt, khaki shorts, white sneakers and matching khaki-coloured cap, and nodded.

He grinned then mounted his bike. She followed suit.

*

"We're almost there. Just a few minutes more," Dominick said twenty minutes into their journey. Andreide was on his left, slightly lagging though she tried her best to stay on par with him. She was relatively fit but his athleticism was far superior. She could not believe how much stamina he had. He was barely sweating.

"Alright. Just one more incline to ride and we're there. It's just past those houses." Dominick pointed further ahead of them where the terrain steepened. Andreide gaped.

"Dominick ..." she said slowly. "This is Lindale."

"Ya, it is."

"Um, are you sure you know where we're going?"

He laughed. He turned back to look at her. "Yes, Andreide. I know where we're going. I'm quite familiar with the area."

She looked around in wonder. Then, it occurred to her. "Dominick, didn't you say you lived close to wherever it is we're going?"

He looked at her and smiled.

"Dominick, you live in Lindale? *Lindale?*" she asked in disbelief.

He chuckled now. "Yes, Andreide. I do. Is there a problem?"

"Uh, no. I just – wow. You live in Lindale." She did not know why it had surprised her. His family was wealthy, so naturally, they would live in such an area.

Dominick adjusted his bicycle's gears. "Come on. Almost there."

Andreide glanced down at her brother's bike and exhaled in relief that it too had gears. She did not know how she was going to make it up that hill without some sort of help.

On their way up the hill, Dominick showed Andreide a road to their left which led higher up the terrain and behind a bend. He told her that his house was located behind that bend and was one of the few properties located that far up on the hill.

Finally at the summit, Andreide inhaled and exhaled deeply. "Wow. That was tough."

Dominick gave her an apologetic look. "I forgot how long and steep this road actually is. It's much different being driven up it."

"It's ok." Andreide said. "I haven't had exercise like that in a long time."

They then turned unto a dirt trail which wound and bent through a small forest of trees and bushes. The path twisted downwards leading them through a beautiful archway of vines and multi-coloured flowers. It seemed too soon when they exited the pretty path. However, the scenery before them was even more breathtaking.

Andreide gasped as they rode into a lush green clearing. Yellow-petalled flowers dotted the grass. There was a small pond in the middle of the glade, where a few small birds were gathered.

They slowed to a stop in the shade of a couple trees with the pond a few feet in front of them. They sat on the soft grass and looked out at the picturesque view surrounding them. Andreide was amazed. She never knew somewhere so beautiful existed in the country.

"So what do you think?" Dominick asked.

"It's lovely," she said in awe. "No, it's wonderful. I've never seen a place like this. How did you find it?"

Dominick chuckled. "Well, actually, Tommy told me about it. His father is a real estate developer and one of the managers of this park. They've only recently done this but it's not finished yet. They're supposed to build a fountain over there and put in more ponds with fish and frogs and the like. Nick loves it here. My mum too."

Andreide leaned back on her elbows and smiled. "Speaking of your mother, why don't you tell me about your family?"

Dominick leaned back as she did. "What do you want to know?"

"Everything. Tell me everything you can and want to tell me."

He looked her in the eyes and smiled slowly. "Alright. And I want to know everything about you and yours too."

"Ok. We'll take turns. You first."

"Hmmm ... where should I begin?"

Over the next half an hour, Dominick told Andreide as much as he could about himself and his family. He told her about his relatives in England and his life there before they started moving. He recounted stories and experiences he had in his old schools and with his friends – many of which made Andreide laugh. His worldly knowledge and experiences made her realise just how intellectual and mature he was; she felt rather small sitting beside him, listening to what she had only dreamed of experiencing.

During the conversation, she asked him about his ethnic background. He confirmed what she and her friends had all thought – that he was of mixed heritage. Through his mother, he had African ancestry while his father's side was mainly Caucasian.

She then told him about her parents and her brothers and described in detail how annoying they all could be, especially Marques. Dominick laughed heartily at her descriptions and told her that he could relate to her problems with his own family. She shared stories about her family with him that made them both laugh. She then told him about her uncle and Chrystal, and her newly blossoming friendship with her cousin. She did not have much to say about her uncle as she hardly interacted with him.

Sheltered under the shade of a tree, the breeze blew cool along their bodies. They looked out at the scenery before them in quiet reflectance, enjoying the tranquillity of the atmosphere. Andreide watched two birds hop along the edge of the pond before turning to her companion.

"What do you like to do, Dominick?"

He turned to her and smiled slowly. "What do you mean? Like sports?"

"Well ... yes. I know you play football and you're really skilled on a bike so I can tell you're a good cyclist too. But you have a golf cap ... you play golf too?"

"Yes, I do." Dominick beamed. "I'm really into sports. I like being out and active. Ever since I was a child I've been playing some sport or the other. My dad really wanted me to be a fit, healthy lad and encouraged me to play. I think what he wanted the most was to collect my trophies." He laughed. "But of course, I'll have to cut back on outdoor time. We can't spend all our dates outside."

Andreide bit her bottom lip and smiled. She tried to remember what she was going to say next. "So um ... do you play other sports besides football and golf?"

"Yup. Cricket, tennis and some basketball."

"Really? So which would you say is your favourite?"

"Well ... I really like them all differently so it would be difficult to say I have a favourite." He paused thoughtfully. "But if I had to choose ... I'd pick cricket."

Andreide raised her eyebrows. "Cricket? Really?"

Dominick laughed. "Yes. Why are you so surprised?"

"Well, I thought football would be your number one. I mean, you're really great at it. I just assumed it was your favourite."

"Oh. Don't get me wrong, I love football. It's just that cricket edges it out by a tiny bit. Just by a slight margin. I'd say football comes in at a close second."

"Ok."

"So ... what about you? Do you play any sports?"

"Me? Well, not really. Track and field used to be my thing but I hardly run anymore. Not with exams coming up. Plus, I kinda lost interest in it."

"Oh. So what do you do if you don't play sports?"

Andreide smiled. "I read a lot. Hang out with my friends. Go to the beach. Go shopping when those lousy stores have something worth buying. Surf the 'net, shop online, whatever." She sighed. "There's not much really to do in this boring place. Believe me, I know. I've been living here for the past sixteen, almost seventeen years."

"Wow. That must be tough." Dominick grinned. "But don't worry, that will change rather soon now that you've got me." He winked. "Wanna be entertained? I'll entertain you, babe."

Andreide felt her cheeks flush. His endearment made her blush even more. She quickly looked away.

"What? I'm serious." He grinned. "I can take you places. We can go to the cinema, to parties, dances, shopping. I can take you to the new plaza that's opening up in a few months. We can go horse back riding and you can come with me and my dad to the races. And I can teach you to play football or cricket or some other sport." He gave her a mischievous grin. "And of course, we can always make our own entertainment."

Andreide laughed. "I already know how to play cricket. I can play football but I'm just not good at it. And as for that last part …" She smiled. "Dominick, you're so … so …"

"Charming? Amusing? Exciting?"

Andreide tried to suppress her smile but it was useless. "You're all of the above and more."

"As are you, my lovely lady." He then leaned towards her and kissed her softly on the lips, lingering there before slowly easing back.

Andreide sighed dreamily. She loved it when he kissed her; his lips were so soft yet all male. She looked at him and saw that he was watching her with a look that made her heart giddy.

"You're so beautiful. I wish I could just lie here and watch you forever." He traced a finger along her arm. She tried very hard not to shiver. His eyes followed his finger down her arm, skimming her soft skin until he reached her hand. She watched as he gently toyed with the sensitive skin of her palm, sending tickling sensations shooting up her arm. She bit her lip and tried to pull away from him but he held on to her palm with his other hand.

Dominick grinned slyly as he traced his fingers tantalisingly slow along her palm, making equally slow circles. Andreide bit her lip harder and tried not to squirm as he gently pinched her palm in several places. He raised her palm to a horizontal level with his mouth and looked her in the eyes as he slowly blew along the indentations he had made in her skin. She could not hold it in anymore.

"Dominick! That tickles!" she squealed as she pulled her hand away.

He grinned then chuckled. "I was beginning to wonder if you could feel that or not. So you *are* ticklish then?"

She tried to hide her smile with a defiant pout. "No! I am *not* ticklish. That was just … an effect of your irritation. Only babies and little children have such sensitive reactions."

Dominick grinned, amused. "Oh, really? Why don't we test your theory then?"

Andreide tried to keep a straight face. "Dominick, don't even think about it. I'm not ticklish. No matter what you do –"

He rolled over her at that instant, trapping her legs under his as he swiftly captured both of her wrists with one hand; he pinned them on the grass above her head. Her startled expression turned into one of annoyance and amusement. He laughed.

"Dominick! Let me up!"

"No." He planted his legs firmly, securing hers between his and tightened his grip on her wrists, ensuring that she could not writhe free. He shifted his weight unto his left so that his right arm was free for his mission. He looked down at her and a grin inched along his lips.

"So … you were saying you weren't ticklish?" He had an amused, deviant gleam in his eyes.

Andreide tried not to grin. She frowned some more. "That's right."

"Well, let's see now, shall we?"

Dominick raised his right arm dramatically above them. He swept his eyes along her body before quickly lowering his fingers, tickling her wildly. Andreide broke her mock defiance as she wriggled beneath him, twisting with laughter. She tried her best to get away from his roaming fingers as they crawled with spider-like grace along her body.

"Hey, hey! Keep still! I thought you weren't ticklish."

"S-S-Stop … Eeee! Stop!" Andreide shrieked amidst her laughter. She struggled against Dominick's unyielding grasp as she tried to free her hands; freeing her legs was virtually impossible.

Dominick grinned. "Stop? Are you sure? But you're not ticklish. Why should I stop?" He increased the speed of his fingers as they skimmed up her arms, teasing the sensitive softer areas of her skin. She squirmed and screeched gleefully as he made his way back down.

"Dominick!" she gasped. "Stop it! I'm going to … Eeee! Dominick, stop!"

"No way, babe." He grinned. "Admit it. You're ticklish. Just like my little brother and like every other child out there."

Andreide struggled to control herself but the tickling sensations were overcoming her. She laughed and with one last shriek, gave in. "Ok, ok! Stop! I admit it. I *am* ticklish."

Dominick chuckled. "Good. Now that wasn't so difficult, was it?" He stilled his hand, freeing her arms. She then gave him a few light, playful slaps on his chest. He laughed. He leaned down, planted a quick kiss on her lips then eased himself off her body. He reclined on his side and gazed at her.

"You're such fun, Andreide. I've never met a girl quite like you."

She smiled. "And I've never met a guy quite like you either. I can't believe I actually enjoyed that. Normally, being tickled annoys me more than anything else."

"Really?"

"Yes. You must have the magic touch … or something."

Dominick smiled. "Or something …" He softly touched her chin, tracing his fingers along her jaw. Andreide's heart beat faster.

"Andreide, I really like being with you. I wish we could stay here all day."

"I wish the same. It's so beautiful and quiet up here. I like how it's so private too."

"Yes, it's amazing here, isn't it?" He looked around before returning his focus to her. "Any plans for tomorrow? What do you think of a picnic?"

Andreide shook her head wistfully. "Sorry, I can't tomorrow. I already skipped church last weekend. I can't do it again this weekend. Marques will probably tell my mother again if I do and she'll go nuts. Plus, she's coming back on Monday and I'll need most of tomorrow to get the house in order before then." She rolled her eyes. "My mom is a neat-freak. She can't stand to see dirt or disorder anywhere."

Dominick chuckled. "Sounds like my mum. If she isn't cooking, she's cleaning something."

Andreide smiled.

"But anyway," he continued. "If we can't find time during the week, you have to come to our football match on Friday. Duncan's versus St. James High. Interested?"

"Oh, yeah, definitely." Andreide grinned. "Another chance to see the most talented footballer in the country play? Of course, I'll be there."

Dominick gave a modest smile. "I'm not all that great."

"Of course you are! You're spectacular. And this time I'll be in the front row cheering you on. I'll be your number one cheerleader, the loudest of them all. You won't be able to miss me then!"

Dominick grinned. "Even if you're as quiet as a mouse and in the highest, furthest row, there's no way I won't be able to find you. Not now, not ever."

Andreide was caught by the look in his eyes. "Why?"

"Because ..." He lifted a finger and slid it slowly, up and down her arm. She sighed. "Because, you're a magnet. An intense magnet that pulls me from my core to you. I can't help being attracted to you."

Andreide swallowed slowly. Did he really just say that?

"Does that answer your question?"

At a lost for words, she nodded. He took her hand and squeezed it. Still holding it, he looked out at the view in front of them. Andreide watched him silently for a few seconds.

"Dominick." He turned back to her. She leaned forward then kissed him softly, her heart accelerating as it usually did from his touch. She parted from his lips then gazed into his eyes.

"I can't help being attracted to you either," she whispered.

They both gazed at each other then smiled shyly before looking away at the surrounding greenery. The wind blew caressingly around them.

h1>*Chapter 13*</h1>

The American Airlines flight arrived on time, in the early afternoon on Monday. Rose Marie was relieved when they cleared customs and collected their baggage. Although the trip had been successful, she was exhausted. She could hardly wait to get home to her bed.

"Busy day for travelling, huh?" said Jean as passengers flowed out of the arrival doors. They had pulled their luggage to the side of the pavement after exiting the terminal.

"Yes, it is. I'm just glad we're done with it." Rose Marie shifted her handbag as a man rushed past her.

"Just for now, you mean. There are still more tours to come."

Rose Marie sighed. She did not need the reminder.

Victor looked around at the busy travellers hustling to and fro before glancing at his watch. "I don't mean to hurry you ladies but I have a meeting in less than two hours. How are you getting home?"

"Assuming that we're going home, you mean?" Jean winked at him.

He smiled slightly.

Rose Marie glanced around, scanning the idle vehicles in line awaiting passengers. She had called home already and told Charles the time that her flight was to land but their car was no where in sight. As far as she could see, it was not in the small parking lot either. She looked at her watch and noted that they had arrived twenty-five minutes ago – more than enough time for her husband to have driven from work or home to the airport. What was worse was that he had told her that he would come for her. She hated his unreliability.

"I was going to call my friend to come for me but you know what?" Jean grinned. "I suddenly feel for a drink. A nice strong drink. How about it?"

Rose Marie declined the offer. "No thanks, Jean."

"Victor?"

He shook his head. "No, thank you. I don't drink after flights or before meetings. You shouldn't either." He glanced to their left where a line of multi-coloured tourist buses were parked.

"I don't have any meetings today. How is it that you have one so soon? We've hardly been here an hour. You're quite the busy man, aren't you?" Jean dug in her purse as she looked at Victor for his response. This time, he barely smiled.

"I have a job, Jean. A job that keeps me occupied. I haven't taken time-off today therefore a meeting at four is within my working hours." He took out his iPhone and looked at it a while before slipping it back into his pocket. He glanced at Rose Marie. "Is someone coming for you, Mrs. D'Averette?"

She sighed. "My husband was supposed to but I haven't seen him as yet."

"Oh." Victor scanned the vehicles passing by. He stepped back as a group of businessmen walked briskly past him. "I would hate having to wait here with this crowd. Does he know you're here?"

"I told him what time we were to arrive. I tried calling him when we were in customs but his cell seems to be off."

"Maybe it's the reception," Jean butt in. "You should try again later. But then again, these networks don't work very well with all the interference around here."

Victor glanced at her just as a blue minibus pulled up near the sidewalk in front of them. The driver, wearing a garish tropical shirt and khaki pants climbed out of the taxi and hurried to greet them. The shiny watch on his outstretched hand was as fake as his cheap American accent. He hastened to shake Victor's hand.

"'Afternoon folks! How was your flight? My name's Jeff and welcome to the beautiful St. Kitts. This your first visit here? These your bags, sir?"

Rose Marie bit her lip to prevent herself from laughing as she watched the man put on his show. His overdone accent and eager-to-please mannerism were quite ridiculous and comical.

Victor indicated his bags before turning to Rose Marie. "Since no one's here for you yet, you can come with me if you'd like. Spare yourself the wait."

Rose Marie looked around one more time then nodded. "Thanks, Victor. I really don't want to wait here much longer indeed."

He smiled then inclined his head slightly. Before he could say anything, Jean jumped in.

"Well, excuse me, people. Aren't you forgetting somebody?"

Victor raised an eyebrow. "I thought you had your own arrangements?"

"Well ... well," Jean stalled. "Carpooling is much more economical and environmentally friendlier than having a whole car come just for me, wouldn't you say?"

"Oh, I agree, ma'am. What with all this pollution going on, it's best to economize. Keep the air nice and fresh. But don't y'all worry – this beautiful country got the freshest air there is!" The driver grinned, his large teeth glowing in the sunlight.

Victor regarded him with a touch of humour. "Yes, Jeff, you're right. Now, could you take these ladies' bags on as well? They're coming too."

Jeff beamed. "Oh, yes, sir! No problem, sir! These beautiful ladies coming too? That's good, good. My taxi got lots of room. Here, let me get that door for you." He pulled the handle on the passenger door and slid it back, revealing eight cushioned seats. He ushered his three passengers in before loading the remainder of the luggage into the trunk. Less than a minute later, Jeff started the minibus. He launched into animated chatter as he sped out of the airport.

*

When Rose Marie arrived, she met a silent, spotless house much to her surprise. Everywhere was clean and not a soul was to be seen. She could not have wished for a better welcoming for all she wanted to do then was sleep. She deposited her bags in the corridor, then wearily climbed the stairs to her bedroom.

In what seemed like five minutes, though it was a couple hours, the silence of the house was shattered by the loud shouts and excited cries of her children as they ran up the stairs. Marques bounded in first, followed by Andreide, both of whom flung themselves upon her. She smiled despite her tiredness, for she was in fact happy to see them. After answering their many questions then listening to their many other complaints, Rose Marie shepherded them out so she could have a few more moments of peace.

However, before she could blink twice, a car horn hooted outside then a second later, her cell phone rang; Jean's excited chatter resounded from the other line. She had just received news that a well-known international bookstore with a local franchise was interested in buying copies of Rose Marie's book. The representative had requested a meeting with Jean as soon as possible. Jean thought it would be better promotion if Rose Marie herself was there as well. She pleaded with her to attend the meeting. Reluctantly, Rose Marie agreed. If this bookstore deal was as great as Jean claimed it was, she supposed she could put aside her fatigue.

She took a quick shower then changed into one of her new business suits. A few minutes later, she was back on the road.

*

Over the following two weeks, life quickly changed for Rose Marie and her family. The meeting she attended with Jean was quite fruitful as the bookstore had agreed to stock Rose Marie's new book and promote it locally. What made the deal even better was the advance she had received from it. She had not expected it to be so much. Her family was just as shocked, even more so ecstatic. Before she could deposit the money in the bank, her children had already drafted lists of all the things they had ever wanted which she could now afford to buy. She had agreed to do the best she could but she was not one to splurge unnecessarily.

However, she did buy some things that were more wants than needs. The most expensive of them all was the metallic blue Toyota Corolla that she drove home one afternoon which drove her children wild. Much to her expectation, Charles was the only disgruntled one, grumbling over the cost of the car. Later that night Rose Marie told him that he could continue to use their old broken down station wagon if he were not pleased with their new vehicle. He then muttered something about wasting money before marching out of their bedroom.

Nevertheless, her children could not be happier. Their beaming faces, bursting with joy were all she needed to see to maintain her own cheery mood. She took them on a shopping trip to Puerto Rico one weekend, and needless to say they had all come back loaded with bags; naturally, Andreide's and Chrystal's were the biggest.

Rose Marie too had gotten her share of new things, she had made sure of that. The first thing she treated herself to was a pair of sparkly diamond earrings which she had been longing to have. She could not remember the last time Charles had bought her jewellery; she was not even sure if the tiny diamond on her engagement ring was real. If she continued to wait on him, she would never get what she wanted. After twenty years of marriage he was not going to suddenly become generous. He was not going to change. She had to accept that fact.

Rose Marie covered her mouth as she yawned while reclining in the new armchair she had bought for her study. She had been at a book-signing the night before and had not returned home till late; she was now feeling the effects of sleep deprivation. Her new recliner invited her to take a nap, but thoughts of her even newer, soft, queen-sized bed offered a greater temptation. She sighed longingly as she dragged herself from the comfy chair and towards the door. She was glad it was Friday.

However, the phone rang, disrupting her movements. Reluctantly, wanting nothing more than to sleep, she answered the call.

"Hello, good morning."

"*Hello,*" a low, sweet-sounding voice replied. "Who is this?"

Rose Marie frowned. "*You* called my house. Who's speaking?"

A few seconds elapsed before the caller responded. "Is Charles there? I have to speak to him."

Rose Marie was now beginning to get annoyed. Who was this person? She did not know the voice but could tell that it was a woman. "Who is this?"

Again, the caller took her time in answering. "Are you Rose Marie D'Averette?"

Wary, Rose Marie replied cautiously. "Why?"

The caller chuckled. "Well, maybe I should talk to you too. You'll find out anyway. But your husband prefers we keep it a secret for now."

Rose Marie stiffened. What was this woman about? And how did she know her name or Charles? "Who are you?"

The caller laughed lightly. "Let's just say I'm representing someone who's been robbed of what is rightfully his ... legally his."

"What? What are you talking about? You must have the wrong number."

"How long have you been married to Charles, Rose Marie? What ... twenty years or so?"

Rose Marie paused. It was one thing for this person to know her name but she knew how long she had been married too? She looked at the phone's screen but the caller ID was blocked.

"Who is this?" she repeated.

The woman laughed.

"Look, if you don't tell me who you are, I'm going to hang up."

"You could have hung up already. But you're not going to because you're wondering who I am and how I know you and your husband. Am I right?"

Rose Marie was now extremely annoyed. "No. You're wrong." She hung up the phone. Who did that woman think she was? Rose Marie took a deep breath and exhaled. Jean had warned her about this though she had not taken her seriously. But did people really stalk psychologists?

She jumped as the phone rang again, shattering her thoughts. On an impulse, she grabbed it up. "Look, woman! I'm going to have this number traced and I'm going to call the police if you don't –"

"What? Tell you who I am?" The woman laughed again, a low, cold laugh. "You can go ahead but it won't do you any good."

Rose's Marie's jaw clenched. "What do you want?"

"Now that's a loaded question. But let's start with your husband. How's your marriage?"

"*What?*"

"Has Charles ever cheated on you?"

Rose Marie sputtered, caught off-guard by the question.

"Who the hell do you think you are asking me these kind of personal questions? What my married life is like is none of your business!"

She was just about to hang up when the woman responded with another question, which instead of irritating her, alarmed and confused her. "Do you remember 2003 – June 15th, 2003? Your wedding anniversary, right?"

Rose Marie's breath caught. She knew the date of their wedding anniversary? But what was more troubling was the memory of the year in question. She did not like thinking about it for it was one of the most upsetting moments of her life – the first and only wedding anniversary that Charles had not been present for, nor had he acknowledged.

"I'm sure you remember. How can you forget?" said the woman. "But do you remember the excuse your husband told you for not being there to celebrate your … memorable occasion?"

Rose Marie gripped the receiver tightly.

"Did he tell you he had a business trip? A business trip that suddenly came up out of nowhere just around the time when you two hit a rocky spot in your marriage? Have you ever thought about the coincidence of that meeting with your anniversary? I bet you have. I'm sure you're a smart woman. After all, you are a psychologist…."

"*Who – are – you?*" Rose Marie hissed.

The woman laughed. "I'm the business trip."

"*What?*"

"You heard me. You can't really believe that Charles had a business meeting, do you?" Her low, cold laugh resounded through the phone line. "You have to be an idiot to believe that."

"Excuse me? I don't even know who you are. How dare you call my home, insulting me and accusing my husband of absolute rubbish!"

"I'm not insulting you nor am I accusing your husband of anything. I'm simply stating the facts."

"Charles has never cheated on me."

"Oh, come on, woman. Stop playing the ignorant wife. You're in denial. You and I both know."

"I am *not* in denial. We may have had a rough patch in our marriage but we got through it and that's the past. What you're proposing is preposterous!"

"I have proof."

"I don't give a damn what proof you have! There's nothing you can say that will prove otherwise. Charles and I have always had a completely faithful marriage."

"Yeah? Well, we'll see how much *faith* you have in that belief pretty soon. I have physical proof that your husband has been unfaithful to you."

Rose Marie clutched on to the phone, her heart beat accelerating. "What are you talking about?" she uttered in one breath.

From the silence on the other end of the line, she could tell that the woman was smiling.

"Maybe I *should* tell you who I am. It might make things easier for when Charles decides to tell you himself."

Rose Marie held her breath, tense with anticipation. She dreaded hearing what the woman was going to say for she knew it could only be bad news. And she was right.

"My name is Latricia Davis. I'm your husband's ex-girlfriend and the main object of that so-called business trip. You know, the trip that you believed he went on for business and in fact, the only thing that kept him busy and working was me." She laughed bitterly. "Well, I bet you know what's coming next – the physical proof. And I'm not talking about sweaty sheets because I didn't keep those." She laughed again, sinisterly. "I'm talking about what I did keep." She paused. Then her voice took on an accusatory tone. "You husband knocked me up and now I think it's time I collect thirteen years worth of overdue child support."

Chapter 14

A group of five merry young people sang joyously as they sauntered through the streets of St. George. Actually, only three of them were singing. Andreide and Alisa exchanged an amused look as they watched the boys perform their song, each singing to his own tune.

"*Duncan's footballers are the best ...*" Tommy sang in his deepest baritone.

"*We kick our rivals from the east to the west ...*" Dominick supplied with a grin, glancing at Andreide.

"*Knock 'em down, knock 'em 'round, we never ever rest!*" Will finished with gusto.

They all laughed.

The boys had just finished playing a practice match against a visiting regional team and had won by two goals, much to their delight. They were euphoric and had decided to take a victory walk through town. Alisa had been interested in seeing the Duncan's team play again and had asked Andreide if she could accompany her to the match. Andreide had not minded and apparently neither the boys. They had even suggested the girls tag along with them. To Andreide's surprise, Alisa, who was usually shy around boys, agreed to go with them and seemed to be enjoying every minute of their company so far.

"So ladies," Tommy grinned at them as they crossed the street. "How'd you like our singing?"

"Oh, it was great!" Alisa piped up before Andreide could respond. "The way you guys rhymed – that was so poetic."

The boys laughed. Andreide shook her head and gave Alisa a 'Are you for real?' look.

"What about you, Andreide? Were we great too?" Will grinned at her.

Andreide raised an eyebrow. "I must have a hearing problem or something because all I heard was something like a trio of dying toads."

Dominick, Tommy and Will threw back their heads and laughed. Alisa grinned at them then playfully hit her friend. "Andy, you're too mean. They weren't bad at all."

Tommy glanced at his two friends before grinning at Alisa. "Why thank you, darling. You're so nice. Come here." He reached out and pulled her to him, draping an arm around her shoulders. He kissed her on the cheek. Alisa giggled, shooting a quick glance at Andreide who raised an eyebrow and grinned at her.

"Heh hey, Tommy! What's this?" Will teased. "You see this, Dominick?"

"Oh, yeah." Dominick grinned before turning his gaze to his girlfriend. "Which reminds me …" He stopped and took Andreide's hand, pulling her into a close embrace. Andreide looked up at him with slight surprise on her face.

"Dominick! What the –"

He cut off her last words as his mouth met hers in a sweet kiss.

"Woohoo! Go, D!" Will cheered. Tommy and Alisa also stopped to watch them.

Andreide's heart pummelled against her ribs as Dominick kissed her; she was sure he could feel it too. As he pressed her closer to him, quickening her breathing and sending familiar sensations shooting through her body, she became painfully aware of the three people staring at them. She quickly pulled back.

"Dominick! Wh-What are you doing?" She chuckled nervously. Alisa's eyes were wide in amazement as she looked at her.

Dominick grinned. "Kissing you."

"But not in public in front of *everybody!*" she squeaked.

Dominick chuckled. "Why not? They know we're together. It's not a secret how I feel about you. And these guys don't mind, do you boys?"

"No, no! Of course not."

"Don't stop 'cause of us."

Andreide rolled her eyes. She shoved Dominick good-naturedly, who laughed and grabbed hold of her hand.

Ten minutes later, as they were heading into the centre of town, Tommy's cell phone rang. After he answered it, he grinned at his companions. "Guess what, guys? My folks are out for the weekend. Who wants to hang out at my place? Gordon's gonna pick us up on Green Street."

"Sweet, dude! I'm game. PS4 time!" Will punched the air with his fist.

Andreide looked at Dominick who gave her a slightly calculating look that she could not quite read.

"D? Coming, pal?" Tommy asked.

Dominick shook his head. "Sorry, Tommy. Not now. I promised Andy I'd show her my house ... today."

Andreide glanced up at him, slightly confused. She was about to question him when he squeezed her palm then gave her a quick discreet wink. She tried not to smile as she suddenly understood. He wanted to be alone with her, she was sure of it. She had had the same desire ... especially after that kiss.

Tommy nodded at Dominick before turning to Alisa, who was still by his side even after he had released her. Tommy nudged her gently and smiled. "How about you, miss? Wanna see my pad?"

Alisa noticeably blushed then nodded. Andreide stared at her in shock. She agreed? Alisa?

"Uh, Alisa," Andreide began cautiously. "You sure you want to go? I mean, these guys are PS4 freaks, you know."

The boys laughed. "Don't worry. We'll find other games to play." Tommy grinned.

That was what she was afraid of. Plus, Alisa did not even know those guys.

"Well, that's settled," said Will. "Come on, guys. I can't wait to beat you at FIFA Tommy."

"Yeah, right! You wish." Tommy grinned. "Come on, Dominick, Andreide. I'll have my brother drop you guys off one time. That alright with ya?"

Dominick glanced at Andreide, who smiled shyly at him. He looked over at his friend and nodded. "Oh yeah, that's fine."

*

It took about fifteen minutes before they arrived at number fourteen, Girard Avenue, Lindale. After she gave Alisa a significantly warning look, Andreide followed Dominick on the most elaborate tour she had ever been on. His house was three storeys tall, excluding a basement and an attic. She was stunned from the moment she set foot in the huge, marble-floored entrance hall.

Dominick led her through every room, pointing out certain features of interest before leading her to another room which astounded her even more than the previous one. Never before had she seen a kitchen so large and well-organized, nor a dining room so magnificently decorated. There were crystal chandeliers in almost every room on the first floor – the hugest of them all sparkled majestically above the foyer.

By the time Dominick showed her the attic then ended the tour at his bedroom, Andreide was overwhelmed.

Dominick grinned. "Pretty big, huh?"

"Are you kidding? It's enormous! I've never seen a more fabulous house. Wow! This place is *amazing*."

Dominick smiled modestly. "It is kind of spectacular, isn't it? A bit too much if you ask me." He gazed around. "Well, anyway. Here we are. This is my bedroom." He opened the door revealing a spacious, blue-carpeted room.

Andreide stepped into his bedroom and took it all in with as much amazement as she had with the rest of the house. Even though his room was not as fancy as the others, it had a regal touch that was impressive all the same. After a few minutes, she turned to face the room's inhabitant.

"Dominick ... wow," she said in awe. "I can't believe you live here. I love your house. It's more of a palace than a house really."

Dominick chuckled.

"And your room is amazing! It's stately but it has more of your touch to it."

Dominick grinned. "Thanks. But when you say my touch –" He wrapped his arms around her, reeling her in towards him, "– what exactly do you mean by that?" He gave her a devilish grin. Andreide felt her heart leap to her throat. His honey coloured eyes kept her gaze, drowning her in their sweetness.

Andreide swallowed. "I ... I ... don't know."

Dominick arched an eyebrow. His handsome face smiled down at her. "You don't know? You don't know your own boyfriend's touch? That's a crying shame, Andy. We have to do something about that. Right now, in fact."

Before she could respond, he pulled her tightly against him. She inhaled sharply a second before his lips descended unto hers, more forcefully than he had ever kissed her before. The eager force of his mouth on hers sent shivers down her limbs; she felt an odd sense of weakness.

His hands roamed her body as he kissed her – gliding up and down her back and along her sides. Her pulse raced as his fingers brushed the side of her breast through her t-shirt. Her heart hammering madly, she clutched to him. But he suddenly pulled back, abruptly ending the kiss.

She opened her eyes to his gaze, now heated with the desire she felt mirrored in her own eyes. Just as she felt like her legs were about to collapse, Dominick bent and swooped her up and carried her over to his bed.

"Dominick," Andreide murmured, her eyes half closed as he laid her on his king-sized mattress. Her heart pounded as she gazed at him standing next to the bed; he was by far the most gorgeous guy she had ever laid eyes on. As he slowly smiled at her, making her heart flip crazily, it was then she realised that she was completely in love with him. She felt her eyes moisten.

Dominick lowered himself over her, placing a jean-clad leg on either side of her as he eased himself onto the bed. Andreide waited with bated breath as he hovered over her face, longing to feel his lips on hers again. But instead of kissing them with the passion of before, he stroked her lips softly with the tips of his fingers.

"You are so beautiful, Andreide," he whispered. She all but melted. Dominick kissed her cheek tenderly then kissed a trail down her neck, leaving each spot tingling from his touch. Andreide moaned as she felt the warmth of his mouth against her shoulder. He retraced the path up her neck, teasing her skin with his lips and breath. He gently nibbled along her jaw and she gasped.

"Dominick ... I ... I ..."

His mouth found hers, silencing her murmurs. His tongue flickered tentatively along the line of her mouth, leaving an enticingly moist trail on her skin. Instinctively, she parted her lips inviting him in. His tongue met hers creating new, pleasurable sensations. Andreide moaned. She had never been kissed like that before.

All too soon, he eased back and looked down into her eyes. "So ... do you know my touch now?"

A slow, mischievous smile spread across Andreide's lips. She ran her finger down the bridge of his nose. "I think so. But I'm not all that sure ..."

"Oh, yeah? Well, someone needs more demonstration." With an equally teasing smile, he resumed their kiss with renewed fervour.

Andreide felt like her heart would explode as Dominick's hand slid down her body. He lingered for a few seconds at her breasts before continuing down to her stomach. She gasped in shock as his other hand slithered over her jeans, over her hips and up and down her thighs. But the playful smile at his lips reassured her of his intentions.

"How about now? Or do I need to demonstrate further?"

Andreide shook her head. "No. I'm sure I know your touch now."

"Damn. I was hoping you would need more convincing."

Andreide laughed and wrapped her arms around his neck. He leaned down and kissed her cheek noisily. She giggled as his lips strayed to her ear, nibbling her earlobe, making her squeal. "Dominick! Stop that!"

He looked at her and grinned. His expression contained such warmth, that she felt like melting in his arms. She sighed.

Dominick looked at her carefully. "Andy, what's wrong?"

She smiled softly. "Nothing. It's just ... I ..." She sighed and looked away.

"What is it?"

Her eyes flickered back to his. Seeing the look of deep concern in his gaze, her heart beat faster. She had to tell him.

"I love you, Dominick. I love you."

His look of anxiety was quickly replaced by the soft, glowing smile spreading across his lips. "I love you too, Andreide. So much. I've been meaning to tell you for a while now."

"Really?" she asked, her voice higher than usual.

Dominick nodded. A blush crept up his cheeks as he gave her a bashful smile. "I really do. Now I can give you this." He eased off her and reached under his bed. Andreide sat up, watching him curiously as he dug under the bed. He emerged a few seconds later with a small, blue velvety box.

"I had to hide it where Nick wouldn't find it," he chuckled sitting up. He smiled at Andreide as he extended it to her. "I was trying to find the best moment to give this to you but I think there's no better time than the present."

Andreide's expression was full of curiosity as she took the box from him. She could not help comparing its size to that of a jewellery box which usually contained an engagement ring. And she suddenly felt excited. But ... it couldn't be. Her heart pounded as she quickly looked up at him.

"Open it," he urged her quietly.

Her fingers shook slightly as she did so. She bit her lip and held her breath, then slowly opened the box. A gold ring shone up at her and she gasped. It held a single red gem in the shape of a heart, embedded between a cursive 'D' and 'A'. She traced her fingers over the engraving, staring at the sparkling red jewelled heart.

Dominick's voice was soft. "I wanted to give you something that would remind you of me and my feelings for you. Jewellery was the most valuable thing I could think of."

Andreide tore her eyes away from the ring and looked up at him. Her eyes were filled with the love she felt for him. "Dominick, it's so beautiful. I love it."

He exhaled in relief then smiled. "Good. I had a hard time deciding which ring to get you until Mum suggested I personalise one. May I?" He indicated the box. She nodded and gave it to him. "Now, which finger would you like it on?"

Andreide smiled. "You choose."

"Alright." He removed the ring from the box. He frowned thoughtfully before taking her right hand. He slid it gently unto her fourth finger. It fit perfectly.

"Wow. It's just the right size. How did you know?"

He shrugged. "Took an average. I reckoned you were about a size below Mum." He smiled. "And I was right."

"Yes, you were. It's so incredibly beautiful, Dominick. You shouldn't have. It must have been expensive."

Dominick took her hand and kissed her finger sparkling with the ring. "Nothing's too expensive for you, baby."

Andreide's heart felt like bursting for the umpteenth time that afternoon. She never knew she could feel love so strong for anyone. But Dominick wasn't just anyone – he was the love of her life.

Her eyes filling with tears, she leaned forward and kissed him tenderly.

*

Andreide had never had a happier day. After giving her the ring, Dominick had showed her around his room. When she caught sight of a childhood picture of him on his dresser, she had asked him to see his baby pictures. He had been reluctant but was easily persuaded by her pleading smile. They then spent the next half an hour looking through his photographs.

While they were looking at pictures of Dominick's eleventh birthday party, his door swung open and in bounced a boy with big, black curly hair. His mouth fell open and his eyebrows shot up into his curls as he stared at Dominick and Andreide lying on the bed. He covered his mouth and giggled, still standing in the doorway.

Dominick shut the album and quickly got up from the bed. His expression was more of annoyance than anger at being interrupted. Andreide also got up as he walked over to the boy.

"Nick! What did I tell you about knocking?"

The boy gave an apologetic shrug. However, his expression was far from contrite. "Sorry, Dominick. The door wasn't locked. I didn't think you were busy."

"Well, I am. Whether my door is locked or not isn't the point. You always knock. Can't you see I have company?"

Nick shot a glance at Andreide and grinned. "Is she your girlfriend?"

Dominick frowned. "Yes, but that's none of your business. Now, can I help you with something or did you just come to spy on me?"

"Oh, right. SpongeBob is starting and I was wondering … if you wanted to watch it with me?"

Andreide stifled a chuckle. Dominick watched SpongeBob? She grinned at him as he gave her an awkward, apologetic smile.

"I … I don't really watch SpongeBob, you know. It's just when Nick has it on and I'm sitting there and –"

"It's ok, Dominick." Andreide chuckled. "It's funny and lame but I watch it sometimes. I just find it amazing that you watch it too. Sort of relieving, actually."

Dominick's look of embarrassment faded slightly. He smiled and shook his head as he turned back to his brother. "Well, sorry Nick, I can't. Unless Andreide wants to –"

"Oh, I don't mind," Andreide said. She walked over to Dominick and placed her hand on his arm. "Do you, Dominick?" She looked into his eyes with a smile sweet enough to melt his heart.

"No, no. Of course not," he replied at once. He gazed at her with an expression so cute, she would have kissed him if his brother had not been there staring up at them.

Nick grinned. "Good." He tapped Andreide on the arm. Slightly surprised, she looked down at him. "Hi. My name is Nicholas Michaels but everybody calls me Nick. I'm ten but I'm much smarter for my age. I'm glad you're my brother's girlfriend. You seem pretty nice."

Andreide laughed lightly, slightly taken aback by the boy's forthrightness. "Hey, Nick. I'm Andreide D'Averette but you can call me Andy. Thanks for the compliment. You're not so bad yourself. And really cute too. I love your big dark curls!" She playfully tussled his hair.

Nick blushed. He glanced up at Dominick before lowering his gaze and smiling shyly. "Thanks. Follow me, please." He took Andreide's hand and started down the hall to the stairs.

As she was being led away, Andreide looked back at Dominick, who appeared amused. She mouthed the words, "He's so sweet!" Dominick shook his head and whispered, "If you only knew...."

*

Andreide tried not to giggle as Dominick's hand slowly slid up her thigh. She kept her eyes focussed on the screen in front of her and firmly removed his hand, placing it on the cushion between them. She heard him chuckle.

"Hahaha! That was really funny, wasn't it? Patrick is such an idiot!" Nick laughed.

"Uh, yeah." Dominick glanced at his brother, who was lying on the rug in front of the television before returning his attention to his girlfriend. He swiftly tossed the cushion separating them aside then shifted closer to her. He caught her eye and flashed her a mischievous, boyish grin.

Andreide bit back her smile as she looked at the television again. Dominick pretended to yawn widely, then placed his arm surreptitiously on the sofa behind her head. He grinned as she shot him a quick glance before looking away.

"Hey," he whispered.

She looked, and he leaned in quickly and kissed her.

"Dominick!" Andreide whispered, pushing him back. "Stop. Your brother is right in front of us!"

He grinned. "So what? Nothing can distract him from that nonsense. Want to see?" He took her chin and kissed her again, this time lightly tickling her neck.

She grabbed his fingers and pulled back. "Dominick, stop." She giggled. She glanced nervously at Nick who still lay rooted to the spot in front of the screen.

"See?" Dominick grinned. "He wouldn't care for anything. Now, do we have to watch this or can we go back upstairs and continue where we left off?" He moved nearer and nuzzled her neck.

Andreide stifled a giggle and edged back. As much as she loved to say yes, she was not sure how far they would end up going if they did go back to his room. And she was not sure if she was ready for that. As she was about to respond, her cell phone vibrated in her pocket, making her jump.

Dominick watched her as she took it out and read the text message. She frowned as she stared at the screen.

"What is it?" he asked.

"It's my cousin. She says something's up with my parents. I think I should go see what's going on."

"What do you mean? As in they're having a row or something?"

"I don't know. I have to go." She placed her cell phone back into her pocket then faced him. She sighed as she saw the concern in his expression which had replaced the good-humour he wore only a few seconds ago. She touched his cheek.

"I'm sorry, darling. We've been having such a great time and I hate for it to end so soon, but I have to go. I don't know what could be happening at home – Chrystal didn't explain. I just hope it isn't really bad."

"It's alright, babe. I hope it's not anything bad too." He got up. "I'll call our driver, Prakash, to give you a ride."

"You're coming for the drive too, right?"

He smiled. "Of course."

*

Chrystal was waiting at the backdoor when Andreide arrived. She ushered her in and Andreide bombarded her with questions.

"What's going on? What do you mean by they're 'at it'? What happened?"

"Shhh!" Chrystal placed a finger on her lips as she beckoned her cousin to follow her to the kitchen. "I think yuh father cheating on yuh mother."

"What?" Andreide said in disbelief. "You lie!"

"Shhh! Tantie Rosie in there on the phone with him. She say something 'bout some woman and a trip."

"Wait, wait, wait. She's on the phone? I thought they were both here."

"No. But he's coming now anyway." Chrystal peeped out of the kitchen window. "He just reach. Trouble now!"

Andreide looked at her and frowned. What was she talking about? Her parents were arguing over 'some woman and a trip'? What did that mean? What was going on?

Chrystal grabbed her arm and pulled her to the adjoining kitchen door leading to the living room. The door was slightly ajar and they peeped through it. They could see most of the living room before them; Andreide watched with slight trepidation as her mother's angry face came into view. They heard the front door shut seconds before her father made his appearance.

"Wait, Rosie. Before you say anything, please don't be mad." Charles held up his hands in a pleading fashion. He made an attempt to reach out to her but she pulled away abruptly. "Rosie, dear …"

"Just drop the act, will you. And tell me what the hell is going on!"

"Rosie, you're angry."

"Great observation, Einstein! Of course I am angry. How do you expect me to be after some woman, claiming to be your lover, called my house to tell me that you are the father of her child?"

"But Rosie, I told you that's not true. She must have me mistaken with somebody else."

"No! How could she when she knows who you are and who I am and she knows things about us, Charles. She knows the date of our anniversary. She knows about 2003, Charles! Why don't you explain that one!" Rose Marie glared at him.

Charles seemed to falter. "Ah ... 2003?"

"Oh, don't tell me you forgot. Don't tell me you forgot the year when you left me alone with our two little children to go on some supposed 'business trip' ... the day before our wedding anniversary! And you didn't even have the consciousness to call! Charles, how could you forget that?"

Her husband sighed and dropped his briefcase. "Rosie, please. I thought we were over that. That was so long ago. I told you I was sorry, didn't I?"

"That's not the point, Charles. You just upped and left. You knew how important anniversaries and special occasions are to me but you still left without a care."

"But I did care, Rosie!"

"No, you did not! How could you care when you went off to be with that woman!"

"It was a *business trip*," Charles insisted.

"Don't give me that shit!" she shouted. "It wasn't a damn business trip, you liar! Don't give me that."

"Rose Marie —"

"I wanted to believe you that it really was business related. I wished it was so, so badly. As much as I tried to convince myself that you were telling me the truth, deep down, I knew you were lying. And that woman calling and saying what she did, only deepened my belief that I was right all along. You cheated on me on our wedding anniversary." Rose Marie's eyes were glistening with tears. "How could you, Charles?"

The ticking of the kitchen clock vibrated through Andreide's bones as she stared in utter shock at her parents through the crack of the door. This could not be happening, Andreide thought. Maybe her parents were really just practising for a play or something. It must be that. There was no way that the scene in front of her could be real.

Charles looked around at nearly every object in the room before summoning the strength to look at his wife's aggrieved face. "What do you want me to say, Rosie?"

Rose Marie all but screamed. She bit back her mounting rage as the first tear rolled down her cheek. She wiped it away angrily.

"I deserve the *truth*. Tell me the truth now, Charles, as late as it may be and as heart-wrenching as it might be. I want to know ... now."

Charles looked away with a pained, indecisive expression on his face.

"Damn it, Charles, tell me! You owe me that much!" Her voice shook as she spoke.

"I ... I don't know what to say."

Rose Marie swore. She turned from him for a moment before facing him again. Her eyes were dark, shimmering with anger and pain.

"Tell me you didn't meet that woman for more than cocktails. Tell me you didn't sleep with her. Tell me you didn't father her child on the day of our bloody anniversary."

A few seconds passed.

And then he nodded meekly. "I did. I'm so sorry, Rosie, I did."

Wordlessly, arrested by the turmoil of her mottled emotions, Rose Marie sank unto a nearby couch.

Andreide stared in disbelief. Her heart rate rapidly increased as the meaning of her father's words began to sink in.

"Rosie, please!" he said. "I didn't mean for it to happen. You know we were arguing and having a rough time back then. I needed to escape – I needed a break! I had to leave before either of us did anything we'd regret!"

Rose Marie stared at him, her mouth slightly apart, stunned.

"Please, Rosie, believe me!" he continued. "I didn't mean to meet up with her in Antigua. I was at a bar and Latricia just happened to be there too. We talked and I ended up telling her about our problems. She acted like she cared and I really needed someone to give me some kind of support."

Rose Marie found her voice. "And her kind of support was just the kind you needed, right? You had to screw her for comfort."

Charles recoiled. "Rose Marie, please. You have to believe me. I didn't mean for it to happen. I was just caught up in it all. I had too much to drink and the next thing I knew I was ..."

Rose Marie raised an eyebrow. "Yes? Go on, say it! Don't tell me it's easier done than said."

Charles sighed, defeated. "Things got out of hand. I regret ever going to meet her."

"So you did go to meet her! I knew it! All you have ever said to me were lies. Just *what* is the truth, Charles?" She was back on her feet as she glared at her husband.

"I'm telling you the truth now."

"Oh, really? Well, since you're on a truth parade why don't you answer the other question. Is that child yours?"

He paused before answering. "I don't know."

"What do you mean, you don't know? He's yours, isn't he? She said you knocked her up!"

"But that can't be!" Charles denied. "I ... I used protection." He looked away.

Rose Marie glared at him. "You used protection? What, is that supposed to make me feel better? What were you hoping against? Knocking her up or contracting STDs? Because as you can see, you failed big time. You did knock her up and God only knows what disease you got from that whore."

"Rose Marie, stop it." He spoke sternly. "You're overreacting."

She clenched her fists in rage.

"I'm what? How dare you make such a comment? How dare you! After what you've put me through? What kind of a beast are you?" she cried. "I am your *wife!* You cheated on me, sleeping with your ex-girlfriend on our *wedding anniversary* and you got her pregnant and now you're denying being the father. You left me with our two infants so *you* could relax away from it all on your little … sex-capade. And you have the nerve to tell me I'm overreacting? Apart from the fact that you were unfaithful, you risked not only our marriage but the lives of our children, bringing your sinful body back into this house with whatever disease you might have contracted. Did you ever stop to think of that? Of course not, you selfish *bastard!*"

Rose Marie cried before turning and storming out of the room.

Charles hurried after her, catching her at the foot of the stairs. "Rose Marie, please! Listen to me." He reached for her hand but she yanked it away.

"Don't you touch me, Charles! Never again. And to hell with whatever you're going to say. I'm through listening to your lies!" She turned and started up the stairs, pounding each one with her fury. But as she reached the last stair, she turned and looked down at a man who seemed to have shrunken in more than body size.

"And if you think you're taking any of my hard-earned money to pay that bitch child support, you better think twice."

The slamming of the bedroom door signalled the end of more than a conversation.

Andreide slid to the floor, her eyes wide and unblinking; her heart was hammering uncontrollably, and her limbs were lifeless with shock. She did not know what affected her more – her father's adultery and subsequent illegitimate child, or her mother's uncharacteristic reaction. She could not believe what she had just witnessed and prayed to God that it was not true. But as much as she prayed and hoped, she couldn't lessen the growing unease building within her. An unease that brought a mixture of fear, confusion, anxiety, and anger to the surface of her soul.

Chapter 15

Andreide never recalled having a more terrible weekend. Never had she before felt so confused and helpless as she listened to her parents' constant arguments. When they hadn't been arguing, they were either out of the house or barricaded in separate rooms – her mother in her study and her father in their bedroom. Andreide wanted so badly to talk to her mother about it but she could not find the right moment; she also didn't really know what to say that would not upset Rose Marie further. Her mother was in pain and it was all her father's fault.

Andreide felt a surge of resentment for her father as she told her friends the news on Monday.

They stared at her in shock, their mouths hanging open. Their lunches lay forgotten on their desks in front of them.

"Gyul, yuh kidding!"

"Andy, please tell us you're joking."

"Are you serious, girl?"

"No, you think. Why would I make this up?" Andreide's voice was edgy. "You think I just go about saying that my father is an adulterer to get attention?"

"No, girl. We're just shocked, you know that." Harietta gave her a concerned look. "How are you holding up?"

Andreide gave her an irritated look. "How do you think?"

"But Andy," Alisa said. "You could've called us to talk."

"Yeah, well, I didn't feel like talking. Things weren't exactly fine and dandy at home. Calling you girls wasn't the first thing on my mind."

Keisha shook her head. "Man, ah still can't believe that one. Yuh father cheating on yuh mother wit' he ex? And he got a chile with she? Lawdamercy!"

"Yeah, he cheated. But I don't know if he still is. I heard my mother ask him about that but he said he hasn't been with the woman or anybody else since. But I don't know. I never thought he was capable of cheating on her. I never even thought about it. He's just so dead and boring! But now that he has, I wouldn't put it past him that he isn't. He's capable of anything now, the scumbag."

Alisa exchanged a worried glance with the two girls. "You hate him, Andy?"

Andreide rolled her eyes. "Well, of course I do! You expect me to like him after what he's done! That man cheated on my mother and has the nerve to be quarrelling with her when he should be on his knees begging for forgiveness! She's just too good a person – if I were her, I woulda killed him!"

Andreide breathed hard as she fumed. She did not think she would have felt this angry when recalling the events of the weekend. Her friends looked at her with sympathy in their eyes. After a while, Harietta spoke up.

"Andy, I can't say I know how you feel 'cause I don't. I never knew my father and my mother hasn't been married as far as I know. I can only imagine what you must be feeling but I want you to know that I'm here for you, girl. We got your back."

"Yeah, Andy. We're here for you," said Alisa. She reached out and touched her friend's hand.

Andreide smiled. But before she could thank them, Keisha steupsed.

"Well, all you two got life good, eh? Ain't had no real problems in yuh family." She shook her head. "Y'all blessed. I done been through it all. Back when I wasn't living with Granny, it was hell with me mother and father see. He always was never home and when he used to come back me mother used to throw him out. I could still remember all the women she used to accuse him 'bout being with. And I know it was true 'cause I used to see him bring all kinda woman in the house when me mother wasn't there. So I know all about it." She paused. "But then is not like I grew up with him so I wouldn't really feel it like you do. But anyway, gyul. If I was you, I wouldn't ah jus' kill him. I woulda chop off he balls and roast them, then let him dead slowly."

"Keisha!" Harietta exclaimed. "Chile, you got serious problems you know. How you could say that?"

"Well, is true," Keisha replied. "I woulda do just that!"

Alisa stared at her in a mixture of horror and disbelief.

Andreide laughed. Keisha could always speak her mind. However, her laughter was short-lived.

"Well, well, well. Surprised to see *you* in a good mood." The girls turned to see Shauna and her usual followers approach their desks. "Shouldn't you be crying somewhere?" the malicious girl asked Andreide.

"You will be if you don't shut up and buzz off!" Keisha countered.

"Tsk tsk, what a shame." Shauna continued, ignoring Keisha. "Yuh perfect family ruined now, eh?"

"Gyul, ah beg you don't –"

"What are you talking about?" Andreide said hastily giving her an annoyed look.

Shauna laughed. "As if you don't know. Yuh father stepping out on yuh mother. He got a chile by another woman – his ex too, imagine that."

"You won't have to imagine this fist that gonna smash into yuh face if you don't get lost!" Keisha threatened.

A nerve ticked in Andreide's head. How could she know that? She had not been around just now when she was telling her friends, so how could she know?

"Do you actually want something, girl?" Harietta stared at Shauna.

She laughed. "I'm just surprised that this gyul here ain't bawling down the place."

"And why would I do that?" Andreide sneered.

"'Cause yuh perfect little life is over, that's why." Shauna smirked. "Yuh *daddy* an' yuh *mommy* are fighting 'cause he slept with his ex and knocked her up. Now, y'all all upset, ent it?"

"How the hell do you know that?" Andreide glared at her, feeling the beginnings of anger bubble in her veins.

The girl laughed. "It's not like they was trying to keep it quiet. Anybody passing on yuh street coulda hear them shouting at each other and it happen me mother was visiting nearby and she hear it all."

Andreide clenched her jaw as the girl laughed.

Harietta quickly intervened. "Look, girl. Why don't you just go away before you cause any trouble? Andreide doesn't need to hear from you right now." She shot Keisha a warning look.

"Hmmm. Well, alright then. Since you ask nice." Shauna grinned. "But before I go, tell me. How it feel to have another brother? What, that's three now, right?"

"He's not my brother," Andreide said, gritting her teeth.

"Oh, yes he is. And how's yuh mother dealing with that? She in denial too? I bet she never saw that one coming – she wit' she big smart job."

"Don't you dare say anything about my mother!" Andreide snarled.

"Shauna, stop it! Go away!" Alisa implored.

"I bet she still wondering how that happen to her and she happy lil family. Wha' you t'ink, Meesha?" She turned to the stooge on her left. The girl laughed and agreed. "But, Teeky, wha' you t'ink?" She turned to the other one. "You t'ink she gonna pay she man woman child support?" All three of them cackled.

Anger licked her insides and her blood boiled with rage as Andreide glared at their mocking faces, laughing at her, taunting her, trying to humiliate her. That was it. Faster than the speed of light, she was off her chair and flying at Shauna's neck. The momentum of her lunge knocked them both to the floor; Andreide pinned her down as she scratched and clawed at every part of the girl she could put her hands on.

"Andreide, no!"

"Ahhh! Get her off me! Oww! Help!" Shauna screamed, kicking and flapping in vain to free herself from the onslaught. But Andreide refused to budge. She scratched, punched and slapped her with blind fury.

"Get her, Andy! Scrab out she eye for me! Pinch her, pinch her!"

"Keisha, shut up! Andreide, stop it!"

"Andy!"

"Ayyeeee! Help me! Ahhhh! Stop, stop!"

Andreide felt a hand circle her arm, trying to pull her off the girl but she resisted, yanking away. Another hand tugged at her arm but she fought it off too. It was when about three or four pairs of hands simultaneously grabbed her that she felt like her head was going to explode with rage. She lashed out, not caring who received which blow.

"Andreide, stop it! Get up!" Harietta cried.

"Andy, please!" Alisa wailed. Her voice was full of anxiety.

But Andreide did not care. All she cared about was inflicting as much pain as she could on the girl lying beneath her, writhing and screaming in agony.

"What is this? Hey, stop that!" a deep voice commanded from the doorway.

All hands released Andreide and their pleadings were stifled as a sudden silence overcame them all. To her surprise, Andreide felt herself being bodily lifted off a cowering Shauna. Andreide stumbled as she was roughly replanted on the classroom floor. She looked up at the intruding force and the defiance she was ready to display vanished quickly; it was replaced by child-like fear as she recognised the forbidding, giant of a man, towering over her. It was their principal.

"Ms. D'Averette! Have you lost your mind?" Mr. Williams glared down at a scowling Andreide. "You two," He indicated to Shauna's cronies, "Help that child up and take her to the nurse. You –" He turned back to Andreide. "To my office." He turned and headed for the door, fully expecting that his instructions would be carried out.

Before following him to face her inevitable doom, Andreide glanced over at Shauna who was being helped to her feet. She felt oddly pleased. The girl was covered with scrapes and bruises; several of her scratches were bleeding. A devilish grin fleeted across Andreide's face as she saw the damage she had done. She felt satisfied. She could not wait for Shauna to try that again.

She shot one last look at the whimpering girl before walking out the door.

*

"Did he yell at you?"

"No."

"He whip you with Ledda Sergeant?"

"Hell, no! You crazy? He can't touch me."

"What? And he dish out that belt on me for bussing Jimmy face the other day?"

"Any threats?"

"Nope. Just a warning."

"Then … what did he do?"

Andreide laughed as her friends stared at her with a mixture of incredulity and curiosity. She had felt almost the same way after coming out of the principal's office. It was after school now and the girls had just gotten the chance to find out what had transpired.

"Well?"

"He just gave me a warning and told me I have to apologize to the girl." Harietta, Alisa and Keisha stared at her in shock. "Yeah, I know. I was surprised too. Couldn't believe he was letting me off so easy. He told me he had heard about my parents' problem – the fast man – and that he understood how I was feeling. Shocking, isn't it? But then he said I couldn't be expressing my anger like that and that it was unacceptable, blah blah. But then he said since it was my first offence, he would just give me a warning but if it happens again he'll have to punish me like everyone else."

"Wow," Harietta remarked. "I never thought that man had a single compassionate bone in his body. He must like you."

"Oh, please!" Andreide rolled her eyes, flicking her hand dismissively.

"But I got to say," Keisha grinned. "That was sweet how you scrab she up, man! You get she good, gyul. You make me proud see!"

Andreide laughed.

Harietta scowled. "That's nothing to be proud of! Keisha, you're hopeless. Andy could've gotten suspended for fighting that girl."

"Yeah, but she didn't. So what you going on for? How many times you will ever get to see we gyul, Andy beat up anybody, especially that bitch?"

Harietta sighed. "Whatever Keisha. I still think fighting that girl in school was too risky. Mr. Williams musta fallen hard on his head to let you get away with it."

Andreide shrugged.

"You're so lucky, Andy. I wish I had at least half of your luck," Alisa said wistfully.

"Lucky, what?" Keisha scoffed. "I bet Andreide jus' turn on de ole charm for him and had de ole man jaw dropping on the ground. That's how she get outta that one."

The girls laughed heartily.

When they were walking through the school gates, Keisha paused and turned as someone called out to her. It was her cousin, Jamila.

"Keeshy! Whey you been gyul? Hey all you."

Andreide, Harietta and Alisa nodded and mumbled their greetings as she came over. Keisha slapped her on the shoulder.

"Jam-Jam, I here, I here. Wha' happen?"

"Well ..." Jamila glanced at Andreide and from her look, Andreide was sure that she knew too. Jamila tried for a sympathetic look. "I hear 'bout your parents and gyul, ah sorry see. They did seem like a nice couple to me. But after all that, yuh mudda should t'row him out, see! That's what I would do, you hear. T'row he cheatin' ass out! He ain't deserve to stay, making child wit' a next woman."

Andreide was not sure how to reply so she just nodded. The girl seemed to be waiting for her to back it up but she did not feel like going through all that again. Harietta came to her aid.

"Yeah, Andy's real upset by it. It shocked all of us," she said. Alisa nodded.

"Well, gyul. When I don't feel good, I does try to distract meself and that's what you should do. One of me friend t'rowing a party Friday night and you should come, man. All of y'all should come. Down by Gungee Bar. It gonna be de bomb, man. We getting DJ and everyt'ing. So come and just relax and forget 'bout it for a while. Wha' you say?"

Andreide smiled. "Thanks. But I'll think about it."

"Yeah, well while you thinking, I'm gonna be there!" Keisha grinned. "You must see me there, gyul. Me and Harietta."

"Eh heh?" Harietta placed her hands on her hips. "Girl, speak for yourself. I have work to do."

"Wha' work?" Keisha watched her in disbelief.

"Schoolwork."

"Gyul, is the weekend it'll be. What work you talkin' 'bout?"

Harietta rolled her eyes. "Unlike you, some people use their weekends to study and get ready for exams. I know it might sound strange to you but people in fifth form shouldn't be going to parties when exams are just 'round the corner – in less than two months!"

"Alright, alright! You stay home then and study. I know I going to that party and have fun."

"Fine. Go ahead. I don't care. It's your life. When you fail your exams, go tell Mr. CXC is because you were partying. That might help."

Keisha and her cousin laughed. Andreide watched them and shook her head.

*

A bowl of half-eaten popcorn lay on the coffee table as an old black and white film played quietly on the widescreen HD television set. The couple sitting on the couch had long ago lost interest in the movie, but neither of them bothered to change it; what they watched was not important – being together was.

With her head resting on Dominick's right shoulder, and his arm around her, Andreide sighed peacefully as she gazed at the couple onscreen. Luckily that Saturday, Dominick's parents and little brother were not home, guaranteeing them privacy and full reign of the house. However, all they had been doing was watching movies which neither of them seemed to mind. Andreide was content doing just that.

Since the start of the week she had been waiting longingly for the weekend to arrive so she could be with Dominick. She did not know how she had gotten through the week without him. Her whole class now knew about her family's shame. Even though they had not been as bold as Shauna, their whispering and staring behind her back grew to an intolerable level. Before she lost her temper again, she had decided to call Dominick. And what comfort he had been....

On hearing his voice she had felt so much better. His words had soothed her almost as much as his presence had. That night, he spent almost two hours talking to her on the phone, even though they had school the next morning.

She had told him everything – all that her parents had said and done and her trials with school. She had expressed her feelings to him too, amidst tears of anger, worry and confusion. And through it all, he listened patiently, giving her all the advice he could that would ease her pain. He sounded so sweet and caring and even managed to make her laugh through her tears.

She smiled as she thought of this, gazing at his ring on her finger. She raised her head to look at him. His profile was so beautiful and she could not help staring at him.

"Dominick …" she whispered. He turned to her and she kissed him. He smiled, a faint blush colouring his cheeks.

"What was that for?"

"Thanks," she said softly. "Thanks for being there for me this week. I needed comfort and you gave it to me. I'm so glad I have someone like you. You're an angel. I don't know what I would've done without you."

"You mean besides beat up that girl?" he teased.

Andreide chuckled. "Yeah, besides that. You're such a blessing. And I love you for it and more."

Dominick stroked her chin before he replied, "I love you too, baby. I'm happy I helped you feel better. And I'll always be there for you, whenever you need me."

Andreide smiled then kissed him once more.

Chapter 16

"Darling, you must want something for your birthday," Rose Marie nearly pleaded. "You must!"

Her son laughed. "Mom. I told you – I don't want anything. I'm fine." Omarion reached for a book on the dining room table then dropped it into his backpack.

"But, love," Rose Marie said. "You must want *something*. It's your eighteenth birthday! That's a great milestone."

"Yeah, I know, Ma. But I really don't want anything. You've given me everything I've ever needed and all I could hope for." He smiled at his mother. "I really don't want a thing."

Rose Marie sighed softly as she studied her nearly eighteen-year-old son's face. It was hard to believe her first-born was now almost a man. In two days he would be legal – free of her protection. Free to join the real world. She sighed again at the thought.

However, as much as the thought saddened her, it made her quite happy as well. She could not be more grateful for having a son like him; she was even more proud for the young man he had grown to be. She blinked back tears.

"Mom? You alright?" Omarion watched her carefully.

She smiled and nodded. "I'm just so happy to see you all grown up. My little boy will be eighteen on Friday." She sniffed.

Omarion rolled his eyes but a smile tweaked at his lips. "Ma … it's nothing, really."

"Of course it's something! This is the end of your childhood darling and the start of a whole new phase of life. You're a man now. And I don't care what you say. I'm getting you something for your birthday. I must."

He sighed. "Ok, Ma. Ok." He glanced at his watch. "But I got to get to class before one." He winced. "And it's almost one." He slung his bag over his shoulders and gave his mother a sweet smile. "How 'bout a drop? Please, Mommy?"

Rose Marie laughed. She got up from the dining table and placed her dishes on the kitchen counter before meeting her son by the doorway. She took her keys from the rack and chuckled softly.

"What?" Omarion asked opening the door.

"Nothing. I just can't wait for you to get a driver's licence."

He grinned. "Me too, Mom. Me too."

*

Rose Marie paused as she opened the front door an hour later. She could have sworn that she had just heard voices inside. She looked back at the street and confirmed that the old station wagon was not there. So Charles was not home. Thank God, she thought as she pushed open the door and walked in, closing it behind her. She did not feel like being in the house alone with him as she knew her brother, Peter and Chrystal were at work. What she really wanted to do was spend the rest of the afternoon preparing for Omarion's birthday. She was planning to throw him a surprise party on Friday evening. She had just bought decorations and snacks, along with a few presents which were still in the trunk of her car.

She deposited her purse in the bedroom and was on her way down the stairs when she heard low murmuring coming from the living room. There was a clink of glass followed by a soft chuckle – a female, soft chuckle. The voice which spoke next was unmistakeably her husband's.

Rose Marie froze on the steps. He couldn't be as bold as to … No. She shook her head, compelling herself not to believe it. He could not be that bold or stupid. But he was. Rose Marie descended the stairs, crossed the hall and peered into the living room. She stood stock-still at the sight before her – a grinning Charles lounging on a sofa, sharing drinks with a plump, overly made-up woman, whose fat, red-coated lips stretched broadly across her round face. Latricia Davis.

"*What* is *this?*" Rose Marie's voice shook as she stared in disbelief at her husband and his ex-girlfriend.

Like children caught stealing, the culprits hastily looked up, their faces covered with guilt. Charles leapt to his feet, the contents of his glass almost spilling on the floor. But the woman was the first to recover, flashing on a wide, sickly smile.

"Well, *hello*. You must be Rose Marie," she said in her low, irritatingly sweet voice. Unlike her companion who was now on his feet, she remained seated. Seated in Rose Marie's favourite arm chair. Anger now took over her shock.

"What the hell is this, Charles?" She struggled to keep her voice at a controlled level.

The woman looked from Charles to Rose Marie before turning to Rose Marie. She pasted a broad, pretentious smile on her fleshy lips. Her large, dark eyes glinted with something that made Rose Marie as uneasy as she was angry.

"We haven't officially met. I'm Latricia Davis," the woman said smugly, giving Rose Marie a look that made her itch to slap her.

"Yes, I *know* who you are," Rose Marie said with irritation in her voice. "Charles, why is this woman in my house?"

Clearly uncomfortable, he looked from both women before taking a sip from his glass. He avoided his wife's heated gaze and cleared his throat before addressing her.

"Well, um. We had some things to discuss regarding … our situation. And … well, I didn't think you would be here."

"You didn't think I would be here?" Rose Marie repeated. "Where do you think I'd be, Charles?"

"But it's Wednesday! You're supposed to be at work."

"Well, in case you haven't realised, since I've finished my book I've been working at home."

"Oh. Right, well ..."

"Excuse me, Charles?"

Rose Marie looked sharply at the woman, still seated in her arm chair.

"Charles?" Latricia continued. "Maybe this isn't the best time. Maybe we should leave."

"What do you mean 'maybe'?" Rose Marie sneered. "You have some nerve being here."

"And what do you mean by that?" Latricia raised a well-shaven, pencil drawn eyebrow in a manner more challenging than inquiring.

"You know exactly what I mean."

"Really?" Latricia chuckled. "I don't see anything wrong with us being here. I was simply having a chat with your husband."

"My husband?" Rose Marie looked from her to Charles. "You're bold enough to refer to him in that way? Woman, have you no shame?"

"*Excuse* me?" Latricia placed her glass on the coffee table in front of her. She started to rise when Charles intervened.

"Please, let's not argue. Latricia, we'll finish this later –"

"Not in my house you will! I want you out, *now.*"

"Hmph! So much for hospitality. Charles, do something. She's *your* wife."

"How *dare* you? How dare you both? How dare you be in my house and speak in such a manner after what you've done to this family! You harlot!"

"What! Excuse me! You –"

The front door swung open then, causing them all to look hastily in its direction. Their argument halted midstream as Marques bounced in the door, a big smile on his face as he caught sight of his mother; she was the first person in his line of vision.

316

"Hey, Mom!" he sang out. "Guess what? School let off early 'cause of some big teachers' meeting. Calvin and I think it's 'cause of Ms. Rochester and how she's been sleeping in class this week. But then there was this big fat man who came stamping in the school at lunch time and said he wanted to see the principal. He looked like a mobster, Mom, I tell ya." Marques grinned as he dropped his schoolbag on the floor before kicking the door shut. "But anyway, school was alright. Didn't get any homework but I still have to finish that science project Mr. Adams gave us. Hey, Mom? Can I skip piano class today? My hands feel kinda weak from practising that Chopin piece yesterday and Ms. Giuliani will be mad if I don't play it like '*Monsieur Chopin*' himself." He rolled his eyes and grinned. "Mom, I think I'll be better off not playing the piano. Ms. Giuliani is too demanding. Just because I got a distinction in the eighth grade practical exam she thinks she could play me like a banjo, like I'm some super genius. You know she actually called me 'little Ludwig' once?"

Marques paused as he caught sight of his mother's expression. His grin quickly faded as he walked nearer and saw the tense faces of his father and the woman. "Mom, what's going on?" he asked tentatively. "Mommy?"

Rose Marie tried to summon a smile for her son but could not. Her anger and resentment for the two people standing close by overpowered all efforts to remain composed.

Charles cleared his throat. "Marques go to your room. We're having a private talk."

Rose Marie made to respond but stopped herself. Her son's confused gaze shifted from one tense face to the other.

"But –"

"Ooo!" Latricia took a step forward. "Is this the little one?" She glanced at Charles who barely nodded, a grim expression on his face. She leaned forward and grinned broadly. "Hi, sugar. My, aren't you cute! I'm aunty Latricia."

A flare of anger blazed through Rose Marie at the sight of the licentious woman near her child. Enraged and disgusted, Rose Marie reached out and grabbed Marques' hand, pulling him to her side. "Don't you talk to my son, woman! It's bad enough you're in my house as it is. Don't you dare have anything to do with my children!"

Latricia's broad grin seemed to stick on her false face as she straightened up to face Rose Marie. She chuckled menacingly. As she was about to reply, approaching footsteps attracted their attention and they all turned to look at the stairs.

A small bodied, skeletal-looking, big-headed boy stared back at the four people in the living room through large, orb-like eyes. His expression-less face made him look even drearier in the drab, oversized t-shirt and pants that sagged on his bony frame.

"Momma," he croaked in a voice battling with puberty. "I alright now. But the toilet paper done." They all watched as he descended the stairs then walked over to his mother's side, the faint foul odour of his activities tailing him. He gazed at Rose Marie and Marques through his large, dead eyes before turning to address Charles. "Dad, is this your family?"

Rose Marie felt Marques grip her hand. "Did he just say 'Dad'?"

A slow, provocative grin stretched across Latricia's big face as she clamped a meaty hand on her son's bony shoulder. "Yes, Chucky. This is your father's family except the older two aren't here."

Rose Marie felt like she had just been hit with a sack of bricks. "*Chucky?* As in Charles? Did I hear right? You named him Charles?"

"Yes, that's right." Latricia smirked. "It's only fair to name him after the man who fathered him who hasn't been in his life for thirteen years. After all, they have so much in common – just look at them."

But Rose Marie did not want to look nor did she need to. There was no doubt that her husband was his father.

"Mom, what's going on? Why are they here?" Marques whispered quite audibly.

"Your *father* decided it was fitting to have a little get-together in our living room with his ex-girlfriend and son, that's what," Rose Marie replied.

"Rose Marie, please!" Charles implored. "Not in front of our son."

"Whose son? Hers or mine?"

"Rose Marie!" he raised his voice. "Don't. Not now."

"Not now? *Not now?* Yes now! It's now or leave! No. In fact, leave now. I want all three of you out of this house, right now! How dare you be here!"

"Rose Marie –"

"Get out. Get out of this house!"

"Woman, listen to me!"

"No, *man.* You listen to *me*! You get that woman and your bastard child out of my house and you follow them out too, this minute!"

"I will not –"

"Marques, go get me my phone."

"Look. Fine!" Charles turned to the two people next to him. "Latricia, I'm sorry. I'm going to have to catch up with you later." He started walking them to the door, brushing past his confused and worried son.

Rose Marie remained in the doorway to the living room. Her jaw clenched tighter as she heard the brazen woman say in her irritatingly syrupy voice, "Don't worry about *her*, Charles. I'll find us some time alone." Charles mumbled something then she replied with, "Yes, I know. See you soon, sugar."

Rose Marie refused to turn and see what else they exchanged. When Charles came back into the living room, his face was as livid as ever. She motioned for Marques to leave them but did not hear him climb the stairs.

"What the hell was that?" he growled as he turned to face her in the doorway.

"I should be asking *you* that, Charles!" she said just as angrily.

"What?"

"Stop pretending as if you don't know. How could you even think of bringing that woman into our house? And with her child. *Your* child! And apparently giving him full access to the house. What is the matter with you? Haven't you hurt me enough?"

Charles made an aggravated noise. "And what about me? This is my house too. I only wanted to discuss what we were going to do about the boy and thought that maybe it would be nice if he met the children – his brothers and sister."

"Oh, don't you come with that! Don't you link him with my children – our children. I don't want him or that woman anywhere near them! It's bad enough Marques had to witness that."

"Oh, please. You're being unreasonable. He's my child and he has a right to know who his brothers and sister are."

"So you're admitting he's yours now, eh? You're admitting you conceived a bastard child during our marriage."

"Yes! And I don't approve of you referring to him like that. His name is Charl – Chucky."

"Uh! Now don't get me started on that! I can't believe that woman had the audacity to name her illegitimate son after you. And you let her call him that too. In *here*. In front of *me.*"

"So what?" he nearly bellowed. "She's right! He never had me in his life so it was only right to name him after me. So he could know I'm his father."

"Argh!" Rose Marie cried out in frustration. "I don't *believe* this. You are – you are – the most insufferable, selfish, insensitive bastard I've ever known!"

"I'm not listening to this." He started towards the door.

"Yes, you are!" She marched after him. "Do you even know why I'm this upset?"

He turned to face her with an exasperated look. "What do you mean? You've only been bitching about it for the past half hour."

"Damn it, Charles! I'm talking about the significance of this week. Do you even know what Friday is?"

"What? The sixth. So what?"

"So what? So what? That's Omarion's birthday, that's what. Your son is going to be eighteen. But you don't care do you? You never care. Just like you never cared about anything that happens in this house. That's why we are in this mess!"

"Oh, so it's all my fault? You're blaming all of this on me?"

"Well, of course I am! Who else brought this on? Who was the one who went off and slept with that slut and knocked her up? Wasn't me now was it?"

Charles uttered an obscenity before abruptly turning away from his wife and yanking the front door open. Without another word or a backward glance, he stormed through the door, slamming it behind him.

With eyes filling with tears of pain, Rose Marie watched her husband's retreating figure through the glass panes of the door.

*

For the past hour that night, she had been talking to her mother, telling her of all her recent troubles and feelings. Her mother's words of comfort soothed her and for the first time in months, Rose Marie felt a strong surge of homesickness. She would give anything right now to be with her mother – the woman who could solve any problem. She needed her. But at that moment, from the pounding on her door, she was reminded that there were so many other people who needed *her* too. She sighed as she promised to call her mother back then hung up the phone.

Marques was standing at the door, his face stricken with fear and anxiety. Alarm quickly replaced Rose Marie's fatigue.

"Marky baby, what is it?"

"Mommy! Come quick! Daddy and Omarion – they're fighting!" His bottom lip trembled.

"What!"

"Come Mommy, come!" Marques turned and hurried off towards the living room, Rose Marie following anxiously behind him.

Charles and Omarion were standing in the middle of the room when they arrived, both males glaring at each other with open hostility; Omarion appeared to be the more incensed of the two. Rose Marie stared in alarm at their expressions.

"What's going on here?" she said.

Omarion kept his eyes locked on to his father. "I just found out what happened this afternoon and I wanted to make sure I heard Marques right. 'Bout that woman being here in our house – with her son. *His* son. How could you do that to us? To *Mom?*"

"Boy, you don't know what you're talking about –"

"Yes, I do know what I'm talking about!" Omarion shouted. "You brought that whore of your ex-girlfriend in here. And with your bastard child too! Man, what's going on inside your head?"

"Do not talk to me like that!"

"How could you think of something like that? You cheated on Mom with your ex-girlfriend, knocked her up and have the balls to let her into our home with your outside child – and without telling anybody? Man, you are one sick, selfish son-of-a-bitch."

"Omarion!" Rose Marie exclaimed.

"Boy! Don't you talk to me like that!" Charles roared. "You have respect for me, I am your father!"

"Hell, I don't give a *damn* who you are. You cheated on my mother and you're stupid enough to have proof to show for it. And that ain't all. You got us all messed up but you don't care. Mom is always upset and Andreide and Marques are distant and moody. Even Uncle Peter been staying out more to get away from all this.

But you don't care. You can't see nothing but yourself. Bet you can't even see the fact that that gold-digging bitch only come 'round now to try and take Mom's money. You thought 'bout that?"

A vein seemed about to burst in Charles' head; it pulsed furiously at his temple. "*Boy!*" His voice shook with rage. "How dare you talk to me like that?"

"I'll talk to you the way you deserve to be talked to," Omarion replied icily.

Charles took a step closer to his son, his face set stormily. "Boy, I am *this* close to letting you have it."

Omarion bared his teeth in a sneer as he too took a step towards him. Quite insolently, he looked his father up and down before uttering a soft threat. "Go ahead. Try it. But we'll see where that will get you."

Rose Marie looked on in fear as Charles raised a clenched fist. However, to her immense relief he slowly lowered it.

"Yeah ... thought so," Omarion sneered.

His father glowered at him. "You think because you're big like a man that you are a man, eh? You're only a child and I am your father. No matter what I am your father and always will be. You show me respect, boy!"

"I'll show you as much respect as you showed Mom, all of us – none! You have to give respect to get respect. And you're not getting none from me, regardless of who you are. You're only my father by title, nothing more. You've never been a real father to me or any of us anyway. The fact that you cheated on Mom, lied and got us all into this shit now stripped the little of anything I had for you. You're brave to even mention the word 'respect'." His gaze flickered from Charles to his mother then back again to the small man in front of him. Omarion growled, "I have *no* respect for adulterers." He paused, his facial muscles taut. "Which is why I'm moving out of here now. I'm not living with *you* anymore."

Rose Marie gasped. But she was not the only one to do so. Andreide and Chrystal were peeping by the entrance to the living room.

"Boy, what nonsense are you talking? You can't move out, you're a child."

"I'm not a child, I'm a man!" Omarion stated. "I'll be eighteen day after tomorrow. Whether I leave now or then, you can't stop me. I've been waiting for this day for so long but not under these circumstances."

"Omarion, please!" Rose Marie entered the room further. "Don't do this. Let's talk about this."

"No, Mom." He shook his head. "There is nothing to talk about. I've thought this through already and my mind is made up – I'm leaving. I'm not going to be tortured living in the same house with this man any longer."

"Honey, please!"

"No. I'm through with all of this." He started walking backwards. "It's either he goes or I go, and since his ignorant cheating ass ain't going anywhere, I'm leaving." He turned then before anyone could respond and left the room. Charles marched after him. Rose Marie followed.

"Boy, come back here!" Charles ordered, standing at the foot of the stairs where his son had dashed up. He turned to Rose Marie in frustration. "Well? Do something!"

Rose Marie bristled. "Just what do you expect me to do? You are the reason for all of this – you deal with it!"

Charles' scowl deepened but he remained silent. It was then Omarion started back down the stairs; he had a duffle bag in either hand. He was soon followed by Marques. Charles reached out and grabbed his forearm as he cleared the bottom step.

"Omarion, stop this nonsense! I'm warning you."

But his son did not listen. He yanked away from Charles as he headed for the door.

"Omarion, please! Don't go. Not now – it's dark. Where will you go?" Rose Marie looked at him pleadingly. Marques too looked up at him with eyes overflowing with tears.

With one hand on the doorknob, he turned and gave his mother a fleeting, tight smile. "Don't worry about me, Mom. I'll be fine. I'll call you later." He glanced at his sister and cousin standing nearby and at his brother then nodded in their direction. "You all take care of yourselves. Don't let this ass get to you too much."

"Boy!" Charles roared. He started towards him. "You leave this house, you're not coming back! You hear me?"

But Omarion did not respond. He shot his father one last glare before swinging the door open then slamming it shut behind him. And he was gone.

*

Rose Marie closed her eyes and exhaled slowly as the elevator ascended to the fifth floor. She had been trying to keep her emotions in check from the moment she woke up that morning, but now she felt tears threatening to fall as memories of last night's episode flooded her mind. She forced herself to remain composed as the elevator doors opened, welcoming her to the familiar fifth floor of Authentic Publishers.

"Rose Marie!" Jean came bustling out of her office as Rose Marie rounded the corner. "Hey, almost bumped into you. Can't seem to see straight today!" She chuckled distractedly and glanced down at a printed paper in her hand. She looked back up at Rose Marie and gave her a wan smile. "I sort of 'misfiled' a couple documents and the boss-man is having a fit. Can't chat. Got to copy this to give Victor." She winced. "The poor man's taking the heat for me." She chuckled nervously before hurrying off down the corridor.

Rose Marie watched her leave before turning to the door next to Jean's office. Just as she approached the doorway, a young frazzled-looking man swung the door open and made to exit the office. However, on seeing Rose Marie, he paused abruptly and frowned.

"Yes?" His curt greeting – or lack thereof – was loaded with impatience. "If you want to see Mr. Wilson you will have to come back another time. He can't see anyone. I'm afraid we are very busy at the moment." He paused and softened his expression. "Would you like me to give him a message?"

"Um, no. It's nothing," Rose Marie said, suddenly feeling a great sense of disappointment. "No, thank you."

The young man nodded then turned and re-entered the office. Before he closed the door, Rose Marie got a glance of Victor, hunched over his desk, reading through an array of papers. He looked up just as his assistant shut the door.

Rose Marie felt miserable. As she stood in the elevator, a tear trickled down her cheek. She could not believe how her life had suddenly changed for the worse.

She stepped out into the main hall on the ground floor and heaved a great sigh. She needed a distraction. She needed to stop thinking about her family's situation or she would just feel even worse. But she could not. Her mind refused to let it go. Hopelessness overtook her as her shoulders began to tremble. She could barely see through her tears as she hastily retreated to the parking lot.

"Rose Marie, wait!"

She quickly turned around and almost choked on her tears. It was Victor. Oh, God. Why did he have to see her like this … again? She swiped at her wet cheeks as he approached her.

"I'm sorry I missed you. It's pretty hectic today." Concern overrode his expression as he noticed Rose Marie's dismal state. "What is it? What's wrong?" He looked searchingly into her pain-ridden eyes. When she looked away and did not respond, he stepped closer and placed a comforting hand on her shoulder. "Rose, what happened?"

The care in his voice and his soothing touch completely melted her resolve. With one strangled sob, she closed the space between them, stepping into his arms. His warm body and arms around her, instantly alleviated some of her pain as she stifled her sobs in his shirt. He rubbed her back slowly.

"Come, let's get out of here," he said quietly.

She raised her head and looked into his eyes. Her voice was shaky and morose as she spoke. However, she felt a glimmer of hope rise within her at his suggestion. "But … what about the situation upstairs?"

"Jean will have to handle it in the meantime," he said without missing a beat. "She *is* the one who created it. And I've helped her quite enough." Victor lowered his arms then took her hand in his. They silently looked down at their joint hands. Rose Marie swallowed as Victor's thumb slowly stroked the inside of her wrist. She looked up into his warm grey eyes and felt weak.

"Come on. Let's talk over a cup of coffee or something – I could surely do with one. Is that ok?"

She nodded. He gave her a soft smile before gently squeezing her hand and leading her to the employees' car park.

Chapter 17

"Harietta, what would you do if you were me?" Andreide shifted the basket of wet laundry to her hip. She shaded her eyes from the sun's mid-morning rays and looked over at her friend.

Harietta paused from placing a clothespin on a dripping bed sheet and gave Andreide a thoughtful look. "I'm not too sure, girl. But I'll tell you what I wouldn't do. I wouldn't go around thinking the world's out to get me or blame God for this. He didn't make your father do what he did. He gave your father free will like He gave us all and your father decided to screw that up. It's his doing and nobody else's. Not your mother, not your brothers, and definitely not yours."

Andreide sighed. "I know. I'm not blaming God or anybody else but him. But I really did wonder why this had to happen to us. I mean it's not like we're bad people. Why us? Why now? Just when things seemed to be going fine."

Harietta took a few clothespins from a bag hanging on the post then took a small short pants from the basket in Andreide's arm. Her answer came a few seconds later. "You know God works in mysterious ways, just as the devil works in evil ways." She pinned the pants on the line then reached for a tiny cotton dress. "God rewarded your mother for her hard work by giving you all happiness. But now that blasted devil can't stand so much joy and sent that woman with her child to try and destroy what God built for you." She paused from her hanging and turned to Andreide.

"But don't let him win, Andy. Don't let him rejoice in your pain. Show him you're the boss and he can't ruin your life."

"But how?" Andreide moaned. "My family's already in pieces – my brother has moved out, my parents argue all the time, Uncle Peter is back on the bottle, Marques mopes around and Chrystal has been spending almost every night out. I don't think this will ever get better. I just don't see how with that woman and her child being around." She frowned and shifted her weight angrily.

"Anything is possible with God, Andreide and you know that. My best advice to you is to pray about it. Pray and give it time. There's a solution to every problem and yours will be solved, don't worry. But in the meantime, you're just going to have to be patient."

As wise as her words were, Andreide still felt slightly annoyed. "Well, that's easy for you to say. You're not the one having to live with all this crap. How do you expect me to wait for something to happen when I'm only inches away from beating the hell out of that man? I feel like I'm about to go crazy!"

Harietta heaved a weighted sigh. "You know what Andy? Maybe you need to look at this from a different perspective. You need to remember that your family isn't the only one going through problems like this. In fact, there are so many other people with greater problems than yours. Mind you, I'm not saying that your situation is insignificant. I just want you to be aware that this isn't the end of the world for you – your life isn't ruined because of this. You know that, right?"

"Yeah, I know," Andreide muttered.

"Good. Now, what you need to do is get your mind off of it for a while or you really will go nuts thinking about it. Just do what you can to stay calm, especially with exams coming up."

"Yeah, you're right."

Harietta took another item of clothing and resumed her chore. She glanced at Andreide who was looking at one of the neighbour's children playing next door then asked, "So how's things besides all of that mess? Like with Dominick."

Andreide looked at her and smiled. Every time someone mentioned Dominick she automatically felt happier – and much warmer too. She glanced at her nails. "He's good. Things are fine. He has been really supportive of me since I told him about all of this – really supportive. He's such a sweet guy. He knows how to make me happy. I couldn't ask for a better boyfriend."

A grin flashed across Harietta's puffy cheeks. "Ooo! Sounds like somebody is in love! I see you got a ring there. When's the wedding?"

Andreide laughed. "I wish." She raised her hand and gazed fondly at the engraved ring, her eyes latching on to the red heart. She sighed contentedly. "He told me it's to signify how much he loves me. I can't ever take it off. It's like a part of him is always with me when I wear it."

Harietta shook her head in amusement. "Woa, girl. You got it bad. You do realise that's a commitment ring, right? As in you're committed to him."

"Yes, of course."

"And you know what goes with commitment, right?"

Andreide paused. "What do you mean?"

"You mean he hasn't brought it up?"

"What?"

"Oh, c'mon. You know ... sex."

Andreide felt her cheeks beginning to burn. She twiddled with the basket before moving it to her right hip then back again to her left. She knew that Harietta was anxiously waiting for an answer.

"I ... um ... well. We haven't ... talked about it directly. I mean, I thought about it and I know he has – I overheard Tommy asking him about us. But ... I guess there hasn't been the right time to bring it up."

"Wow. He must be a pretty decent guy not to have brought it up yet." Harietta gave her a serious look. "But would you? If he asked, would you do it?"

Andreide shrugged her shoulders, looking at the grass. "I don't know."

"That's not a no."

"And it's not a yes either. I just don't know. I'm still trying to make up my mind about it."

"What's confusing you?"

"You know, this whole morality thing," she said. "I'm a Catholic and the Church preaches about abstinence and this 'no sex before marriage' thing. At first I accepted it since we've been conditioned to anyway. But then with the very priests and bishops and everybody else just doing as they feel, I started thinking about the logic of the rule. I mean, I'm not jumping on the 'everybody is doing it so I should too' bandwagon. I'm not. It's just that I don't think it should be so restrictive. What if you don't want to get married or never do get married? You're supposed to remain celibate till you die then?"

Andreide shook her head then continued. "I think it goes back to the free will part. I think we should be allowed to do it but with moderation, you know? Like maybe … only if you really and truly love the person but you can't get married at that time for whatever reason." She paused and a faraway expression came over her. "And you know that you want to be with him forever … because only together you're whole."

Harietta watched her friend carefully, a small smile tweaking her lips. The basket slipping from Andreide's hand seemed to awake her from her dreamlike state; she quickly tightened her grip on it. Blushing, Andreide glanced at Harietta. "Well, that's just my opinion."

"Wow, Andy. That was deep. I never actually stopped to think of it like that. But then I'm not as indecisive as you are right

now and being in love and all that." She paused. "All I can say is …
listen to your conscience."

Andreide watched her a moment then smiled slightly.
"Thanks Harietta."

"No problem, girl. What are friends for?" She hung the last
piece of clothing on the line then the two girls walked across the
yard then back into Harietta's house.

*

She had been doing her Geography homework that
afternoon when her cell phone rang. She glanced at the caller ID
then quickly dropped her pen and answered, her heart racing.

"Hey, Andy," came Dominick's voice.

"Hi!" she squeaked.

He chuckled. "You ok?"

"Um, yes! I'm fine." She tried to calm her breathing. From
the moment she had returned home, all she could think about was
her conversation with Harietta. His calling her now, only made her
more anxious and excited than she was before. Gosh, how she
wanted to see him.

"What are you doing, love?"

Oooo! He called her 'love'!

"Thinking about you. I mean, doing my homework. I have
this essay to write about the Monsoon in India."

"Oh, I was doing the same thing."

"Really? You have the same essay to do?" she asked all in
one breath. "We have to talk about the factors influencing the
rainfall and the effects both negative and positive for the people –
especially those living on flatland and …" She trailed off as she
realised that Dominick was laughing.

"I didn't mean that." She could tell he was grinning now
and she pictured his cute dimple. "I meant –" He paused for
emphasis. "I was thinking about you too."

Ooooo! She could barely contain her mounting excitement. All thoughts of her schoolwork were wiped clean from her mind as Dominick's handsome face replaced them.

"I was wondering," he continued, "if you'd fancy a swim in my pool with me."

Andreide felt her limbs turn to jelly. She struggled not to drop her phone.

"Andy? Of course if you're busy, I understand. I mean your schoolwork is much more important than –"

"I'd love to! My work can wait. It's just one essay anyway. It can wait." It would *surely* wait!

"Great. I'll send Prakash 'round to get you. What time is best?"

"Uh, anytime. I don't have any plans."

"Ok, so is like now, alright?" He chuckled.

She grinned. "Yah, it is."

"Good. Because Prakash left a few minutes ago."

"Dominick!"

He laughed. "See you in ten minutes, baby."

*

Andreide felt almost as amazed as she had been the first time she had visited the Michaels' house. She tried not to gawk too much as she followed the housekeeper – who kept shooting her watchful looks – through large fancy room after large fancy room. They eventually made it outside, across the patio, down the intricately-lain stone steps, through a mini botanical garden, then finally arrived at the most beautiful, well-designed pool Andreide had ever laid eyes on. It was spectacular – non-definite in shape with mini waterfalls flowing out from smooth rocks, that were covered with vines and purple and white flowers. The crystal clear water sparkled like blue diamonds.

"Hey, babe." Andreide turned and smiled as she saw her barefoot boyfriend stroll over towards her. He sported dark blue swimming trunks, a white t-shirt and dark shades. He looked so cool.

"I bring your guest, señor," the housekeeper said in a Spanish accent.

"Gracias, señora Vega." Dominick nodded at her and she turned and left. Andreide looked at him and grinned.

"My, aren't you the linguistic one," she teased. He grinned then leaned in and kissed her. He then checked out her outfit.

"Nice. Really nice. I thought swimsuits were more revealing but I like it." He grinned.

She laughed. "I'm not swimming in this, you know that. I have my bathing suit underneath."

"Yeah? I hope it's a G-string bikini." He paused. "Um ... did I just say that out loud?"

Andreide grinned. She was beginning to feel quite pleased at which suit she had chosen to wear. "Yes, you did. But it's not that, sorry to disappoint you."

"Oh, I can't take this suspense," Dominick said in mock agony. "And that water is really calling me." He reached up and took his shades off, dropping them on a pool chair nearby.

Andreide watched him in awe as he then took his t-shirt off, tossing it aside by his shades. She stared at his lean body, amazed at his well-defined abdomen and thorax.

Dominick reached up and stretched. He caught sight of Andreide staring at him, her mouth slightly agape, and chuckled. "I try to work out every now and then." He glanced down at his toned stomach and flashed Andreide a teasing smile. "Guess it's been paying off, huh?"

Andreide blinked quickly then swallowed. "Oh yeah, it has. Dominick you look so hot. You're a god."

He laughed. "Why thank you, love. But ..." He stepped closer to her. "If I'm a god, you're my goddess." He wrapped an arm around her waist and pulled her against him. "Now, are you going to take this off or am I going to have to do it myself?" He gave her a devious grin, eyeing her shirt and shorts.

Andreide instantly flushed. She bit her lip and nodded. He stood watching her with a somewhat daring look on his face. Her heart rate sped up as she realised that he had no intention of moving until she was changed. Oh gosh, why did she suddenly feel so nervous? It wasn't as if she had to strip naked.

But the thing was, a bare-chested Dominick stood right in front of her; even if she only had to remove a piece of jewellery she would feel completely self-conscious. But time was going by just standing in the sun and she too longed to get in the pool. Resolutely, she took hold of her t-shirt and lifted it over her head. She unbuttoned her shorts, zipped them down then stepped out of them. She avoided his gaze as she picked up her clothes and placed them along with her bag on a chair next to Dominick's.

"Wow!" she heard him say. She could feel his eyes skimming down her body. But surprisingly she did not feel as bashful as she normally would have. In fact, when she peeked up at him she felt her skin glow with pleasure from the delighted, impressed look on Dominick's face. She smiled awkwardly and toyed with the light pink skirt-tie of her matching pink and white striped two-piece bathing suit.

"Andreide, wow. You look amazing! I never thought – never in my wildest dreams that you'd look this delectable."

Andreide laughed. He reached out to grab her but she swerved then dove into the pool. He quickly followed her, diving headfirst into the cool clear water.

After ten minutes of vigorous swimming, a game of 'tag', and a water fight, Andreide floated listlessly along on her back at the edge of the pool, enjoying the cool breeze and warm sunlight on her face; Dominick was doing laps. After his fifth rounds of the pool, she let her legs sink as she watched him approach her. She shook her head and grinned.

"Remind me again why you're trying to burn out all of your energy?"

He laughed then plunged under the water before resurfacing closer to her. He wiped the water from his face and breathed in and out deeply before replying.

"Coach is trying a new training strategy. He says swimming builds powerful legs faster than our football practices do. So he's making us swim for about an hour a day until he thinks we're good enough to get a break." He chuckled. "I think he must have been a drill sergeant or something, that man. He's completely relentless!"

Andreide smiled. "Good. As long as he doesn't kill you with fatigue and keeps you looking as fine as you do now, I'm not worried."

"Oh, you don't have to worry. I've always been quite energetic." He grinned and moved closer to her, backing her into a corner of the pool. "I can *endure* for a very long time." The look in his eyes made Andreide's face flush again. She tried to tear her eyes away from his but his intense, honey-coloured gaze was riveting. The latter part of her conversation with Harietta came rushing to the surface of her mind.

She slowly exhaled as Dominick's gaze lowered. "Andy, did I tell you how gorgeous you look, and even more so in that swimsuit?" He came even closer to her. "You look –" He was now a few inches away. "– incredibly sexy."

Andreide felt her skin become even warmer.

"You look like the sweetest candy cane ever with those stripes." Directly in front of her, he lowered his head and pressed his lips to the side of her neck. "So sweet. You're edible," he murmured against her skin.

It was so hard for her to resist the moan rising in her throat. But when his mouth started feathering her neck with kisses and the wind blew along each wet spot, she had to release it. She shivered involuntarily as the water lapped around them. She draped her arms around his neck and closed her eyes as she basked in the sensations he was creating. Her talk with Harietta flashed in her mind again.

"Dominick?"

"Mmm?" He kissed a path up to her jaw and back down to the base of her neck. She tried not to swoon.

"I ... I have to ... ask you something."

"Mmmhmm?" He continued back up her neck, tilting her head for full access.

"Dominick, are you ... are you a ..." She trailed off as his teeth nibbled her earlobe. She was grateful for the back support the pool's edge provided. She started over, "Have you ever ... been with anyone before?" Her pulse raced in anticipation of his response.

He eased back slowly. Her hands slid from his neck. When his eyes found hers, she saw the comprehension in them – he knew what she meant. And if she was not mistaken, he seemed slightly flustered by the question.

"No," he said quietly.

Andreide felt relieved. At least she was not the only inexperienced one.

"Have you?" His voice had an anxious tone to it.

Andreide shook her head. "No. Never."

He nodded then looked away. They were silent for a few seconds before they caught each other's eye at the same time. They blushed. Andreide bit her lip as Dominick rubbed the back of his neck.

"Um ... do you want to?"

Of course she wanted to. But whether she should was the issue. However, as they stood there with the water rippling around them, a light breeze blowing and a cloud providing temporary shade, Andreide suddenly felt like throwing caution to the wind. She yearned to do what she wanted and not what anyone else wanted of or for her.

She took a long look at her boyfriend's enticingly toned body, and felt a powerful surge of boldness. She gave him an intense look, steamy with the desire she felt sizzling within her. The look he returned was just as desirous – dangerously so.

In one fluid motion, they were in each other's arms, their lips crashing together in a fierce kiss. Andreide wrapped her arms around his neck, one hand rooted in his wet curls. Her heart pummelled as their tongues collided and his hands roamed her body. His touch tingled and burned her skin. She arched against him as his hand stroked her back, moving upwards towards the clasp of her top. She tensed in anticipation. However, he only lingered momentarily before moving downwards again.

She moaned against his lips as his left hand slid down her back, curving over her bottom, clutching it. His right hand glided along the curve of her waist then up to the curve of her breast, cupping it, caressing it. Again she moaned, grasping tightly to his hair. He responded with fervour, pressing her along the edge of the pool, kissing her with mounting passion.

Her racing pulse skyrocketed as Dominick pulled her even harder against him, her stomach brushing the bulge in his trunks. A searing warmth like she had never felt, surged through her body, lingering between her legs. She clung to him weakly, responding in kind, pressing her semi-trembling body eagerly against him.

A strangled groan escaped his mouth. Breaking the kiss, grasping her hips, he smoothly lifted her a couple inches through the water, and leaned her against the rim of the pool. With her eyes shut tightly, Andreide dug her fingers into Dominick's shoulder as his lips sucked erotically at her neck. She moaned in pleasure. The heat and pressure of his mouth on her skin sent tremors through her body, awakening sensations she had only dreamed of experiencing.

"Oh, God, Andreide," Dominick uttered huskily against her neck. He gripped her thighs, angling her at his hips as he recaptured her lips. His hands at her hips held her in place as he rubbed against her, slowly at first then with increasing vigour. The sheer fabric of their bathing suits seemed nonexistent under the water; they had might as well have been completely naked.

Andreide's face felt like it was on fire – a fire quickly spreading down her neck and to the rest of her limbs as Dominick's mouth left hers, trailing down her neck, her chest … circling her breasts. A low groan sounded in his throat as he planted his mouth over one covered breast, taking possession of the peak printing through her striped bra-like top; his hand found the other, fondling it, tweaking it.

Her gasp was loud, filled with the surprise and pleasure of feeling his hot, wet mouth on her soft, sensitive flesh. Despite their thin clothes barrier, it felt like the real thing.

And it was then as his teeth bit down and something like a spasm trembled through her, an alarm bell echoed faintly in her consciousness. But as she tried not to scream her aching pleasure, she also smothered the warning, knowing that they could not stop even if she wanted to. And hell, she could not stop. She could not stop those unbelievable sensations from cascading through her. And she definitely did not want to. All she could think of was satisfying the exciting, burning, throbbing feeling between her legs.

Her heart thumping madly against her ribcage, Andreide entwined both her hands in his hair and arched towards him as his lips scorched her skin. Her breaths came quickly as the urgency of his mouth and thrusting hips rose, their movements splashing water around and against them.

Just as she felt like she could not take any more, and was about to yank his trunks down herself, Dominick raised up and crushed his lips against hers again; his demanding mouth obliterated every sensible thought in her mind.

Then he suddenly released her. His body took on a different kind of rigidity. Confused, she opened her eyes and looked at him. His face was flushed and the expression in his eyes was far from desirous and inviting. Startled, she wondered what she had done but then realised that he was not looking at her – he was staring at something behind her – *someone* from the approaching footsteps. Alarmed, Andreide spun around then gasped. Mr. Michaels, Dominick's father, was walking directly towards them.

Dominick swore under his breath.

Andreide quickly turned back to him, anxiety and embarrassment darting up within her. His eyes connected with hers but before either of them could speak, his father was upon them.

"Dominick, where have you been? I've been looking for you for over a half an hour until I –" He broke off as his gaze shifted to Andreide. "Oh." He glanced at his son then back at Andreide. "Well ... hello there."

Andreide smiled weakly.

Dominick cleared his throat and ran his hand through his wet curls. "Dad, you said you were looking for me?"

His father returned his attention to his son and nodded. "Yes. It's after four. We're supposed to be going to the races for half past. Have you forgotten?"

Dominick rubbed his face. "Dad, I'm sorry. It slipped my mind. Are you still going?"

"Yes, of course. And you had better hurry up and get ready. Your mum wants to introduce you to some friends of hers who will be there."

Dominick nodded half-heartedly. "Yes, she told me. Well, I'll be right up in a sec."

Mr. Michaels looked down at the both of them before nodding and walking back towards the house.

Andreide and Dominick both released a tight breath.

"Andy, I'm so sorry," Dominick began. "I completely forgot about this."

"It's ok," she said quietly. "But ... do you think he saw us?"

Dominick shrugged, his face becoming noticeably redder. He lowered his gaze as he spoke, "I ... I'm not sure. But I hope not." He raked his fingers through his hair and released a ragged sigh of repressed frustration. "Andy, I'm sorry. I'm so sorry. But I gave my word that I'd go and well … I have to go."

Andreide nodded, her eyes on his chest. Her heart rate had not yet recovered.

"Andy …"

She looked up, the pain in his voice evident. Their eyes met and held for a minute before he leaned in and kissed her on the cheek.

"Come on. I'll get Prakash to take you back home."

*

Despite the premature ending of their afternoon, Andreide could not stop smiling and blushing as she relived their moments of passion. It was her ever-present flushed and excited demeanour which made Chrystal barricade her in their room until she told her everything that had happened. When she found out, Chrystal was even more ecstatic. Both girls pranced about the room, giggling their heads off as they revelled in Andreide's 'experience'.

They were still discussing it a few hours later. Andreide rolled over on her bed and grinned at her cousin.

"See, I told you I wasn't a baby. Bet you think of me differently now, huh?"

"Of course! I mean wow, girl. *You* doing it in a pool with Dominick? Girl, you're hot!"

Andreide giggled. "Oh c'mon. You know we didn't *do* it."

"Yeah, but you might as well had. Gosh, girl. What happened to my little shy, reserved cousin?"

Andreide laughed. "She's all grown-up now. And don't you forget it."

Chrystal grinned. "Oooo girl! You've made me so proud."

They laughed, feeling happier than they had in weeks.

It was about forty-five minutes later when Andreide's cell phone rang. She reached for it quickly but it was only Keisha, inviting her to a party that one of her friend's was having that night. On hearing her hesitation, Keisha begged Andreide to attend it, telling her that she needed to get out of the house, especially away from her family's problems for a while. But Andreide was not ready to tell her that she had already been out for the day and had … well, she had thoroughly enjoyed herself. Just thinking about it made her smile. Before she realised what she was saying, she agreed to go. Keisha hooted through the phone line then arranged to meet her at her house in half an hour.

Chrystal gave Andreide a grin. "A party, eh? Well well, this day just keeps getting better for you, girl. What you going to wear?"

"I don't know. I – Wait a minute. What am I saying? I can't go to the party. Mom isn't here."

"Uh, so what?"

"She went out for a dinner or something. I always have to get her permission to go out to parties and things like that."

"But Andy," Chrystal began. "She's not here. You can go. What she doesn't know won't hurt."

"But …" Andreide paused. "That's dishonest. I'm not like that, you know that."

"Oh, it's not being dishonest! Think about it. If she were here and you asked her, don't you think she would say yes? I mean it is a Saturday night and she knows who your friends are. Why would she say no?"

Andreide frowned. "I don't know."

"Oh c'mon, Andy. What happened to that 'I'm all grown-up' speech? It's not like you're going to rob a bank or anything. It's just a party. A party to relieve your stress and chill a bit. And you deserve to relax – we all do. So what if you don't get permission this one time? You know what I mean?"

Andreide looked at her for a while then nodded in agreement. "Yeah, you're right. It's just a party and it's just this time. But I'm not going to stay long."

Chrystal laughed. "Girl, just go and enjoy yourself. You're a new woman now, remember? Go and have fun. If Tantie comes back before you do, don't worry I'll cover for you. Now go and get ready."

Andreide grinned and hurried to shower.

*

Like most parties that she had attended, the first thing that struck her was the noise. The stereo was blasting the latest dancehall and pop songs and the party-goers were making their own ruckus. Keisha grabbed Andreide's arm, steering them through the crowd and into the main entrance.

"Keeshy!" They turned to see Jamila bounding towards them, her triple Ds bouncing with every movement she made. The usual throng of male followers tailed her.

"Jam-Jam, gyul! This party got people, boy." Keisha grinned.

"Yeah, gyul. Ronny parties always have the big people. And guess who here? Dinga!"

"Wha'? Yuh joking!"

"Nuh uh! Come see for yuhself, gyul. I ain't lying."

Keisha laughed and started to follow Jamila. But remembering Andreide, she turned and beckoned to her. "'Ey, Andy. You can come too you know."

"Uh, it's alright thanks. You go ahead. I'll just mingle out here."

"You sure?"

"Yeah, it's good."

"Alright then. Later!"

Andreide watched them disappear through the crowd towards a room in the back and shook her head. She definitely did not want to mix with their crowd. Keisha was used to it but frankly, Andreide was not keen on Jamila or any of her associates' company. God only knew what or who a 'Dinga' was.

Andreide glanced around, hoping to see someone she knew while trying not to look like she was alone. She slid through the crowd towards the drinks bar. Just as she was about to claim a vacated stool, from the corner of her eye she spotted one of the last persons she ever wanted to be seen with at a party – in fact, anywhere at all. She quickly averted her eyes and pretended to look elsewhere but he had already seen her and was heading her way. She cursed under her breath then quickly changed tactics. She turned on her heel and hastily retreated towards the opposite side of the room.

"Hey, Andreide!" Hal called.

She doubled her steps.

"Andreide! Wait up!"

Oh, shit. He was gaining on her! Spying a doorway, she dashed for it. However, as she reached it, a group of raucous boys came bouncing through, yelling and shouting out to their friends in a corner. Unfortunately for her, they decided to have their shout-out greetings right in the middle of the doorway, blocking her or anyone from passing. She sighed in defeat. Her plan of escape foiled, trapped, Andreide slowly turned around.

"Andreide!" Hal panted as he approached her, slowing his pace, his large mass exhausted from such an exertion. "I was calling you. Didn't you hear me?"

She bit down on her tongue as she willed herself not to respond rashly. She tried to look away from him. But as was the case with Hal Chandani, when he was directly in front of you, there were only so many places one could look. It was like trying to avoid looking at a clothed, talking, hairy version of a glasses-wearing Moby Dick.

Andreide's eyes settled on his midriff then quickly looked away. She bit her bottom lip. Instead of struggling to suppress the usual disgust she felt on seeing him, it was laughter that threatened to burst out of her.

"Are you alright, Andreide?" His large, confused face stared absorbedly at her. She was not sure how to respond. His immense body was enveloped in a massive, lurid orange t-shirt, raggedy brown pants and huge boat-like brown boots; it was just too much to take in a single dose. The raw meat odour wafting Andreide's way only exacerbated the situation and her revulsion returned, squelching her humour. With a tight smile, she turned her head to face him.

"Hello, Hal. I didn't know you were going to be here," she said with a forced bit of cheeriness. "I've never seen you at these kinds of parties."

"Oh, this is my first! And I was invited too! I didn't even have to beg like last time. The guys said I could come." He beamed proudly. "I think they like me now."

Andreide arched an eyebrow but kept her thoughts to herself. "Well, uh, that's great, Hal. You have fun now." She made to turn away.

"Wait!" He stepped towards her. She instantly recoiled. She shot him a wary look as he looked down at his sausage-like fingers and fumbled. "I-I-I-I was wondering if –" He looked up, a bashful expression on his big face. "If you'd like to dance with me?"

"No!" Andreide said at once. "I mean, no thank you."

"But-But why not?" The hurt expression he bore made her wish she could run as fast and as far away from him as possible. "Is it the song? I can ask them to change it for you. Do you want me to? Which song do you want to dance to?"

"No, no. The song is fine. I just don't want to dance right now."

"But why?"

"Why? Because I – don't want to!" Andreide rolled her eyes and turned away. But that did not stop him.

"If the song changed, will you dance with me then?" he persisted, staring desperately at her.

Andreide felt like she could be tolerant no more. What exactly was wrong with this boy? Didn't he understand the meaning of the word 'no'? Or maybe he just liked rejection.

She turned to him and frowned. "Look. I told you I don't have a problem with the song. It's Sean Paul, for goodness sakes. I love Sean Paul. Everyone does!"

"Then why won't you dance with me?"

"Because I don't like you!" she yelled. A few people nearby glanced at them and sniggered. Ignoring them, and ignoring his surprised, wounded look, she continued. "The song is fine, the party is fine, it's *you* I don't like. I *don't* like you. I do *not* want to dance with you or do *anything* with you. I've told you that already so why can't you just give up?"

"But … but I love you! You're the air that I breathe. I can't breathe without you – I'll die!"

"Then die! Whatever it takes, just stay away from me!" Andreide abruptly turned and marched over to the doorway. She shoved a boy aside, squeezed through the entryway and headed for the front door. Once out in the open, she released a deep breath and collected her thoughts. Gosh, that boy was annoying!

She nearly had a heart attack when she glanced at her watch. It was almost nine o'clock. She could not risk being out that late in case her mother decided to go home early. She hurried back inside and began searching for Keisha. She wandered from room to room without any luck and was about to head back outside when she spotted Hal looking around intently. Andreide ducked through the nearest doorway she could find. As she quickly glanced backward, she lost her step then stumbled, bumping into someone passing by.

"Oh, I'm sorry!"

"That's alright. It was my –" He did a double take. "Andreide?"

She looked up, her mouth falling open in surprise. "Dominick! What are *you* doing here?"

"One of my friends invited me." He frowned thoughtfully at her, a smile at his lips. "What are *you* doing here?"

She stared at him, overwhelmed by his sudden appearance. And oh, he looked so gorgeous and smelled so damn good.

"I ... I ... Keisha, she told me about it." She smiled weakly. "I didn't know you were coming."

He chuckled lightly. "I wasn't actually. I decided at the last minute."

Andreide was about to respond when she spotted Hal's orange shirt out of the corner of her eye. She ducked.

Dominick regarded her in amusement. "Andy, what are you doing?"

"Shhh! Don't say my name." From her crouch, she peered around Dominick's side. She could see Hal's bushy head looking around industriously.

Dominick glanced over his shoulder. "Who are you hiding from?"

"My stalker."

"What?"

"It's nothing."

Hal finally left the room and Andreide exhaled in relief. She stood up to meet a confused yet amused Dominick. She gave him a sheepish look. "Can you pretend that didn't happen? You really don't need to know."

He paused, slowly looking her over, a mellow somewhat flirtatious smile tugging at his lips. "Okay. So ... how was your evening, Andy?" From the look in his eyes, she knew that he was thinking about their passionate moment in the pool. All thoughts of annoying Hal vanished. She blushed as her mind flashed back to that afternoon. She glanced at him shyly.

The look in his honey coloured eyes was dark and intense as they searched her face, making her feel warm and tingly. Her pulse race. She desperately yearned for a re-enactment of their passion. And from the expression on his face, she was certain that he was thinking the same thing.

Dominick nodded towards a remote corner of the room where an unoccupied sofa lay. Andreide smiled demurely and he took her hand, leading them to the private area.

It was of no surprise to either of them, when as soon as they were seated they were in each other's arms. But unlike their previous encounter, their movements were smooth and affectionate.

The softness of his lips against hers felt like heaven. As she reclined in his arms, the alluring scent of his cologne drifting up her nose, Andreide felt wonderful. Simply wonderful. Nothing else mattered at that moment. Every worry she had before seemed to evaporate as he held her closer. She felt like she was floating on clouds.

Chapter 18

"Alisa, where have you been all week?" Andreide demanded as soon as the line opened. She closed the bathroom door and locked it before continuing. "I tried calling you about a million times during the week and yesterday but you weren't answering your cell and your folks said you were sick. Is that true? Why didn't you say something? Are you alright?"

"Oh, it's nothing," came Alisa's quiet voice. "I'm fine. It was just ... a touch of stomach flu or something."

"Stomach flu? You mean food poisoning?"

"Um, yes. That. It must have been something I ate."

"What did the doctor say? It must have been pretty bad to miss a week of school."

"Um, well, yeah. Food poisoning is like that – vomiting, nausea, dizziness. It was awful. At least it was mainly in the mornings though. But I'm alright now, really."

"Are you sure? What did the doctor give you for it?"

"Well ..."

"You mean he didn't give you anything? What kind of a quack is he?"

"Andy, I ..." She hesitated. "I didn't see a doctor."

"What?" Andreide asked incredulously. "Why not?"

"Because ... I didn't need one. I assured my parents that I was fine, plus, I *was* really. It was only a slight stomach ache. But Mom forced me to take some Pepto-Bismol anyway. Erk!"

Andreide laughed.

"So what did I miss? Anything exciting happened during the week?" Alisa asked with a new eagerness to her tone.

Andreide grinned, her insides starting to glow with happiness as memories of the past seven days floated through her mind. Amidst all the tension at home with her parents' situation, she could not believe how great her week had turned out to be – how wonderful. And it was all because of Dominick. Dominick. She sighed, feeling as light as a feather drifting in the wind. Just thinking about him made her feel light-headed and euphoric. She did not know how she had managed to live through the past almost seventeen years without him.

After the party, Dominick had walked her home, kissed her goodnight and promised to see her again during the week. And he had definitely kept his promise. In fact, they had seen each other every day for the rest of the week. It was that Sunday that sparked their burning need to be with each other every day – a Sunday, around midnight when Dominick had come calling on his lady to sweep her away on a romantic midnight stroll. He had been at a friend's sleepover and had had an overwhelming urge to see her. It was sheer excitement and a desire to be spontaneous which incited Andreide to sneak out of bed at such an hour.

The rest of the week had been just as exciting and carefree, however torturous, due to the painful hours of school they were forced to endure until their blessed rendezvous in the evenings. They met anytime and anywhere they could, whether directly after school, at each other's house, in a restaurant, or at parties. But they still could not get enough of each other.

Andreide told all of this to Alisa. Her friend's exclamations at her news and her animated chatter barely registered as Andreide slid her fingers into her jeans pocket and extracted a thin plastic packet. She felt her heart beat faster as she tentatively traced a finger along the slight bulge of the square-shaped wrapper. A tingling heat crept up her cheeks as she flashed back to the night before; they had been so enamoured, passionate and reckless that they had almost … Well, it was a good thing her cell phone had started ringing.

There was a knock on the door. "Hey, Andy! You planning on coming out of there any time today? Lana's Boutique closes at two on Saturdays, don't forget. So hurry up, will you!" Chrystal called through the closed door.

Andreide started, nearly dropping her phone. She quickly slipped the packet back into her pocket.

"Hey, Alisa, I have to go. Chrystal and I are going shopping for an outfit for the party tonight. It's too bad you're sick or you could've come. Rick, one of Dominick's friends is throwing it and I heard it's gonna be huge. I'm so excited, I can't wait!" Andreide grinned.

Alisa laughed lightly. "Excited to be with your boyfriend you mean?"

"Definitely! Oh gosh," Andreide moaned. "You can't imagine how much I love that dreamy, sweet boy. I love him so much, Alisa! I just can't stand being apart from him which is why I'd do anything to be with him." She sighed. "I love him *so* much."

"Yeah …" Alisa said softly. "I can tell."

Andreide promised to call her back to tell her about the party. After ending the call, she quickly undressed then stepped into the shower.

*

A few hours later, after sorting through their purchases and picking out Andreide's outfit for the party, the girls lay across their beds, flipping through magazines. They giggled as they imagined what the party would be like. They were about to test out the new make-up they had bought when someone knocked at the door. Before either of them could get to it, the door swung open and Mrs. D'Averette entered, a stern look on her face. They immediately grew silent.

"Chrystal, excuse us a minute. I would like to talk to Andreide alone," she said evenly.

The girls exchanged a worried look before Chrystal got up and left, glancing back at Andreide questioningly.

Andreide sat up as her mother walked in. Her pulse immediately quickened as she saw the serious look on her face. The fact that her mother decided to remain standing was even more reason to worry. She could not know about … could she?

"While you were out, I had a phone call – from that Richardson woman." Something like annoyance flashed through Mrs. D'Averette's eyes. "And do you know what she said? She told me that she was just calling to say that one of her children had been passing by on Regent Street, Wednesday night and saw *you* with a boy outside some house – at a party. But I told her she had to be mistaken because it was during the week and my children are not allowed out on school nights. Then she gave me a detailed description of you and what you were wearing *and* the boy you were with. But I still didn't believe her. Do you think I should have?"

Andreide stared at her mother, her blood slowly draining from her face. At the same time, she could not help feeling a surge of hatred for the wretched Richardson woman and her nosy child – whichever one of the ten million who reported on her. She swallowed.

Her mother continued. "Do you think I should have believed her when I knew my daughter was in her room at that time studying? Or at least I thought I did. Until I found this!" She raised her hand, and Andreide stared in disbelief and shock at the object held between her mother's thumb and forefinger. She looked away, embarrassed.

"Andreide, what *is* this?" Mrs. D'Averette asked angrily, shaking the packet in her hand.

All feeling dissipated from her body as she stared, paralyzed at what her mother held. The lettering on the plastic wrapper reflected in the light, multiplying on her retina – *Trojan*. Her mouth went dry.

"Andreide! What is *this?*" her mother repeated.

But Andreide could not speak. Her mother had found out that she had snuck out and now even worse – she knew what she was planning to do. She *knew*. Oh, God! She could barely meet her eye.

"You know," her mother said, "I'm not sure whether I'm relieved or scared to death by the fact that it isn't opened." She paused. "Andreide ... are you having sex?"

Her daughter's eyes flashed up to hers. "No! Of course not!" she said quickly, her voice slightly hoarse.

"Then what are you doing with *this?*" She shook the packet again. "And who is that boy?"

Andreide's heart pounded. "He's ... my boyfriend."

"Your boyfriend? You have a *boyfriend?* Since when?"

The angry, demanding tone in her mother's voice – instead of making her more timid and self-conscious – triggered an equal anger in her daughter. An anger that was derived mainly from the underscored derision in her mother's tone.

"Since February. But you wouldn't know that. You were too busy to notice anything!"

"Don't try to blame me for this, young lady! And do not try to change the focus here. Where did you get this?"

"That's ... not mine."

"Oh really? Then how did it get into your pants pocket?"

"You searched through my clothes?" Andreide asked in disbelief.

"Of course I did! How else would I have found it – unless you have more hidden in this room?" She paused before continuing. "I was doing the laundry before that woman called. I sent Marques up to get your dirty clothes since they've been piling up for days. And guess what I found when I looked through your pockets?"

"Wait a minute. You sent Marques in here?" Andreide suddenly felt extremely irritated. "Whatever happened to privacy?"

"You are a minor and you are living under my roof. When it comes to matters like these, you *have* no privacy."

Andreide gritted her teeth, willing herself to control her mounting anger. So she had no privacy, huh?

"Who is this boy?"

"What boy?"

"Don't be smart with me!" Her mother glared at her, her voice rising. Andreide boldly met her glower.

"His name is Dominick. His family moved here this year. They're the ones who own that law firm on Bladen Street."

Her mother looked at her for a while before responding. "So, this Dominick. He's the one you've been sneaking out with at all hours and doing God knows what with?"

"Mom, we're not having sex!"

"Then why do you have *this?*" Mrs. D'Averette countered.

"Because –!"

"Yes?"

"I put it there." They both turned quickly to see Chrystal standing in the doorway. "Tantie, it's my fault. Don't blame Andy. I borrowed that pants earlier this week and I must have forgotten to empty the pockets when I gave her back."

Mrs. D'Averette stared at Chrystal for a few silent seconds. Andreide felt a glimmer of hope amidst her anger with her mother. Both girls kept their gaze on her, not daring to look at each other.

"*You* put that there?"

"Yes, Tantie."

Mrs. D'Averette looked at them in turn before replying. "Fine. But you still snuck out, Andreide and don't think you're getting away with it. You're grounded."

"What? What do you mean 'grounded'? You don't *ground* us."

"Well, I do now as your behaviour requires it." She turned to leave then stopped. "You are not allowed to go anywhere other than school and home and wherever else I may allow you to go."

"But –!"

"And that includes no shopping, no hanging out with your friends and especially no contact with that boy. What kind of an influence is he?"

"Mom, Dominick is a great guy. The best. He's not a bad influence!"

"Oh, really? But you have been sneaking out at all hours with him. You've been picking fights at school – "

"He had nothing to do with that, Mom. And I told you I didn't start that fight. That bitch provoked me."

"Andreide!" Her mother looked at her in shock. "What kind of language is that? What is going on with you?"

Andreide looked away, her jaw clenched. Her mother made a living off of studying human behaviour. How could she not know?

"Where is my loving, respectful daughter? I don't recognise who you are becoming."

Andreide did not respond.

Mrs. D'Averette sighed as her cell phone buzzed. "We will continue this later. But you are grounded. You are not to leave this house without my permission. School, home and back. Got it?"

"Mom! I have a life. That's not fair!"

"That's enough! You betrayed my trust *and* you put yourself in unnecessary danger. Don't talk to me about what's fair. I have half a mind to ship you off to a convent right now."

Andreide glowered at her mother. She could not believe how unfair she was being. There was nothing outlandish about her behaviour that warranted such punishment.

"As of now, consider yourself under house arrest until further notice. Don't even think about going anywhere tonight. I hope I made myself completely clear." Without waiting for a response, she turned and left the room.

Andreide released a violent oath. "Who does she think she is to ground me? And can you believe her banning me from seeing Dominick … and my friends! God!"

Chrystal walked over to her cousin and sat beside her. She gave her a sympathetic look. "Well, at least she forgot to take your cell phone and your new laptop."

Andreide grunted. "Oh boy, lucky me."

Chrystal sighed.

Andreide glanced at her. "Thanks by the way. For saving me just now. Don't think she bought it but anyway."

"Well, it was worth a try. Plus, I already told you I got your back. We're not just roomies, we're blood." She paused. "And if you don't want a repeat of what just happened, I suggest you keep those rubbers out of your clothes and somewhere your mother won't find them. And another thing," She touched Andreide's hand. "If you are, you know, doing it with Dominick? You can always talk to me about it." She grinned. "I'm a store of advice just waiting to be sampled. Plus, you know I just want to hear the juicy parts!"

Andreide smiled. "Yeah, thanks."

They lapsed into a few seconds of silence.

"So, what are you gonna do? About tonight I mean."

Andreide gave her a determined look. "I already bought my outfit for the party. You think I'm going to let that sexy number go to waste?" She stuck her chin out defiantly and folded her arms. "Grounded my ass! I'm going to that party no matter what she says!"

*

Once she made up her mind to do something, she got it done. It only took two hours of pouting and stormy looks; she stomped through the house in her pyjamas, irritating both her already testy parents until her father grabbed his car keys and left, and then her mother locked herself in her study. She grinned in satisfaction as Marques gave her a curious look from his place in front of the television set.

After marching back upstairs, stamping as hard as she could to more than make her rage be known, Andreide darted into her bedroom and quickly changed her clothes. Chrystal seemed just as excited as her cousin as she applied Andreide's make-up and arranged the long curly braids she had put in earlier that week. After waiting for her mother to retire to her room, Andreide tiptoed down the stairs and stealthily sneaked out the back door.

It was after ten when she arrived, having caught a ride with one of her friends. As was the norm with Duncan parties, the house was huge. Everywhere she turned there were people laughing, talking, dancing to the loud, rap songs blaring from the DJ's corner – just generally enjoying themselves. But as she went from room to room, she felt a bit unsettled as she realised that many of the partygoers looked like they were in their twenties. And not only were they older but they were drinking and smoking too.

Andreide quickly turned away from a motley crew of red-eyed smokers who were sharing a joint among them. The unmistakeable smell of marijuana permeated the air. She stifled a cough and hastily exited the room.

"Andy?"

She whipped around and gasped. "Alisa? What are you doing here? You're supposed to be sick!" She placed her hands on her hips and frowned at her friend. However, she could not help smiling.

Alisa gave a guilty shrug. "Well, uh. After you called me, Tommy called and well, it didn't make any sense to stay home when I was feeling a lot better. So here I am!" She grinned.

Andreide chuckled. "Your parents let you out at this hour to go to a party?"

"Uh … did yours?"

The girls gave each other a knowing look then giggled.

"Hey, there you are! You made it." They turned to see Tommy strolling over to them, his red hair appearing even more vivid under the party lights. He placed an arm around Alisa then gave her a peck on the cheek. She blushed and looked away.

"Hey, Andreide." He nodded at her. "D's around here somewhere. I just saw him a while ago. He's been looking for you forever."

Andreide felt her heart flutter. Dominick ...!

Tommy chuckled. "He was planning on sending his driver for you but I told him not to bother since Gordon's here. He and some of his buddies decided to crash the party but I don't think Rick cares anyway. Actually, I was just going to find Gordon when I saw you. D's gonna be really happy now that you're here."

Andreide grinned. She glanced at Alisa who had an odd almost unnerved look on her face. But she quickly donned a small smile. Andreide was not sure what to make of it but she didn't think on it long.

Tommy turned back to Alisa. He whispered something in her ear and she bit her lip then nodded. He grinned, glanced at Andreide then started walking away. The look on Alisa's face as she met her eyes made Andreide bite back a chuckle. She arched an eyebrow at her blushing friend.

"Well, um. I'm just gonna follow him."

"Uh huh." Andreide grinned. Alisa smiled, fiddled with her hands then turned, disappearing into the crowd.

Andreide wandered around again, looking anxiously for her boyfriend. After about ten minutes of searching, she had seen almost everyone but him – Will, Hans, a guy named Kurt, Jocelyn, Duncan's football and basketball team players and a few people she knew in passing. She had even glimpsed Richard to her dismay, laughing quite loudly among a group of scantily dressed giggling girls. Andreide rolled her eyes. As usual, he was the spectacle of the show.

It was while she was heading over to the dance floor that she finally spotted him across the room. He was chatting with two of his friends from school. As she gazed at his happy, easygoing expression, she felt a great surge of affection for him. He looked up and caught her eye, his face lighting up even more in the process. Her heart pounded excitedly as he excused himself from the conversation and jogged over to her.

"Andy! At last! Where have you been, love?" Dominick's smile was so incredibly heart-melting. Andreide's knees almost trembled.

"I ... dunno ..."

Dominick chuckled. "Come here." He stepped forward and wrapped his arms around her in a warm hug. He felt and smelled so good, she all but swooned. He released her and smiled his delight as his eyes travelled up her body.

"Mmm. I like. Wow, baby, you look so hot." His gaze seemed stuck on her designer mini skirt.

She batted her eyelashes in a coy, girly manner then leaned towards him and said in a husky voice, "I wore this just for you. And this." She traced a finger along her body-hugging, off-the-shoulder peach top. "And something else too but I'm not going to show you out here." She gave him a teasing smile.

Dominick groaned. "God, Andy. You should be illegal." She giggled before he pulled her against him and kissed her. She laughed then pulled back, grabbing his hand.

"Come on, let's dance. I just love this song!"

He chuckled and let her lead him to the dance floor.

And dance they did. It amazed her how incredibly in sync he was with her movements. As the music changed to a faster beat, they tore up the dance floor.

Eventually the tempo slowed and Beyonce's *'Dance for You'* began to play. Andreide's heart thudded harder in her chest. Her face felt hot as Dominick wrapped his arms around her waist, her back towards him. She felt an even greater thrill when out of the corner of her eye, she spied Shauna skulking to the side. How did *she* get invited? The girl's eyes were on her and Dominick; the expression she wore sizzled with rage and envy.

A devious smile crept across Andreide's lips. She took Dominick's hands and placed them on her hips; she slowly gyrated, pressing against him. The look on Shauna's face was to die for. Andreide longed to laugh but she wasn't yet satisfied – she could torture the girl a lot more.

She swivelled around to face him and draped an arm around his neck. She stared Shauna in the eyes as she kissed his neck, his jaw, his cheek. Her other hand rubbed his firm chest slowly ... then moved lower ... and lower. It was a strong surge of boldness and possessiveness that lured her hand further. And as her palm made contact with the jean-clad bulge beneath his pants, their gasps were of equal shock. Andreide almost forgot Shauna's existence. She was snared by the dark, desirous look in Dominick's eyes, until an enraged shriek came from the girl's direction.

However, before she could look, Dominick pulled her hard against him, his mouth taking hers ravenously, regardless of the people around them. Her hand now trapped between their bodies, somewhat unintentionally tightened its grip. Dominick moaned, grasping her bottom.

Andreide did not know how to describe the sensations that were shooting through her. But whatever they were, they were deeply affecting her body and soul. Her breathing laboured, her mind rampaged by wild, hungry thoughts, she drew back, breaking the kiss, and looked desirously into his darkened eyes. She could not resist any longer.

"I need you. I *want* you," she rasped. "Now."

"Yes?" His voice was low and husky.

Andreide swallowed then quickly nodded.

They looked at each other for a while before Dominick took her hand and led them off the floor, down a corridor and towards a more secluded area of the building. With every step her pulse raced faster. As he paused outside a door, her breath seemed to stick in her lungs. There was no turning back. He opened the door and allowed her to enter the bedroom before him.

As soon as the door was locked behind them, Dominick pulled her towards him. He recaptured her lips with equal urgency, his hands skimming all over her body. Andreide latched on to him with a desperation she had never known before.

She moaned as his hand found its way under her skirt, over her panties, clutching her closer. His other hand travelled up her skin-fitting top and over her breasts, squeezing and fondling them.

Andreide's mind was reduced to mush as his mouth continued to command hers, driving her crazy. His hands caressing her body were just as nerve-racking – exciting, frustrating and pleasurable.

Oh, God, how she wanted him!

As she thought this, her foot bumped into the room's huge bed, and the next thing she knew, they were tumbling onto the soft white sheets of the sturdy mattress.

Dominick blazed a trail of hot kisses across Andreide's face, down her neck and along her exposed shoulders, while his hands slithered down her sides. He grasped the hem of her top and hastily pulled it up; Andreide rose up slightly as he pulled it over her head. He paused for a second as he stared intently at her pink lacy bra before reaching for his shirt and yanking it off, tossing it to the side.

As he hovered over her, his breathing hard, his eyes trained on hers, she made a mental imprint of his image, knowing that she would never ever forget this moment.

She reached up and grabbed him, pulling his gorgeous body on hers, and wrapped her arms around his neck as she claimed his lips in an impassioned kiss. Oh, how he smelled sensational!

Dominick moaned. Easing back, he kissed a path down her throat, her chest, between her breasts, down her stomach – each kiss sending tiny shivers of anticipation through her body. She threw back her head and closed her eyes as his mouth went lower.

She gasped as she felt his wet tongue flicker over her navel, circling and toying with it, snaking a moist trail below it before teasing it again. She was vaguely aware of her naked thighs quivering as Dominick unzipped her skirt and pulled it down her legs.

But his explorations did not stop there. He parted her legs and caressed her thighs, while gazing at her intently. Then slowly, he lowered his mouth to the area where no one else's had ever been.

Her intake of breath was sharp – almost a cry of surprise. Andreide buried her fingers into his hair, and arched slightly as his mouth settled over her damp, lacy pink panties. The heat from his breath seemed to evaporate the thin layer of her underwear as his mouth lingered between her legs. His lips grazed her flesh and again she gasped, gripping his hair even tighter.

"Dominick," she moaned.

His grunted response against her sensitive skin sent darts of pleasure shooting through her body. His fingers soon joined his mouth, adding to the delightful, burning sensations building up within her.

As he kept his fingers rubbing against her, Dominick moved back up her body, planting steamy kisses on his way up. His hot mouth made her tremor as it found her breasts, his lips zeroing in on her hardened peaks through her bra. The increasing pressure was almost unbearable.

Andreide dug her fingers into his back and tried to suppress a squeal of pent up frustration and delight. But Dominick could not contain his.

"Oh God," he groaned, then slid a hand beneath her back, pulling her closer. He scooped his other hand under the delicate material of her bra and cupped a bare breast, his thumb stroking its hardened tip.

Andreide arched towards him, her hands digging further into his back.

Dominick groaned. With one hand, he quickly undid his pants, fumbling slightly with the buckle before pulling down his zipper. Andreide waited anxiously as he kicked his pants away before grabbing his hand and replacing it over her breast.

His darkened gaze met hers for a moment before he uttered a low growl; he sank his teeth into the side of her neck.

Andreide cried out, a mixture of pleasure and pain coursing through her. She slid her hands from his back and down his sides, along his lean hips and into his boxers. One hand glided over his cheeks as the other wandered further down.

Her pulse raced even faster. By the deep groan resounding from her boyfriend's throat, she had found her treasure. She didn't need to look to see it clasped between her fingers – she could feel his arousal. Her breath caught in her lungs.

"Oh, hell! *Andy* ..." he rasped against her neck.

He placed a hand over hers to guide her as she initiated her stroking movements.

Suddenly, a rattling sound startled them both and their heads jerked towards the door. Someone was twisting and shaking the doorknob, trying to get in. Thankfully, the door was locked.

"Oy! Anyone in there?" came a tipsy male voice. A female giggle accompanied it.

Dominick swore under his breath. "Piss off!" he directed at the two outside the door.

It appeared they understood the message as their attempts to unhinge the door ceased and their drunken voices faded into the distance.

Dominick made to resume their love-making but stopped. His groan was heavy with irritation.

"Damn," he uttered softly, placing his head between her breasts. He looked up at Andreide's flustered expression then gave a small smile. "You know, those idiots couldn't have come at a better time. Well actually, they could have but ..." He trailed off then noticed her perplexed look. "I forgot my wallet – Will borrowed some money from it and didn't give it back to me. It has the um … you know." He saw the understanding in her eyes and her face flushed more than it had already.

He ran a finger down her waist then gave her a firm kiss on the lips. He stroked her chin, looking her in the eyes. "Don't move, baby. I'll be right back."

His whisper sent shivers of longing down her spine. She watched as he got up and retrieved his discarded clothing, pulling on his shirt and pants, lacing up his sneakers.

With one last glance in her direction, Dominick flashed her a gorgeous smile before unlocking the door and closing it behind him.

Andreide closed her eyes and sighed blissfully.

A few minutes later, she jerked up from the bed, realising that she was practically naked and Dominick had not turned the lock. She quickly found her clothes and dressed then headed for the door. However, as she was about to bolt it, laughter from outside intrigued her. She opened the door and peeped out.

Three girls with cameras were dashing up the corridor, laughing their heads off as a half naked boy hollered after them; he was holding on to his pants as he raced after the girls.

Andreide chuckled then stepped out of the room to get a better look. But before she could follow them any further, they disappeared around a corner. She then decided to wander along the hall to pass the time.

With each step, she felt her face glow brighter with excitement as she thought of what was to come after Dominick's return. She could not believe how wonderful she had felt a few moments ago, how passionate and sensational it all was. To think that was only a prelude! She could hardly wait for the real thing. And she had made up her mind – she was going to do it.

Unable to bare her anxiety and excitement for another minute, Andreide turned and started back to the room, her body tingling from her thoughts. However, as she was about to turn the corner leading to their room, she nearly jumped out of her skin as someone suddenly appeared around the bend.

"Hey! Watch it!" she said in alarm. She placed her hand over her chest to calm her galloping heart. When she looked up and saw who it was, her previously happy glow vanished. She frowned at the boy regarding her with a lazy, insolent smirk.

"Hey, yourself," said Richard. "What you doing back here?" His usually demanding, antagonistic tone was muddled with curiosity.

She gave him a scathing look before replying. "Let me guess. You're going to tell me that this is a 'Duncan's party' and I have no business here, right? Well for your information, at least half of the people here aren't from your stupid ole school. And you can threaten me as much as you like but I ain't leaving! So there!"

She waited for his heated retort but was surprised to see the slow grin spreading across his lips. She was even more unsettled as the usual contempt he had in his penetrating blue eyes when they were focussed on her, contained nothing of the sort. In fact, they gazed at her with unnerving interest.

"That's a really short skirt you're wearing there. Really short. Mini. Short. I like short skirts. Really short skirts."

Andreide stepped back uncertainly. "Did you even hear what I just said?"

"Yeah, 'course." Richard's gaze stuck on her skirt and her legs beyond. He shook his head and grinned. "Dominick's one lucky guy. Saw him just now lookin' all happy and grinning. Knew it had to be you to have him acting like that." His eyes flickered up to hers and darkened. "Knew that from experience. 'Member that?"

Andreide stared at him, not believing what she was hearing. What the hell was wrong with him?

"You always had that way about you. Could always trap a guy and bewitch him with one look. Just a glance, not even a touch." He stepped closer to her and as he did so, she could smell the alcohol on his breath.

"But then when you did touch –" He chuckled. "– that was amazing. Dominick must be going wild. 'Specially with the way you dance."

Andreide stepped backwards. "Look, um, I'll see you later, alright?" She made to leave but Richard quickly turned, blocking her path.

"What's the rush? Meeting someone?" He smirked. "Oh yes, of course – *Dominick*. I'm curious. What does he have that I don't got?"

Andreide raised an eyebrow. "Are you serious?"

"Yes, I am." He frowned. "What, you think I was joking?"

Andreide rolled her eyes. "Well, I thought the answer was obvious. What's it to you anyway?"

"Just tell me," he said impatiently.

"Look. Aren't your groupies missing you? Shouldn't you be elsewhere, like getting blown by some cheerleaders or something?"

What looked like anger flashed through Richard's eyes. The look he gave her was frightening as he stepped closer to her, backing her against the wall.

"I think I already offered you that position. But since you're so keen on reminding me about it why don't you do the honours yourself?" He sneered. "*Head* cheerleaders are my favourite."

Andreide gave him a cold stare. "And you wonder why I prefer Dominick."

"No. He doesn't have what I do."

"That's right. He has a lot more. In fact, he's *bigger* and *better* than you! Bigger than you in so many ways. Better than you in so many more."

Richard stared at her for a few seconds before replying. "Oh really?"

"Yes!"

"Yeah?" His gaze lazily flickered up and down her body. A slow, taunting smile tweaked his lips. "If your boyfriend's such a good guy, he wouldn't mind sharing his goods, right?"

Andreide glared at him. "Don't even think about it."

He grinned. "Why not?"

Before she could respond, Richard reached out and grabbed her skirt, yanking her towards him. He wrapped one hand round her waist as the other groped at her thighs, heading up under her skirt.

"Hey! What the hell! Stop it!" Andreide cried. She shoved at his chest but he refused to relinquish his grasp. "Richard, stop!"

"Why? Quit pretending. You want me to give it to you, don't you? You want a *real* man to give it to you." He growled in her ear, "Your boy can't do it how I can. And I'll show you."

Panic shot through Andreide's veins as he grabbed both her wrists with one hand. But as much as she struggled against him, he would not let go. His grip was like the jaws of death.

"Richard, I'm serious. Stop it!"

He pulled her closer and lowered his mouth to the side of her neck. He clamped both hands over her bottom, squeezing her roughly.

Andreide cried out in alarm more than pain. Her hands now free, she shoved him back then delivered his face a mighty slap; her other hand clawed and scratched at his chest.

"Ow! Hey, what's wrong with you? What the hell you do that for?" Richard exclaimed. Andreide struggled to pass him. "Oh, no you don't! You're not going anywhere. Stay here with me. You know you like it."

He recaptured her hands then pushed her against the wall, trapping her body with his. He anticipated her scream and quickly leaned in, covering her mouth with his own. Her startled and enraged cry was muffled by the sudden, forceful entrance of his tongue. The strong, disgusting odour of beer mixed with what tasted and smelled like cigarette smoke on his breath was nauseating. Andreide was revolted.

"Ugh! Get off of me, you creep!" She pushed hard at his chest.

"Damn it, bitch!" He swore. "Keep still!" He grabbed her back, plastering his mouth over hers, invading and polluting her with his toxins.

Andreide now felt the beginnings of hopeless frustration. Her body shook as she began to cry, hot tears streaming down her face. The more she struggled, the more determined her attacker became. She had might as well surrender for there was no point in fighting a losing battle. He would have his way no matter what she did.

Just as Andreide had given up, Richard released her as he was forcefully jerked backwards. She gasped for breath as she tried to recover from the attack, her body and mind reeling from conflicting emotions. She managed to look up in time to see her rescuer grab hold of her attacker before he could escape. Her hope began to restore as her tear-stricken gaze settled on her saviour.

"What the bloody hell do you think you're doing?" Dominick said, his face contorted with rage and disbelief.

Richard wrenched free from his grip and met his friend's incensed gaze with a challenging, sneering one of his own. "Sampling your goodies. What does it look like I'm doing?" He brought his face close to Dominick's. "But get in line – I was here first."

Dominick lunged backwards then boxed Richard in the face. He stumbled and cried out in shock, his hand flying to his cheek.

"What the –! Dominick, boy! You crazy?"

Richard's look of astonishment was nothing compared to Andreide's. She stared completely astounded by her boyfriend's action. Although she had seen him angry, she had never witnessed him become violent. He was such a gentle person, it never occurred to her that he was capable of such behaviour. But as she stood there against the wall, watching the fury transform his beautiful, soft eyes into unrecognisable dark pools of dangerous intent, Andreide felt almost scared herself.

"Dominick." Her voice was barely audible. But he heard her. His eyes instantly softened as they looked at her, but the dark anger still hovered over them. He walked over to her.

"Andy. Are you alright?" His voice was strained. She barely nodded.

Richard chuckled. "'Course she is. Why shouldn't she be? I was just giving her a taste of some lovin'. Showing her what a real man can do. And since she's with you, I know she ain't been getting nothing proper." He grinned. "So I gave her a treat, didn't I, babe?"

Dominick's fists balled at his side as he turned to face him. A vein in his temple pulsed as he glared at his schoolmate. "Shut up, Richard. You don't know what you're saying."

"Yeah?" He stepped up to him. "Why's that? You think you better than me? Huh? That what you think?"

Dominick turned away from him.

Richard persisted, grabbing his arm. "Hey, I'm talking to you! You feel you're all that don't you? You feel 'cause your daddy's big and rich and you're white-looking that you're something special, huh?"

Dominick whipped around, his eyes smouldering with anger. Andreide felt unease like she had never felt it. She looked on fearfully.

"Let go of my arm," Dominick said, his voice low and tense.

Richard sneered, "Is that all you have to say?" Dominick's silent glower was his response. Richard narrowed his eyes and stepped right up to his face. "You think you got it like that, huh? Well, you don't and I do. I got more money, more rides, more girls, more everything!" He shot a glance at Andreide then looked back at Dominick. He grinned. "I even got your bitch in the bag! Bet you didn't know 'bout –"

Wham!

Richard rocked backwards as Dominick slammed him in the jaw. Dominick grabbed the scruff of his neck before he could fall and delivered another blow to his face.

Andreide gasped in shock. She made to move but could not, transfixed to the spot.

Richard released a howl of pain. He charged forward and lunged at Dominick, who quickly ducked his flying fists. Swooping back up, Dominick rammed a tightly clenched fist right into his opponent's stomach. Richard doubled over, his eyes watering in pain and shock at the sudden deprivation of oxygen. Dominick started towards him again but Andreide's startled cry halted his movement.

"Dominick, stop!" she pleaded. Her face was contorted with anxiety and her eyes were filling with moisture as she met his enraged gaze. But his fury seemed to melt as she hurried towards him.

"Dominick, don't." Andreide reached for his hand and held it tightly. "Please don't."

"I *can't* have him talking about you like that! Or touching you like that – I saw him," he growled.

"I know, baby. But it's alright –"

"No, it's not alright! I'm not going to stand here and let that piece of scum disrespect you like that!"

"Yes, but –" Andreide gasped. "Dominick, watch out!"

He turned around but it was too late. With a warlike cry, Richard rushed forward and grabbed him round his middle, throwing them both to the floor.

Andreide screamed.

With blind rage, Richard threw punches in every direction, several catching Dominick in the face, while the others he deflected with his arms.

"No! Stop!" Andreide cried. She ran forward and tried pulling Richard off her boyfriend but he roughly shoved her backwards. She stumbled and fell.

Dominick released a roar of rage. He heaved his assailant off him then rolled over his body, pinning him to the floor. His teeth gritted, kneeling over him, Dominick pummelled every part of the boy he could reach. "Don't – you – ever – refer – to – Andreide – like – that – again!" He punctuated each word with a heavy punch then repeatedly cuffed him in the face and chest. Over and over again he landed blow after blow, Richard helpless to defend himself, flailing his arms aimlessly.

"Dominick, no!" Andreide wailed. She got to her feet just as a group of people appeared around the corner.

"Woa! Fight!" a boy shouted then ran off to spread the news. The others swarmed nearby, looking on gleefully as Andreide hurried forward.

"Dominick … please! He's bleeding. You're going to kill him!" She tugged at his arm.

But Dominick either did not hear her or refused to care, for he continued to pound his foe mercilessly, despite his bleeding knuckles and Richard's swollen and bloody face.

Tears flowed down Andreide's cheeks as she tried fruitlessly to stop her boyfriend from pulverizing his old friend. It wasn't until someone pulled her backwards that she released Dominick's arm. She barely glimpsed Will's face before she clutched to his chest and sobbed.

"Hey! D, Rich … what the hell?" Tommy emerged through the crowd, followed by Hans and Kurt, surprise etched across their faces. They pushed people aside as they rushed forward and grabbed Dominick, hauling him off Richard with difficulty.

"Getoffme! Letmego!" Dominick hissed, struggling against his friends' grip on him.

"Dude, relax, will you!" Tommy pulled him away from a semi-conscious Richard who was now being helped off the floor. "What happened, man?"

Dominick glared at a whimpering, wounded Richard before switching his incensed gaze on his friend. Tommy flinched. With a sharp twist of his arm, Dominick freed himself of his comrade's grip then turned away from him.

"Dominick –" Tommy reached out to him.

He turned and gave him a scorching look. "Leave me alone." Without another glance, he stepped past him and cut his way through the crowd.

Andreide made to follow him.

But after disentangling herself from the throng of nosy people, and searching the nearby rooms, he was no where to be found. She headed for the front door then paused as someone called out to her. She turned to see a pale-faced Alisa hurrying towards her.

"Alisa! What is it? Are you ok?" Andreide gave her friend a worried look. At the same time, she wondered how the evening – which had started out so well – had turned into such a nightmare. And just as she was hoping that it would not get any worse, Alisa clamped a hand over her mouth and raced through the front door. She leaned over the porch railing and threw up.

"Oh, God! Alisa! You're still sick – I knew you shouldn't have come. Oh gosh. Does it hurt really bad? Did you eat something to upset you again?" Andreide rubbed her friend's shoulder.

Alisa shook her head slowly.

"Then what is it? Your stomach just started hurting like that?"

"I … I'm …" Alisa gave Andreide a hesitant glance before looking away. She shook her head again.

Andreide frowned. "Alisa, what –"

"Hey, Andreide, you caught up with Dominick yet?" Tommy appeared in the doorway. His gaze flickered to Alisa and a smile tweaked the corner of his mouth. "Hey you, I was wondering where you disappeared to. By the way, have either of you seen my brother? Can't seem to find him anywhere."

Andreide shook her head then glanced at Alisa. She started at the anxious expression on her friend's face. "Alisa, what's wrong?"

She shook her head hastily and began backing away. "N-Nothing. I have to go."

"Alisa, wait!" Tommy called out and started after her.

But it was too late – she had dashed down the steps and fled through the gates, disappearing into the dark night surroundings.

"What was that all about?" Tommy exchanged a confused, worried look with Andreide. She did not have a clue herself. But whatever it was, she knew it had to be something grave for Alisa to hide it from her.

"Tommy, I'll see you later. I don't think she's feeling well."

"Yeah, ok. Would you tell her I'll call her?"

Andreide registered his concern before nodding and starting off in the direction in which Alisa had left.

Ten minutes later, after following the main road and not finding a trace of her friend, Andreide said a quick prayer, hoping that she had returned home safely. She then turned and headed for her own house. She had called Alisa's cell phone several times to no avail and could not stop her mind from thinking the worse. She had also tried Dominick's number with no success. She hoped that they were both alright. These thoughts and more occupied her mind as she walked home.

Suddenly, a rustling noise nearby caught her attention and Andreide froze. Her pulse raced as she quickly looked over to the trees at the side of the road, her eyes skimming the dark branches for movement. It was only when a cloud shifted and moonlight shined unto the trunks of the trees, that she saw the source of the noise. Her heart leapt up into her throat as she spied a person slouched at the base of a tree, half-shrouded by shadows.

Andreide felt her fingers grow cold as she stood indecisive in the middle of the deserted road. She did not know whether she should run or scream or do both. But her dilemma was solved when the person shifted slightly, and the moonlight illuminated his face.

She shrieked. "Dominick!"

"Andy?" His voice was quiet.

She ran over the pitch and across the grass, hurrying to her boyfriend's side. "Oh, God, Dominick! You scared me so much!" She flung her arms around him then kissed his cheek. She eased back and looked into his face. "Baby, are you alright? I was so worried! You just stormed off like that. And what are you doing here on the side of the road? You could have been kidnapped or attacked!"

Dominick smiled. He took one of her hands and laced his fingers between hers. "I'm fine. Sorry for worrying you but I had to get out of there. I needed to be alone – to cool off." He glanced around at the trees. "Nature's my thing and this seemed like a good spot." He gazed into her concerned eyes. "I was planning on coming back, you know."

"But ... but back there. At the party." She looked down at their locked fingers. "I never knew you to be the fighting type. Why did you do it?"

He was silent for a while before responding. "Because I love you." The softness of his tone captured her heart. "I saw him with you, touching you, hurting you. And I just had this insane urge to strangle the life out of the bastard. To knock the daylights out of him ... and I did. Or rather tried to." He sighed and looked down. "You were right. I was going to kill him. But I just couldn't think straight after seeing that ... seeing him ... Ugh! I hate that foul creature so much."

Andreide looked at Dominick with deep love in her eyes as he rested the back of his head against the trunk of the tree. She stroked his cheek gently then stopped as he winced.

"You're hurt," she said sympathetically, now noticing the slight swellings on his face and the few scrapes and bruises on his arms and chest. He closed his eyes and nodded slowly.

"It's nothing. I know I got him a lot worse."

"Oh, baby, I'm so sorry. I was thinking about this and it's all my fault. I shouldn't have left that room. You told me to stay. I'm so sorry."

It was then Dominick sat up and took both of her hands in his. He had a serious expression on his face and an intense look in his eyes as they focussed on her. "It's not your fault. Don't say that. I knew all along the kind of guy Richard was but was too much of a trusting fool to stand up to him or do anything about it. But tonight changed it all. I hadn't planned on beating him before but seeing him with you like that changed everything. That fight was inevitable – he had it coming to him, whether it was tonight or some other time. So don't think it's your fault."

"But ... your friendship. It's over ..."

"And bloody good riddance to it too!" Dominick said vehemently. "Having his friendship is worthless if he's going to take advantage of you. Nothing will make me compromise your safety, Andreide. Nothing." He pulled her closer, his gaze unwavering. "You mean the world to me, Andy. I would do anything for you. I would kill for you if I had to."

Andreide gasped. "Dominick ...!"

"I would. I mean it, Andy. I truly mean it." He paused as his eyes roamed her face, taking in her touched expression. "Anything at all, and I'll do it. I love you."

A sob of joy escaped Andreide's lips as she threw her arms around him and kissed his neck. "I love you too, Dominick. So very much! You're the best thing that has ever happened to me. And I can't thank you enough."

Chapter 19

A cool afternoon breeze ruffled the leaves of the sturdy lime tree in the D'Averettes' yard. Despite the gentle wind, kneeling among her bed of flowers, pulling weeds, Rose Marie felt irritated. She yanked at a stubborn root which refused to part with the soil. Frustrated, she grabbed her hand-spade and dug at its base, scooping the surrounding earth away. But as much as she tried to uproot it again, the weed still refused to budge – not even an inch. Frowning, she tossed the spade aside and wiped the beads of sweat from her face.

All day that Monday, she had been marshalling her thoughts, trying to think straight. But no matter how hard she tried she could not stop herself from fuming over last night's argument. They had cursed each other in the foulest way possible before Charles marched out of the house; he still had not returned and she could care less. Her face tensed as she thought back to the ignorant, selfish comments her husband had made and felt a scream of annoyance threaten to burst out of her. How dare he stand up for that woman? How dare he argue in her favour?

Rose Marie stabbed fiercely at a clump of weeds as her mind brought that abominable woman into focus. She – the subject of almost every single recent argument they had had. Although by reference she seemed to be ever present in their home, as Rose Marie thought about it, she realised that the woman was rather scarce of late. In fact, Rose Marie had not seen her all weekend much to her relief. But the fact that she was not buzzing around as usual, was cause for concern in itself. She had to be up to something.

Rose Marie took off her gloves and gathered her tools, then started for the house. She had made up her mind. It was more than time for this nonsense to be over and it certainly was high time that that woman and her bastard son left her family alone for good! Her gardening would have to wait. She was going to find Latricia Davis.

*

It was not hard to locate the dump where the woman and her child stayed. Rose Marie was hardly surprised as she pulled up in front of the tiny, shabby apartment building which was practically built on the sidelines of the road. She checked the page that she had ripped out of her husband's daily planner, and made note of the room number. She then locked her car and stepped out onto the nonexistent, litter-strewn front yard. The place was disgusting.

After finding room nine and hammering for several minutes on the dirty, rickety door, Rose Marie stood back and frowned in thought. It was late afternoon; the boy did not attend school there as far as she knew. Someone had to be home. But as she began pounding on the door again, a cohabiter of the filthy dwelling stuck his mangy head out of a dilapidated window of a neighbouring cell and shot Rose Marie an annoyed look.

"What's with the noise, woman? You ain't from here are yuh? We like tings nice and quiet so pipe it down, will yuh!" He started to retract his dishevelled head through the window but Rose Marie stepped forward and called out to him.

"Excuse me, wait a minute!"

He paused and gave her a lazy look. "Yeah?"

"Do you know if anybody for this room here is home? Latricia Davis, maybe?"

The man shook his unshaven face. "Don't know no names. But a thick woman and a scrawny, big-head child used to stay there though."

"Used to?" Rose Marie's brow creased.

"Yeah. They was here for a while 'till Saturday when I see she and de boy bussing out ah here wit' a ton load ah speed. De skinny boy look like he woulda fall over dragging them big suitcase fast-fast 'cross de ground to de taxi."

Rose Marie's heart began to beat faster but she tried to suppress the rising excitement she was starting to feel.

"You mean, you mean she's gone? They've gone?"

He shrugged. "I suppose. After they went racing out and into de taxi I ain't seen them come back. I tell you though, she did look really scared see!" A nasty, guttural laugh emitted from his scruffy face.

Rose Marie managed a small smile then thanked him for his information, turning to leave.

For the duration of her journey home, all she could think of was what the man had revealed. But the more she thought, the more confused she became. Sure she was overjoyed at the news that they had left, but just like that? With no warning? Running scared? But why? What could have possibly made Latricia Davis, such a bold, nasty woman, flee so suddenly? What had frightened her? *Who* had frightened her?

These questions were still on her mind an hour later as she reclined in her office armchair. She kept replaying her last confrontations with the woman and tried to recall if either she or Charles had let slip any indications of the woman and her child's departure. But as much as she tried to rake her memory, nothing of significance struck her.

It was while she was thinking over the past week that it occurred to her. A rather curious suspicion which intrigued her. Could it be? Was it him? But the more she thought about it the more curious she became until it was the only belief occupying her mind. She had to find out for herself. With this thought in mind, she hastened upstairs to shower and change her clothes.

A few minutes later, after checking on Marques who was doing his homework and informing Andreide that she was going out for a while, Rose Marie headed down the stairs and out the front door. Andreide had been writing in her diary when she came in, and had given her a rather surly look. She thought back on her daughter's reaction but soon dismissed it as teenage behaviour. She had more pressing matters to deal with. As she started for her car, her mind preoccupied with her earlier notion, her pulse sped up as his face swarmed her mind's vision.

*

It took about five minutes for Rose Marie to gather her thoughts and steady her nerves before she left her car and headed into the lobby of the stately Raltz building. It took another three minutes after getting into the elevator before she arrived at the eighteenth floor – a floor home to the penthouse suites. As she stepped into the hall, clutching her handbag, she took a deep breath before pressing the buzzer outside suite 1806.

She waited a couple minutes before the lock disengaged and the door swung open, presenting her with a view that left her speechless and temporarily paralyzed.

Victor stood in front of her in the doorway, dressed in a grey vest and matching grey *Reebok* track pants, a white towel draped across his shoulders. The expression on his face as he looked up and saw her was as taken aback as she was stunned.

"Rose Marie! Wow, what a lovely surprise." He gave her a bright smile, his eyes shining pleasantly as they rested upon her.

Prying her eyes away from his sweat soaked vest, muscular biceps and hairy forearms, Rose Marie swallowed. She lifted her gaze to meet his, her pulse quickening on doing so.

"Victor. I didn't mean to interrupt. I'm sorry, I didn't realise you would be busy. I should have called."

"Nonsense. It's quite alright. I'm not busy at all. In fact, I just came back from the gym as you can see." He glanced down at his attire and flashed her a grin. "I was on my way to shower when the door sounded and here you are."

"Victor, I'm sorry. I don't know why it didn't occur to me to call first. I just assumed … You know what, maybe I'll come back later."

"No, don't." Victor moved forward. "It's not a problem, believe me. Monday evenings are normally slow and this one in particular seems work free." He grinned. "Well, at least I'm taking the night off. Plus, it's not everyday I'm blessed with your presence at my door."

Rose Marie felt a slight flush to her cheeks as she looked up into his charming face. She smiled and lowered her gaze.

"Would you like to come in?"

She hesitated before meeting his eyes and nodded. He stepped aside, allowing her to pass before closing the door behind them.

As he led them along a corridor, Rose Marie took in the layout of his apartment with silent admiration. It was rather big and spacious, well-designed to meet the condominium's first class status. The smooth, pale-coloured walls beautifully reflected the light from the sparkling chandeliers and wall lamps. The interior decoration was first rate.

"Welcome to my bachelor pad!" Victor announced as they ascended a few steps to a sitting room decked out in black leather armchairs, matching rugs and glass tables. A large, fifty-five inch flat screen HD television set lay perched on the wall surrounded by a state of the art stereo system and a rack of DVDs. Rose Marie smiled as she took it in, musing to herself how perfectly male-oriented it all was.

"This is a really nice apartment, Victor. Looks like the complete male haven."

He laughed. "Yes, it is. I just wish I had the time to fully enjoy it. These last couple months I've been really living in the office."

"I know what you mean."

He smiled at her. "Well, at least you don't have it as bad anymore – work wise that is."

"Yes … work wise." Rose Marie sighed and glanced around.

Victor watched her for a while then started towards her. "Rose, I –" He stopped then exhaled slowly, placing a hand on the end of his towel. He gave her a soft smile. "Could you give me a few minutes?"

"Sure, Victor. Don't let me get in your way."

"You're never in my way," he said quietly. "I'll just take a quick shower. Please, make yourself at home. I'll be right back."

Rose Marie watched him leave the room and sighed. What was she doing here disturbing him when he most likely had other things to do? And why did she think that he would know anything about the woman's disappearance? He had never even met her – the thought was ludicrous.

She wandered over to the adjoining kitchen and sat at the black marble-topped bar which served as a divider between the two rooms. She aimlessly traced a finger along the cool, smooth surface of the counter as she quietly observed her surroundings.

"Something to drink?" She started at Victor's voice a couple minutes later. She quickly looked up as he entered the room. He took two glasses down from a kitchen cabinet. She stared at him in slight amazement, her eyes wandering from his dark damp hair to his close fitting black jersey, his dark grey trousers and bare feet, and back up again. Her heart jerked suddenly as he turned and caught her eye.

He smiled, his teeth dazzling. Her heart raced.

"What will it be? I'm all out of iced tea but I do have quite a selection of alcoholic beverages."

"Um, whatever you're having is fine."

"You sure? I like my drinks strong, you know." He took a dark bottle from the mini bar and began pouring into the two glasses. "But let's mix things up, shall we?" He capped the bottle then took out another, this one containing an orange liquid. He stirred both drinks then handed one to Rose Marie, his lips tweaked to the side. "Rum punch and brandy. Think you can handle it?"

Wordlessly, she accepted the glass. She took a long sip and daringly met his eyes as the harsh liquid burned a path down her throat. Unflinching, she replaced the glass on the counter and arched an eyebrow at him. Victor looked shocked.

"Wow. I guess that's a yes. I'm impressed." He chuckled as he took up his drink and rounded the bar, taking the stool next to hers. "I was almost certain you would be coughing that concoction up."

She laughed. "I've been known to handle my drinks. You should have bet me."

He grinned. "Good thing I didn't."

They were silent as they sipped their drinks. A few seconds elapsed in which neither of them spoke, both aware of the tentative air between them. With each second, Rose Marie felt her face grow warmer in the air-conditioned apartment, a tingling sensation spreading from her neck downwards to the rest of her limbs. She was not sure if it was an effect of the drink, or the result of the divine cologne wafting off Victor's freshly showered body. The fact that his eyes kept drifting over her intensified the feeling.

"So …"

She quickly looked up.

"To what do I owe this honour?" He took a couple sips from his glass as he waited for her response.

Rose Marie's previous mood immediately died down as she recalled her reason for being there.

"I went to find that woman this afternoon, to really give her a piece of my mind. But she wasn't there." She turned the glass around between her fingers, her gaze following her movements. "A man living there told me that she and the child had left. And that they had looked frightened. I was so happy and relieved to hear that. But then all these questions kept popping up in my mind, like why did they go and what made them – her, so scared?" She looked up at Victor but his gaze was focussed on the countertop. "Oh, you must think this silly, Victor," she continued, "but the more I thought about who could have been involved in her leaving, the more my thoughts strayed to you. I had this odd suspicion that you knew about it."

Her brow creased slightly as she noted his reluctance to meet her eyes. She gasped, the dots beginning to connect in her mind. "Victor! They left on Saturday. We went out to dinner Saturday night." Her mouth twitched in wonder. "You know, now that I think about it, I do remember you seeming a bit too happy about something. Victor ... did you have anything to do with that woman and her child leaving?"

He finally looked up and met her eyes, a guilty smile on his lips. "Ok, you caught me. I admit I played a part."

"But Victor ..."

"I had to. I had to, Rose Marie!" A serious expression was now on his face. "I couldn't bare the thought of you suffering so much by the deeds of that woman and your husband. They had caused you enough pain. I wanted to do something about it, Rose. I had to. And I thought the best option I had was to see that that woman left you and your family alone."

"But ... how ...?"

"You told me she was from Antigua. I have some friends in high places and I had her checked out. And I mean fully investigated. It turned out that she had some run-ins with the law – petty offences but charges all the same. But even better, she had been recently indicted for fraud and wasn't allowed to leave the country. The fact that she'd left meant that she must have been in serious trouble and I had my guys check that out too. Turns out she had conned a notorious money launderer into giving her half a million dollars and then did a disappearing act."

"That bitch," Rose Marie said, shaking her head. "I knew all she wanted was my money but it never occurred to me that she would be using it to pay off her debts! She used that child like a cheap trick. But it's a good thing it didn't work on me."

"It surely worked on your husband though. He gave her twenty thousand."

"What!"

Victor nodded grimly. "According to one of my sources, a withdrawal was made from an account in Royal Bank with his name on it. The sum was transferred to an account in Latricia Davis' name to a branch in Antigua."

Rose Marie stared at him in disbelief. "You *cannot* be serious. Charles doesn't have an account in Royal Bank."

"Oh, but he does."

"That son of a bitch! All these years … he has never once mentioned having a separate account in another bank. Not once. How could he keep that hidden from me? And why? I have my own money and I've always been the one taking care of the finances. Now it turns up he had a stash hoarded away all this time? No no no! That's it!"

She got up from the stool and took a few steps away. "I've had it. I think I've been patient enough. I have endured enough of this shit!" She dashed away a tear that had streamed down her cheek. She made a sound of frustration and turned her back away. "God! I hate it when you see me like this."

Victor stood up but remained by his stool. "It hurts me to see you like this too," he said quietly. "But the main thing is, she's gone. I personally got into contact with her and gave her the status quo. She was shocked at first when she realised how much I knew about her dodgy dealings. After I gave her the ultimatum, I threatened to inform the police and her creditor of where she was. Her fear set in and that was it. I gave her until today to be gone but she left within the hour." He paused. "I doubt you will ever be hearing from her again."

Teary-eyed, Rose Marie turned around and lifted her eyes to Victor's. Her gaze held the burden of pain and sorrow compounded with unmitigated fatigue. "Why?" she whispered. "Why would you do this for me? You have nothing to gain in return."

"But I do." His voice was quiet. "Your happiness. I want you to be happy, Rose Marie. You've been sad for far too long."

The soft look in his eyes captivated her. Her pulse quickened. "I don't understand."

"Or do you?" He walked towards her, closing the gap between them. He held her eyes as he raised his palm to her face. "Rose," he breathed her name, gently stroking her cheek.

She could feel her limbs go weak from his touch and she struggled to remain upright. Oh God, how could his fingers affect her so?

"Tell me what you want, Rose," he whispered, brushing his lips against her ear. "Tell me what you want and it's yours."

Her heart racing, her lips parted, her eyelids halfway closed, the scent of a man drifting up her nose, Rose Marie was going to tell him what they both wanted. But then the voice of her momentarily suppressed conscience pushed to the forefront of her mind.

"Victor, no." She quickly stepped back from him. "We can't. This isn't right."

"What isn't right?"

"Oh, Victor. I'm married!" she wailed. A groan of frustration escaped her lips as she turned and walked a few feet away. She ran her hand through her hair and sighed. "You don't know the number of times I've wished … if only things were different."

"Then what?" His voice was low and quiet.

After a few seconds, she turned to face him. "Then I wouldn't be in this predicament. I wouldn't be feeling as trapped and angry and hurt and completely fed up as I do now. I would be free to live as *I* want to. But you know what? I'm tired of wishing because that's getting me nowhere. I have to *do* something. I've had more than sufficient time to think things through and I've come to a decision." She paused. "I'm going to divorce Charles."

For a moment, Victor just stared at her. Then, what looked like shock and relief overcame him all at once.

"Are you serious?"

She nodded. "Yes. I am. I can't stay married to him anymore, Victor. Not after what he has put us all through. I cannot live with him anymore. I won't. And after twenty years, I've more than reached my limit with him."

Victor looked down at the floor for a while before meeting Rose Marie's eyes. He searched them before responding.

"Are you absolutely sure? Is this what you truly want?"

Gazing back into his eyes, she gave him his desired answer.

"Yes. Don't you?"

"Yes. I do."

Rose Marie's heart skipped a beat. "You do?"

Victor's face flushed. He lowered his gaze. "I um ... I ... What I meant was —" He stopped and suddenly cursed, startling Rose Marie. "Damn it! I'm not going to make any more excuses. I'm tired of covering up how I feel. I know I said I just want you to be happy but that's not all I want. I want *you*, Rose. I want you and I love you and I can't hide it any longer."

It was stunned disbelief that froze Rose Marie to the spot as she stared at the man in front of her. She could not dare believe what he was saying, especially since she had secretly dreamed about it for so long.

Victor continued. "You don't know how hard this has been for me — feeling how I do and not being able to do anything about it. Especially at times when it's just us and I want to tell you everything." He stepped closer to her. "Especially when those beautiful eyes are misty like they are now."

Rose Marie's bottom lip quivered. "Victor ... you can't ... you can't say that."

"Why not? Why not when I feel this so strongly?"

"You can't ..."

"I can. And I do." He moved closer, his eyes intimately on hers. "And I know you feel it too."

"Victor," Rose Marie whispered feebly, shaking her head slowly. She stepped backwards.

"Tell me I'm wrong. Tell me that there was nothing in those moments we shared, in those looks. Tell me you didn't feel anything in Miami or even before that. Tell me."

"Oh, Victor ..." Rose Marie's voice trembled. "I can't."

"Then prove me wrong, love."

In less than a second he bridged the space separating them, his eyes dark and intent on hers. She barely had a chance to gasp before his arms closed around her. His head lowered and his lips met hers with crushing force.

Shock kept her rooted and senseless until her initial surprise wore away and Victor's roving mouth drove all thoughts of protest out of her mind. She moaned as he pulled her against his hard body. His shower-clean aroma and the feeling of his skin beneath her palms, reminded her of exactly how long she had been deprived of such affection. As his hands roamed her body, the thought made her shiver with longing.

Her pulse racing wildly, her heart pounding out of control, Rose Marie clutched to Victor as she returned his kiss with equal desire. She could hardly think beyond the fact that he was completely right. She loved him, she wanted him – God, how he was right.

He uttered her name with breathless yearning, pressing her closer as he feverishly kissed along the side of her neck. She moaned, closing her eyes, tilting her head and holding him tighter. She couldn't possibly resist.

Victor bent and lifted her off her feet. Their breathing ragged, their gazes said more than words possibly could. She kissed him as he turned and carried them in the direction of his bedroom.

Chapter 20

Andreide waited anxiously as Harietta rang the doorbell. She glanced at Keisha who too looked worried, her thin eyebrows contracted in a frown. Harietta, despite her earlier stalwart façade, appeared just as nervous as her friends as she stood back and waited for someone to answer the door.

It was Friday and for the entire week, Alisa had been absent from school – yet again. According to Mrs. Smith, her parents had said that she was sick but they could not get any more information about their friend's condition. They had called her house and cell phone several times, each time getting no answer. They had even stopped by her house but no one answered their call. The fact that she was sick was reason for concern but the fact that Alisa seemed to have disappeared off the face of the earth or was otherwise ignoring them was rather unsettling. The girls were worried.

"C'mon Alisa. Open the door," Harietta pleaded, pressing the doorbell for the umpteenth time.

Keisha made an exasperated noise. "Look, this is jus' dum. How she could be ignoring us like this?"

"Oh gosh, maybe she's really very sick! What if they took her to the hospital or something and we don't know."

"Andy, don't worry," said Harietta, "I'm sure she's ok. Let's not think the worst."

Keisha rolled her eyes and made another annoyed noise. "Look, jus' move. If they pretending they can't hear the doorbell, they can't pretend they can't hear this!" She nudged Harietta aside then began pounding on the front door. "Alisa, open de blinking door now!"

"Keisha, stop shouting!" Harietta said harshly. But her friend ignored her.

"Open up! Open up!" Keisha banged harder.

"Keisha! You're going to break down the people's door! What's your prob –?"

Suddenly, the inner lock clicked and the door swung open, nearly throwing Keisha off balance. Harietta steadied her before the girls looked up into the irritated face of their friend's mother.

"Yes?" she asked tersely.

"Mrs. Bretford?" Andreide began cautiously. "Is everything alright? We noticed Alisa has been missing school and we got worried when we couldn't get through to her."

"We told the school she was sick. You should have been informed."

"Yes, but –"

"There's no need to worry. Alisa will be fine."

Andreide took a moment before responding, trying to figure out the best way to continue without sounding rude. At the same time, she felt that Alisa's mother was deliberately keeping them in the dark.

"Mrs. Bretford, could we somehow speak to Alisa?" Andreide asked.

"Yeah, so we could actually know she's alright for *ourselves*," Keisha butted in, perhaps a bit too insolently.

Mrs. Bretford frowned. "Alisa isn't allowed to see anyone at the moment so I'm sorry, you can't." She began to close the door but Keisha quickly moved forward, jamming her foot in the space between the door and its frame.

"Wait! You *have* to let us see her. You know how long we been out here, nuh?"

"Excuse me?" Mrs. Bretford said, her tone affronted. "I don't have to let you do anything. Now please, go away."

"Mrs. Bretford, please!" Andreide stepped forward. "Please let us see her. Or at least tell us what's going on because I know something's up. Alisa isn't answering her phone, e-mails or anything."

"That's because those privileges have been taken away, of course!"

"What? What do you mean by *that*? Look woman –!"

"Keisha!" Harietta warned.

"Mrs. Bretford," Andreide spoke up quickly, shooting her incensed friend a glance, beginning to feel quite annoyed herself. "What's going on? Is Alisa sick? Did she do something wrong? We just want to know so we could help her. We're her best friends, please tell us."

It seemed like forever before their friend's mother answered, a length of time which confirmed Andreide's belief that something was not right. But it was not only Mrs. Bretford's contemplation time, but the pained expression which marred her otherwise pleasant face which confirmed Andreide's suspicion.

Mrs. Bretford sighed. "I suppose you should know. But I shouldn't be the one to tell you." She opened the door wider and stepped aside. "Alisa is in her room."

The girls glanced at one another before tentatively stepping inside. They quickened their steps as soon as they were clear of Mrs. Bretford and hastened upstairs. Keisha was the first to reach their friend's bedroom; she flung the door open.

"Alisa! Girl, you don't know how many times we tried calling you and –" Keisha broke off as they entered the room. Their friend was lying flat on the carpet, one hand clutching a brown raggedy teddy bear, the other a wad of Kleenex tissues. She raised her head as they came in before flopping back down again, emitting a strangled sob.

"Alisa! What happened?" Andreide hurried in, dropping on the carpet next to her. "What's going on? Why wouldn't your mother –" She stopped mid-sentence as she saw her friend's tear-stricken face. "Oh gosh, Alisa. What's wrong?"

Alisa slowly sat up, still holding on to the stuffed toy. Her lips moved but no sound followed.

"What is it?" Harietta asked, joining them on the floor. "Are you sick?"

Alisa shook her head.

"You in pain?" Keisha watched her closely.

Again, she shook her head.

"Then what is it?"

Alisa clutched her teddy bear closer to her chest, looking down at the carpet. Her bottom lip trembled before she burst into tears.

"Oh, Alisa." Andreide reached for her friend, wrapping her arms around her shaking body. "Tell us what it is so we can help you."

"Yeah, it can't be so bad, can it?" Harietta rubbed her back gently.

"But ... it is," Alisa sniffed. "It's ... it's ... terrible!" she sobbed, her shoulders shaking as tears poured down her face. "I'm the ... biggest ... fool!" she managed between sobs. "I'm such an ... idiot."

Andreide frowned. "No, you are not, Alisa."

"Yeah, girl. How can you say that?"

"I am!" Alisa pulled away from her friends and threw her teddy bear aside. "My life is ruined. It's all over."

"Chile, what de hell you talking 'bout?" Keisha scowled, her arms folded across her chest. "You said you ain't sick. And you's one of the last people who could commit a crime. So what is yuh story?"

Alisa looked away from her concerned friends with an aggrieved expression on her face. Andreide felt a sinking feeling of dread. Her heart began to beat faster with anxiety. They waited in suspense for about a minute before Alisa turned back to face them. Her tear-filled eyes remained lowered as she made the announcement of her life.

"I'm pregnant." Silent tears trickled down her cheeks.

The girls were speechless. They stared in stunned disbelief at their friend for several minutes before Keisha broke the silent stupor.

"I know you didn't jus' say what yuh jus' said. 'Cause I know you didn't jus' say something dum like you pregnant." She snorted in disbelief, looking from Andreide to Harietta then back at her.

Alisa gave a big sob, wringing her hands.

Harietta closed her eyes, shaking her head. "No no no. Alisa you were sick – you had the flu. You're not pregnant."

"I am. It wasn't the flu. I was pregnant. I *am* pregnant!" she wailed.

Andreide stared wordlessly at her sobbing friend, finding it difficult to believe what she was saying.

Keisha gave a snort of a laugh. "How could *you* be pregnant? You're the shyest thing alive! You got to be joking!"

Alisa shook her head, tears streaming down her face.

"Well, if you're not joking," Keisha continued, "then you must be really stupid for real."

"Keisha!" Harietta glared at her.

"What? Is true. She must be stupid to be sixteen and pregnant in this day an' age. I didn't even know she had a man!"

"Keisha, you're not making the situation any better. You're only making it worse! We're her friends. We have to support her and not make her feel any worse than she is already."

"Well as her *friends*, we're supposed to hold her accountable for her actions. And what I'm saying is what other people gonna be tinking and saying 'bout she too! They gonna be calling she a slut and all kinda thing now!"

393

"Keisha!"

"What?"

"This isn't the time for that now. Argh!" Harietta pounded her fist on her thigh. "Can't you be sensitive for once?"

"Fine!" Keisha abruptly stood up and started for the door. "You stay there and sugar-coat things for she. I won't though."

Harietta got up. "Girl, come back here!"

But Keisha was already through the door. Harietta glanced back at her friends before marching after her. The door slammed shut behind them.

Alone with Alisa, Andreide gave a deep sigh. She looked at her friend's trembling shoulders and puffy eyelids then sighed again.

"Alisa?" she said quietly. "How sure are you that you really *are* pregnant?"

"Positive," Alisa replied. She sniffed. "My parents took me to the doctor a few days ago which is when we found out."

Andreide shook her head. "But Alisa ... how can this be? You're a virgin!"

Alisa gave an involuntary sob. "I'm not ... anymore."

Andreide felt at a loss for words. This could not be happening. Not now. Not to her friend. How could it?

"Alisa. Who's the father?"

Again she sobbed. "I-I can't." She covered her face with her hands and a fresh batch of tears flowed from her eyes and between her fingers.

"Is it Tommy?" Andreide asked.

Alisa shook her head and her tears flowed even more profusely which alarmed Andreide. Tommy was the only person she could have thought of. "If it isn't him Alisa, then who is it? *Who* was it?" she asked more forcefully.

But again Alisa shook her head, her tears subsiding. "I can't."

"You have to. I have to know."

"He'll kill me."

"Who will?"

"Gordon!" Alisa said, then immediately gasped, her hand flying to her mouth.

"Gordon?" Andreide's brow creased in bewilderment. "Tommy's brother? What does he –?" She then gasped, suddenly realising. "No. No! Alisa, you didn't!"

She was silent, her head lowered, a tear trickling down her nose.

"Alisa! Gordon? You don't even know him! How did this happen? No, forget how. When did it happen? No, not just when – how and when. Alisa!" Andreide paused, realising how loud her voice had become. She took a few breaths to calm herself then began again. "Alisa? Was it a one-time thing or were you planning on having a relationship with him? Because as far as I know, he has a girlfriend, doesn't he? And I thought things with you and Tommy were going well."

Alisa remained silent, looking everywhere but at her friend.

"Alisa, please. You have to tell me. How else can I help you if I don't know the situation? You trust me don't you?"

Alisa nodded meekly, her eyes brimming with tears as she timidly met her friend's gaze. "I didn't even like him. I don't. Andy, I *so* didn't plan this."

"I know you didn't, Lissy. You couldn't have."

"And it was just once. That time when we went to the Duncan match and we were walking back with the guys and Tommy invited us over. Remember you went off with Dominick? Well ... it was then."

"Oh God, Alisa. I knew you shouldn't have gone with them! I just had this feeling that you shouldn't have."

"I know. And you tried to warn me but being the stupid trusting fool that I am, I went along."

"Alisa –"

"No, Andy. I *was* stupid. I couldn't see past Tommy's cute face and I wanted to spend more time with him."

"But it wasn't Tommy."

"No. Gordon picked us up. He seemed nice, like a regular guy to me. But after watching Tommy and Will play their games for a couple hours, he invited me to watch TV with him in his room."

"You went to his room ... alone with him?" Andreide asked incredulously.

"I know, I know. I wasn't thinking properly!" Alisa wailed. "He'd given me a drink earlier and I guess it was alcoholic or something 'cause I could hardly remember much after we got in his room."

Andreide sat up straighter. "You mean he spiked your drink?"

"I guess. I dunno," Alisa said pitifully, shrugging her shoulders.

"Alisa, you do know what this means, don't you?"

"Wh-What?"

"He raped you!"

Alisa stared wide-eyed at Andreide. "No!" she gasped. "He didn't hurt me. At least I don't think so."

"He doesn't have to hurt you for it to be rape. He slipped something in your drink – he took away your ability to consent."

Alisa gaped. "How do you know that?"

"Pfft!" Andreide gave a dismissive wave. "I watch a lot of *Law & Order SVU*. Anyway, the point is you're the victim here. You deserve justice. You have to report him to the police, Alisa."

"No, I can't!"

"Yes, you can! You have to."

"No! I *can't!*" Alisa cried. She pushed herself off the floor and began to pace the room, twisting her hands. "He practically exploded when I told him I was pregnant. He said if I don't 'get rid of it' he's gonna do it for me!"

"What?" Andreide exclaimed. "He said that? The bastard!"

"Yes. But the thing is he's gone. So even if I were going to press charges against him I can't because he's fled the country."

"Where did he go?"

"I don't know."

"There must be a way to find him. Oh God, this is terrible. Do your parents know about him?"

Alisa shook her head. "I couldn't tell them. That's part of the reason why they're so angry with me. You're the only person I told about him."

"But what about Tommy? Aren't you going to tell him?"

Alisa stopped pacing, her face turning ashen. "How? How can I?"

"Alisa!" Andreide exclaimed. "It's his brother's child you're carrying! He deserves to know."

"Oh, God. He's going to hate me! He'll never want to talk to me or see me again. Oh, Andy!" She slumped unto her bed and covered her face with a pillow and began to cry. "How can this be happening to me? What did I do to deserve this? It was just *one* time and I can barely remember it. This isn't fair!" she sobbed through the pillow.

Andreide got up then joined her on the bed. She took the pillow from her friend's hands, removing it from her face. "This really seems unjust. I know. You're the last person I thought would end up in this situation."

Alisa nodded, blinking back her tears. "What am I going to do, Andy? What about school? What will everybody say?" She sat up, suddenly looking scared. "How can I raise a baby? I've never had any siblings to practise on. I don't even know how to change a pamper. Andy, I can't be a mother. I'm not even finished being a child!"

Andreide hugged her as Alisa broke down and cried. She wished she could help her. If only she knew how ... but then she did know how. She was after all, her best friend.

After her crying subsided, Andreide released her then took hold of her hand, looking her squarely in the eyes. "Alisa, I can't begin to imagine how you feel but I want you to know you have my sympathy. And as your best friend, I promise you, right here and right now that I'm going to do everything I can to help you get through this. Don't worry what people think, they don't matter. They don't know how you got into this situation and if they were in your shoes, they couldn't do any better. And don't worry about that bastard Gordon. He will get what's coming to him."

Alisa gave a half-sob.

"Don't worry," Andreide continued. "You're going to be a great mom because you're a great person. And you have us, your best friends to help you and your parents, even if they're upset with you right now."

Alisa nodded.

"But above all, Lissy, don't get to thinking that you're a bad person because of this. Because you're not. We love you and God loves you no matter what you do." Andreide gave her friend's hand an encouraging squeeze. "You're going to get through this. Okay?"

Alisa smiled through her tears and nodded.

*

Andreide sighed as she sat in the shade under a large tamarind tree in the Michaels' garden. Although the day was cool and a light breeze blew, she felt far from comforted. All week, all that occupied her mind was Alisa's predicament. Alisa still had not returned to school and Andreide had only heard from her once for the week. And her panicky state had done nothing to help assuage Andreide's feelings of worry and guilt. In fact, they had triggered the most disturbing nightmares that Andreide had had in a long time. Ones in which Andreide herself was pregnant and all her friends and family had abandoned her, including Dominick. It was a recent dream like this which forced her to arrive at a decision.

She gazed down at Dominick lying on his back beside her and pondered on how to approach the subject. He was reading a literature novel and Andreide did not want to disturb him. However, as he was about to turn a page, he looked up and caught her eye. He regarded her for a couple seconds before marking his page and closing the book.

"What's bothering you, Andy?" Dominick sat up, concern in his eyes.

Andreide sighed.

"It's Alisa, isn't it?"

She nodded.

"Baby, I wish I could help. I really do." He gently rubbed her arm. His hand felt comforting; the soft touch of his fingers along her skin was oddly calming. "You know, I could talk to Tommy."

"Don't. Alisa has to tell him herself." Andreide paused uncertainly, started to speak again but hesitated.

"What is it, Andy?" he asked.

"Dominick, I ... I need you to promise me something," she said quietly, looking at her palms.

"Anything," he responded just as quietly, taking her hand in his.

She raised her eyes to his. "Promise me if I ever ended up in Alisa's situation, you wouldn't abandon me."

"Of course I wouldn't. I'd be there for you no matter what. You know that, Andy." He held her hand tightly as he looked at her intently. She could see the truth clearly in his eyes.

"Andy," he said continuing, "You shouldn't worry. Alisa will be fine and so will you. You won't end up in her position, I promise you that."

Andreide shook her head slowly. "But Dominick, no matter how much protection we may use, there's no guarantee I won't get pregnant."

He was silent at this, lowering his gaze in thought. "You're right," he said after a while. "So what are we going to do?"

Andreide's heart pounded as she formulated the words that she had been seriously thinking about since the torture of her first nightmare that week. She knew her decision would pain them both but she had to say it.

"I want us to wait," she said somewhat hurriedly. She exhaled slowly before repeating herself, more evenly this time. "I think we should wait. I thought I was ready but what with Alisa ... I'm not ready to be a mother at sixteen or seventeen. I don't want that responsibility just yet."

Dominick nodded, his eyes on a blade of grass.

Andreide continued, "I know this must be hard for you – it was even harder for me to come to the decision. And I'm sorry, but I can't take that kind of risk right now. I'm sorry Dominick, I –"

"No, don't," he said cutting her off gently. Their eyes met. "Don't apologize, Andy. You're right and I completely understand. We *should* wait. I don't want us to be in your friend's situation. No way."

"Are you sure? I mean, you're a guy and all ..."

Dominick gave a light laugh. "Baby, my emotions don't control me. I can wait." He continued on a more serious note. "Andy, I love you. And the love that I have for you is greater than any physical need." He touched her cheek. "I don't want you to be hurt in any way. I respect your decision. I can wait till whenever you're ready, baby. I can. I will."

Andreide smiled feeling a glowing warmth of relief and happiness. She leaned forward and kissed him. "Thanks, love. You're so incredibly mature."

Dominick wrapped his arms around her and his lips tweaked to the side in a tantalising smile. "So what do we do now?"

Andreide's grin was equally teasing. "Hmm ... how about demonstrating how well you can control your emotions. Are you up to the challenge?"

The intent gleam in his eyes was her answer.

*

It was Monday afternoon and Andreide was walking home from a long day at school. She had spent most of the morning and afternoon practising past exam papers. Drained of her energy, she looked up in relief when she realised that she was a few feet from her front gate. However, on approaching it, a sudden loud voice shattered the stillness of the air.

Andreide started in fright. Her pulse raced as she looked quickly at her house. She felt a sickening sense of dread as she realised that it was from there that the sound had emanated.

Her eyes flickered to the open garage and her pulse raced even faster. Both her parents' vehicles were there, along with a familiar, shiny black BMW car. Before she could fully grasp the situation, she watched in confusion, as a glossy, chrome-coloured Cadillac car sped up their street and turned into their driveway; it pulled up behind the black BMW. Andreide stared at the magnificent vehicle as the driver's door opened. Out stepped a man in a classy dark grey suit, with close-cropped, freshly-dyed black hair. She did not get time to examine him further as he took a briefcase from his car then hurried to the front door, disappearing inside.

Suddenly energized, Andreide opened their gate then rushed up the pathway to the house. She was about to open the front door when a head bobbed around a corner of their house and called out to her.

"Hey, Andy! Come here!" Chrystal waved enthusiastically. She beckoned her over and Andreide followed, intrigued.

"Girl, what's going on?" Andreide asked. "What's with all the cars? And who was that man just gone in there?"

"I ain't sure but I think he's a lawyer. Fine-looking isn't he?" Chrystal grinned.

"A lawyer?" Andreide frowned. "Chrystal, what's going on?"

"Shhh! Come and see for yourself." Her cousin turned and led them around the house where she had a bucket overturned on the grass outside one of the kitchen windows. Andreide stepped up on the bucket, raising her eyes to the level of the window. She peered in but the kitchen was empty.

"No one's in there, Chrystal!" she hissed.

"Then they must have moved to the dining room. Come let's go."

They picked up the bucket then sneaked around the other corner to the dining room window. "Girl, they're not in there either!" Andreide whispered, looking in. "Oh, wait a minute ... crap! They're in the living room. I can see them now. They're talking but I can't hear anything. Who closed this window?"

"Lemme see." Chrystal exchanged places with her cousin then tried pulling at the sliding window pane. But it did not budge. "It's locked from the inside. But at least we can see in."

"Don't you have something I can stand on too?"

"This is all I found."

"C'mon, Chrystal. I wanna see!" Andreide whined.

"Shhh! I think I can hear something." Chrystal stuck her ears to the window. She was silent for a few seconds then she gasped, turning her head to look in at the occupants.

"What is it?" Andreide quickly asked. Her heart was pounding in anticipation. She yearned to know what was happening. "Chrystal!" she hissed, "Tell me what's going on."

But her cousin looked like she was in shock. Her mouth was slightly parted as she continued to stare inside.

"Chrystal!" Andreide called from below. "You better tell me or move over. I'm dying here!"

Chrystal shook her head slowly. "Tantie ... Tantie say something 'bout divorce."

"What!"

"She standing next to that white man," she said somewhat in a daze. "And the lawyer-man on Tantie other side." She paused, her eyes widening. "Uncle Charlie look vex-vex!"

Andreide groaned in frustration before yanking at Chrystal's jersey, pulling her down from the bucket. She quickly took her place before she could protest.

Her cousin was right. Through the window, Andreide could see all four people standing in the next room, each possessed with varying degrees of tension. However, her father took the crown, standing alone on the opposite side of the sofas. His stance was stiff, his face contorted with rage as the lawyer opened his briefcase and handed him a file of papers. Andreide could see the lawyer's mouth moving but could hardly make out the words. Her father was silent. Silent and angry.

Her mother's stance was also tense as she stood with Victor at her side. Her arms were folded and her soft features were hardened by the resilience and determination on her face. She now spoke and Andreide watched as Victor supported her, a stern expression on his face as he concurred with her statements.

Her father was livid. She watched in shock as he made a sudden movement towards her mother, the back of his hand connecting sharply with her mother's face. Andreide's startled cry was muffled by the commotion erupting inside the living room.

Victor had leapt forward as Rose Marie stumbled backwards, shoving Charles away, who tripped over the coffee table. Charles got up and lunged wildly at Victor, who sidestepped the inaccurate blow. In a rage, Charles jumped at Victor, knocking them to the ground. All the while, the lawyer's voice was raised, his face flushed as he implored the men to stop. Rose Marie was in shock, staring at them in horror.

The sparring duo rolled across the floor, knocking furniture aside as each tried landing punches on the other. For a moment, Charles was on top before Victor propelled him off, kicking him into a nearby settee. It was at this moment when both men were scrambling onto their feet to continue the brawl, that the lawyer stepped quickly between them. His arms were outstretched, separating the two as he shouted, "Enough!"

Their warfare disrupted, the men stood at opposite ends, their chests heaving as they glared at each other with undisguised animosity. Andreide looked on in utter disbelief, her eyes wide, her fingers gripping the windowsill, unaware of her cousin pulling at the end of her school blouse.

"Andy, what's all that noise? Let me see!"

But Andreide could not move. Her gaze was riveted to the shocking scene happening in her living room.

Rose Marie seemed to have recovered from her shock as she was now looking daggers at her soon-to-be ex-husband. Although Andreide was not proficient at reading lips, she did however, understand the "Get out!" uttered from her mother's gritted teeth.

Even from such a distance, Andreide could see the rage shaking her father's bony frame. He glared at all three of them in turn, his eyes burning their hatred into Victor the most. Victor took a step towards him, his fists clenched but was restrained by the gentle touch of Rose Marie's hand. It was then the lawyer intervened again, saying something to both men. Charles glowered at him then turned on his tail and marched out of the room.

The front door swung open with a bang, startling both girls perched outside the window. They quickly abandoned their position and ran towards the front of the house. They slowed to a stop and peered around the corner, catching sight of an angry, humiliated man storming down the pathway. Andreide watched as he gave a violent kick to the gate; it sprung open with such force that it recoiled, hitting Charles in the thigh. But he kept going, not caring for the pain in his leg.

Andreide's gaze turned to the front door where her mother, Victor and the lawyer were now standing. She observed Victor's arm around her mother's shoulders before switching her focus back to her departing father. She watched as he marched further down the street, never looking back.

A silent, lone tear trickled down Andreide's cheek.

*

Jenny's Ice-Cream Parlour was unusually empty for a Saturday afternoon. Or so it seemed to Andreide who sat alone in a booth, slowly swirling the contents of her kiwi strawberry smoothie. It was the second week in May and exams had begun, which was probably the reason why the shop was nearly empty of her schoolmates. All week Andreide had been pressured for time to study having exams scheduled every day of the week. When she had checked her timetable that morning, she was relieved to note that she had a whole week's break until her next exam. It was then she decided to give herself the day off. She continued to swirl her drink as she made a mental study plan for the coming week.

While she was figuring out Wednesday's schedule, she caught sight of someone standing behind her in the reflection of her glass. Without turning around, she knew who it was by the shiny blonde hair. Her pulse immediately quickened as she saw that he was coming towards her.

"Andreide," Richard said in greeting. He paused a few feet from her at the opposite end of the table.

Andreide stared at him, somewhat stunned and confused at his sudden presence.

"I was wondering if we could talk," he said, his voice quiet and his tone mellow.

Andreide's confusion deepened. "About what?"

"About us."

"What?" Andreide's brow furrowed. "Are you kidding?"

Richard's gaze lowered, as did his voice. "No. I know you probably don't want to talk to me but could you please give me a chance? You don't have to talk, just hear me out."

Andreide looked at him carefully before indicating the vacant seat opposite her. He slid into it and clasped his hands together on the tabletop, his eyes focussed on his twiddling thumbs. Andreide watched him cautiously, unsure of his current demeanour.

"So ... why are you here again?" she asked.

He cleared his throat and glanced at her. "I came to apologize. About everything."

"What? What did you say?" Andreide must have been mistaken.

Richard appeared clearly uncomfortable. "I'm here to apologize," he repeated, his voice sounding strained.

Andreide simply stared at him, blinking in disbelief.

"Look, I'm sorry," he said in an anxious tone, leaning forward as he spoke. "I'm sorry about how I treated you at that party. The fact that I had been drinking doesn't excuse my behaviour and I'm sorry. It was wrong of me to treat you like that and I regret those things I said to you. I was stupid. I *am* stupid. And you were right." He paused, looking desperately at Andreide for a response, but she could only stare at him in shock. He released a ragged breath and ran a hand through his perfectly-styled hair, dishevelling it.

"You were right," he continued, "that I was jealous. I knew it but I refused to believe it. I couldn't stand to see you with Dominick. The more happy I saw you with him, the more jealous I got."

Andreide's lips were parted as she gazed at Richard, feeling as if she had just woken up in a different realm. How could *he* be saying this? What had happened to him?

"You must think I'm crazy," he said, as if reading her mind. "Hell, I think I'm crazy to be telling you this right now! But I got to. I have to."

"Wh-Why?" Andreide stammered in shock. "Why are you telling me this ... now? Who put you up to this?"

"Nobody did," Richard replied. He gazed at Andreide through blue eyes which had suddenly turned soft, void of their usual sharp resentment and contempt. The look he gave her was alien to her coming from him, and she was speechless.

"Nobody did?" she echoed.

"No." He shook his head. "Ever since that party and when Dominick and I had that fight I've been thinking about this. You know ... I think he literally knocked sense into me." He chuckled. "Well anyway, it was then I began to think things over and I realised just what an ass I had been. And my conscience just wouldn't let it go."

"Your conscience?" Andreide stared at him in amazement. "You have a conscience?"

He laughed and Andreide started, not expecting the oddly familiar sound.

"Yes, I actually do have a conscience. It hasn't been functioning properly for the past couple years but it's starting to click in."

"Oh. That's good, I suppose."

"Yeah ..." Richard's gaze flickered from Andreide's eyes to her glass then back up again. "Andreide, I'm really sorry." He sighed. "I know my apologizing now can't change what I've said and done before but I hope you can accept it."

Something moved within Andreide as she looked at the humility he was now showing after so long. But she still felt confused, more so than ever.

"Richard is that all that you want?" she asked.

"Huh?" He quickly looked at her.

"For me to accept your apology?"

"Oh ... Well, no, I suppose not." He met her eyes. "I was hoping maybe ... things could change ... between us."

Andreide glanced down at the glass between her hands then began fiddling with the straw. She suddenly felt shy. "We used to be friends, didn't we?" she said softly.

"Yeah ... we were." His eyes were on her. "We used to be more than friends."

She quickly looked up at him then looked away, feeling her cheeks beginning to grow warm. "That was a long time ago. Things have changed."

"It wasn't that long ago ... Andy."

Again their eyes connected and a flood of memories washed through her mind. Richard's gaze had suddenly become intense again.

"Andy, what if we could –"

"Richard, Dominick is my boyfriend."

"But –"

"Things have changed, Richard," Andreide stated evenly, finding it difficult to maintain eye contact. "Our lives are even more different than they were before. You know that."

"Yeah. And now you have Dominick," he said slowly. His tone was mellow, almost wistful.

"Yes, I do. And he's wonderful."

Richard leaned back and watched her for a while. He sighed in resignation. "Yes, I know. He's great. Wish I knew his secret."

Andreide smiled then laughed. "He has no secret. He's just a good person."

Richard nodded in reflection. "Well, I'll have to start taking notes from him then. That is if he'll let me."

"Dominick is a pretty forgiving guy."

"Yeah. And assuming that you've forgiven me, I'll use that as leverage to get myself back into his good graces."

Andreide smiled, feeling happier than she had in days. "I forgive you, Richard. Honestly."

The bright-eyed smile he gave her was heart-warming.

"Well, that's good to hear!" He eased himself off his chair then stood up. "Well, I'll be going now. Got to find your boyfriend for part two of my apologies." He smiled. "I'm glad we had this talk."

"So am I," Andreide concurred.

"Friends?" He extended his hand to her.

She took a second before she smiled and shook it. "Friends."

"Well, I'll be gone now," he said, starting to walk backwards. "Looking forward to talking to you again. See you around?"

Andreide nodded. "You will. See you later, Richard."

"See you later, Andreide."

She watched as he turned and left, then smiled to herself. Richard was back. She did not know it was possible, but it was. And as she mused on this, she had a feeling that everything else was going to fall back into place too, however different the format.

Epilogue

On the twentieth of December, Alisa welcomed her son, Bradley Bretford into the world and Andreide became a proud seventeen-year-old godmother.

As she stood outside her friend's room in the maternity ward, Andreide gave a big sigh then smiled. It had been a tough delivery but Alisa had managed surprisingly well, giving birth to a healthy, beautiful baby boy, whom she had christened Bradley, after her father. The new mother was now resting in bed. She was looking on quietly as her overjoyed parents sat at her side. They were gazing in adoration at the pink-faced, redheaded baby lying serenely in their arms.

Andreide could not describe the extent of her happiness as she watched the proud Bretfords through the glass pane in the door. It had been a challenging few months for them, but in the end it had all been worth it. Not only had Alisa had the support of her parents and friends, but Tommy as well, who had taken the news rather well. However, he had severed ties with his brother, who, when confronted, had blatantly denied the whole incident.

Before, it had hurt Andreide when she thought about Gordon's behaviour, angering her more than anything else. But the more she had thought about it, the less significant he became, as Alisa had all the people she needed to help her manage. Tommy's pledge to support Alisa and his nephew was far more valuable than any monetary compensation the child's biological father could have given.

Andreide shook her head in wonder, amazed at how life had turned out for all of them. In such a short space of time, so much had happened that she never could have predicted a year ago.

She had graduated with honours from St. George's Public High School, having received distinctions in all her exams. Harietta and Keisha had also graduated – Keisha managing to scrape through, having passed only four subjects. As she lacked the qualifications necessary to be admitted to the local tertiary schools, Keisha had to get a job. Harietta had gained entry into a college where she was currently studying fashion designing; it was her dream of opening her own plus-sized clothing store one day.

Despite the trials of her pregnancy, Alisa had passed the majority of her subjects; Andreide was quite proud of her. Dominick too had passed all of his exams with distinctions, as was expected. His parents had given him the option to study in England but he had decided against it, attending Andreide's sixth form college instead, much to her delight.

But that was not the only cause for her joy. Her family life had also improved.

Her parents were officially divorced, having signed the last set of legal documents in September of that year. Her father had moved out months before, rather by force than by choice. He had been staying with a relative of his, somewhere in the countryside the last time Andreide had visited him. However, his absence was not the only change in the household.

Much to Andreide's disappointment, that August, Chrystal had returned to St. Vincent along with her father. Uncle Peter had decided that it was time that they had left; he had been offered a stable job in his home country and his drinking was now under control. But Andreide had not fully bought his excuse. He was indeed sober but she believed that her mother's new relationship had been a significant factor in their departure. Nevertheless, the girls had remained in contact.

A soft smile tweaked Andreide's lips as she reflected on her mother's newfound happiness. Ever since her father had left, her mother seemed to be walking on sunshine. In fact, the entire household appeared to have caught her infectious joy and there was no mystery why. Rose Marie had a man who loved and appreciated her, and who made her happy. Victor was that man and Andreide was glad.

She sighed, feeling at peace as she gazed at her seven pounds, seven ounces, rosy-faced godchild. Life had a way of working out in the strangest ways possible, and she knew it now more than ever.

Andreide's thoughts returned to her family. Her mother was home more often and Andreide was happy – even more so as their relationship was back to normal. She had missed being able to tell her about her friends and the events in her life. Now, they talked about everything. Her mother had met Dominick and thoroughly approved of him, much to Andreide's relief. She had even met Dominick's parents. Rose Marie had found a new lease on life and had even decided to start writing a new book. This time, she had said, it would be about family.

Andreide's relationship with her brothers had also improved. A few days after his twelfth birthday, Marques had all of a sudden assumed a more mature disposition; it both pleased and unnerved Andreide. To her mother's delight, Omarion had returned home and he was remarkably more pleasant. He was fulfilling his dream, working as a chef in a new Italian restaurant in town.

Approaching footsteps distracted Andreide from her thoughts. She glanced in their direction and smiled. Dominick and Tommy were walking towards her, holding between them a big, blue teddy bear and a bouquet of roses. They had all been at Richard's party that night celebrating their Christmas break, when Andreide had received the call that Alisa was in labour. Andreide had left at once for the hospital, getting a ride from Richard, while Dominick and Tommy had opted to stop first at a gift shop.

Tommy nodded at her with a slightly awkward grin before opening the door to Alisa's room. He stepped inside hesitantly. Her parents looked up as he entered, their faces still beaming; they beckoned him over to see their bundle of joy.

Dominick remained outside with Andreide as they looked in at the family, both in awe. He held the roses in one hand, and wrapped his other arm around Andreide's waist. She sighed again in contentment. Dominick leaned down and placed a soft kiss on her cheek. She smiled at him, amazed at how wonderful her life had become.

As she returned her attention to little Bradley, now in his uncle's arms, her heart felt heavy with emotion. A large chapter of her life was over and a new, even greater one was now beginning.

About the Author

Giselle Mills was born in Trinidad and Tobago but spent her childhood in St. Kitts and Nevis. She holds a Bachelor of Laws degree from the University of the West Indies and a Legal Education Certificate from the Hugh Wooding Law School. *Through It All* is her debut novel which she wrote when she was sixteen years old.

Most recently, the novel was used by the University of the West Indies as the main text for analysis in the Caribbean Civilisation course for the academic year 2017/2018. Giselle is also the owner and editor of the new online magazine *Patrice Magazine* which features articles on female empowerment and highlights issues surrounding Caribbean identity.

Additionally, Giselle is the author of the non-fiction guidebook *How to Survive Law School: Year 1*. She is currently developing this series and working on her next novel.

Follow Giselle on Twitter @Giselle_Mills and Instagram
@gisellezmills or visit her blog:
www.gisellemills.com